The Bentleys Buy a Buick

PAMELA MORSI

The Bentleys Buy a Buick

MIRA®

Recycling programs
for this product may
not exist in your area.

ISBN-13: 978-0-7783-2985-5

THE BENTLEYS BUY A BUICK

For questions and comments about the quality of this book please contact us
at Customer_eCare@Harlequin.ca.

www.MIRABooks.com

Printed in U.S.A.

First Printing: September 2011
10 9 8 7 6 5 4 3 2 1

The author would like to acknowledge the help and advice of William Cole, owner of DIVERSE CUSTOMS auto shop in Rutherfordton, NC, who knows a lot about classic cars and is willing to tell all.

And to Jennifer Morsi who knows a lot about me, but has the good sense to keep her mouth shut.

Chapter 1

FOR TOM BENTLEY it was love at first sight. She was beautiful, there was no denying that. She was graceful, sophisticated, enticing. Her long sleek lines were unmarred by even the tiniest defect. It was as if everything about her had been designed to catch a man's eye, to lure him to her, to make him want to possess her. To make him want to take her home. And that's what Tom wanted.

His heart beat faster and he verbalized his thoughts with a loud wolf whistle.

"Gorgeous," he declared as he took a step back to get a better perspective.

"Yes, she's still a mighty pretty girl," the older woman beside him agreed. "But she's not as young as she used to be."

Tom nodded. The hints of her age were visible, but somehow her beauty was unaltered, timeless. And just the sight of her tugged at something in him, something buried deep but which now sprang to the surface, causing the blood to tingle in his veins and his breath to catch in his throat.

"Just gorgeous," he repeated. "How many miles has she got on her?"

The elderly woman chuckled. "Isn't that as unwelcome a question as asking a woman her age?"

Tom managed for a moment to tear his eyes away from the car to grin at the little old lady who'd invited him here. Gladys Gilfred, Guffy to her friends, was at least eighty, a few inches short of five feet and weighed about as much as Tom's toolbox. Her steel-gray hair was clipped in what could only be described as a crew cut. In the day's slightest nip of fall weather, she was clad in a couple of thick, heavy sweaters, some men's gray trousers and a bright orange beret. She was a bit hard of hearing, but made up for it with a quick wit.

He smiled at her. "My apologies, ma'am," he said. "I didn't mean to offend you or your Buick."

"You are forgiven," Mrs. Gilfred said. "Neither Clara nor I were ever very good at holding a grudge."

"Clara?" Tom asked. "Is that what you call her?"

She nodded. "I named her for my best friend from childhood," she said. "Clara was always pretty and fun."

Pretty and fun. Tom's eyes were drawn back to the car. What more could a guy want?

He hadn't expected to fall in love that afternoon. He'd spent the entire trip across town in a state of annoyance. Cliff, his best friend and most dependable employee, had just disappeared in the middle of the morning with no real explanation. Tom wasn't able to leave the shop until he got back. And that had made him more than an hour past when he'd said he'd be here. People never remember when you show up on time. But they never forget if you made them wait. That wasn't the impression he wanted to give of himself or his business. But sometimes things happened that you couldn't anticipate. And they affected other things in ways you couldn't predict.

"She's a real beauty," Tom said as he walked slowly around the car, taking in every view of the vehicle with appreciation.

He hadn't wanted to come out on a house call. He preferred his customers to come to the shop. But his business was less than two years old. He still had to take work where he could find it. And this morning it was in Leon Valley, a small Texas town that had become part of San Antonio's urban sprawl.

Tom stopped just behind the car and reached out to run a hand along the sweep of chrome on her side.

"Nice, really nice," he said almost under his breath. "Her body couldn't be in much better shape."

"She's not just nice to look at," Mrs. Gilfred assured him. "Back when she was running, Clara purred like a kitten."

Tom smiled. The Buick Roadmaster convertible was an all-around top-of-the-line machine. Sleek styling, lots of chrome and just a hint of fins in its future, this particular model was exceptionally appealing. She had a two-tone color palatte, the upper third and the convertible top was a deep royal, almost navy. Beneath the curved chrome and the four characteristic ventiport holes, she was powder-blue. The huge jet-plane hood ornament and shiny grill dominated the front. Between the fuselage-like headlights was a stylized circle with the year 1956 impressed into the emblem. The extended back bumper sported the "continental kit," a chrome-and-metal cover to carry the spare tire in style.

"How long have you had her?" Tom asked.

"I drove her off the showroom floor when she was

brand-new," Mrs. Gilfred answered. "I've done every lick of maintenance on her myself. Clara and I have been through our whole lives together."

The Buick was certainly a feast for the eyes, Tom wouldn't deny that. But there was something else, too, something that tugged at him in some primitive snippet of desire or memory. It spoke to him on a level that was the totality of his whole life's yearning.

"She's been here in this garage for ten years or more. My vision has gotten so bad I can't even see enough to change the oil, and I sure wasn't about to get her out on the road."

Tom couldn't resist another minute. "Can I open her up?" he asked.

When Mrs. Gilfred nodded, Tom slipped his fingers into the grill and released the latch. He lifted the hood to gaze inside, holding his breath for an instant of anticipation.

"Not too bad," he announced.

Tom bent over the big 322 V-8. The engine, known among its adherents as the Nailhead, definitely looked its age. The belts were rotten and the hoses cracked. Of course all that would have to be replaced, but that was easy.

"Once I can get her started I can give you a better idea of the shape she's in."

Tom unscrewed the wing nut atop the breather and removed it to get a better look at the carburetor. Using the flat tip of a screwdriver he pried open the choke plate. Inside the throttle valve looked fine and it was clear of debris. But it would probably have to be rebuilt anyway. Neglect was a carburetor killer.

"Mrs. Gilfred, I'd love to get a chance to work on her. I'll try to get her running again as inexpensively as I can."

"Good," the older woman said. "Clara needs to be driven. There is a lot of life in her yet."

"Let me get my phone out of my truck and I'll call to have her picked up."

"You're going to tow her to your shop?" Mrs. Gilfred asked.

"We'll put her on a trailer," Tom assured her. "It's never good to tow one of these old automatic transmissions."

"Yes, she is automatic."

Tom nodded absently. "Variable pitch Dynaflow," he said in a whisper that was almost reverent.

Mrs. Gilfred nodded in agreement.

Tom walked the length of the driveway toward his own vehicle. The Ford pickup that he'd bought a couple of years before he married was a fun, functional little truck. Stenciled on the doors was his business name, Bentley's Classic Car Care, and the logo that his wife, Erica, had drawn. It was a winged emblem harkening to the luxurious and historic British car company Bentley Motors. But rather than the graceful winged B, Tom's B3C logo was cartoonish and featured the less awe-inspiring feathered span of a domestic chicken. He always smiled when he saw it, because it reminded him of his wife. Erica was down-to-earth and self-effacing. She had a clear-eyed view of the world and a great, good humor that came out in very unexpected ways.

Quickly Tom made his phone call. From the lock-bin in the truck bed he retrieved the spare battery that he always carried and lugged it back to the Buick. The cables were corroded almost solidly onto the old posts and it took him several minutes to get them loose. Once he'd put his battery in place he cleaned up the connectors as best he could and then connected them tightly.

As Mrs. Gilfred watched, he tried the ignition.

The key clicked on, but nothing happened.

"We're not getting a spark," he told her. "The plugs may be just too dirty."

Mrs. Gilfred leaned beside him, squinting under the hood's dark interior. Even her poor eyesight couldn't inhibit the desire to see the engine in action.

"I know you can get her running again."

"Oh, she'll run," Tom assured her. "She's going to need some work, but I can get you back to driving her for sure."

The old woman smiled slightly at him and then sighed. "No, I can't see to drive anymore," she said. "I'm getting Clara fixed up to sell her."

Momentarily Tom's excited heart skipped a beat. Then rational thought came over him in a wave.

"I'm sure you won't have any trouble lining up a buyer," he said.

Mrs. Gilfred straightened to her full height. "I'm not willing to sell her to just anybody," she said. "Half the tattooed hoodlums in this town have tried to buy her. My good-old Clara deserves a better fate than to be glass-packed and hot-rodded into somebody's muscle machine. She may be able to do a hundred, but she's not a fast woman, she's a lady."

Tom laughed at the description. His heart was beating quickly again. Once more he forced mature thinking to crowd out the kid inside him. With a business barely two years old and a son who'd just started first grade, the last thing his family needed was for him to spend good money on a cool car.

"My shop attracts a lot of collectors," he told her. "They're guys who really love these vehicles just like they are. I can put the word out that you're looking to sell. I'm sure the right person will step up."

"That's what I was hoping," Mrs. Gilfred said. "That's

what I was hoping exactly. And I'm willing to pay you a ten-percent commission."

Tom nodded, pleased. He and Erica could always use the money.

"Husbands are just like used cars. You can get them all over town, they're cheap and unreliable."

The women around the cafeteria lunch table at University Hospital hooted with appreciation at Callie Torreno's joke. Erica Bentley, seated at the edge of the group, laughed, too. The camaraderie at the table was contagious, even if the jokes were old.

"Yeah, you know I used to think I should date older men because they were more mature," Rayliss Morton chimed in. "Then I realized none of them are mature, so I might as well just enjoy the younger ones!"

The women liked that one, too.

Erica was the "new girl," still trying to fit in. Though she wasn't really new. She'd come to work here the first time when the ink wasn't quite dry on her credentials as a Registered Health Information Technician. But she'd quit work when her son, Quint, was born. Now after six years as a stay-at-home mom, this was her second week back on the job.

"It wouldn't be so funny if it wasn't true," Darla Ingalls said. "My husband, Kyle, is such a kid. If it were up to him, we'd eat pizza seven nights a week and he'd decide what to wear to work based on which dirty shirt stinks less."

"But at least you can trust Kyle with the kids," Lena Wallace declared in a case of one-upmanship. "I leave the kids with Aiden to go shopping and he lays down on the couch for a nap. He takes a nap while he's supposed to be watching a three-year-old!"

"Kyle is good with the kids because he's like one of them," Darla told her. "There is nothing positive about that."

Callie turned her attention down the length of the long cafeteria table.

"What about you, Erica?" she asked. "Is your husband an idiot? Or are you married to Mr. Perfect, like Melody here."

The last was said with heavy sarcasm. Erica glanced over at Melody. Melody Garwin was the sour apple in their tasty dessert dish. The least popular member of the group, she typically evoked eye rolls as she described her husband, Gabe, as either "a genius," "a hero" or "someone I look up to."

"Tom isn't perfect," Erica answered. "But that works out well for us, cause neither am I."

The self-deprecating humor was a good response. The group seemed to like her. And Erica was eager to make friends at the office. Having work buddies was, in her memory, one of the nice bonuses of full-time employment.

The cafeteria at University Hospital was a huge expanse of tables and chairs set next to a wall of two-story windows. Glancing around the room provided a short course in the diversity of the community. The majority of the people were Hispanic, but there were almost as many Anglos. A good number of African-Americans. Some Asians. And other people who by virtue of heritage or home country didn't quite fit into any of the large designations. They were all together eating lunch in little groups here and there. The groups were not divided by race or creed or color. At the hospital cafeteria, people were self-segregated by job description.

The housekeeping staff clung together in noisy good humor in the southwest corner, never sharing a word with laundry personnel just across the aisle. The X-ray techs perhaps recognized each other by the radiation meters they wore. And the nurses always found lunch companionship with other nurses. Doctors, of course, whether in lab coats or scrubs were given a wide berth by everyone.

And the women from Medical Records, attired more or less chicly in business attire, sat every day between noon and twelve-thirty at the table parallel to the east wall's brick facade. It had been the same when Erica had worked here before.

She didn't know what occurred at other tables, but Erica imagined that over lunch the doctors discussed patient protocols. And the nurses mused about the prognosis of the sweet old man just admitted from the emergency room.

However, transcription and coding was basically translating Latin names of diseases and technical descriptions of procedures into a classification of numbers. Not the kind of interesting stuff people wanted to chat about over salad. Instead they filled their lunch break with family news and hospital gossip.

Callie and Darla were the ringleaders of the group. Callie, in her mid-forties, was happily divorced and funny to the point of caustic.

Darla was a couple of years younger than Erica. She obviously admired Callie's power and freedom and lived vicariously though the stories of her dating life.

Rayliss had never been married, but was an expert on the subject. Lena was pretty and peppy, wrapped up in her home life with husband and kids. Melody, despite being married to the self-described "perfect man" was humorless, ill-at-ease and tended to overeat. And Mrs. Converse, the supervisor of the department, had the good sense to take her lunch at her desk every day.

Erica imagined herself eating alone, but she didn't want that. She'd just spent the past six years being home full-time. She'd eaten thousands of lunches alone. Though mostly she'd eaten with Quint. In memory she could see him negotiating over squash.

"You need to eat five bites to know if you like it," she informed him.

"It's yellow," he replied. "So I already know that I probably don't."

Erica smiled to herself.

"What are you grinning about?" Callie asked. "Do you know Dr. Carnegy's wife?"

The discussion had moved from the faults of men in general to the faults of specific men, namely Dr. Carnegy. And the fault in question was that he was cheating on his wife.

"Oh, no," Erica assured them quickly. "I was thinking about something else. I was thinking about my son."

"Aww…" Rayliss said, drawing the sound out extravagantly. "Isn't that sweet. How old is he?"

"He's six," Erica answered. "He just started first grade."

"How's that going?" Darla asked.

Erica nodded. "He went to half-day kindergarten last year, so he's very excited to be in 'big school' all day."

"So, who's your after-school care?" Lena asked. "I think the school system's extended day program is just not the place for the younger ones."

"Quint's not in after-school care," Erica answered. "My husband does that."

"Your husband doesn't work." Melody made the statement flatly, but the tone of superiority couldn't be missed.

"He does work," Erica quickly corrected. "Actually he owns his own business, so he picks up our son after school. And then Quint hangs out at his shop until I get off."

"Oh, that's great," Lena said. "What kind of shop is it?"

"It's Bentley's Classic Car Care," Erica answered. "He'll

service whatever drives in, but he specializes in older vehicles."

"So he fixes junk cars," Melody said.

Erica caught Darla trying to hide a grin behind her hand. It stiffened her backbone.

"That's pretty much the kind of thing my mother would say," she commented easily. "But Tom makes a good enough living that I only had to come back to work when I decided I was ready."

Erica was proud of that. She knew plenty of women who'd only been able to take minimum leave for each child. Even getting the new business off the ground, she and Tom had been very clear about their priorities.

Melody piped in. "So your mother doesn't like your husband?"

Erica shrugged. "My mom thought that working at a hospital, I would marry a rich doctor."

That statement provoked guffaws all around the table.

"The myth of the handsome single doctor," Rayliss replied shaking her head. "I think everybody's mother has bought into that one."

"They're all married by med school," Callie stated as a matter of fact. "'Cause somebody has to support them when mommy and daddy are all tapped out. You might catch one in midcareer, divorced and on the rebound. But by then, all he's got left is the debt."

Everyone nodded in agreement.

The "docs," as they were known collectively to the hospital staff, were mostly nice people, professionally respected, endlessly fascinating to watch, but not held in the kind of awe more typical of the community at large.

"It's just another of those inescapable facts of life," Callie said. "So many men, so many reasons *not* to hook up with them."

"That is, except for Dr. Glover," Darla said with a sly glance toward the far end of the table.

Callie blushed and shook her head. "He's a pharmacist not an M.D. I know it's likely that I might break his heart, but he does bring out the cougar in me," she said. "He's got to be at least ten years younger."

More like fifteen, Erica thought but kept the observation to herself. A romance around the table was an entertaining interlude for everyone. And Erica was so happy, contented with her own marriage, that she couldn't help wanting that for everyone.

A few minutes later, the group finished eating and bussed their table. As they headed back to the department, Erica made a quick stop at the ladies' room to freshen up. She surveyed herself critically in the mirror.

She wore her long, light brown hair up in a neat twist on the back of her head. It gave her a more serious, businesslike appearance. The reading glasses helped, too.

The pink-and-black tweed suit was a retread from her prepregnancy days. It was still a good-looking outfit and it still fit, but it looked different. Erica turned sideways and surveyed the lines of her body. She'd lost all of the baby weight and exercised herself into the best condition since her volleyball days in high school, but to her own eyes, she didn't look the same. That young, fresh, twentysomething was now somebody's mommy. And wearing these clothes from her former life reminded her of the passage of time in a way that her thirtieth birthday last summer hadn't.

Erica decided that a little midday pep talk could go a long way and began rooting through her designer knockoff handbag. When she found her cell phone, she immediately punched in her speed dial. After only one ring, the voice of reassurance answered.

"Hello, gorgeous working woman."

Erica smiled into the phone.

"I just wanted to hear the sound of your voice," she answered. "What's up at the shop?"

"I've got two cars on lifts, if that's the question you're asking," he replied with a teasing lilt to his voice. "If that 'up' inquiry is more personal, I think I could be lured from this grindstone for a quickie with a hot babe like my wife."

She laughed, just as he intended that she would.

"I'm not such a hot babe anymore," Erica said. "These days I'm somebody's mommy."

"Woman, you are hotter than a '48 DeSoto with a bad radiator," he said.

Erica shook her head, smiling into the phone.

"So how's your day going?" Tom asked her.

"Well, I spent the morning coding like a crazy woman. I ate a slightly limp taco salad for lunch and I'm now hanging out in front of the bathroom mirror missing my man."

Tom chuckled lightly. "It sounds like you might be asking yourself why you were so anxious to go back to work."

"I know exactly why I wanted to come back," she corrected. "I like my work. And we need my wages to cover our household expenses so we can give our business some room to grow."

"And it's growing," he assured her. "Wait till you see this car I brought in today. I swear, Erica, it's the most beautiful car ever built."

"Yeah, I bet you say that to all the '57 Chevys," she answered.

He laughed. "Actually, it's a Buick. A '56 Roadmaster convertible. Great condition."

"Only driven by a little old lady to church on Sunday mornings?"

"Sort of," Tom answered. "Although I think this little old lady may have been more interested in whiskey dens on Saturday night."

Erica listened to her husband's enthusiasm. He loved cars. He loved everything about them. She didn't really understand it, but she was grateful for it. A car had brought them together in the first place.

She'd just finished her afternoon classes at St. Phillip's College. It was raining heavily and the traffic was challenging enough. Then her sad old Honda began acting weird. The motor raced, but she had no power and the unmistakable smell of burning wires began to permeate the interior. All around her cars honked impatiently. Erica barely managed to get the sedan off to the side of the road. She opened the hood and got out in the pouring rain to look underneath. The only thing she knew about engines was how to check the oil and the radiator. Both of those seemed fine, but the smell of burnt wiring was still pungent. She stood there pondering who to call. Her mother would never come to help, but she would undoubtedly find a reason why a broken-down auto was Erica's own fault. Her girlfriends were not any more knowledgeable about cars than she was. And her kid sister, Letty, was smart and quick-thinking, but she was only twelve.

As she pondered which direction to walk for help, a flashy new pickup pulled up behind her. From behind the wheel a big, burly guy with thick, black hair and a scar across his nose got out. He looked a little scary. But Erica realized pretty quickly that her pulse wasn't racing from fear. Tom Bentley was strong, streetwise and sexy. He was also the sweetest guy she'd ever met. How could she not fall for him?

"I can't wait for you to see this Buick," he was saying on the phone. "There's something about it…it's like…I don't know, it's so familiar in a really good way."

"Maybe you used to drive it in another life," she teased.

"I've got my fingers crossed that I can fix it well enough to be able to cruise it around the corner in this one," he answered. "So what does your afternoon look like?"

"Charts," she answered. "I'm just coding charts. I'm still so slow. It's frustrating when I think how efficient I used to be."

"You expected that," he reminded her. "You're a little rusty, but you are really good at what you do, Erica. They're lucky to have you back."

She sighed, feeling much better. She could always count on him to have confidence in her. Talking to Tom was like refueling her self-esteem.

"Future view!" he challenged in an infomercial announcer voice. "The Bentleys—ten years from now."

Erica laughed lightly. Future view was a silly little game the two of them had made up. They'd been playing it since their dating days. It was ridiculous, but somehow funny and encouraging as well. It lifted them out of the everyday and kept their dreams on track.

"Ten years," Erica mused. "Okay. In ten years for sure, I'll be the boss of this place."

"If there's any justice," Tom agreed.

She laughed.

"In ten years we'll have paid off the small business start-up loan," she said.

"Whoo-hoo!" Tom cheered. "And we'll decide to celebrate by taking a second honeymoon."

"I believe that technically it would be a first honeymoon," she pointed out.

"I was never that good with math," he answered, before feigning over-the-top sincerity. "And every minute with you, lovely wife, is a honeymoon for me."

"Shut up, you idiot," she responded playfully.

"Ten years, your mom will be married like three more times," he suggested.

Erica sighed and nodded at that. "And my sister will be some amazing something, so busy we will hardly ever get to see her."

"She will never be too busy for you."

"I hope not," she answered. "Ten years, Quint will be sixteen. He'll probably be as tall as his dad."

"Probably," Tom agreed. "But with any luck at all, he'll look more like you."

"At the very least, he won't have the broken nose."

Tom laughed. "He'll be old enough to drive."

"Wow, that's hard to get my mind around," Erica said. "We'll have to get him a car. Maybe that Buick driven by an old lady."

"Be careful what you wish for," her husband warned. "You might prefer that he fall in love with a real live girl."

"You think he might not?"

"For us testosterone producers, a beautiful car can be very, very seductive."

Chapter 2

RICK'S ROADSIDE SERVICE showed up with the Buick about two-thirty. Tom hardly had time to supervise the unloading and get it safely tucked into bay four before it was time to head over to pick up Quint.

He left his truck parked in the lot and took the aging, rusty sedan that Erica had when they married. It was ugly, but he kept it dependable. And, unlike his truck, it had a perfect place for a car seat in the back. Within a few minutes of three o'clock the street in front of Woodlawn Elementary was clogged with traffic. Moms, grandmas and babysitters all waited patiently for their turn to pull up to the sidewalk in front of the school. Tom was fairly certain he was the only guy involved in this ritual. At least, he had yet to see another man waiting. He didn't mind. He figured it was a lesson in patience, something much required in being a dad, and it gave him a few minutes to make phone calls away from the noise and interruptions of the shop.

He called to let the owner of a '38 Studebaker know that he'd finally located a rear-seat deck at a salvage pick-and-pull in Ohio.

He gave the bad news to the fellow who'd just bought a "cherry Mustang" that the engine had been rebuilt.

And he reminded the very wealthy developer from Olmos Park that he still hadn't been paid for the drivetrain work on his 1970 GTO.

One of the calls he made was to Mrs. Gilfred.

"I just wanted to let you know that 'Clara' made it safely to the shop."

"What you say?" the older woman hollered into the phone. "Who is this?"

Tom repeated himself more loudly a couple of times before Mrs. Gilfred understood.

"Oh, thank you for letting me know," she said. "I watched them pull away and I honestly felt as if I was waving goodbye to an old friend."

Tom smiled. He could understand that connection. "Try to think of her as going to a vacation spa for a little rest and rejuvenation," he said.

"Say what?"

Tom repeated again.

Mrs. Gilfred chuckled. "That certainly sounds better," she said. "I only wish I was there myself."

He patiently went over everything that he'd told her earlier about his impression of the vehicle's condition and he reassured her that as soon as he'd made a complete assessment, he'd be back in touch.

"I didn't get most of that," the old lady complained. "I can't hear a blame thing over this telephone."

Since Tom was already yelling into his cell, he found that

fact almost as frustrating as she did. He made a mental note to find a way to communicate with her directly in the future.

When he edged up to the pickup spot in front of the school, he put his phone away. He flipped down the passenger-side visor, displaying the bright yellow number 214. But it was unnecessary, Mrs. Salinas, the first-grade teacher, recognized him. Quint did, too. His son was all bright smiles as he hoisted his book bag and came running in his direction.

"Good afternoon," he said to the pretty, young teacher as she opened the rear passenger door.

Quint scrambled inside and into his booster seat. He managed to buckle himself in.

"See you tomorrow," Tom said to Mrs. Salinas.

"Yeah, see you tomorrow," Quint echoed.

His son's smile for his teacher was absolute adoration and the one she returned to him was equally genuine. With parents she was more guarded, but that was okay, too. She obviously loved her job, and if Quint's enthusiasm for school was any measure, she was good at it.

Tom pulled away from the curb, slowly, carefully, cognizant of all the kids being kids, not paying attention, and their parents distracted. He didn't mind taking it slow.

"I was like the smartest kid in my class today, Dad," Quint confessed excitedly. "I did better than anybody, except Maddycinn Guerra and she's like the smartest every day, so that doesn't count."

Tom grinned. "Just so you do your best," he said. "Your mom and I are always proud when you do your best."

Quinton Bentley was six years old. His light brown hair was cropped closely to his head, making his big brown eyes seem even larger and brighter than they were. He was a little bit small for his age. Perhaps the remnants of his early struggles as a preemie, born six weeks early, or maybe it was some long-ago ancestor who was short and slight. It didn't matter to Tom, he was just happy that his child was healthy. And it didn't seem to matter to Quint. He'd been blessed with a temperament that looked at the world to see all the positives, not the negatives. Other boys might be bigger, but they could never win at hide-and-seek by scrunching inside the radiator closet. And none of them were ever small enough to slide beneath the chain link to retrieve the softball when somebody hit it over the fence.

Tom paused for traffic at the street in front of the school. Their home was to the right. The neat little two-bedroom, postwar house was on French Place just on the other side of Woodlawn Lake. But he turned left instead, toward Zarzamora. From there he drove north to Fredericksburg Road toward his shop on West Avenue.

"Did you know my teeth are going to fall out?" Quint asked him.

Tom raised an eyebrow as he glanced in the rearview mirror. "Do you have a loose one?"

"No, I don't think so," Quint answered, and then continued to try to talk as he tested each one.

"There's no need to be in a hurry," Tom assured him. "Baby teeth usually start coming out next year, I think."

"Baby teeth?" Quint scoffed at the description. "I'm no baby! Mrs. Salinas calls them *deciduous teeth*, Dad. Babies don't have teeth at all."

He nodded. "I guess you're right," Tom said.

"All our deciduous teeth come out and then we get permanent teeth that are bigger and stronger," Quint informed him. "Do you know what that's called?"

Tom shook his head.

"Exfoliation."

"That's a big word," Tom pointed out.

Quint agreed. "I like big words," he said.

Tom smiled.

"Cody Raza said that when our teeth come out, we can put them under our pillow and get money. Is that true?"

Tom was thoughtful for a moment. "I don't know," he answered truthfully. "I think we'll have to ask your mother on that one."

Erica was the one who knew about what families did and what traditions they should or shouldn't have. Tom knew nothing about families until he had one of his own. His life before Erica had provided the kind of education that most people never acquire. It had prepared him for a lot of things. Love and family, however, were not among them. He was feeling his way through parenthood one day at a time. His wife always assured him that love, patience and good intentions were all that was needed. Still, some details required a breadth of experience that Tom simply didn't have.

"I hope it's right," Quint said with great seriousness. He pulled a very scary look as he counted his teeth, speculating how much money they might bring him.

Tom chuckled.

A few moments later, he turned into the driveway of their family business. Bentley's Classic Car Care or, as they called it, "the shop," was a dream come true. It had been Tom's dream, but it would have never come true without Erica.

The long brick building with four service bays was set far back from the street, surrounded by ten feet of metal fence and twenty-four-hour video surveillance. Tom kept the place neat as a pin and free from the marks of taggers and graffiti artists. He was asking car owners to trust him with valuable vehicles. Even the ones in sad disrepair were irreplaceable. His customers needed to see that he understood that.

Tom drove through the gate and parked his car in the back of the building. Quint gathered up his book bag and the two headed inside.

His young son announced his presence with a general yell, "I'm here!" he said, as if everyone had been waiting for him. Tom's three employees stopped what they were doing long enough the acknowledge the six-year-old.

Hector Ruiz was forty-something. He was an excellent mechanic and really knew his way around old cars. Unfortunately, he was also overly familiar with alcohol. He was a binge drinker who would disappear without warning for weeks at a time. None of his former employers would tolerate that. Tom did. Because when Hector was on the job, he was the best.

Gus Gruber would never be that good. Gus was short, fat and nearing sixty. He was a capable mechanic. He knew how things worked and how to replace parts that weren't functioning. But his real skill was bodywork. He was an artist, in his own way. And like an artist, he had a temperament that might be mistaken for laziness.

Cliff Aleman was Tom's oldest friend and the guy most like Tom himself. They were both a couple of years past thirty. They both had great wives. Cliff had two kids, a boy and a girl.

Tom and Cliff had been roommates at Job Corps. Later they'd been bachelors on the town, sharing a cheap, stripped-down apartment with mattresses on the floor and a fridge full of beer. Back then, both of them dreamed about owning their own business. Cliff's dream was still in the dream stage. And it didn't look to Tom like it would get out of that phase anytime soon. He and his wife, Trish, had just bought a new house in Westover Hills. It was in a clean, pretty, just-built subdivision with a brand-new elementary school. It was hard not to be envious, but Erica talked him out of it.

"Owning a business is not like working for wages. We're investing in the future," she told him. "And besides, living in Woodlawn insures that we'll never have to enroll Quint in Spanish immersion."

Tom had laughed. It was true. Their son had already picked up enough street Spanglish to understand and obey all the scolding grandmothers at the playground.

Tom opened the side door separating the work floor from the office of Bentley's Classic Car Care and ushered Quint inside. He and Erica agreed. It was too dangerous for their son to spend his time among the lifts and machinery of the bays. A mechanic shop was a hazardous place even for adults. So they made a deal with Quint. He would be the after-school office manager. He would sit at his dad's desk, do his homework, keep himself busy. And he could answer the phone and then use the intercom to page the right person.

From the office fridge at the back of the room, Tom retrieved a carton of milk, a Baggie full of grapes and a chunk of cheese.

"Do you have a lot of homework?" he asked.

Quint nodded. "I have spelling words," he answered with a sigh. "And some of them are really long."

Tom grinned at him. "You like big words, remember."

"I like to say them, not to spell them."

"Holler at me on the speaker if you need something," he told his son.

Quint took him at his word. The door to the office had hardly shut behind him when he heard the little voice reverberating through the shop.

"I love you, Dad!"

Tom couldn't help smiling and the other guys didn't even bother to try to tease him.

Chapter 3

ERICA GOT OFF WORK AT four-thirty. The longest, hottest part of her commute was the walk from her office to the bus stop. She didn't complain much about the distance. Even those employees who drove their own cars were assigned to lots and garages some distance from the building's air-conditioning. She was really looking forward to the new BRT, the bus rapid transit service, that was scheduled to run from the medical center down Fredericksburg Road. The Fred Burg Line, as they called it, would supposedly get her to within blocks of their business in less than fifteen minutes. The current bus was more like a milk run, stopping block after block as it edged toward downtown.

They'd decided on leaving her car at the shop both to save money on parking fees and to free them from buying another vehicle. Her old sedan was dependable enough to get around their neighborhood, but if she was to take on real commuting, she'd have to get something better.

With a young family, it always seemed that money was in short supply.

Though there was some good news on that account. She'd been called down to payroll late in the day to inform her that an error had been made when calculating her pay rate. She was actually going to be bringing home almost forty dollars a month more than she'd thought. It wasn't a fortune, but she was humming as happily as if it were.

As she stood at the bus stop her cell phone began beeping. She glanced at it to see her mother's name on the display screen. Erica groaned aloud, but then stuck a determined smile on her face as she answered.

"Hi, Mom."

Ann Marie Maddock was not the kind of mother who tolerated *attitude* in her children. Attitude was rather broadly interpreted to include everything from petulance to grief, and even ordinary exhaustion was forbidden. Ann Marie was the absolute center of her own universe and the only person in her sphere allowed to have emotional ups and downs.

"What are you doing?" she asked Erica.

"I'm just getting off work."

Her mother made a sound of disapproval. "I warned you that if you married that grease monkey he'd never make you a decent living."

"We're doing just fine, Mom."

"Not fine enough that you can stay home and do for yourself," Ann Marie pointed out.

"I'm ready to go back to work," Erica insisted. "With Quint in school all day, well, I'd much rather be at the hospital than hanging around the house."

Ann Marie sniffed. "I should think that now that the boy is out from underfoot and is big enough not to ruin the furniture, you'd be fixing up the house."

"My house is fine, Mother," Erica said firmly. It was an old argument, a never-ending one, and one Erica knew she could never really win.

"It's a disgrace," Ann Marie said. "Every stick of furniture you have looks like it came from the thrift store. I suppose if you're going to live in such a tacky little house, you don't see any need to buy anything nice. But you should at least make an effort."

Erica rolled her eyes and fortunately, her mother couldn't see her face.

"I painted the living room just two months ago," she said by way of defense."

"A gallon of paint doesn't equal redecorating," Ann Marie said. "Don't think that everyone who walks in doesn't notice the worn spots in that rug. That sofa is not vintage, it's just old. And those tacky curtains, I wouldn't have those hanging in my garage."

Erica had bought the couch when she was still single. And the curtains had come with the house. They were pretty bad, but Erica wasn't about to concede the point.

"We like our house, Mom," Erica said. "It suits us."

"Nonsense," she said. "You don't spend money on your home, because every penny is going into your husband's business."

"It's not Tom's business it's *our* business," Erica corrected. "And then there's Quint's college fund. Both of those things are more important to me than new draperies."

Her mother's sigh was long-suffering. "Well, I hope your sister ends up having better sense than you do," Ann Marie said. "Though I don't see any evidence of it yet. With her looks, why is she wasting her time studying science? Only unattractive women go into that field."

"I don't think that's true, Mom," Erica said. "And if it is, well, Letty has always been a trailblazer."

"Well, that girl certainly hasn't been blazing a trail home lately," her mother said. "Have you seen her?"

"Uh, no, not really," Erica hedged, but then decided that she shouldn't be deceptive. "She's babysitting Quint tonight."

"Oh, really? You and Tom are going out? On a Friday night?"

It sounded like a criticism and Erica was immediately defensive. "We haven't been out for ages," she said. "And Tom doesn't know it yet, but we have a reason to celebrate."

"Oh?"

"Yeah, well, it's no big deal, really, but the payroll office made a mistake and I'm going to be bringing home more money than I thought."

Erica explained more than she needed to about how education and experience were calculated in the University Hospital employment contracts.

"So, Tom doesn't know about this extra money?" Ann Marie asked.

"Not yet."

"Then don't tell him."

"Huh?"

"Don't tell him," Erica's mother repeated. "What he doesn't know about he'll never miss."

"What do you mean?"

"I'm talking about a way for you to have some money that's your own. Some money for you to use for things you want."

"Mother. I have all the money I need. I'm the one who makes sure the bills are paid. I even do the accounting for the business. I am the finance director of the family."

"But you're not acting that way," Ann Marie pointed out.

"You never stick anything aside for fixing up the house or buying new furniture. You're just completely locked into going along the path that best suits *his* goals. Sometimes a woman needs to strike out on her own. She needs to buy some things simply because she wants them. Heaven has just handed you a way to do that without causing your family even the slightest sacrifice."

"That's doesn't make any sense," Erica said.

"It makes perfect sense," Ann Marie insisted. "If you throw this extra money in with the rest, it will just disappear. Every dime will go to some sort of metal something in your husband's shop and it will not bring you one moment of pleasure or joy. But if you took this bit that nobody even knows about, or will ever miss, and put it into your own little nest egg, very soon you'll have enough to buy a new rug or a new couch or decent drapes. That's the sort of thing that feeds a woman's soul. And you've been soulless too long."

"Mother, that is just ridiculous," Erica told her. "Buying stuff doesn't feed my soul. That's not me. That's you. And if you come up with some extra money, please, feel free to go out and buy whatever you like."

Her mother huffed in displeasure. "You should be saving money to add on another bedroom at the very least."

"We don't need another bedroom."

"Yes, you do," Ann Marie insisted. "What if you change your mind about having another baby?"

"That is none of your concern and not up for discussion," Erica stated firmly. "We have one healthy, happy child. That's enough for us."

"Fine, if you say so, but you'll still need another bedroom if I have to come and live with you."

"Mother, you will not be coming to live with us."

"I may have to," she said. "I'm not as attractive as I used to be. This thing with Melvin may not last through the week. I may be out on my ear and with no place to go, except your tiny, tacky, cramped little house."

"May God forbid!" Erica said with genuine abhorrence. Her multidivorced mother was currently living with a wealthy widower. Ann Marie had very bad luck with men, or perhaps she made her own luck. But under no circumstances did Erica ever want her mother to move in with her.

The rest of the conversation was as tight-lipped and disapproving as Ann Marie could make it. Erica's relationship with her mother had never been the best. But Ann Marie was, for all intents and purposes, her only parent.

Stuart Maddock, Erica's father, had been a lawyer, tall, good-looking and athletic. According to Ann Marie, he had a wandering eye for the ladies. Her mother divorced him. More than that, she proudly claimed to have stripped him of every dime he had and sullied his reputation so badly he could no longer make a living in his home town, not even in his home state. He'd moved to Florida to take a job as a golf pro. Except for an occasional Christmas or birthday card, Erica hadn't heard from him since.

She'd had two dads in the years right after that, Dale and Doug. In her mind they were interchangeable and she had no idea which was which. They both just disappeared and those divorces were rarely commented upon.

Then Ann Marie married Cesar, Letty's father. What she mostly remembered about him was that he left, too. And he left Letty behind.

Some women took up needlepoint. Others gambled at bingo. Ann Marie's hobby became divorce. She spent her years in conflict and court cases trying to wring the last dime out of every man who'd done her wrong.

Nobody who knew that about her ever wanted to get on her bad side. Erica included. She was grateful when she saw the bus crest the top of the hill at Medical Drive. It was a perfect excuse to get off the phone.

"Got to go, Mom," she said in a rush. "I'll remind Letty to call you."

Erica didn't wait for her mother's response, but quickly hit the end button. She heaved a sigh of relief and shook her head before stepping onto the bus and slipping her pass under the bar-code reader.

She made her way toward an empty seat near the back and settled in as the bus began to move. Glancing around, she recognized most of the faces. After only a couple of weeks, she already felt familiar with those she thought of as "the regulars." They travelled the same time of day that she did and that sort of cheered her. She knew already that commuting was sure to become a hot, tiring daily task, but for now it was still a new enough experience to be sort of strangely enjoyable. After six long years of simply running errands with Quint, she was once more a part of the community of working people. That was exciting. The isolation of being a stay-at-home mom had had its challenges. She hadn't realized how much she had missed just being out in the world, talking about other things and seeing other people.

A lot had changed over the past six years. There were new hospitals and a lot of opportunity for a smart, experienced professional coder like Erica. But this old job was appealing because it was fairly close to home and she was familiar with it. She didn't like stress and she avoided risk. Stress and risk were her mother's drugs of choice. Erica was determined to be drug free.

When she arrived at her stop, she exited out the back and waited at the corner to cross with the light. She walked the four blocks to Bentley's Classic Car Care, mentally taking note of everything she needed in the next few hours to perfect the evening out with her husband.

She heard the whiz of hydraulics and the clink of wrenches just before her husband's shop came into view. Through the glass in the front office she could see Quint at Tom's desk. He was bent over a paper, looking very official.

As she crossed the lot she glanced into the work bays. There were three cars parked inside. Erica didn't immediately spot Tom, but Gus waved at her, so she knew her husband would get the word that she was here.

As she approached the doorway her son glanced up, and when he saw her a big grin spread across his face.

She walked through the front office door. A loud horn blared announcing her entrance. Erica was so accustomed to it, she didn't even flinch.

"Good afternoon, sir," she said with feigned formality. "I'd like to know if Bentley's is the best classic car repair in the city."

"Of course it is, Mom," Quint answered. She always pretended to be a customer and he always pretended that the game was silly, but she knew he liked it.

"Are you doing homework?" she asked him.

"All done. It was only one math paper and my spelling words."

"So what are you working on?"

"Just drawing," he said. "There is nothing else to do here." Erica nodded.

"How was school?"

"Good," he answered, nodding.

"Learn anything interesting?"

The little boy shrugged. "I guess so," he said.

The side door opened and Tom came in, grinning.

"Hi, favorite woman," he said. "How was your afternoon?"

"Busy, exhausting," she answered honestly, then added, "but it's about to get a lot better, spending some time with my guys."

Tom was near enough to snake an arm around her waist and pull her close to him. In front of their son, he gave her a very chaste kiss on the end of the nose, but he also managed a surreptitious pat on her backside.

"I'd better get this bored little boy home," she told him. "His aunt Letty is coming to see him tonight after supper."

Tom raised an eyebrow. "Is she coming to visit all of us?"

"No," Erica answered. "She wants to spend all her time with Quint. So I guess you and I will just have to make ourselves scarce."

There was a smile in Tom's eyes, but he kept his voice appropriately grave. "Do we have any plans for this…ah… 'scarcity'?"

"Not as yet," Erica told him. "But I'm sure we'll think of something."

He nodded, grinning at her. "I'm sure we will."

Quint had already packed up his papers and gathered up his backpack. Knowing Letty was coming to babysit was a big incentive to get moving.

Tom and Erica managed one more peck on the lips before she was out the back door and into her old sedan. Quint seemed a little tired, a little quiet. When she used to pick him up after kindergarten, he was always very chatty and full of information. But his after-school wait with Dad at work seemed to wind him down. Glancing into the rearview mirror, Erica saw a big old yawn contorting his face. She silently mused that she could go for a nice nap herself. But she knew she couldn't and that he wouldn't.

Once they were home, she resisted the desire to sit down and put her feet up. Instead she changed her clothes and headed straight for the kitchen. She quickly threw together a meat loaf and put it in the oven. While it was cooking she straightened the house, put a load of towels in the wash and commented positively on Quint's efforts on his video game karaoke.

By the time she was setting the table, she was about half-way hoping that her sister would call up and cancel her visit. But she did not. Letty showed up early, before Tom had even gotten home from work.

The two sisters didn't look much alike. Erica was medium height and curvy. Letty, on the other hand, was almost six feet tall. She was as long and lean as any runway model, which was what her mom had wanted for her. Erica was supposed to marry a doctor and Letty was supposed to grace the covers of fashion magazines. Neither had chosen to live out Mom's fantasy.

Now a senior at UTSA, Letty had gotten a bare-bones scholarship and, with a lot of hard work, had turned it into exceptional grades and top-tier opportunities for graduate school. Her first love was physics and she had worked the previous summer cataloging condensed matter at Rice University's Ultracold Lab. She wasn't sure exactly what she wanted to do with her life yet. Whatever it was, Erica was certain it would be exceptional, because that's what her sister was all about.

"I love eating over here," Letty told her. "It always feels like a real home."

"It *is* a real home," Erica replied, laughing.

"I know, but I like how you make a big deal of it," Letty said. "Most of the people I know, their kids eat fast food in the car on the way to somewhere. With you it's like Norman Rockwell or something."

Erica shrugged. "It's important to Tom," she said.

Letty nodded as if she understood. Truth was, Erica wasn't sure if she understood it all herself. Tom's childhood had been strange and fragmented. His expectations for himself and his family were high. But his understanding of what typical home life entailed was gleaned from sanitized after-school specials and Disney movies. Real people could never replicate that. But Erica tried to foster what she considered the best aspects of family life. Two parents, committed forever, was at the top of her list.

Quint dragged Letty away to his room for some fantasy fencing. Erica put together a salad. The house was small enough that she could hear every thrust of the sword as her son vocalized, "Take that, you scoundrel!"

To which her sister responded with a pirate's "Argh!"

The noise of battle went on uninterrupted and was finally joined by the sound of Tom's pickup in the driveway. He came in through the garage door into the kitchen and kissed his wife on the top of her head.

"Do I have time for a shower?"

"If you make it quick," Erica told him.

He winked at her by way of agreement and then called out a hello to Letty as he went down the hallway.

Alone in the kitchen with the warmth of the meat loaf just out of the oven, Erica smiled to herself.

Life is good, she thought. She had a healthy, happy child and a great marriage. They weren't rich, but they weren't living in dread of their mortgage payment. She had a job she liked, the closeness of a dear sister and even her mom was better than no mom at all. Life was very good and she wanted to hang on to these ordinary moments that made up so much of that.

"Ta-da!"

Erica looked up to see Letty blocking the dining room doorway. "For your enlightenment and edification, may I present, the one, the only, Quintasma the Magnificent!"

She stepped aside to reveal Erica's adorable son, clad in a sparkly shawl from the back of her closet and a weird head-dress made from plastic dinosaurs chained together with pipe cleaners.

"I am Quintasma," he announced. "And I can read your mind."

"Really? What am I thinking?"

Quint placed index fingers on each of his temples and closed his eyes to take a deep, dramatic breath.

"You are thinking that we need to wash our hands before we sit down to dinner," he announced.

"OMG! Alert the media," Erica responded. "My son is psychic. And also very cute." She tweaked his cheek.

"Please, ma'am, I'm thinking so hard that my brain might *explode*. And that would be very bad and a big mess."

"Yes, it would. Brains everywhere."

"Brains everywhere?" Tom said as he walked up, looking clean and neat in jeans and a sports shirt, his hair still damp from the shower. "That sounds like my wife's side of the family."

"Your son can now read minds," Erica told him.

Tom raised an eyebrow and then bent forward, pressing his forehead against his son's. "What am I thinking?" he asked.

"That you're hungry," Quint answered.

"You *can* read my mind!"

His declaration of incredulity was so well faked, Quint was compelled to confess the truth.

"Not really, Dad. It's just that you're always hungry when you get home from work."

"You're very smart to figure that out," Tom said. "And, really, it's better to be smart than to read people's minds."

"You think so?"

His father nodded. "What people are thinking is sometimes so confused, they don't even understand it themselves."

The women at the table laughed in agreement. Quint joined in with a giggle as well.

Erica spooned out generous servings of meat loaf and salad. The conversation was lively. They listened to Letty's stories of life at school. Quint had a couple of those as well. His mostly involved who jumped the highest, ran the fastest or threw the farthest. He had to be encouraged not to get up and demonstrate.

When they were finished, Letty began gathering the plates.

"I can do that," Erica said.

"No you can't. Quint and I are on cleanup. Go get ready for your romantic rendezvous with your husband."

Erica shook her head, but as she passed Tom's chair he grasped her arm. With a glance toward the kitchen, making sure Quint and Letty were out of hearing distance, he whispered, "Why don't you put in your diaphragm."

Tom whistled appreciably as Erica walked into the living room. He watched her smooth down the sides of her short, black dress, which looked even shorter in impossibly high heels.

"It's a little tight," she said apologetically.

"Tight is good," Tom told her.

"You look beautiful, Mom," Quint agreed. He and Letty were seated cross-legged on the floor playing slapjack and crazy eights.

"It's fits fine," Letty assured her sister. "Not your usual, but a dash of hotness never hurts."

Erica laughed as if the suggestion was incredulous. For Tom it went without saying. His wife was hot. Not in the slutty outward way of some, but in that simmering-beneath-the-surface kind of way that made a guy just desperate to get his mitts on her.

There were kisses and hugs for Quint and promises not to be too late. Tom wrapped his arm around her waist as they headed out.

"Where are we going?" she asked.

"It's a surprise."

She grinned at him. "I love surprises."

He escorted her to the passenger side of his truck. Tom was feeling very lucky. His wife looked great. She smelled great. She was irresistible. As he opened the door with his right hand, he casually allowed his left to slide down to the generous curve of her backside.

"Have I told you how crazy I am about this butt?" he asked her.

She laughed. "I don't think you've mentioned it lately," she answered. "But you have shown some fondness for it in the past."

He patted it affectionately. "It's better now than when I married you."

Erica shook her head in denial. "It's certainly bigger now, but I think better may be up for debate."

"Just easier for me to get my hands on."

He gave her an exaggerated leering expression, complete with tongue hanging out.

She giggled at him.

Tom closed her door and rounded the truck to get in behind the steering wheel. Carefully he pulled out of the driveway and headed up the street. He reached out to clasp her wrist.

"Come over here, closer to me," he said.

Erica scooted across the Ford's bench seat to sit beside him. The move edged the hem of her skirt higher and he couldn't resist slipping a hand between her thighs.

"That's much better," he said.

At the stoplight at Zarzamora, he kissed her. It wasn't his typical husbandly peck, but rather a full-throttle, pedal-to-the-metal, I-can't-get-enough-of-you, kiss.

When their lips parted she sighed into his neck and it pulsed through him pleasurably.

A honk from the vehicle behind them prompted Tom to get his eyes back on the road and his foot back on the accelerator.

Erica leaned her head against his shoulder.

"You make me feel like a teenager," she told him.

Tom grinned at her as he moved his hand higher on her thigh. "Can I feel you up like a teenager?"

She laughed. "Not in traffic."

When he turned onto West Avenue, Erica questioned him.

"Are we stopping by the shop?"

"I want to show you the Buick," he said. "You won't believe how great it looks."

Her token agreement was a bit lackluster, but Tom was certain that was because she just hadn't seen the car. Still, he tried in words to do it justice.

"Even the finish is good on it," he said. "And 1956 was

before they'd invented clear coat. They were just covering lead enamel with lacquer."

She nodded absently.

"The convertible top is in excellent shape," Tom continued. "Not a lot of sun damage or cracks. I'll be able to just clean it up and apply some protectant."

"Uh-huh," Erica responded.

"And I think I'll be able to get the original engine in top shape," he said. "It's going to be a collector's dream."

"Great," she said as she managed to pull out a smile for his enthusiasm.

Tom drove in through the gate, making sure that it was securely locked behind them and getting the lights on before he ushered her inside.

"I just knew you had to see this," he told her.

Tom led her back through the shop to the fourth bay where the two-tone blue Buick sat with its hood up. He switched on the hanging utility light, which exposed the well-aged V-8. He leaned over it and sighed with pleasure before glancing back at his wife.

"Come have a look," he told her.

Erica took one step forward, but maintained her distance.

"I don't want to get grease on my dress," she said.

Tom nodded. "Oh yeah, right. Of course not," he said. "Come have a look at the interior."

He walked around and opened the driver's door for her. Erica peered in and then glanced up with a smile.

"It's very nice, Tom. How did the owner keep it in such good shape?"

He shrugged. "I don't know if it was all good luck or all good care, but she sure did great."

Erica was bent forward from the waist and Tom allowed his gaze to drift from the Buick's well-preserved upholstery to the curve of his wife's backside and the length of her bare legs.

"Let's try out the backseat," he said.

He flipped the seat forward before taking her hand. Stepping inside, he urged her to follow. Erica slid in beside him, running her hand along the decorative V of upholstery.

"Nice," she said. "I wonder why vinyl doesn't feel like this anymore?"

"Maybe it ages like good wine." Tom deliberately softened his voice, making it velvety and, he hoped, seductive.

"It's really roomy in here," she said.

With a sigh of pleasure he pulled her into his arms. "It's a 127-inch wheelbase," he whispered.

She made a noise, but whatever she intended to say was lost when his lips came down on hers. Still, the slight sweet sound deep in her throat was easy for Tom to interpret.

His wife was a great kisser. Tom was never sure exactly what made that so. It wasn't as if she had some unique process or unusual lips. It was something else entirely. It was as if she brought her entire being, all her emotions—sexual, intellectual, nurturing—to this one place and lavished them upon him.

"Oh, baby," he moaned against her neck.

Her answer was a sweet, breathy sigh.

He pulled her into his lap and sat her nice round butt right atop the ache in the front of his trousers.

She wiggled a little bit, giggling, and then she kissed him again.

His fingers found their way to the zipper at the back of her dress and he quickly drew it down past her waist.

"Tom!"

Her near breathless call of alarm as their lips parted only encouraged him.

He pulled the little black dress down on her arms, exposing a tiny bit of a bra that had clear plastic straps and the thinnest layer of sheer black fabric, through which her nipples were visible. He covered one with his mouth.

She was wiggling again, but this time it seemed not so much to entice him as to move away.

"Tom! What are you doing?"

He gave her nipple a naughty nip before pulling away to answer.

"Honey, I need to test the suspension on this old Buick," he teased. "And I warn you, we're going to need to do some serious up and down before I can come…to any serious conclusion."

"Tom!"

"So what do you think? Let's work on those shocks and struts. I want to check the bushing for random vibration."

He slid the tight skirt up around her waist and was pulling down her panties when the panic in Erica's voice penetrated.

"Stop!"

He did so immediately. "What?" he asked.

"We can't have sex in somebody else's car," she said.

"Sure we can. The shop door is locked. It's as private here as in our own bedroom."

"But this is not our own bedroom," she pointed out firmly. "This is the backseat of some stranger's car."

Tom shook off her concern. "The owner will never know. I doubt seriously if she'd care and she probably has nice memories of this backseat herself."

"That is not the point," Erica said as she moved off his lap and began straightening her clothes. "We are not crazy teenagers at some lover's lane. We are…we are responsible parents. We don't go around having sex in other people's cars."

"Just because we're grown-ups doesn't mean we have to be boring."

"Are you saying there is something boring about having sex with me at home?"

Tom recognized a slippery slope when he saw one. "There is nothing boring about having sex with you anywhere," he assured her. "I just…I just like this car a lot and thought it might be fun to…try it out a little on this well-aged uphol-stery."

Erica shook her head. "I don't mind making out a little, but I am not having sex in some stranger's car. It's just gross, Tom."

His disappointment was bigger than sexual, but he didn't want to whine.

"Okay," he said. "You want to go catch a movie or some-thing?"

"We don't have to," she replied quickly. "I mean, if you want to hang out back here, have a few kisses, I think that's okay."

"No, it's fine," he said. "I'm fine. We had a few kisses. Come on, I'll take you to a movie."

With some reluctance, she agreed.

However, they'd missed all the seven-o'clock showings and if they hung around till the nine-o'clocks they'd really get in too late. So Tom took her to a dimly lit bar where the place was filled with mostly singles on the lookout for each other. After consuming a beer, they ventured out onto the tiny dance floor. The DJ played a slow, romantic tune and Erica snuggled up close to him, wrapped her arms around his neck. He knew she felt bad about turning him down. It was a rare occasion when that happened. When she said she had a headache, he knew she must really have one. It was fine and she was right. If she didn't feel comfortable about having sex in a client's car, then the sex wouldn't have been that good anyway. Still, rejection felt like rejection. He didn't like it.

The thing about loving her however, was that even things he didn't like, the things she did that drove him crazy, paled in comparison to what he saw as his great luck in finding Erica and getting her to marry him.

In the dim blue and green lights of the dance floor, she pressed herself next to him and laid her cheek against his chest.

"I love you," she whispered.

"Me, too," Tom answered.

Their romantic history had included only a minimum number of noisy bars and crowded dance floors. Before meeting Erica, he'd been very involved in the San Antonio nightclubbing scene for a couple of years. His "dating" life, if you could call it that, involved having a few drinks and hooking up with a woman who'd had a few of her own.

It was a crazy time, working all day and partying all night. He and Cliff were both running up the score, buying condoms by the gross and screwing everything that moved. After a while, all the girls at the bars looked familiar, their names ran together in his head. A woman would wave him over and he'd couldn't remember if she was the giver of a great blow job or the one he'd bent over the bumper of her BMW.

Tom deliberately kept Erica away from that. He didn't want anyone to see her as his latest conquest. In truth, he didn't want anyone to see her at all. He wanted Erica all to himself. He wasn't sure exactly how to do that. But he went for quiet restaurants, moonlit parks and darkened movie theaters. They'd held hands and he'd talked softly and he'd kept his desire for her in check. Desperately he had wanted to make love to her. But even more desperately, he'd wanted her to be in love...with him.

It wasn't until he'd met her, until he'd seen himself in the reflection of her eyes, that he saw his party life for what it had been. His own version of the rudderless existence that he'd grown up in. That was not what he wanted. He wanted this. Solid. Stable. Substantive. For Tom, that was what was truly seductive.

"Future view," Erica said, interrupting his memories to get his predictions. "One year from tonight."

He grinned down at her. "One year from tonight, huh."

"Yep."

"Well, with Quint, our budget and our schedules, it might very well be the next time I take you out dancing."

She laughed and then shook her head with resignation. "You might be right."

"Maybe next year, we'll get out early enough to make the movie," she said.

He nodded. "Or perhaps this time next year I'll be smart enough to stay at home with you."

"Oh?"

"The floor will be a lot less crowded and we'll have the option of dancing naked."

"When you look at me that way," Erica whispered, "I feel naked."

"Let's get out of here."

Chapter 4

THE NEXT MORNING, a couple of inches of gray, soapy water covered the laundry room floor and it was beginning to flow into the kitchen.

"Mom said a bad word," Quint announced gravely to Letty as she stumbled into the kitchen, her hair still tousled from sleep.

"Oh, yeah? I didn't think your mom *knew* any bad words," Letty told him.

Erica shot her sister a look for the snide comment.

"Sorry, sweetie," she said to her son. "I didn't mean for you to hear that."

"It's okay," Quint assured his mom. "Cody Raza says a lot worse."

That was not exactly good news.

"Could you go play quietly in your room for a few minutes?" Erica suggested. "And I'll clean up this mess."

The little boy sighed and then complained to his aunt.

"She said the bad word, but I'm the one who has to go to my room."

"Just go, Quint, before you hear me say something else."

Letty ruffled his hair as he passed, then grinned at her sister.

"What happened?"

"Stupid…fudging washer," Erica faux cursed as a reply.

"I thought Tom fixed it weeks ago."

"He did fix it weeks ago and a week after that and last week, too," Erica told her. "The cranky old machine springs more leaks than an old man on the incontinence ward."

Letty shook her head sympathetically. "Do you have another mop?"

Erica handed her the one she was using and then waded into the laundry room to get a second one from the broom closet. Together the two sisters worked to sop up the water and wring it into a bucket.

"You may just have to bite the bullet and buy a new washer," Letty told her. "This one continues to cause more problems than it solves."

"I keep trying to make it last another month and another month," Erica explained. "I keep hoping Tom will have one good month with especially good receipts. You know how I hate to buy things on credit."

"Maybe you should get over that," Letty said. "You are not at all like Mom. You are never going to run up a bunch of credit card bills."

Erica shook her head. "It's a bad habit to get into."

"Don't you have a savings account?"

She shook her head. "If we get a dime we don't put back into the business, we put it in Quint's college fund."

"Well, maybe you should think about putting something aside for household emergencies."

Erica glanced up at her sister suspiciously. "Have you been talking to Mom?"

"Mom, no. I'll try to call her on Sunday maybe."

"I talked to her yesterday after work," Erica said. "I made the mistake of telling her that the hospital miscalculated my pay rate and I'm going to get more money than I thought."

"Oh, that's great," Letty said.

"Yeah," Erica agreed. "Mom suggested that I not tell Tom. That I just put the money aside to buy stuff for the house."

Letty laughed. "I bet Tom loved hearing that."

"I forgot to tell him," Erica said. "I forgot to even tell him about the pay-rate thing."

"How could you forget to tell him?"

Erica paused to squeeze more water from the mop to the bucket. "Last night just got really weird and complicated."

"Oh?"

"Oh," Erica mimicked.

"Come on, tell me," Letty said. "If not me, who else are you going to tell?"

Erica glanced toward the living room, making sure that Quint was still out of earshot.

"We went down to his shop and he has this old Buick that somebody wants him to get ready for sale."

"Yeah."

"He wanted to have sex in the backseat."

Letty hooted with laughter.

"It wasn't that funny."

Letty's laughter continued and evolved into snorts of hilarity. "It sounds as if Tom came up with a great plan to mix the two things he really likes."

"Oh, shut up!"

Erica attempted to focus her attention back on the soaked floor.

"So how was it?" Letty asked, too amused to let it drop.

"How was what?"

"Sex in the stranger's car."

"I didn't do it."

"You didn't?"

"Of course not."

"When did you get to be such a prude?"

"I am not a prude," Erica insisted. "I just…I mean, who would have sex in somebody else's car? I don't think that would be…it wouldn't be good business. If I were to leave my car in a shop, I wouldn't want people using it for a romantic rendezvous."

"Hey, if Ford Motor Company didn't want people screwing in cars, why did they call it an Escort?"

Erica rolled her eyes. "You're an idiot," she told her sister.

"Better that than a prude."

"I am not a prude. And it wasn't a Ford—it was a Buick."

"Oh well, a Buick then, that makes it all different," Letty said with exaggerated sarcasm.

Erica ignored her.

"Poor Tom," Letty said with a sigh. "I hope you gave him an 'I'm sorry' blow job when you got home."

Erica dropped her gaze. Deliberately she kept her eyes on her mopping.

"Oh gosh, you did!" Letty said, snorting with laughter.

"Shut up!" Erica said, more embarrassed than annoyed.

"It's true. It's true. I can see it in your face."

"It's none of your business."

"No, it's not," Letty agreed. "But I'm glad to hear it. I really like my brother-in-law a lot. Mostly because he makes my sister very happy."

After the mopping was done, the sisters tried wringing the water out of the clothes in the washer and then loaded all of the week's dirty laundry in Erica's car.

Letty needed to get back to her own life. The apartment she shared with two roommates was always overflowing with friends and fellow students on the weekend. But she liked the camaraderie of it all.

"Don't forget to give Mom a call," Erica reminded her. "If you don't, she'll blame me for not telling you."

"One Mom phone call coming up," Letty promised.

Quint whined considerably about spending Saturday afternoon at the Laundromat. Erica felt like whining herself, but she forced a smile to her face.

"It's just an hour and a half, two at the most and you'll get to play video games the whole time."

Unfortunately, it was a very crowded place of business. All the washers were in use and Erica had to wait her turn. When it was her turn, however, another woman, who had come in after she did, grabbed the one Erica had been intent on using.

"That's my washer," Erica told her.

The woman eyed her unpleasantly.

"I don't see your name on it," she answered.

"We don't see your name on it," her son, who looked about ten, echoed more loudly.

Erica decided that getting into a public argument with the woman was more trouble than it was worth. But as she sat on a dirty plastic chair waiting for another machine to open up, she thought longingly of the comfort of her own little laundry room. She really did need a new washer. And if she held back the extra money in her paycheck, she could buy one in a couple of months. But she wouldn't keep it a secret. She would tell Tom. He would understand. He'd been patching the old machine back together time and time again. He knew how much she needed a new one. He'd be fine with using the extra money she made for the purchase.

Blushing, she remembered the information Letty had wheedled out of her. Her sister had called her a prude. Okay, she could plead guilty to a bit of that. But falling for Tom had never really been very prudent of her. And she might very likely have allowed the relationship to die a natural death. She supposed that she had Ann Marie to thank. If her mother hadn't stuck her nose in it, the love of her life and her wonderful child might never happened.

She and Tom had been dating for a couple of months when he'd finally confessed his personal history. Erica had already sensed that something was off. Ordinary questions like "where did you go to school?" or "which did you like better, soccer or little league?" provoked nonanswers and conversation shifters. But she had never, in her wildest dreams, suspected the facts. Revelations about a life of homelessness among addicts and drug traffickers had shocked her, frightened her. She'd managed to keep the horror out of her expression and the pity out of her voice. But when he kissed her good-night, she imagined it to be the last time. She had her own demons about growing up different. She wanted a normal guy from a regular family who'd be interested in an ordinary life. Erica didn't believe that Tom could be that. She stopped taking his calls.

Ann Marie noticed.

"You're not seeing the big grease-monkey fellow anymore?"

Erica shrugged a noncommittal reply.

"Well, it's good news, if you want my opinion."

Erica didn't.

"He's a nice guy."

Ann Marie had shuddered and shook her head. "He's so… so big, so brutish," she said. "I understand how that type can inspire a certain amount of animal magnetism, but he is definitely not the kind of man you should ever get serious about."

In an act of pure defiance, Erica had called Tom. And that very night, under the stars, they'd made love for the first time.

With a sweet sense of nostalgia she remembered that cool, crisp evening. They had been out for dinner and music at The Cove. She'd been nervous with him, anxious. Never much of a drinker, she had downed two glasses of red wine before Tom suggested that they get some air. They drove through the darkened streets to Woodlawn Lake, the westside's jewel of an urban park. In the center of the quiet water, a small, striped lighthouse was a decorative addition that skipped a bright, shimmery gleam along the dark water.

Tom parked his truck in the smallest, most distant lot from the shore. The clubhouse and docks were deserted in the evening chill. He urged her into the truck bed, with a view of the lake and the stars in the night sky. If it seemed a bit purposefully convenient that the truck carried an array of cozy blankets and a camping mattress, Erica pretended not to notice.

"Let me just hold you in my arms while I gaze at heaven," he said to her.

She snuggled against him before pointing out the obvious. "You're not looking at the sky, you're looking at me."

"Exactly," he answered before he kissed her.

There was tenderness on his lips, his mouth. There was tenderness in his hands as he caressed her. But there was demand as well. Tom went after what he wanted and he wanted her. Her secret places were no secret to him. He claimed them, exploited them, until she begged him to rip her clothes off. He didn't so much as snag her sweater as his big, masculine hands worked every button, hook and zipper with the precision of a man who knew his way around a carburetor, was an expert in stoking a spark and could rev her engine until it squealed in high gear.

Erica recrossed her legs on the plastic laundry-room chair as she recalled that passion. She'd had sex with guys before and she'd enjoyed it in a thrilling, titillating kind of way. But her previous experience bore no resemblance to the wanton, world-rocking intimacy of having sex with Tom. He completely satisfied her and, at the same time, kept her craving his touch.

There was no going back from a night of passion and a declaration of commitment in the back of a pickup truck under the stars. Erica realized that no matter who Tom had been, he was now the man she loved.

Saturdays were busy days at the shop. All the guys who worked nine-to-five all week needed to bring their cars in on the weekend. And those that didn't need work, just wanted to hang out and talk with the guys who did. It was almost a party atmosphere and Tom didn't like it much. Unlike many in his business, Tom had never preferred the company of men. He'd had no father, not even so much as a hint of who that person might be. And he'd grown up in a situation where the males were especially untrustworthy and often quite dangerous. The shoulder-punching camaraderie was a foreign language that he'd mastered but never felt quite comfortable with.

Still these loud braggarts, practical jokesters and tobacco spitters were some of his most loyal customers. And it was their word of mouth that he counted on to bring in new people and more work.

So he tolerated the Saturday hangout.

He had, however, put his foot down when Bugg Auflander wanted to furnish a cooler of beer. Tom had trouble keeping them out of the work area as it was. He didn't want to spend his Saturdays as a bouncer for the overinbibed.

Even without the added incentive of alcohol, the mere presence of the gang really stuck a wrench in the shop's productivity. Gus pretty much gave in to the distraction and did no work at all. And Hector was little better.

Tom's only consolation was their sociability freed him up for doing actual repair.

Except this Saturday, that wasn't quite working. All the guys wanted to look over and talk about the Buick. And Tom couldn't quite keep himself from joining in.

"Is this like a '54?" Kyle Gibbons asked.

"No, no," Dave Lofts said. "The '54 was the one with the sad eyes."

"Sad eyes?"

"Yeah, the headlamp piece was long and droopy to include the parking light," Dave said.

"Oh yeah," Nick Vallarta agreed. "From the front view it kind of had the face of a basset hound."

Dave nodded. "This is a much rounder headlamp. It's got to be a '55 at least."

"No, it's not a '55. That year they had the headlight and the parking light separate," Manny Felde said. "It's either a '56 or '57."

"It's a '56," Tom called out to them. He had his head stuck under the hood of a 1975 Gremlin.

"I'd love to customize her," Perry Pickets declared. "Can't

you see her rolling down the street with a four-forty and some glass packs?"

"Are you out of your mind?" Dave Lofts's question was rhetorical. "You could search a lifetime for a better original condition vehicle and you want to turn it into some lowrider. That's just crazy."

Immediately sides were drawn up and opinions shot across the bow.

Tom heartily agreed with Lofts. He would really hate to see Mrs. Gilfred's "Clara" turned into some jacked-up or bagged whammy tank. Even customizing her would be like forcing a beautiful actress into plastic surgery. The result might look new and flawless, but those things are a poor substitute for natural beauty.

Eventually he couldn't resist straightening up and walking into the discussion.

"I think the owner wants her to be restored, not redone," he said.

"But she's selling it, right?" Pickets said with a chuckle. "So what she don't know won't hurt her."

That might be true for Mrs. Gilfred, but the motives of the buyer would probably be obvious to Tom. He would not allow this Buick to end up in the wrong hands.

"We've got to get some work done around here, guys," Tom announced.

The statement forced him to move away from the Buick and he hoped that it would be a hint to his employees to get busy.

Gus was actually sitting on a lawnchair in the driveway, in the middle of some long tale. Hector, at least, was under a Chevy pickup, lubing the joints.

"Gus, are you going to get to the wiring on this Gremlin?" Tom called out.

He nodded and waved without even pausing in mid-sentence.

Tom glanced around for Cliff, but he didn't seem to be anywhere. Mentally shrugging, he figured Cliff must be in the john. However, when he walked around the back, he noticed that the restroom door was open and the tiny room was empty. He surveyed the interior of the shop again. Clearly Cliff wasn't anywhere inside.

Tom walked into the office, but it was all old men focusing on their never-ending Saturday morning discussion of "cars I once owned."

"Have you seen Cliff?" he asked generally.

The discussion paused only long enough for negative responses all around, then commenced once more just where it left off.

It was very strange. Cliff was on the clock and he wasn't supposed to just disappear. Tom walked out the back to see if his shiny, vintage Cutlass was still in the employee parking.

It was there, parked near the end. Tom's brow furrowed. There was an unfamiliar blue Mazda minivan parked right next to him, and it seemed to be swaying slightly. A sure sign that Cliff was working on it, though why he hadn't pulled it around to the front was puzzling. Maybe because the minivan was new, but Tom's policy had always been to fix whatever showed up. And he didn't care if people knew that.

"When we're struggling to keep a business in the black," he'd told his staff many times. "You can expand the definition of 'classic car' to include everything north of a riding lawnmower."

Tom walked toward the vehicle to see what was going on and to suggest to Cliff that he move it into the driveway.

When he reached the space between it and Cliff's Cutlass,

he stopped in his tracks. The side door to the minivan was wide open. As were the legs of some feminine person who had them wrapped around Cliff's naked butt.

"What the hell!"

Tom spoke before he thought. His words had the expected result. Cliff jumped to his feet as if he'd been shot. His trousers dropped all the way to his ankles and he bent forward frantically, grabbing at them. The woman, too, pulled at her discarded clothes attempting to cover herself. But not quickly enough that Tom hadn't had a very good look at a slim body with visible tan lines. He recognized her face, of course. She was Stacy from the Auto Parts Store. He'd seen her, spoken to her a thousand times in the past few years. Now he knew for a fact that she wasn't a natural blonde. It was not a piece of information that he'd ever wanted to acquire.

"I can explain," Cliff said, belatedly remembering to stand in front of the doorway, partially shielding Stacy from view.

"You can?"

Tom's tone was incredulous as he turned his back and walked to the front of the vehicle. Cliff followed him while he zipped up.

"It's not what you think," Cliff told him.

"*What I think* is that you're having sex with some woman in my parking lot."

Cliff ran a hand through his typically perfect gelled hair, smoothing it into order. He was tall and lean with the kind of congenial personality that made all the men want to be his buddy and all the girls want to be his squeeze.

"Usually we sneak off somewhere, but the shop's so busy today that I thought I should stay close," Cliff said.

"Usually?"

Cliff shrugged. "It's been going on awhile," he admitted. "It's not like…it's like…it's a Saturday thing."

"A Saturday thing?"

"Yeah, on Saturdays when Stacy's husband is home with the kids, she cuts her aerobics class and we have a quickie."

Tom shook his head as he looked at his friend. It had always seemed as if they had so much in common, shared so many dreams and aspirations. He thought he knew Cliff as well as he knew anybody. But apparently he didn't know the guy at all.

Stacy came out of the back of the van wearing jogging shorts and a T-shirt with an athletic logo. She jerked open the driver's door of her Mazda as if she intended to flee without a word, but then she hesitated. She raised her head and looked Tom straight in the eye.

"Please, you can't say anything." The words were pleading, but the tone was authoritative. She wasn't asking him not to tell. She was ordering Tom to keep his mouth shut. "It would cause trouble and hurt my kids. You don't want to hurt my kids."

"No, of course I don't want to hurt your kids," Tom assured her.

"Don't worry," Cliff piped in, offering the woman an almost lighthearted reassurance. "Tom's my best friend. We can trust him."

Her smile was hesitant, but Tom saw that it was indeed a smile.

"See you next week," Cliff said.

Stacy nodded, jumping into the minivan and backing out of the parking space.

As Tom watched, a sick, sad feeling settled on him with a dampening weight.

"I can't believe you're doing this," he said.

Cliff shook his head. "You need to forget you ever saw anything," he told him.

"What about Trish?"

"Trish?" Cliff asked, feigning puzzlement, as if Tom had abruptly changed the subject.

"Yes, Trish. Your wife, Trish. Remember her?" Tom was angry and his tone was sarcastic.

"I love Trish," Cliff answered. "I love my kids. I'm not falling in love with somebody or quitting my marriage. I'm just getting a little bit on the side. Hey, I've known you a long time. I remember those days when our policy was screw first and ask questions like 'what's your name?' later."

"That's when we were stupid kids with dicks for brains," Tom pointed out.

Cliff shrugged. "We may be older," he said. "But that part of a guy never gets wiser. Come on, you can't tell me that you've never got a little bit on the side."

"Uh, yes, *I can tell you,*" Tom answered. "I'd never cheat on Erica. You were best man at our wedding. I'll bet you heard me promise not to."

Cliff snorted derisively. "Everybody promises," he said. "I doubt if anybody really means it."

"I meant it. I still mean it."

Cliff waved away his words. "Okay," he said. "So you're Mr. Straight Arrow these days. Good for you. But I need variety." Cliff was calmly buttoning his shirt. He was relaxed, relieved. As if a crisis had been successfully averted. "Trish is a good wife and a great cook," he told Tom. "She's fixed up our house real nice. And she's the best mom our kids could ever have. But we've been married almost eight years. She's not exactly a hot tamale in the sack."

"That's not what you said when you two were dating," Tom pointed out. "You told me that she had moves that nearly made your eyes roll back in your head."

Cliff shrugged. "Yeah, well, she does have great moves.

And it's not like I don't still do her a couple of times a week. But Stacy has different moves and it's all just sex with no sappy 'I love you' stuff. I don't even have to kiss Stacy. She just takes off her pants and we do it. It's all fun."

"How fun is it going to be when Trish finds out?"

"She's never going to find out," Cliff said. "Unless you're determined to tell her. If you want to break up a couple of marriages and cause a lot of grief for everybody, I guess it's your right to do so. If that's really what you want to do."

"It's not what I want to do," Tom said. "It's not what I'm going to do. But this kind of stuff always comes out. Trish will find out and it won't be worth it."

"Trish will never find out," Cliff said confidently.

"You'll have to stop meeting Stacy," Tom said. "You've got to stop taking the risk."

"Aw, come on," he answered. "I'm not giving up Stacy. Not till we're both really done with it." His statement was adamant and without the slightest hint of self-reproach or regret. "You're not thinking about how smart this is," Cliff continued. "I could be picking up hookers. Paying out money for it and bringing home diseases. Doing Stacy is… it's almost like a gift to Trish. I'm a better husband because I'm a happy husband."

"I don't think Trish would see it that way."

Cliff laughed and slapped Tom on the back. "No, she wouldn't," he agreed. "Females are all possessive and ter-ritorial about stuff that's just strictly physical. It's a craziness in them, but they can't help it. So what's a guy to do except protect them from the things that they just don't need to know?"

Tom agreed to keep the secret, but he didn't like it.

"You can't even tell Erica," Cliff cautioned. "Women stick together. She'd be on the phone to Trish is ten minutes."

"I won't tell Erica."

"Good," Cliff said. "There are some things in married life that a man is just better off keeping to himself."

Chapter 5

ERICA CONTINUED READING ALOUD, slowing down, allowing her voice to go softer and softer. Beside her, snuggled up in his Lightning McQueen bedding, Quint had fallen asleep. He had an almost perfectly heart-shaped face with soft, blemish-free skin and a sturdy chin that had just the hint of being like his father's. His eyelashes were amazingly long, his small nose was upturned a bit, and his mouth opened slightly as he slept.

He was beautiful. She'd thought that the first moment she'd seen him, even when he was all red and slippery and screaming. She'd thought it every day since. But you don't say "beautiful" to boys. They get all squirmy about a word like that. Instead she told him that he was "tough" and "smart." But she wanted him to grow up to be "kind" and "honest" as well.

They had not been so sure about having children. Tom had worried that he might be as ill equipped for parenting as his own mother had been. Her addiction problems and stunted sense of responsibility had left Tom to make his way through life mostly on his own. She had dumped him on strangers, forgotten him in strange cities and even once had him taken from her by Protective Services before she'd moved him south of the border.

"It turned out to be good for me, in the long run," Tom had assured her long ago. "I figured out at about five or six years old that nobody was going to take care of me, but me. So I became self-reliant. I can always depend upon myself."

Erica looked down at her sleeping son of that same age and shuddered at the thought of him being alone and vulnerable in a dangerous border town while his mother floated somewhere on a cloud of booze, pills and cocaine.

That had happened more than once to Tom. He'd had almost no upbringing at all, no experience to draw upon. From the time they began talking about children, he looked to Erica to provide the framework with which he was so unfamiliar.

Erica had had her own concerns. Her family history of constant divorce with her and Letty caught in the middle, caused Erica to fear the extra pressures of having a child. She understood and supported Tom's desire to own his own business. But she knew there would always be lean years and inevitable uncertainty. Financial risk was hard on the best marriages. And what would she do if ever forced to choose between the security of her child and the ambitions of her husband?

Tom and Erica had talked openly of both their dreams and their worries about expanding their family. Their marriage was so good, the idea of voluntarily choosing to rock the boat seemed almost foolish, as if they were asking for more problems, more stress. Strangely, stating up front what they felt about themselves and about each other brought them closer together. And when they finally made the decision to try for a baby, they were united, confident and eager.

And having Quint had turned out to be so much more than they had imagined. The depth of love that one can feel for a child came as a surprise to both of them. Regret was a sheer impossibility.

Erica set the book aside and leaned down to plant a featherlight kiss on his temple. She turned off the lamp and tiptoed out of the room in the glow of the night-light.

From the living room she could hear the television. Tom was all settled in to watch the basketball game. It would be an excellent time for her to take a long leisurely soak in the bath. Or she could clean up the kitchen. The latter seemed much more pressing than the former, but she decided to do neither. Instead she went into the living room, kicked off her shoes and snuggled up next to Tom on the couch.

"How are we doing?" she asked.

"Manu is incredible," he answered, referring to one of his favorite NBA players. "How can a guy make a shot on one leg with his off-arm while falling down? Only Manu can do that."

"Well," Erica said. "Manu, and my husband, Tom."

He chuckled. "That's one of the things I love about you, babe. I guess blind loyalty comes with very bad eyesight."

"I think you play great."

"If you call 'playing great' beating my six-year-old at a game of H-O-R-S-E, yeah, I'm totally great."

"You should play with the guys again," she said, referring to the pickup games at the park down by the lake.

Tom shook his head. "Why should I spend my spare time with those dunderheads when I can spend it with you and Quint?"

"Guys need other guys."

"That's all I've got all day is guys," Tom said. "Believe me, when I get home I want to sit next to someone soft and nice smelling."

She laughed a little and he wrapped a muscled arm around her neck to pull her close enough for a kiss on the end of her nose.

The noise from the TV crowd heightened and they both turned their attention just in time to see Manu steal the ball from Chase Heddington, star guard for the opposing team. Manu went galloping at top speed toward the Spurs' basket. Heddington, now chasing him, was unable to block the shot and settled for giving him a nasty push into the photographers crouched at the sidelines.

Tom and Erica responded in unison with a cry of complaint.

Manu was awarded two free throws.

"It should have been a flagrant," Erica said.

"You almost have to go for the head to get that call," Tom said. "It was an intentional and there's no bonus for that. Heddington can afford the foul."

"I don't like him anyway," Erica said.

Tom eyed her questioningly. "Heddington? He's a great player. He'll be a Hall of Famer one day for sure."

Erica snorted in derision. "I don't care how well he plays basketball," she said in a very matter-of-fact tone. "All that stuff that came out about him cheating on his wife with that porn star. She was his high school sweetheart and she stayed with him when he was injured in that car wreck. She nursed him back to health and struggled financially until his career got back on track. Now she spends half the year raising their kids by herself while he's on the road. And what is the thanks she gets? He's out canoodling some tattooed skank who wants to use him to get fifteen minutes of fame."

Beside her Tom was silent, thoughtful.

"You know I'm right," she stated.

Her husband shrugged an agreement, but there was a definite lack of fervor on his part. "I think the guy made some very bad choices," Tom said. "But that's about as far as I can go. We don't know anything about their marriage."

Erica was surprised.

"We know he made vows he didn't keep," she said. "In my book that makes him a low-life jerk."

She watched a frown appear on Tom's forehead. "Sometimes guys, and women, too, they just get their heads messed up for a while. I don't think that it always means that they don't love their wife or their husband or that they want to throw out their marriage. They're...just messed up. Temporary insanity or something."

At that moment Tim Duncan got the rebound, took two lumbering, long-length steps and made a ridiculous last-second shot that flew more than half the length of the court before it swished through the net as the buzzer went off.

The discussion of infidelity was sidetracked. But during the half-time break, as Erica soaked in her hot bath, the remembrance of it kept her from truly relaxing. She couldn't stop herself from wondering when and why her husband's views on adultery had become so moderated.

It was not marriage, it was basketball, she assured herself. Tom was defending an NBA star, not stating his own inclinations. Tom was not the cheating kind, Erica reminded herself. When he gave his word, he kept it.

She leaned back in the tub and laid a washcloth over her eyes, willing herself to relax.

"Men cheat, it's just their nature," her mother had told her when she was just a teenager. "They will say they love you. And they'll even mean it. But if you're a smart woman you never trust them."

Erica snorted derisively at the memory. Her mother was angry and bitter. Maybe the men Ann Marie fell for were like that, but Erica had Tom. And Tom was just not that kind of guy.

The beginning of the workweek was a busy one in the shop. Cliff was in a great mood, but from Tom's perspective it was for all the wrong reasons. Every peep of his cheerful whistling made Tom feel as if he were part of a conspiracy, a conspiracy to deceive their wives. Cliff even showed up early one morning to work on the restroom plumbing.

"What are you doing?" Tom asked.

"I'm getting this shower working again," Cliff answered.

The bathroom's shower was in disrepair. No one had ever used it since the day they'd moved in. It mostly was utilized as a closet for storage. Cliff had removed the boxes to the shop floor, scrubbed up the tile and attached a showerhead to what had formerly been a capped pipe overhead.

Tom's brow furrowed in confusion. "If you're looking for jobs, Cliff, there's half a dozen on the clipboard. I don't think we really need a functioning shower."

"I think we do," Cliff said, grinning at him like the cat that swallowed the canary. "We can wash up here so we don't go home smelling of grease or oil or gasoline…or another woman."

Cliff chuckled delightedly at this last. Tom didn't find it funny at all. He'd agreed to keep his friend's secret. But he did not appreciate its broadening scope.

"I've got work to do," he said, turning his back on Cliff and purposefully getting on with his day.

From the clipboard he sorted out the jobs that needed to be done and assigned them based on the talents of his employees and the time typically needed for completion. He tried to be smart about who was best at what. But he also tried to be fair. He never asked anyone to do more work that he did. And he took his turn on the crappy tasks that nobody really wanted to do.

Tom not only did his share of the mechanic work, but he handled all the estimates, set the assignments and kept up with the money.

Still, he made time to devote himself exclusively to the Buick. He'd been in, out, under and over her and he felt as if he had a very thorough knowledge of the car. Clara, he began to call her. She wasn't just a pretty Buick—she was unique, and Tom found himself thinking about her, referring to her, by Mrs. Gilfred's pet name.

Besides the problems with the carburetor and the worn belts, he thought the transmission was leaky and there were some serious rust problems on one of the ankle boots. Still, it would all be fixable and increase the value of the car beyond the price of repairs.

With Mrs. Gilfred's hearing problem, Tom thought she was not quite as good on the phone as in person. So on Tuesday he left a message on her answering machine that he would be coming over. He gathered all his paperwork on the vehicle and drove over to her home in Leon Valley.

There was no answer when he rang the doorbell loud enough to wake the neighborhood. He waited on the porch for several minutes. With no car to drive, she couldn't have gone far. A bus trip to the grocery store, maybe, or visiting with friends down the street.

Tom pushed a little pile of newspapers out of the way and seated himself on the porch steps, reading over his work sheet as he waited for her. It was several minutes before the presence of the newspapers clicked in his head. He turned to check her mailbox and sure enough it was overflowing with junk mail and ad circulars.

His brow furrowed. Maybe she was out of town, visiting family or seeing the sites.

Down the street he saw another woman, probably twenty years younger than Mrs. Gilfred, raking the leaves in her yard. Tom loped over to her calling out a "Good Morning!" as he approached.

She stopped her work long enough to give him a look of acknowledgment.

"I'm Tom Bentley," he said, by way of introduction. "I own Bentley's Classic Car Care. I've got Mrs. Gilfred's Buick in my shop. Have you seen her lately?"

He handed the woman his business card. She looked it over before she answered.

"An ambulance came and took her away on Sunday afternoon. That's all I know," she said. "Ask Miss Warner in the blue house. I think she's a friend of the old lady."

Tom did exactly that. The neighbor just on the other side of Mrs. Gilfred seemed very pleased to have a visitor of any type and insisted that he sit on her porch for a glass of lemonade.

"Poor old thing," Miss Warner said of Mrs. Gilfred, who couldn't have been more than a few years senior to Miss Warner herself. "I don't know if it was her heart or a stroke, but something happened and she fell. She's lucky she didn't break a hip as well as the rest of it. The nice man from the EMS said he thought she probably lay unconscious on the floor for hours. Then she came to and crawled to the phone to call 9-1-1 herself." The woman tutted and shook her head. "She was always like that. Very self-sufficient. My mother said those women always end up alone, because men just don't feel the need to take care of them. But then, if rumor can be relied upon, she was never truly interested in men."

Tom's eyebrows momentarily shot up at her words. Then he deliberately concentrated on the ice in his glass.

"So you're fixing up that old car of hers?"

"Yes, ma'am. I had it towed into my shop a week ago."

"That is so silly! Why in the world would she spend good money on that old rattletrap junker?" Miss Warner giggled. "She used to drive me and Mama around sometimes, but she hasn't gone farther than the grocery store in years."

"It's a very valuable car," Tom explained.

Miss Warner, a pudgy woman with a face framed in graying ringlets, giggled. "Well, I wouldn't have it myself. I don't drive, of course, but if I did I'd have a sturdy sedan. A convertible, in the sun we have in South Texas? It's just silly and showy."

Tom uncomfortably listened to several more complaints about the woman that Miss Warner called "her friend" before he finally managed to get the information he needed out of her.

"She's in Christus Santa Rosa," Miss Warner told him. "I haven't talked to her, but as far as I know, she must still be there."

Tom thanked the woman for the lemonade and got away as quickly as he could politely manage. He had liked Mrs. Gilfred the day that he met her. His empathy for the woman had now increased considerably. With *friends* like Miss Warner, the old lady wouldn't need enemies.

As he walked back to his truck, he checked his watch. Maybe he should run by and see her. Find out if she still wanted him to work on the Buick. He pulled out his phone and called the shop to let the guys know that he might be longer than he'd thought.

Gus answered.

"Hi, Gus. I'm just checking in. Everything going okay around there?"

"Uh…yeah, I think so."

The uncertainty in his voice was not particularly encouraging.

"So what are you doing?" Tom asked.

"Oh…I've been talking to Sparky. He's still thinking about pulling the engine."

Tom rolled his eyes. Sparky was a nice old man who'd been talking about that for years. And he could talk about it for hours. And Gus would likely let him, rather than accomplish anything concrete.

"What else is going on?"

"Oh, Hector has Murphy's Chevy step-side up on the lift. He's doing the brakes and lubing, I think."

"What about Cliff?"

"Cliff's gone."

"What?"

"That Stacy woman, you know the one at the parts store," Gus said. "She came by and said that they'd gotten in some pulled parts and she needed Cliff to come take a look."

"He left with Stacy?"

"Yeah."

"When?"

"Oh…I dunno, maybe a couple of hours ago. Right after you left really."

Tom offered a silent curse.

"Okay, I'm on my way back there," he told Gus. "Send Sparky home to his wife and get busy! I want to see that you accomplish something today."

Tom was shaking his head as he pulled his truck away from the curb. Cliff's "Saturday thing" was seeping into Tuesday and Tom didn't like it a bit. It was not his business if his employee cheated on his wife. But it was definitely his business if his employee spent time cheating while he was on the clock.

He thought about Mrs. Gilfred up at the hospital. Maybe he could get away this afternoon to go see her.

Erica sprinkled her bowl of lettuce and tomatoes with just the very fewest of bacon bits as Melody Garwin stepped up beside her at the salad bar.

"They're not even real," she said.

"Huh?"

"The bacon bits, they're not real, so it's not like it's eating real bacon." The pudgy young woman punctuated her pronouncement by ladling a hefty quantity of the crunchy brown condiment onto her own salad.

"Actually I think they are made of bacon," Erica said. "Dried-out bacon, I guess, but they do say *real* bacon bits."

Melody stared at her plate as if it had turned into a snake. "How many calories do you think that is?"

Erica felt a surge of sympathy for her. "I…I don't know. I guess most of the calories would be in the fat and the fat's gone."

Melody nodded slowly. "Right, the fat's gone. That's got to be good."

She was smiling again as the two walked to their usual table. Most of the crowd from their department were already seated. Erica took her usual chair on the end opposite Callie Torreno. Melody sat catty-corner to her, next to Lena.

Erica had barely gotten her napkin unrolled when Darla Ingalls rushed up, scooting in next to Rayliss.

"I've got the scoop on Dr. Carnegy," she said in an excited whisper.

"I thought we already had the scoop," Callie said. "He cheated."

Darla nodded. "But there's more and I have it straight from the horse's mouth."

"Which horse?" Rayliss asked her, clearly eager for details.

"I talked to Celia Rey, she's an R.N. on Five-South and the woman who babysits her kids has a sister who works in Dr. Carnegy's office. You know the office staff always know everything."

They all nodded in agreement.

"So tell us, tell us," Lena urged excitedly.

"Well, according to Celia's babysitter, Mrs. Carnegy has a certain squeamishness about some of the doctor's favorite bedroom games. So he's been quietly buying those services from professionals for years."

"Prostitutes?" Rayliss exclaimed in a whisper.

"Celia didn't think they were like streetwalkers or some-thing like that," Darla said. "It's much more likely that they were expensive call-girl types."

"Still, that's pretty gross," Lena said.

"It's not clear whether Mrs. Carnegy knew about it all this time," Darla continued. "But now he's fallen for some one-stop full-service sweetheart still in her twenties."

"Yikes! Dr. Carnegy must be fifty if he's a day," Rayliss said.

"More like sixty," Callie piped in.

"Anyway, he's in love and he's the one who asked for the divorce."

"So he's divorcing her?"

"Well, not now, not officially. He's wanted a no-fault split.

But when she found out about the twentysomething, she and her lawyer decided to go after him for adultery."

"That pays better than an amicable split any day," Callie said. "So good for her."

It didn't sound to Erica that it was actually good for anyone, but she kept that opinion to herself. She had been down the divorce road so many times with her own mother, she felt like an expert on the subject. But it was not a mastery that she enjoyed sharing. And she knew that no amount of financial settlement could make up for the anger, disappointment and basic disruption of a marriage falling apart.

"Still," Rayliss said after a moment, "the woman brought it on herself."

"The twentysomething?" Melody asked.

"No, silly," Rayliss answered. "The wife."

"The wife?" Melody sounded as surprised as Erica felt. "How is it the wife's fault?"

"Because she should have let him."

"She should have let him…what?"

"Whatever it is that he wanted," Rayliss said.

Callie nodded agreement. "If a wife has any chance of keeping her husband at home, she'd better never say no."

"She won't if she's smart," Darla agreed.

"If she does, she gets what she deserves," Rayliss said.

Lena giggled. "I'm lucky that Aiden has a short attention span. When he comes up with something I'm not crazy about, I try to distract him."

"Well, don't count on that always working," Rayliss said. "Men can be easygoing about a lot of things, but not about sex."

Erica saw Melody shaking her head. She was tempted to warn her to stay out of it. But she decided it was better just to stay out of it herself.

"That's not right," Melody declared. "Sex is for mutual pleasure. Two people who love each other want to please each other. If there's something that somebody doesn't like, then find something that you both enjoy. That's not such a tough challenge. Gabe would never ask me to do anything that I'm not comfortable with."

Erica agreed with the sentiment. However, Melody's condescending tone and superior attitude certainly didn't encourage anyone to agree with her.

"So you never do anything you don't want to do?"

"I give my husband the kind of respect that he's due. So he always treats me with courtesy. Everything we do in bed is…is nice."

"Courtesy?" Darla repeated.

"It's *nice!*" Rayliss put an emphasis on the word that was incredulous.

Lena giggled. "I'd say our bedroom was more naughty than nice."

Laughter filled the table. Even Erica couldn't stifle a giggle. Only Melody remained unamused.

"Perhaps if you showed more respect for your husbands, they would show more respect to you."

"I *respect* my husband," Lena said. "But I don't worship him."

"She's got that right," Rayliss agreed. "It's better to have equality in the rest of the house than to demand it in the bedroom."

The insinuation that Melody's marriage might not be ideal pushed her even further.

"If you were better wives and held your husbands in higher esteem, perhaps they wouldn't always be the butt of every joke."

"Since he hit forty, what's left of my husband's butt is a joke," Darla said.

That statement brought more laughter.

"Just a word to the wise," Callie told Melody. "There are no perfect men. If you keep treating Gabe like one, he's going to start believing it. And you've got nothing but trouble from then on."

All the women nodded sagely.

"Keep your eyes open," Rayliss said. "You've made him think he's God's gift to women. So if he's not looking elsewhere already, then he certainly will be when he hits that midlife thing."

"Gabe loves me," she said with certainty.

"Of course he does," Callie conceded. "But it's not about love, it's about sex. When it comes to men, sex and love are two different things."

"If he loses interest in you, says he's too tired, that's one of the first signs." Rayliss, the single female who was an expert on marriage, made her statement utilizing a fork as a pointer.

"Or he may want more sex," Darla suggested. "And changing it up in new ways, ways he's picking up from somebody else."

"I've heard that watching the money is the thing to do," Lena said. "If he takes out a new credit card on his own or opens some kind of account without asking you, then he's spending money on restaurants and hotel rooms."

Around the table the women nodded in agreement.

"Gabe doesn't do any of that," Melody insisted.

"He doesn't do any of it...yet," Callie said, by way of correction.

"The biggest clue is the shower," Rayliss said, speaking as if she had eons of experience. "You've got to pay attention if he starts taking a shower at the gym. If a husband showers at the gym then you know there's someone else."

"He plays racquetball," Melody defended. The only response she got were knowing nods.

"I'm not going to listen to this," she stated adamantly. Melody got to her feet and stormed off.

"Well, crap," Darla said. "I didn't mean to make her mad. I guess we shouldn't have done that."

Erica thought she was undoubtedly right.

"It's for her own good," Lena said. "I'm crazy about my husband, too, but I don't think he's some all-powerful superhero. Marriage is for people, not gods and goddesses."

"Melody's too sensitive by half," Callie said. "And the way she's got that man of hers up on a pedestal, it's about time somebody gave her some straight talk."

Chapter 6

TOM WAS MAD FOR most of the day. Just after ten that morning, Cliff had disappeared and left the rest of them to pick up the slack. As Tom silently seethed, he felt as if he couldn't say anything to anyone. The boss cannot complain about one employee to another. And he couldn't even vent his frustrations to his wife. He'd agreed to keep Cliff's infidelity a secret. And there was no explaining what was going on without revealing that piece of information.

Cliff had been cagey enough to return while Tom was gone to pick up Quint. By the time Tom confronted Cliff, he was busily engaged in pulling the engine on a 1985 Trans Am. Tom wanted nothing better than to chew his employee up one side and down the other, but with an 800-pound engine swaying slightly on a hoist, he decided it was the better part of valor to bite his tongue and let the work proceed as necessary.

He decided to go to the hospital and told Cliff that he was

leaving and for him to keep an eye on Quint until Erica got there. At least the responsibility of babysitting would keep his friend on the job.

"I'm going to go visit a lady in the hospital," Tom told his son. "She's sick and I need to talk to her about her car."

"Are you going to take her flowers?"

"Flowers?"

"Mom says that when people are in the hospital, you take them flowers," Quint told him.

Tom grinned at his son. "That's a very nice idea, Quint," he said. "Maybe I'll stop down at the grocery store and get her one of those little bouquets they have."

Quint nodded sagely. "I think bouquets are just like flowers," he told his father. "Or they mostly are."

Tom chuckled and ruffled his son's hair lovingly. "While I'm gone, you behave like you always do. If you need something, call the guys on the intercom, but stay here in the office."

The boy nodded solemnly.

"Your mom will be here in a half hour, forty-five minutes, tops."

"Okay."

Even after assuring himself that everything would be fine, Tom was a little hesitant to go. Still, if he waited for Erica, he'd miss visiting hours.

He got in his truck and drove to the hospital, stopping only for a two-dollar bunch of posies as his son had suggested. He was glad that he had then when he got to Christus Santa Rosa. Somehow it seemed better to be standing at the information desk with flowers than not.

Mrs. Gilfred was a bit tricky to locate. Tom was told that she'd just been moved out of ICU, but when he got to her room, she had yet to arrive.

"Are you a family member?" a woman in pink scrubs asked him.

"No, no I'm…I'm just a friend." He knew he was being presumptuous, but he didn't want to go into explanations about his shop and her car and her hearing problems. The nurse left him to wait in the empty room. He paced unhappily.

What on earth am I doing here? he asked himself.

He was ready to bolt when the nurse returned and handed him a green plastic pitcher. Tom stared at it questioningly.

"We sometimes use these discarded ones for vases," she said, pointing at the flowers he still held. "I just got the call, Mrs. Gilfred should be in the elevator on her way up."

Tom nodded as the woman left. He looked at the pitcher and shrugged. Flower arranging was not something with which he had any experience, but at least it was something purposeful to do while waiting.

He filled the pitcher at the sink. He tried just stuffing all the flowers in at once and found that it didn't work so well. Tom set the pitcher on the windowsill and placed the blossoms in it one by one, as if he were attaching connector assemblies to an ignition coil. When he was finished, he surveyed his work solemnly. It didn't look great, but it looked friendly. That's what it should look like, he decided. In the cold hospital room the flowers were actually welcoming.

Although he'd been waiting for Mrs. Gilfred to arrive, the sudden opening of the door startled him a little. They wheeled the bed already in the room out into the hallway and then replaced it with the one in which a gray, pale-looking Mrs. Gilfred lay.

"You've got someone here to greet you, Gladys," the nurse in the pink scrubs called out loudly.

"Nobody has called me Gladys since my Uncle Walter," the woman answered more strongly than her frail appearance would have suggested possible.

"What do they call you?" the nurse persisted.

"My *friends* call me Guffy," she answered. "As I am famous for not taking guff off anyone. You, young lady, may call me Mrs. Gilfred."

Tom hid a smile.

There were several minutes of getting everything in order, including taking her vital signs and making notations about the IV fluids. Tom tried to make himself as unintrusive as possible. He wondered seriously why someone didn't suggest he leave the room. After all, he was just the woman's car mechanic. He surely shouldn't be present when the nurse was asking questions like *Do you know where you are? And Can you remember the year you were born?*

To the latter, Mrs. Gilfred replied with heavy sarcasm, "I don't recall that first year too clearly, but Mother always said I spent most of my time sleeping."

Tom didn't even attempt to hide his humor at that statement. He grinned broadly at the woman, which apparently sparked her attention for the first time.

"Oh, it's you!" Mrs. Gilfred said, sounding delighted. "I thought you were another one of those long-faced young doctors. How is my dear Clara? Are you taking good care of her?"

"I'm certainly trying, Mrs. Gilfred. That's why I came... uh, to see how you're doing and to talk to you about Clara."

"Good. That will be infinitely more interesting than the typical conversation in this place. Try not to get old. When you do, all anyone wants to discuss with you is the medications you're taking. And all they ever ask about is your last bowel movement."

The flock of caregivers finished their tasks quickly and efficiently and in a short time Tom found himself alone with the old woman. She fumbled around the bed railing until she found the controller and raised the head of the mattress into something that resembled a sitting position.

She smiled again at Tom and he was uncomfortable. He felt silly for having come to see her and didn't really have any idea what to say.

"I brought some flowers," he told her.

"Well, isn't that nice," she said. "Your mother certainly raised you to have good manners."

That was so far from the truth, Tom could have rightly offered an adamant denial. Instead he gave credit where credit was due.

"Actually my son told me to bring them," he said. "Quint's only six, but I value his opinion. He said that you don't visit the hospital without bringing flowers."

Mrs. Gilfred chuckled. "Well, he sounds like a very bright boy," she said. "He's either observant and sensitive or he's angling for an endorsement contract from the Society of American Florists."

Tom grinned at her.

"So you've come to talk about my Clara," Mrs. Gilfred said.

He nodded.

"Please pull up a chair and tell me what you think."

Tom did just that.

Although he'd written up a complete assessment, which he'd brought to her, he found himself simply telling her what problems he'd found and what options he thought she had.

"The carburetor damage is worse than I'd thought," he told her. "The throttle valve and choke plate are both seriously frozen and the intake manifold is completely shot. There's not really a good rebuild option. The transmission is in surprisingly good shape, except for the torque converter, which has corroded pretty badly. The cooling system needs an overhaul, the radiator is badly rusted, you'll need all new hoses. The crankshaft seems okay, but you'll probably need a new water pump. As I said initially, Mrs. Gilfred, the body is in excellent shape, though the running gear, the suspension and steering are going to need some TLC."

"You've got to call me Guffy," the woman told him.

Tom grinned at her. "I thought that name was only for your friends," he said, referencing her previous comments upon her nurse's familiarity.

She raised an eyebrow at him before returning his smile. "Any friend of Clara's is a friend of mine."

Tom laughed.

"So how much is this going to cost?" she asked him.

"That depends a lot on the direction we go," he answered. "If we do it quickly, buy new parts or parts available, it's going to run a fairly high price tag. And along with that, since you are planning to sell, you need to know that one of the things you've got going for you in this car is that it's in virtually original condition. If the car is up and running and in original condition, collectors pay a premium for that. If we put new, off-the-shelf parts in…" He shook his head. "If we do that, we might as well just pull the engine and start all over. We get no credit for the original parts we've saved."

Guffy nodded slowly.

"If Clara were your car, Mr. Bentley, what would you do?" she asked.

"I'd try to have patience," Tom said. "There are junkyards and pick-and-pulls all over the country that have parts for these Buicks. If you can sit tight and give me time, I may be able to do everything with vintage parts scavenged from other vehicles. It will, I think, ultimately be a little cheaper and enhance the value, but it's going to take time."

She thought about that for a minute.

"I know the phrase, 'time is money,' so if you just want me to get on with it, I can absolutely do that."

"Time is money," Mrs. Gilfred repeated, and then smiled. "From where I sit, time is in very short supply and no amount of money can make up for that."

Tom nodded.

"Still, I'd like to find the right person for Clara," the older woman said. After another thoughtful moment she smiled broadly, her eyes nearly disappearing in the creases. "Perhaps I should think of it as the choice between having her come out as a debutante or just trying to meet men in a honky-tonk."

Tom shook his head and chuckled. "So which should it be?" he asked.

"Clara never really had the temperament of a debutante, so I'm counting on you to smooth over the rough edges."

Tom laughed. "I'll do my best, ma'am."

"So the next question is, I suppose, how do I pay for this?" she asked. "Beyond my house and Clara, I only have a small pension."

Tom thought about that for just a couple of seconds. "You can pay me out of the profit from the sale," he said.

"It could be months, you said so yourself," she pointed out. "Can you afford to carry me that long?"

"I'll work something out," he assured her. "Besides, you need to be figuring out how to break out of this place. That jailer I saw on the way in looked pretty formidable."

She laughed as he hoped that she would.

"You get Clara running, get her revved up and in the driveway outside the back door, and I'll make a break for it," she promised.

Erica still hadn't told Tom about the extra money. It wasn't on purpose, she assured herself. It was just that it hadn't come up in conversation. She was going to tell him. Of course, she was going to tell him. But that fact had not kept her from checking out prices on washing machines.

As she rode the bus from work to the shop, she was thinking that her mother was not completely wrong. A little household fund to pay for things that break down or get damaged or just need to be replaced—there was nothing wrong with that. In fact, it could be completely right. An unexpected expense could make a terrible mess of their monthly budget. Sure, losing the washer was only a big inconvenience, but what if the refrigerator went out? She sure couldn't take the groceries to a coin-op cold storage. She'd made up her mind completely that the extra money would be for the house. Tom was sure to go along with that. If he didn't get it at first, she'd just convince him.

However, when she got to the shop, he wasn't there.

"Dad went to visit a lady at the hospital," Quint told her.

"Really? Was it a friend of ours? Did he say who was sick?"

Quint shook his head. "No, he didn't say."

"Is she in my hospital? Where I work?"

Her son shrugged. "I dunno."

"Okay," Erica said. "Well, when Daddy left, did he drive up the street or down?"

"Down," Quint answered quickly, as pleased with himself as if it were a question on a math quiz.

"All right!" Erica answered, praising his observation.

"I remember because he was going to the store to get her flowers."

"Flowers?"

"Yep, a bouquet," Quint said. "*Bouquet* is a big word that means flowers."

Erica gave her son a smile. "Actually bouquet and flowers are the same size, seven letters."

Quint screwed up his face in disappointment. "Why even have a harder word if it's not bigger?" he asked.

Erica had no answer for that.

"Put your stuff in your book bag and I'll tell the guys that I'm taking you home."

Her son nodded and Erica went through the side door into the shop. Cliff was under the hood of a Trans Am nearby. He was noisily using hydraulic wrenches to reseat an engine block. She didn't really want to yell at him over the noise. From the open back door, she could see Hector and Gus talking together in the shade of the building. Their backs were to her, but she could see that Hector was casually drinking a can of cold cola and Gus was puffing on a cigarette. She could tell them as easily as Cliff and without any disruption of their work.

She stepped out of the back of the building and walked toward them, hearing just a snippet of conversation before she caught their attention

"You're an idiot if you think a man and a woman go off together for hours to look at car parts," Gus told Hector. "They're looking at parts all right…each other's."

The two men laughed lewdly, before Hector spotted her.

"Mrs. Bentley! Uh…good afternoon."

Gus turned in her direction as well and gave her a half-bowing kind of nod. "Miz Bentley."

She smiled sweetly at them both, letting them believe she

hadn't caught the two of them gossiping like a couple of old maids.

"Quint and I are headed to the house," she told them. "So if you miss your office help, well, he's been recruited away for work as an assistant room straightener and table setter."

Hector smiled and Gus nodded as he tamped out the dregs of his cigarette with his boot heel. "He's a good little boy," the man said.

"Hey, Quint," Hector called out.

Erica turned to see her son was at the door, his heavy backpack slung over one shoulder.

"We'll see you tomorrow, guy," Hector told him.

The six-year-old grinned and waved as he made his way toward the old sedan.

Erica met him there and, after turning on the car, rolled down the window to allow the worst of the autumn afternoon heat to escape the car. She glanced in the rearview mirror to see Quint buckling himself in his seat without conversation. He was yawning. The word *nap* could never be mentioned in her son's presence, but this time of day he was always dragging a bit. She missed not having their regular conversation, but let him lapse into sluggish silence as she drove home.

Mentally she took inventory of the refrigerator, hoping to come up with an interesting idea for dinner. She was still debating chicken cutlets versus chicken curry when she turned onto her street and spied a familiar car parked in her driveway. The aging silver Mercedes was shiny and immaculate—it looked brand-new. Erica knew, however, that it took a lot of her husband's time and effort to keep its worn-out engine running. The Mercedes, like its owner, had a beauty that was mainly skin-deep.

"Ann Marie is here," Quint piped up from the backseat.

Erica didn't correct her son's appellation. Ann Marie had never really liked designations such as mommy, mama or ever mother. She positively hated anything that smacked of "grand." She had insisted since babyhood that Quint call her by her given name.

Erica pulled into her parking spot as her mother stepped out of the car.

Quint made quick work of his seat belt and rushed out to meet her. Erica saw her mother hold her hands out in front of her at Quint's rushed approach. Some might have thought she was reaching for the boy, but Erica knew the intent had more to do with protecting her clothes.

Ann Marie managed to grasp her grandson by the shoulders. She was smiling at him, speaking to him, charmingly and congenially. She was also keeping him firmly at arm's length.

Erica almost laughed at the sight. There was a certain dark humor to Ann Marie's uncomfortable grandparenting. It would have been truly funny if her own heart hadn't ached in sympathy for her ever-optimistic son.

"Would you like to see my race-car track?" Quint was asking. "Aunt Letty helped me put it all together and we fixed it so the upside-down part actually goes right through a Lego block tunnel."

"That sounds very nice, Quinton," she answered. "Perhaps I will see it later."

Erica had raised the door on the garage. When her mother caught sight of it she frowned.

"Erica, you have a perfectly acceptable front entrance to your home," Ann Marie said pointedly. "Only tacky women who live in little cracker-box houses enter through the garage."

The fact that there was more love in Erica's little cracker-box home than any of the larger, lavish houses her mother had shared with her daughters was not something that Erica felt it was politic to mention. Her mother preferred to cavort with the well-heeled. The Monte Vista manse that she shared with her current gentleman friend, Melvin Schoenleber, was filled to the brim with fabulous objects and beautiful clothes, collected by the man's late wife. The gossip was that Ann Marie had been working for the caterer that served at the poor woman's funeral reception. Ann Marie had taken one look at the house, and the widower had taken one look at Ann Marie, and they made a mutual decision that she would simply never leave.

Erica would never ask for the whole story. But she knew her mother well enough to know that she trusted men about as far as she could throw them. Mr. Schoenleber was generous with gifts. Still, she was certain that the old man's children, similar in age to Ann Marie herself, would never let her walk out of that house with so much as a silver toothpick. But the old man was currently hale and hearty and liked nothing more than attending parties and being a fine-arts patron with the youthful and well-garbed Ann Marie on his arm. Her mother was apparently content to enjoy the high life while it lasted.

And a part of that enjoyment, Erica was sure, included looking down her nose at those, like her daughter, living a more mundane existence.

Erica closed the garage and followed her mother to the front door. Quint was at Ann Marie's side, talking a mile a minute and skipping with new energy.

Her mother gave the little boy wary attention as if fearful that at any moment he might suddenly demand something from her. Once inside she actually shooed him away as if he were a neighbor's pesky pet.

"Why is it so hot in here?"

"Because we've been gone all day, Mother."

Ann Marie gave her a disapproving look, as if an empty house were a personal failing.

"Would you like something cool to drink?"

Ann Marie sighed gratefully. "A chablis would be very nice," she said.

Erica raised an eyebrow. "I've got iced tea, orange juice, water or milk."

"Oh well, then, water I suppose."

Her mother followed as Erica headed toward the back of the house, pausing to open the windows. In the kitchen, she retrieved a glass from the cupboard and found a few ice cubes in the freezer before filling it under the tap.

When she turned around her mother was already seated at the table, removing her date book, a notepad and a small stack of papers held together with an oversize clip.

"What's going on?"

"I have some paperwork that I need you to fill out," Ann Marie said.

Her mother's tone was so matter-of-fact that Erica immediately suspected a scheme of some sort. She sat at the table across from her and eyed Ann Marie warily.

She pulled one sheet out of the stack of papers and pushed it toward Erica.

"Just fill this out for Tom's business and don't worry about the fee, I'll take care of that."

Erica read the heading at the top. "Entry form—Chamber of Commerce Christmas Parade?" The question mark was in her tone.

"It's not for you, it's for Tom's business," Ann Marie told her.

"Tom's business?"

"Yes, of course. This is how businesses raise their profile. They advertise, and this is like advertising."

Erica glanced down at the paper. "Bold lettering in the phone book, maybe. But I don't think entering a float in a Christmas parade is exactly Tom's kind of advertising."

"Well, he doesn't actually have to do it, you just say you're going to do it."

"Huh?"

"It's a community project and I'm involved."

"Okay," Erica replied warily. "*You're* involved, but I'm not."

"I'm not asking you to be," she said. "I just want you to fill out the entrant's form. I told Cissy Womack that I could sign up five businesses. That prissy old harridan said, 'Well, do the best you can' as if I wouldn't know five business owners to ask."

"Do you know five business owners?"

"Of course! There is Melvin and there's Tom and there's Richard, the owner of the salon where I get my nails done. I know plenty of people and I'm determined to get my five, Cissy Womack be damned."

"What do you care what that woman thinks?" Erica said.

"I don't. I absolutely don't. But it's the principle of it. And it's a learning experience for her."

"A learning experience?" Erica eyed her mother dubiously.

Ann Marie tutted her dislike and explained herself. "She looks down her nose at me because she's a *wife* and I'm not. It's important that she understand that my being single is a strength not a weakness."

Ann Marie's tone was very emphatic.

"Still, I doubt this is something Tom will want to do. And that time of year is so busy for all of us."

"You don't have to actually do it," Ann Marie said. "You just sign up and I pay the money. My point will be made and by the time the holidays roll around, no one will ever notice that you don't show up."

Ann Marie handed her the pen. Still Erica hesitated.

"It's no big deal, just do it. I would have filled it out myself, but I was afraid someone would recognize my handwriting."

With a sigh, Erica began writing the requested information.

"So," Ann Marie said, "did you tell Tom about the extra money you're getting paid?"

Erica's first thought was to lie to her mother, but she had never been very good at that.

"No," she answered with feigned casualness, not raising her eyes from the paper. "We've been so busy, it just hasn't come up yet."

Ann Marie laughed lightly.

"Good for you," she said.

"What do you mean?"

"You've taken my advice. And it's about time. If you let Tom decide how to spend your money, every dime of it will be tucked away for a rainy day."

"Rainy days do happen," Erica pointed out defensively. "More often than we like to imagine."

"Of course they do," her mother agreed. "But wouldn't it be better to struggle through hard times on a decent couch with some nice curtains?"

Erica shook her head adamantly. "I have every intention of telling him," she said. "It's just…it's just that we're going to need a new washing machine and I know it will worry him. Once I save up the money, we'll go together and pick it out. It will be a nice surprise."

Ann Marie was nodding, but her expression was still self-satisfied. "Yes, I'm sure it will be," she agreed.

Chapter 7

AS THE SECRET RELATIONSHIP at work continued, Tom became hesitant to leave the shop. Everybody was busy, working, earning their pay. Still, he and Cliff were virtually not speaking. And he no longer felt confident about leaving his best friend in charge.

"You told me this was a Saturday thing!" Tom had railed at the first private opportunity after Cliff's midweek disappearing act.

"Stacy is important to me," he answered. "If I get a chance to be with her, I want to take that chance."

"Your job ought to be important to you," Tom pointed out angrily. "Running off with a girl like some love-crazed teenager is not what I expect from a responsible employee. You're having sex on my time clock and it's got to stop."

Cliff shrugged. "Dock my pay," he said. "It's an hour on Saturdays and four hours yesterday. I'll keep track of it and you can just subtract that time from my check."

"How will you explain that to Trish?"

He snorted with disgust. "I'll tell her I broke something and you're making me pay for it," he said.

"She'd never believe that."

"You're my boss," Cliff replied. "That automatically qualifies you for SOB status. It'll piss her off. But it'll be at you and not me. And you don't have to live with her."

"Five hours cut out of a two-week paycheck is big," Tom reminded him. "A loss like that will put a heck of a dent in the household budget."

Cliff shook his head. "Trish will just have to deal," he said. "If she doesn't like it, she can get off her lazy butt and get her own job. Stacy works, even Erica works. If Trish needs money, let her go out and earn it, like I do."

Tom didn't like the sound of that at all. Just a couple of weeks ago, Cliff was declaring he loved his wife and kids and this thing with Stacy was just sex. Now it was beginning to sound like being with Stacy had a higher priority than the security of his wife and kids.

Tom said as much and Cliff responded with an off-color suggestion of where Tom could stick his stupid opinion.

It was the good news/bad news aspect about putting friends on the payroll. You knew them, cared about them, trusted them. But they knew you as well. And Tom was pretty sure that Cliff had no fear of being fired. He probably didn't even think that Tom would follow through with docking his pay.

Tom wasn't sure if he would follow though himself.

Reluctantly, he left the shop a few minutes after nine in the morning to take receipts to the bank. Erica had handled all the billing and bookkeeping from the day they'd opened the shop. Now, with her hours at the hospital, Tom needed to take on some of that himself.

The paperwork wasn't all that complicated. Having everything set up was great. Sometimes he didn't know why things were singled out like they were. But he was beginning to get a handle on what went where, when to tally up and send in his sales tax and where to find the numbers required for his workers' compensation insurance.

He didn't like having to make second and third calls to customers who owed him money, but he was pretty sure Erica wouldn't have liked it that much, either.

And he'd come up with his own payment plans policy. He would never again extend credit to a painter, a politician or a preacher. Those three professions, he'd determined, seemed uniquely unwilling to make paying Tom a priority.

He was very grateful that, by far, most of his patrons paid in full and on time.

Tom ignored the convenient drive-through at the bank and parked his truck in the branch parking lot. He didn't really like doing business through a video screen. And besides, just inside the bank's lobby area was a table with free coffee and cookies. Tom was whistling as he went inside.

He only stood in line for a couple of moments before he got to talk to the teller.

"I have two accounts here—I want to make sure this goes into the business one," Tom said.

The young man made a couple of clicks on his computer.

"Actually, you have three accounts," he said. "Looks like your wife just opened a new personal savings."

Tom shrugged. "Well, whatever, just make sure this one gets into the business."

The young man double-checked the contents of his bank bag, totaled it all up, entered it on the computer and handed Tom his receipt. Pocketing the paper, he headed directly for the free food. He doctored his coffee with a packet of fake cream and picked up a cookie that looked like oatmeal but appeared to have chocolate chips instead of raisins. That seemed like a good idea.

"Good morning, Tom, how's it going?"

His mouth was full as he glanced up at the greeting. Bryce Feldon, the local bank branch manager, was an occasional customer over at the shop. The staid and slightly balding thirty-something in the charcoal-gray suit looked very different in khaki shorts and a brightly colored Hawaiian shirt behind the wheel of his 1970 yellow Torino.

"Oh, I've been keeping busy," Tom responded. "How's the car?"

"I took her out a couple of weekends ago," he answered. "We went up to the Hill Country. You know how she loves to hug those curves."

Tom nodded, smiling.

"I just wish I had more time to get her out on the road."

It was the upside/downside of vintage vehicle ownership. In order to afford to keep a fine car in working order, a guy had to work so many hours at his day job that he rarely had time to drive.

"When are you going to get yourself some classic wheels?" the banker asked.

Tom shook his head. "Probably never," he answered. "I can only afford to love them from afar."

Bryce nodded and chuckled.

"But there is a real beauty of a car in my shop right now," Tom continued. "I'd almost give my eyeteeth and my kid's college fund to own it."

"Oh, yeah?"

"It's a '56 Buick, original condition, owned by a little old lady who is looking to sell."

"Mmm," the banker said, as if Tom were describing

something deliciously tasty. "Come here. Step into my office for a minute," Bryce continued. "Bring your coffee."

Tom followed him into the glass-walled room at the north corner of the building. It was a masculine office with lots of dark wood and duck-hunting motifs. Bryce sat down in the big leather desk chair and indicated that Tom should take the seat across the expanse of mahogany desk from him.

"I was kidding about Quint's college fund," Tom joked. "There's not enough in there yet to even buy a good set of tires. But if my eyeteeth will help, let's get the dentist on the phone."

Bryce grinned. "Tell me about this Buick," he said.

Tom raised a brow. "Are you interested? Clara's a real beauty."

"Clara? You've named the car already? That's a dangerous sign, my friend. I can almost see a *man-tique* in your future."

The guy-term slang for classic cars and motorcycles, most preferred by male collectors, made Tom smile.

"Her owner calls her Clara," Tom corrected. "But somehow the name fits. She's a real beauty. Two-tone blue convertible with a continental kit."

"You don't come across many of those."

"I've never seen one," Tom said. "Or I haven't seen one in decades." A distant memory, grainy and indistinct, clicked in his brain. "I think I rode in one once when I was a little kid."

"Sometimes," Bryce said, "when the right deal comes along, a man has just got to take it. I hope you know your credit is good with me. I'm sure we can work something out."

Tom made a sound that was part chuckle, part sigh. "Car collecting is a little rich for my blood," he told the banker. "And I sure wouldn't go into debt to buy one."

"Is it debt?" Bryce asked. "Or an investment? I saw those mini-index numbers that showed collector cars have held their value better than the stock market or gold."

Tom made a tutting sound and shook his head. "You know as well as I do, Bryce, that those sales were almost handpicked and represent the very pristine, the top of the luxury market. And the survey was done during a recession."

Bryce shrugged an agreement.

Tom continued, "I tell guys all the time, if you want to buy a classic car, you do it because you want to own it, not because you hope to sell it. The little guy is never going to make the kind of deals the big brokers can manage."

"But a beautiful car, one that you can maintain yourself, does hold enough value that you'd probably never lose money," Bryce said. "It is a tangible asset. And it would be there if you ever had to sell it."

"If I ever owned the Buick, I'd be hard-pressed to part with her. I hate to think about letting her go even now. And she's just sitting in my shop, belonging to somebody else."

Bryce nodded. "I'd hate for you to let her go. Have you considered the tax incentive?"

"What tax incentive?"

"With a business like yours, a classic car business, I'm sure that an argument could be made that owning and maintaining a beautiful classic car with your logo on it could be a tax write-off as a promotional expense."

"You're kidding, right?"

"It sounds reasonable to me. You'd have to check with your accountant, of course."

Tom grinned. "Erica is my accountant," he said. "And I'm pretty sure that she would say exactly the same thing your wife would say."

Bryce sighed. "Women," he complained. "They just don't understand the romance of the internal combustion engine."

Tom chuckled. "There are plenty of gals as car crazy as we are," he said. "Erica just doesn't happen to be one of them."

"I'd still hate for you to let a car you love get away from you," Bryce said.

"Aren't you supposed to be talking me into buying certificates of deposit or investment services?"

Bryce laughed. "Bor-ing," he said softly, dragging the word out to great length.

Tom shook his head. "Now I know you're lying," he said. "You're crazy about all this money counting and deal making."

"Yeah," Bryce admitted. "But numbers on a page can never compete with the sight and sound of a great old car."

In the end, the only thing that Bryce talked Tom into was a new credit card.

"With all the parts buying you're doing on the internet, you need to have a separate credit card. There are lots of scammers and hackers out there. If they happen to get into your card account, you want to limit your exposure. This card won't have any ties to your accounts at this bank. No one will be able to use it to worm their way into your information."

Tom took his advice and filled out the form.

"It says 'number of cards,'" Tom said. "Should I get one for Erica, too?"

"No," Bryce said. "One is enough. This is not the kind of card that anyone is going to have in their wallet. You're just going to keep it locked up and use the number."

"That makes sense," Tom agreed.

He handed in his paperwork and stopped to grab another cookie on the way out.

"Keep thinking about that car," Bryce told him. "When fate brings something like that your way, it just seems down-right ungrateful not to snap it up."

Tom laughed off the suggestion. As he walked out to his truck, however, he couldn't quite resist the fantasy of owning the beautiful Clara.

Once again that faint remembrance niggled at his brain. The Buick in his memory had been yellow and white and the convertible top had been up. He was in the backseat with other children. Who those kids were and who the driver might have been, he couldn't imagine.

Tom shook his head. The memory was a strangely pleasur-able one. Although, who wouldn't be happy riding around in such an incredible car?

Erica had just returned from her morning break. In fact, it hadn't been much of a break. She'd filled her coffee cup in the staff lounge and gone back to her cubicle to retrieve an energy bar from her desk drawer. She had just taken a bite and leaned back in her chair to sip her coffee when Mrs. Converse suddenly appeared.

Erica startled guiltily and splashed a bit of coffee on her skirt.

"Could you please come into my office," the supervisor said.

"Yes, ma'am," Erica replied. She got to her feet and quickly cleaned up the evidence of the spill on her clothes before following the older woman.

It never seemed like a good idea to get called into the boss's office; however, Erica couldn't pinpoint anything that she might have done to get herself into trouble. She'd picked up the pace on her charts and she was gaining confidence in her skills every day. She wasn't a "real" newbie, but she couldn't take her veteran status for granted, either.

Get a grip! You are very good at your job, she mentally chided herself. It was one of the unfortunate facts of her upbringing that her mother's constant criticism lingered in her psyche as self-doubt. Like a patient who'd been administered a potent prescription—the residual side effects often took a long time to dissipate.

Mrs. Converse was already seated behind her desk when Erica stepped over the threshold. She was a small woman, with diminutive facial features and tiny hands and feet. Her brown hair, streaked with silver, was cropped close to her head. And her eyeglasses seemed oversize. But somehow her presence never seem to conjure up words like "dainty" or "petite." Her appearance evoked ideas of efficiency and sparsity, as if her whole being were devoted to a conservation of resources.

"Please close the door," her supervisor said.

Erica turned to do her bidding and caught the eye of Darla Ingalls standing next to Rayliss Morton's cubicle. She was watching Erica and appeared to be reporting her visit to the office to the woman hidden behind the short, blue fabric wall.

With a wan smile, Erica closed the door and seated herself across the desk from her boss.

Mrs. Converse was glancing through some paperwork on her desk, but when she looked up she smiled.

"You seem to be settling in very well," she said.

Erica felt the muscles in her shoulders relax. "Yes, ma'am," she said. "I guess it's like riding a bicycle, it all comes back."

Mrs. Converse nodded. "That's true. Still a lot of things have changed since you last worked here and I see that you are able to adapt to that."

Erica shrugged. "We didn't have nearly as many digitized records coming in when I left. But clicking through screens is much easier than shoveling paperwork. The new coding manual is actually more user-friendly than the older edition. So yes, there are changes, but it seems like good change."

The supervisor chuckled lightly. "For many in this department no changes are good changes. But you've always been very capable and competent."

"Thank you."

"And I've been positively impressed with your grasp and skill at using the EMRs. You're quickly becoming my best producer."

EMRs, electronic medical records, were rapidly changing the nature of Medical Records. When Erica had left the job, they were the newest, latest thing and had only been implemented on a trial basis in certain areas. Now they were hospital wide, the norm rather than the exception. Occasionally a paper record would arrive through the emergency room or with a transfer from another hospital. And there were still whole storerooms of old documents kept in files. But the future was already upon them and savings in manpower and accuracy made EMR a winner even before a discussion of tree-saving or ease of retrieval.

"I like having a neat desk," Erica replied, smiling. "Remember when we would come to work and there would be so many piles of charts that there wasn't room to put down a cup of coffee?"

Mrs. Converse chuckled. "I do remember that. And I don't have a lot of nostalgia for it."

"Now, if we can only get the rest of the health-care community on board," Erica said. "I know that small hospitals and doctors' offices are going to love this as soon as they get it implemented."

"I'm glad to hear you say that," Mrs. Converse replied. "I thought you would be in my corner on this, but it's good to hear you voice it aloud."

The woman tapped her pencil thoughtfully against the desk for a half minute before she continued.

"Erica, I've had my eye on you as a potential team leader, even before you left to have your baby," she said. "I wasn't planning to rush into anything until you were thoroughly back into the routine, but you seem to be doing well and I need you."

Erica felt a flush of pride in her cheeks. "Whatever you need me to do, Mrs. Converse, I'll try my best."

The woman accepted her assent gratefully.

"I want you to take on the EMR Training Workshop," Mrs. Converse said.

University Hospital had developed course work to teach records professionals from smaller facilities as well as staff from private physicians' offices and clinics how to implement electronic charting and maintenance where they worked. Among older physicians and community-based services in lower income areas, the transition to digital had gotten stalled. While grant funding was still available for equipment purchase, the real stumbling block had become the lower level of computer literacy and the foot-dragging that sometimes verged upon intransigence.

The software companies provided excellent staff training once their product had been purchased. But getting these facilities knowledgeable enough to make an informed decision about what software to purchase was a community challenge that Mrs. Converse had taken on as her own. She had for the past two years utilized her department's resources for broadening EMR use in South Texas. And it was working, slowly but surely, it was working.

"I want you on the team," she told Erica. "Melody will still be in charge. Nobody on my staff knows more about how systems work than she does. But like a lot of those who truly understand computers, she's not always at her best among people."

Erica nodded.

"I want you to work with her," Mrs. Converse said. "I especially want you involved in all the interdisciplinary collaborations."

Erica frowned. "I thought Callie Torreno was doing that," she said.

Mrs. Converse's hesitation was so slight Erica might have thought she imagined it.

"Callie *has* been on the project," the supervisor said. "But she and Melody have not been a good fit."

It was a tepid criticism. Erica assumed Mrs. Converse was measuring her words.

"Callie is an excellent employee with a very good grasp of the material," she said. "But it is Melody who is by far the best on my staff in explaining what we do and answering why we do it for those who have yet to understand that good records are vital to quality care."

Erica nodded in agreement.

"Melody is not, however, a particularly warm person. As you can imagine, many of our workshop attendees are not as enthusiastic about going digital as we are. New things can be threatening. The stress of that occasionally comes out in resistance. Melody's response to that is not always the best. She seems to alienate more than she consoles."

From what Erica had seen of her coworker, Mrs. Converse was putting it lightly.

"Many of our attendees were sent here by their supervisors, occasionally against their will. They are angry and frightened about the effect of these changes on their job. But they've got to keep all that bottled up on their own turf, in front of their own boss."

That made sense.

"Here, within the safe confines of an unfamiliar place full of strangers, it sometimes bursts to the surface."

Erica was not surprised. It was a lot to expect of people who'd done their job a certain way for an entire career to suddenly have to learn something new and almost totally foreign. Especially when that investment in time and effort was perhaps not expected to pay out fully until long after you were retired.

"Melody knows her material," Mrs. Converse said. "But she cannot teach it to a roomful of unhappy professionals who find reasons not to like her."

Erica's own encounters with Melody bespoke the truth of her supervisor's words.

Mrs. Converse gave a long-suffering sigh.

"I decided she needed some backup," she told Erica. "I need another staff member who could be competent in conveying our vision to others. The position requires an almost infinite patience and a willingness to help. I had high hopes for Callie—she has a very bright mind, she's personable and a natural leader. But she has not been the best choice."

Erica found that surprising. "I can't imagine what Callie would have done wrong," she said.

Mrs. Converse looked sharply at her for a moment and then tapped her pencil thoughtfully.

"Suffice to say that it didn't work out. And that I expect your behavior to be completely professional and with the best interests of our department in mind. Furthering our goals here should be your paramount consideration."

"Of course," Erica answered.

"I have great hopes that, with your help we will be able to do that," Mrs. Converse said.

Erica nodded because it seemed like the thing to do.

"I am aware of your workload, Erica. And I know you're still getting your bearings," Mrs. Converse continued. "But I do believe that you are an excellent choice to take this on. There is still time for you to have some input on the syllabus. All the department chiefs have agreed to either participate or provide staff to speak for them. Brush up a little on note requirements and the forms. You can let Melody answer the technical questions. I just want you ready to be the friendly, welcoming face of our department and our institution."

Erica noticed that somehow the request that she take this on had morphed into the assumption that she would.

"Absolutely." She answered the question that hadn't been asked. "I will be ready and I will have Melody's back."

"Good."

"Have you told Callie that I'm replacing her?"

"Not yet," Mrs. Converse said. "But she does know that I'm giving the task to someone else. She'll be completely cooperative."

That may have been true, but Erica realized very quickly that there was some unspoken reason her coworker had been taken off the job. And that she was not happy about it. Not that Callie said anything to Erica. In fact, nobody said anything to Erica. The lunch table had never been so quiet. Rayliss and Darla gave her furtive glances. Lena acted nervous, as if she were in on a secret and she didn't know what to do with the knowledge.

Only Melody seemed completely normal. She was contentedly enjoying her plate of grilled chicken and summer squash. But she was itching for an argument with Callie.

"For the record," Melody announced, her nose in the air haughtily. "I spoke to Gabe last night about the accusations I heard at this table. He denied them as ludicrous. And he agrees with me that you think like that because your own marriage was such a disaster."

It was unfortunate that her timing was such that she baited her coworker while she was wounded.

"Did you think he would admit it even if it were true?" Callie asked her. "I'm just warning you to keep your eyes open. There are signs for cheaters and only women who are fools ignore them."

"I am not a fool," Melody said. "And my husband would never be unfaithful. He loves me."

"Of course he does," Darla agreed. "But you know men… or maybe you don't."

Rayliss agreed. "I see it all the time," she said. "I go out to clubs and most of the men there, they're all married."

Darla and Callie nodded.

"Not all men are like that," Melody insisted.

"Maybe not *all* of them," Darla said. "But *most* of them."

"It's no surprise," Callie said. "A guy may love his wife, but she's getting older and usually putting on the pounds." She glanced pointedly at Melody, who visibly paled before setting down her fork. "It makes perfect sense to them to go out looking for something younger and hotter."

"I…I…it's hard work to lose that last ten pounds of baby weight," Melody pointed out. "And when you sit at a desk all day."

"Don't I know it," Lena agreed. "These young girls sure aren't sitting at desks. They're in the bars all night and at the gym all day. They'd never eat a salad. They get all their calories from tequila."

Darla laughed. "I remember those days, kind of."

"And you never dated any married men," Melody pointed out as evidence for her side of the argument.

Lena shrugged. "Who knows? Married men look just like single men."

"Especially when they've got their pants down," Callie said.

Her trio of henchwomen giggled delightedly.

"Don't worry," Rayliss told her. "These guys are never planning to just blow up their marriage."

"Although that does happen," Callie said. "Remember Dr. Carnegy."

The women nodded to each other sagely.

"Just remember the signs," Darla said. "Changes in your sex life. New clothes. Secret spending."

"Unexplained absences," Lena added.

"You should be watching him like a hawk," Callie told her. "Men are very good at this kind of thing. But if you watch closely enough, you'll pick up clues."

"But don't do anything about it," Rayliss reminded her. "Don't confront him unless you're ready for a divorce."

"And you're not ready for a divorce until you've got photos of the two of them in a cheap motel."

Darla giggled at her own statement and the other women laughed, too.

Erica smiled halfheartedly. These women were beginning to sound like her mother. Inexplicably, she suddenly recalled her discussion with Tom during the basketball game. Then somehow the infidelity humor just didn't seem quite as funny as it once had.

Chapter 8

THE FOLLOWING SATURDAY, Erica simply could not bring herself to visit the laundromat again. Instead she called her mother.

"I need to use your washer and dryer," she said.

"I'm going to be out most of the day," her mother answered. "I've got a massage at Ric Marmolejo and then I'm having my hair done. After that I have a facial with Iga."

"I don't need you, Ann Marie. I just need your laundry room."

"Oh, all right," she said with a huff. "Are you bringing Quint with you?"

"Well, I can't exactly leave him at home."

"Don't let him break anything," her mother said. "This house has so many irreplaceable pieces that it would break Melvin's heart if anything were damaged. And it would be just one more excuse for his children."

Her mother sighed heavily.

"I promise he won't break anything," Erica said. "I'll do laundry and I'll leave. That is it."

But of course that wasn't exactly it. Her mother's gentleman friend, Melvin Schoenleber, was just back from temple, still wearing his suit and yarmulke. He was not a particularly tall man and his back was slightly bent with age. But behind his glasses was a sense of good humor that was unmistakable. Erica was fairly certain that a sense of good humor would be essential for living with Ann Marie.

"Come in, come in, it is always so good to see you. And especially to see this young man. How are you, Quinton?"

"Hi, Mr. Schoenleber," Quint said. "Cool hat."

"Cool hat?" Schoenleber repeated, and then laughed delightedly. "Did you hear what the fellow said? He said, 'cool hat.'"

"I'm so sorry," Erica apologized. "He's just barely familiar with his own religious heritage, we haven't actually branched out to other faiths yet."

Mr. Schoenleber was laughing. "You have to admit, he's right. It is a cool hat."

Erica was embarrassed.

"We are very sorry to intrude upon you on the sabbath, Mr. Schoenleber," she said.

"It's my sabbath not yours," he pointed out. "And you've got to call me Melvin. I am so disappointed that you don't call me Melvin."

"Of course, of course, Melvin," Erica managed to get out.

"Quinton, Quinton, I think there are some toys in that far cabinet in the living room. Go see what you can find in there."

"Be careful," Erica cautioned. "Don't break anything."

"The room is full of useless tchotchkes. You can break whatever you want," Melvin called after him.

He smiled broadly at Erica. She wasn't sure what he'd just said, so she smiled back.

"I need to get started on the laundry," she told him, and headed off in that direction.

She carried in one basketful, which she started washing immediately. Then she returned to the car for another basket.

Mr. Schoenleber's home was on a wide, graceful boulevard in the old Monte Vista section of the city. On house-tour brochures it was described as a two-story Italianate villa built in 1927 on a half-acre lot just above downtown. How long the Schoenlebers had actually lived here, Erica didn't know for sure. But his four children had grown up in this house. They had a great attachment to it. And, according to Ann Marie, they weren't all that keen on Erica's mother making herself at home.

That was understandable, even to Erica. If a woman who seemed to make her living divorcing well-to-do men moved in with an elderly parent, there was reason to be concerned.

She'd parked in an area between the main house and the building that housed both the garage and the guesthouse. It was convenient to the kitchen entrance. She lifted out another basket and then topped it with a couple of pillowcases stuffed with dirty sheets. Erica carried that inside and had just set it on the laundry room floor when she turned to find Melvin behind her, holding the final basket.

"You didn't have to do that," she said, immediately taking it from him.

"It's not so heavy and I'm glad to help."

"Thanks," she said. "And thanks for letting me just barge in over here."

"You and your sister are always welcome in this house," he said. "And don't let anyone ever tell you otherwise."

"Thanks Mr. Scho...I mean Melvin."

"Do you drink coffee?" he asked. "I make a mean pot of joe."

"Please don't go to any trouble," Erica said.

"It's not trouble, it's a pleasure," he said. "Coffee's always best when shared with a good conversation."

"Okay then, I'd love a cup."

In the kitchen, Erica seated herself at the glass table in the windowed breakfast nook that looked out on the garden.

Mr. Schoenleber didn't just throw a filter in the Mr. Coffee, he ground the beans by hand and then slowly brewed them in a moka pot. Erica watched him as he moved around the kitchen with purpose and confidence. He was almost eighty, and age had marked him in many ways. But there was no sense of him as a defenseless old man. He seemed completely in control of his own universe.

Quint came running in, excited. In his hand he carried a wooden biplane with a U.S. Mail insignia on the side. Its paint was fading and the wood had a dark glossy patina.

"I found this, Mr. Schoenleber," he said. "I found it in the back of that cabinet. Can I play with it?"

"Of course you can," the old man said.

"That's an antique," Erica said. "Maybe you should just look at it, you wouldn't want to break it."

"It's a toy," Mr. Schoenleber corrected. "Toys are meant to be played with. Why don't I give it to you—that way if you break it, it will be your loss, not mine."

"Wow, thanks," Quint said. "This is so cool."

Her son immediately headed back down the hall, swooping his plane up and down and making engine noises in an imitation of flight.

"You really shouldn't give him something so valuable," Erica told Mr. Schoenleber.

The old man shrugged. "He likes it. Who else should have

it? He's the youngest of all the grandchildren. The rest are all too old for toys."

Erica raised an eyebrow at that statement. At first she thought just to leave it alone, but decided she couldn't.

"Quint isn't really your grandchild," she said. "And your actual family might not appreciate having you hand out family treasures to him."

Mr. Schoenleber carried the moka pot to the table and set it on a trivet.

"Technically he's not my grandson," the man conceded. "But when you're that young, technicalities don't count for much."

Erica couldn't argue with that.

He retrieved a pair of beautiful china cups with matching saucers from the cabinet and asked Erica to pour. She managed to fill them without spilling a drop. The smell was wonderful, but when Erica brought the cup to her lips, it was too hot to drink. She'd just have to wait.

Mr. Schoenleber, however, had his own method. She watched as he sloshed a small amount of the coffee in the saucer, then drank out of it instead of the cup.

Her surprise must have shown on her face, as the old man answered the question that was never asked.

"It cools more quickly this way," he said. "The wider area of the saucer diffuses the heat more efficiently, so you can drink it. Give it a try."

It was not as easy as it looked. Getting the right amount from the cup to the saucer was a challenge. And then drinking from the saucer without spilling it was even more difficult. Erica was grateful to have a napkin.

"It's an old trick I learned," he told her. "A very good trick for a man who loves coffee but who never had a moment to linger."

Quint came flying in, delivering a fake letter to the table. Mr. Schoenleber gave him a pile of sales circulars requesting air mail service to several different sites in the house. Erica watched her son happily participate in the game.

Alone at the table once more, she sipped her coffee, directly from the cup.

"I love your mother, you know," Mr. Schoenleber volunteered without preamble. "But I worry about marrying her."

Erica was momentarily caught off guard, but recovered as quickly and as graciously as she could.

"I understand."

"No, I doubt you do," he said. "You probably think, like my children, that Ann Marie is a gold digger and I have just enough functioning brain cells left not to tie the knot."

Erica deliberately focused on the coffee in her cup.

"The truth is, your mother doesn't need my money," he said. "She's tucked away enough from all those losers she married to live like a baroness. Of course, she doesn't believe that. There's not enough money on the planet to make Ann Marie feel financially secure."

Mr. Schoenleber chuckled as if that fact were humorous. "Lucky for me," he added.

Erica glanced up, forcing herself to meet his eyes. At least her mother wasn't pulling something over on the old guy.

"That's why I hesitate to marry her," he explained. "We have a wonderful time together. She's fun and full of life. She likes parties and concerts and the productions at San Pedro Playhouse. We eat great food at Biga or Il Sogno and we truly enjoy each other's company."

He took another sip of coffee, as if appreciating his own thoughts.

"But we both know her history," Schoenleber said. "And I've no doubt that it could repeat itself. The minute that a man says 'I do' to Ann Marie, she starts to believe that he doesn't."

Erica was surprised at the man's insight. She thought he might be exactly right about her mother.

"In order to keep her on the hook," he said, "I've got to keep stringing her along." He chuckled lightly at his own little joke. "But I don't want you and your sister to imagine that I'm not committed to Ann Marie. I fully intend to spend the rest of my life with her, however long or short that might be. But I may not be able to manage being listed as husband number nine."

"Nine?" Erica asked. "I thought there were only seven exes?"

He shrugged. "With a woman like Ann Marie anybody could lose count."

Tom had a long list of car parts that he was chasing down over the internet. He could put a 2001 valve assembly in a '91 model or change out a Chevy drive train for a Mercury. But when it came to a 1963 Impala bumper or an interior door panel on an '81 T-Bird, his customers counted on him to scrounge through the almost infinite number of vintage dealers, antique metal specialties, hobby sites, pick-and-pulls and ordinary junkyards. He had to find the exact make and model. He couldn't even bid on a restoration if he didn't know that he could get the part and how much it was going to cost.

This was the kind of work that he could do at home. And with the shop as busy as it had been the past few weeks, he found himself playing catch-up. After dinner, he'd logged onto the laptop. In some ways it was a treasure hunt. It was exciting, especially when he found something that he needed, or stumbled on something that was really rare. But a lot of the salvagers were barely inventoried and lacking quick search capabilities, which forced him to read through long lists of car parts until his eyes nearly crossed with the effort.

With a sigh, he closed his computer and rose from the kitchen table, stretching tall and wide to snap out any kinks in his not-really-meant-for-desk-work frame.

He walked through the quiet house, curious about his family. Glancing out the back window, he saw Quint and Warren, Quint's friend from down the street. They were running around the yard like crazy, occasionally freezing into a martial-arts stance before wildly kicking at the air. This was undoubtedly some game the two had made up. They might be kung-fu fighters. Or superheroes who did kung-fu fighting. Or androids with superpowers programmed for kung-fu.

Tom smiled. Even in his weird, disruptive childhood there had been moments of blissful fantasy. All kids deserved as much of that as they could get.

Sitting at the picnic table nearby, Erica had dragged outside a lamp attached to a long extension cord. She was bent over a thick pile of paperwork.

She'd told him over dinner about the new training assignment and that she needed to familiarize herself with the syllabus. They'd both agreed to spend the evening doing "homework." Tom had done his in a quiet silence conducive to concentration. Erica chose to do hers on the picnic table with a background noise of hollering six-year-olds.

Naturally, somebody had to watch the boys. And just as naturally, that fact had not occurred to him in advance. He shook his head. Erica was not big on complaints. Nor was she likely to make demands. It might have been easier on Tom if she did. He knew exactly what to do to keep a car running in top shape. He could listen to an engine and diagnose a problem before he even raised the hood. But he had no idea about how a happy marriage worked. He wanted his to last forever, but he had no idea about what kind of regular maintenance was required.

"Okay," he said aloud to himself. "She's doing something just because it needs to be done. Look around and find something that needs to be done and do it."

He walked through the house, looking for hinges that needed tightening, bulbs that needed replacement, boxes that needed to go up into the attic. Nothing. He walked through the kitchen. Dishes were done. Floor looked good. He even opened the fridge to see if it needed cleaning out. Everything looked fine.

He moved to the bathroom. Everything looked pretty good in there, too. As he was leaving, however, he noticed the hamper. Sure enough it was not only full it was stuffed.

Almost as pleased as if he'd just stumbled onto a radiator cap for a Stutz Bearcat, Tom carried the hamper out to the laundry room. He sorted everything on the floor and put a load of towels into the washer. With a quarter cup of detergent and a flick of the wrist, he started the machine up. He left the hamper there and went back through the kitchen.

The sounds of Erica and the kids drew him to the living room. The two boys looked worn-out.

"Did you get much work done out there?" he asked her.

"More than you'd think," she answered. "Why don't you walk Warren home and I'll get Quint bathed and into bed."

"Do I have to take a bath?" Quint's words were more a whine than a question.

"Yes," Erica answered, brooking no excuse.

"Yeah," Tom added. "As dirty as you are, we'd have to throw that bed out if you slept in it."

His son was still grumbling when he said goodbye to his friend, but he did head for the bathroom without resistance.

It was almost dark as Tom walked the half block to Warren's house. The little fellow was yawning and beginning to drag his feet. They passed an SUV parked on the street. A teenage girl sat in the passenger seat. A guy, maybe twenty years old, had the hood up and was gazing cluelessly at the engine.

Been there, done that, Tom thought to himself. For car trouble there was no better teaching tool than being stuck on the side of the road. It made a young man think through all the pieces of the engine and how they worked together. Then he'd either figure it out or get some exercise with a long walk home.

Tom turned Warren safely over to his mother at the front door and headed back up the street toward home.

As he approached the SUV again, the young woman had stepped outside. She was heavily pregnant, her big belly as round as a basketball.

Tom sighed. He could let the boy fend for himself. But the girl needed help and he wouldn't just pass her by.

He stepped off the curb and made his way toward the front of the vehicle.

"Hi, I'm Tom Bentley," he said, offering his hand.

The young guy glanced up, defensively at first, but when he saw Tom's hand, he shook it. "I'm Briscoe and this is my girlfriend, Kera."

The pregnant person gave Tom a shy smile and a wave.

"I work on cars for a living," Tom said, pointing to the logo on his shirt. "Why don't you let me see if I can get you back on the road."

"Great!" Briscoe said. "That would be great."

The kid took a step back and folded his arms. There was

an anger in him that belied his words. But Tom was not about to let him hand off his troubles to a passerby.

"Check the obvious things first," Tom said, as if he were a teacher and the young guy his student. "Have you got plenty of gas?"

Briscoe nodded. "About a quarter of a tank, I think. All the gauges went dead just before she broke down. So I'm thinking it's electrical or something."

As Tom leaned in, he could feel the heat from the engine block. It was too much heat.

"Have you got a flashlight?"

The young guy didn't. In fact, he didn't have any tools at all. Even his jack was missing the screw. Tom was irked. It was on the tip of his tongue to tell the kid that he had no business driving a car even around the block if he wasn't prepared for an emergency. But instead of biting the boy's head off, he walked to his house and got his own tools from the garage.

"Of course, this kid is no kind of emergency planner," Tom grumbled to himself. "Otherwise his little girlfriend wouldn't be as big as a house."

He grabbed a big jug of coolant as well and walked back to the stalled vehicle. The young woman had opened the back doors of the SUV and had seated herself on the floorboard. She was talking on her cell phone. Tom wondered if she was chatting with a friend or reassuring a worried mother.

The engine was still hot and it took him several moments, but he finally located a leak in the radiator hose. It was only a hairline crack right next to the clamp, but it was at just such an angle to blow hot steam against the fuse box.

"These may all have to be changed," he told Briscoe. "But first try just taking them out and putting them back in. Do it one at a time, so you don't get any in the wrong slot. They may surprise you."

The young guy nodded appreciatively.

Tom unclamped the hose and wrapped the cracked area with several layers of duct tape before reclamping it.

"This will hold for a while, but this hose has got to be replaced," he said. "What you might do, is take this one off. Just loosen the clamps top and bottom, and take this one with you to the parts store. That way you'll be sure to get the right one."

"Okay," Briscoe said.

"You're going to be able to do this repair yourself and it's going to save you a lot of money," Tom said. "You'll also have the assurance of knowing that it was done well, because you did it yourself."

He could see from the guy's expression that he wasn't there yet, but that's how people learned about cars. One repair at a time.

Tom filled the radiator with coolant that had been lost in the overheating. Before he shut the hood, he had Briscoe start it up. The engine sputtered a little and the battery whined, but it turned over and the motor sounded fine.

Both Briscoe and Kera cheered as if a touchdown had just been made at the football game.

"Wow, thanks!" Briscoe said. "This is great."

"Now you're going to get that hose taken care of tomorrow, right?"

"Tomorrow. Right. I'll take care of it tomorrow."

Tom nodded.

"Do I...do I owe you something?" Briscoe asked.

The words "no, nothing" came to Tom's lips, but the sight of the heavily pregnant teenager attempting to hoist herself into the SUV's passenger seat silenced him.

"Fifty dollars," Tom said instead.

"Fifty?" Briscoe repeated, his voice unnaturally high.

"That's the minimum charge for roadside service."

"Oh…okay." Briscoe pulled his wallet out of his back pocket and opened it wide enough to see inside with the aid of the flashlight. He counted out what he had and then went to Kera in the car. Tom waited patiently until the young guy returned. He handed Tom the money. They'd come up with the whole fifty dollars though three dollars of it was coins, including nickels.

Tom held the money in his hand for a few seconds and then stepped a couple of paces away from the vehicle and motioned to Briscoe to follow.

"I am going to give you this money back," Tom said, holding the cash out to the young man. "Not that I don't need it. I've got a wife and a son that count on me for support. But I see that you have Kera and a child on the way yourself. You may need it more than I do."

"Thanks," Briscoe replied, his voice tentative.

"Now since I'm giving you this money, that gives me some right to say what ought to be done with it," Tom continued. "It will be yours and you can do what you like. You can pay for a radiator hose. For that much money you could probably buy three of them. Or you could just put it in your pocket and piddle it away. But there's something I want you to think about spending it on."

"Okay."

"If I were you, I'd take my fifty bucks and go down to the courthouse and buy a marriage license."

The young guy's eyebrows shot up, clearly surprised at the suggestion.

"There is a lot more to being a parent than just getting somebody pregnant," Tom said. "Your girl is getting ready to do something tough and painful and very scary. There is not much you can do to make it better. This is one thing you can do. You can make a commitment that says, 'you're not in this alone.'"

"I, uh…uh." The kid looked genuinely scared.

"Being a husband is like changing a radiator hose," Tom told him. "Once you figure out that it's what you should do, all that's required is the determination to follow through and the patience to keep working at it clumsily, until it finally begins to feel natural."

Tom watched them drive off before making his way back home. He hoped, without a lot of optimism, that he'd made a difference in the kids' lives. It wasn't likely. People weren't like cars. You couldn't just spot the trouble, repair or replace the parts and make it run as good or better than new.

But people could change. Tom knew that. He'd seen it. He'd lived it. Sometimes unexpected things could turn a whole life around. And those things didn't have to be big and dramatic. It could be little things. Maybe one little thing or a lot of little things.

Tom wasn't even sure what had turned his own life around. He certainly wasn't born heading in the right direction. Drug-addicted mother, father unknown, residence variable, concepts like home, family, stability were as foreign as some of the countries he'd awakened in. When he should have been in preschool, his mother, with or without her boyfriends, had dragged him through places like Medellín and Cali. By the time he was nine or ten, he'd occasionally been left on his own in Guadalajara and Juarez.

Tom's mother died when he was eleven. It had been some force of personal will, some drive that came from an unknown source that had propelled him to step away from that life, where he knew he'd be welcome as a runner or a lookout, and seek the less-than-warm welcome of the overwhelmed caseworkers of the Texas Child Protective Services.

What made people decide to ride their life off into the sunset rather than down the rabbit hole or into the toilet?

Tom didn't know. But he was grateful for the direction he was headed. And if there was a way to pay it forward, he wanted to do that.

Inside his house, all was quiet. He walked down the hallway and peeked inside Quint's room. In the glow of the night-light he could see his sleeping son, mouth open, face angelic.

He checked the master bedroom, but Erica wasn't there. He wandered through the house and finally into the kitchen. In the door to the laundry room he spied his wife on her hands and knees mopping up the floor.

Tom's question of why she might be doing that was completely obliterated from his thoughts by the sudden surge of testosterone that ignited his brain. Erica's position fired up old porn flick fantasies of the sexy French maid. But his wife's luscious backside didn't require a frothy little skirt and black stockings. Her typical sleeping attire of a tank top and boxers with little pink hearts was just as sexy.

Tom dropped down behind her, his knees straddling her own. Erica made a startled, almost guilty sound. He wrapped his arms around her waist, pressing himself tightly against her before allowing his left hand to skim upward along her torso and his right hand to wander lower along her abdomen. He kissed her throat and whispered to her.

"Do you remember when we bought this house and I promised to make love to you in every room?"

"Uh-huh," she answered, followed by a sharp intake of breath as his right hand reached its sought destination and he spread his fingers wide to take her entire genital area in his grasp.

"I think this room got left off our list."

He pulled her tightly against him and, as if he couldn't get close enough, he flipped her body around to face him and brought his lips down upon her own.

Tom lost himself in the kiss, the taste of her, the entry of her mouth, warm and wet and welcome. He could stay there forever...or maybe not. He had to get her clothes off. He had to get his clothes off. He had to discard the thin prison of fabric that kept her skin from his own.

He ended the embrace just long enough to grab the hem of her top.

"Tom, I need to tell you something," Erica whispered.

"Just tell me that you want me," he answered. "That's all I need to hear."

He pulled her shirt off over her head. Even in the stark light of the laundry room fluorescent, her breasts were gorgeous. They were, he thought, the perfect size, the perfect shape, with just the right amount of upward tilt offering perky, aroused tips.

"Oh, babe, you are so beautiful."

He hesitated over whether it was more important to get his hands on her breasts or get her out of the rest of her clothes. He settled on doing both, taking his time to tease and caress, reacquainting himself with the hills and valleys of her that he found so thrilling to explore. He lifted her close enough to tongue her nipples—he loved the sound she made deep in her throat when he did that. Then he skimmed the pink heart boxer shorts down her legs and tested her reaction to that same tongue on more intimate parts of her anatomy. The noises she made now were more like little yelps and he had to hold her pelvis still to get her the way he wanted.

Erica was now pulling at his clothes, too. His shirt was easy enough to dispense with, but his jeans wouldn't come off over his work boots. Unwilling to take the time and trouble to free himself, he decided the best position for them was having her on top. However, the minute his bare butt touched the laundry room linoleum, he realized that it was damp and cold.

Tom got to his feet and picked up Erica, sitting her on the edge of the dryer and parting her legs in front of him. He thrust himself inside her all the way to the hilt.

Erica gasped.

Home! The word screamed so loudly in his own brain Tom was sure she must be able to hear it.

Deliberately he crawled back from the edge of the sexual precipice he teetered upon.

Take your time, he told himself. *Make it last. Make it good. Make her scream. Get her there and then get yours.* He repeated some version of this mantra several times. And the clothes dryer, warm and gently, rhythmically rocking, added a new and pleasurable element to the experience of laundry-room lovemaking.

Chapter 9

"I TRIED TO TELL HIM last night," Erica confessed on the phone to her sister. "But the timing was bad."

"When it's bad news, the timing is always bad," Letty pointed out.

"Well, it's not all bad news," Erica said. "I've already saved almost half of what I need for a new washer."

"Yeah, and we know now that you'll never be able to part with that dryer."

Erica giggled. "You're just jealous," she teased. "But don't worry, sis, someday you too will find a man who will have sex with you on laundry equipment."

Erica was still laughing as she swiveled around in her chair. Standing in the opening of her cubicle was young Dr. Glover, the pharmacist whose name was so often linked with Callie Torreno.

"Letty, I gotta go," Erica whispered hurriedly into the phone and then clicked the off button before waiting for a response. She tamped down her embarrassment and spoke in her most professional tone. "Hello, Dr. Glover, may I help you with something?"

He was not a particularly tall or imposing man; instead he was cute. Cute in the way that teen idols are cute, well proportioned with soft features, perfect teeth and great hair. Yes, Erica decided, Dr. Glover was like a teen idol, all grown up and wearing a white coat.

He held out his hand. "I don't think we've officially met. I'm Zachary Glover."

She shook his hand. "Erica Bentley."

"Mrs. Converse said that I should speak to you," he began, his boyish grin countering the formality of his words. "I've been tagged to orient the workshop participants on basic e-script and digital pharmacy operations. Ms. Torreno has been giving me some help on that, but now I understand that's been handed over to you."

"Uh…yes, I suppose it has," Erica answered. "Although if you've been working with Callie and Melody, you probably know more about it than I do."

"I've only worked with Ms. Torreno," he corrected. "Apparently I make Ms. Garwin nervous."

Dr. Glover added a quizzical eyebrow to the flashing white smile, badly feigning befuddlement. The young pharmacist clearly understood his effect on women and enjoyed it completely.

"Well, you won't have that problem with me," Erica told him. "I'm the mother of a six-year-old backyard daredevil. Nothing makes me nervous anymore."

He laughed lightly, appreciating the opportunity for camaraderie. Dr. Glover borrowed a chair from the conference room and took a seat in Erica's cubicle. They shared notes on what they felt were the key presentation points.

Dr. Glover's boyish good looks apparently camouflaged a quick, sharp-thinking brain and the skills of a natural teacher. He gave Erica more ideas than she gave him. Yet she was still able to come up with some insights of her own.

"A blank form is informational, but doesn't teach anything," she said. "A filled form with arrows indicating the sources where the information originated, now that's a slide you can really use."

Dr. Glover nodded in agreement and wrote the idea in the margin of his notes.

The guy spent close to an hour brainstorming with Erica before taking his leave. Her regular work had piled up in the interim and she doggedly dug into it, trying to complete as much as possible before lunch.

As it happened, she almost missed lunch completely. Typically, someone would walk by and announce she was headed to the cafeteria and everyone would quickly finish what they were doing and follow. Erica's stomach grumbled and she checked the clock to see that it was after 12:20 p.m. It was then she noticed how unusually quiet it had become. Puzzled, she stood up and looked around. The entire maze of cubicles were all empty.

She just stood there for a half minute, staring in disbelief. Only Mrs. Converse, eating a sandwich at her desk in the glass-fronted office was still in the department. Erica shook her head, unlocked her file drawer to retrieve her purse and headed down to the cafeteria.

By the time she got her lunch and settled in at their regular table, everyone else was nearly finished.

"I need to get back early," Darla announced the instant Erica sat down.

"Me, too," Callie said.

They rose, as did Rayliss and Lena. Melody hesitated only a moment or two and she got up and took her tray as well.

Erica wasn't sure what was going on, but she shrugged to herself and started on her salad.

A couple of minutes later Melody returned, furtively glancing around. In an ill-fitting gray pantsuit and sensible shoes, it was almost as if the woman dressed to blend in with the background, like office camouflage. She slipped into the seat at an angle next to Erica's. The room was noisy, but her words were matter-of-fact.

"You're persona non grata today," she said.

"Oh, yeah?"

Melody glanced around again and then nodded. "Callie is furious about you taking over Dr. Glover."

For a moment Melody's words didn't even translate in Erica's brain. When they did, she was incredulous. "I didn't 'take him over,' Mrs. Converse sent him to me about the EMR workshops."

Melody made a huffing sound, signifying disbelief. "How long could that take? Fifteen minutes? The man was in your cubicle laughing and joking with you for nearly an hour."

"I don't know how long he was there," Erica admitted. "But all our discussion was about the workshops. We don't have anything else to talk about."

"Callie walked by a half-dozen times, listening. She thought you were flirting," Melody said.

Erica was incredulous. "I wasn't flirting."

"Well, maybe he was flirting with you," Melody said. "Whatever, Callie had her eye on him first. Those two have gotten way too familiar. I had to tell Mrs. Converse. So Callie's out and now you're in. I hope you're not going to make the same mistakes that she did."

Erica shook her head. "I have no interest in Dr. Glover.

Yes, I spent, maybe, an hour with him. But it was totally about the training. Nothing personal at all. I'm married, remember."

Melody allowed her gaze to roam over Erica as if she'd never quite seen her before. "I don't think that kind of explanation makes any difference with Callie. She's hurt and she's offended."

"Well, I'm sorry for that," Erica said. "But nothing happened. I have no interest in Dr. Glover and there is no reason for Callie to be offended or hurt."

Melody's brow furrowed and her brown eyes were serious. "I think, perhaps, you should watch your back. Women, especially women like Callie, can be very petty and vengeful. It's their nature."

Erica chuckled. "You're overstating it a bit, don't you think?"

"Not at all," Melody said. "I've known Callie a lot longer than you. And I know a lot of women like her. If you get between them and the man they want, then you're on the enemies list and one-hundred percent in trouble."

"Enemies list?

Melody nodded. "Women like her don't like to be crossed, and when someone does it, they make sure they are sorry."

Erica searched Melody's face for hints of humor or deceit. Surely she couldn't be serious. Melody's high opinion of her husband seemed to often contrast vividly with her low opinion of most everyone else. Still, it was worse than Erica thought if the young woman could imagine her coworker as some sort of crazed avenger.

"I haven't 'crossed' anybody," Erica told her calmly. "That's the absolute truth."

Melody shrugged. "I don't think it matters. Even if it's not true, if Callie thinks that it is, well, that is just as bad."

"Melody, you're giving her a lot more power than she has."

"You just don't know how vindictive women can be," she replied. "A couple of years ago up in the Admitting office, one employee got under the skin of the coworker at the next desk and ruined the woman's marriage."

"Nobody can ruin somebody else's marriage," Erica stated flatly.

"They can if they target the husband," Melody said. "And that's what happened. She stalked the man at his job and he got all flattered and macho and stuff. Before the wife even knew what was happening, her coworker had him on tape talking sex."

Erica raised her eyebrows at that. "You're kidding?"

Melody's face remained grave. "I heard all the details right here at this table. It was all over for them. The wife felt like she couldn't trust him anymore. And once the husband had started thinking about himself as some kind of God's gift to young gals, he was dissatisfied with what he had at home. Within six months they were divorced."

"They may have gotten a divorce," Erica said. "But the coworker's part in it sounds like the stuff of rumors."

"It's one-hundred-percent true," Melody assured her. "The evildoer bragged all over the hospital about breaking them up."

"Well, even if it did happen just like that, there was something wrong in that marriage to begin with. You can't exploit problems unless the problems are already there."

"A lot of women, like Callie, know how to create problems."

It was obvious that Melody and Callie didn't get along, but Erica didn't believe that either of them could justifiably be called an "evildoer."

"People are not as easily manipulated as you think," Erica told her. "And if Callie is upset with me today, by tomorrow she'll realize that I haven't done anything. It will all blow over."

Melody nodded, but her expression suggested she wasn't convinced. "I just thought it was only fair to let you know," she said. "A jealous woman can be very dangerous. And right now, Callie is jealous of you."

Erica smiled gently at her, hoping to be reassuring. "I appreciate the heads-up. I promise you, it's going to be all right. By next week, Dr. Glover will walk by her desk and say something nice and Callie will forget all about me and the EMR workshops."

"For your sake, I hope so," Melody answered.

She walked away stiffly, as if annoyed that her warning had not been taken seriously enough.

Erica went back to her salad. She liked Melody, but she had to admit the woman was a little weird. Nobody should go through life so sour and certain. Callie might be a pill, but she wasn't a danger. Erica was sure of that.

Through the fog of a sleeping dream, Tom saw the Buick. Clara was parked in her spot in the fourth bay of the shop. Tom walked the unexpectedly long distance to the driver's door, opened it up and slid in.

Once inside, however, he was not behind the wheel but in the middle of the backseat. He was small again, very small. He could see his feet in canvas sneakers, new white canvas sneakers.

Those people were there, they were talking and laughing. Tom was laughing, too. It felt good. It felt safe.

Who were these people? What were they saying? Were they speaking Spanish? Tom wasn't sure.

Deliberately he tried to turn his head to look at the person beside him. If he could see them, he was sure he would recognize them. But when he turned his head, beside him sat Erica.

"What are you doing here?" he asked her.

She smiled. "I brought you."

Tom startled awake. The scene in his head had been vivid. But he was lying comfortably in his own bed. Erica murmured in his arms. His dream had disturbed her sleep as well.

He lay staring up into the darkness for several minutes. It was not unusual for his work to intrude upon his slumber. And he spent a lot of his waking time these days thinking about the Buick. But there was something about that car, something about that car and the memory it brought back that he couldn't quite put his finger on. He tried to examine the dream, recall it more completely, but it was just impressions and flashes. How did he know it was this Buick? Most of what he saw in it was his own shoes. And why was bringing it back so pleasant? Maybe for the novelty of it, he thought to himself. In that car he felt different. He tried to examine that idea but it was tough trying to conjure up remembered feelings. Had he felt loved in that car? Or maybe it was just that he felt safe. *Safe* was not one of the typical words that he'd used to describe his childhood. Was that what it was? He felt safe with those people?

Tom was fully awake now. A quick glance at the alarm suggested that he had a couple more hours before it would buzz. Still, he was alert, his mind active. He was not likely to capture another forty winks. As quietly as possible he got up and tiptoed out. After a trip to the bathroom, he walked down the hall and peeked in on Quint. His son had kicked off the blanket and was scrunched into a fetal position on top of the sheet. Tom covered him up and tucked him in without causing so much as a catch in his breathing. Quint was a pretty sound sleeper. He and Erica often joked that an explosion could go off in the next room and Quint wouldn't even wake up. Tom wanted him to get all the rest he could. He'd need it to carry around all those big words he was so fond of. The little guy looked like such an angel; he was tempted to ruffle his hair, but he managed to resist.

Tom went to the living room and turned on the television at a very low volume. He clicked through the channels, finally settling on what he thought might be the least boring of the bad choices. Then he picked up his laptop and began perusing the internet pages for classic car sales. Anytime he wasn't actually working, Tom was thinking about the Buick. He'd promised Mrs. Gilfred, Guffy, that he'd find a buyer. And he'd expected to get her an excellent price. But, he didn't like what he'd been seeing. Despite what Bryce, his banker, had said, prices for classics like the Buick had really taken a hit from the downturn in the economy. The cold truth about these cars was that they were only worth what people were willing to pay for them. And while the wealthy collector was still in the market, the Buick held more appeal to the regular guys and gals. And in this market they were selling off or, at the very least, not buying. That drove prices down. Everybody likes a bargain and lots of vintage dealers could afford to buy low and wait for prices to rebound.

Normally these kinds of fluctuations wouldn't bother Tom much. But he felt a responsibility to Guffy. She wanted a certain kind of buyer and she deserved a good price. Tom was afraid that he couldn't deliver both.

Erica shuffled in. She was tousled and groggy, wearing a long sexy nightgown of pink satin and lace. The outfit's dazzling effect was effectively countered by a pair of his white cotton work socks. The sight made him smile.

"Did you make coffee?" she asked.

Tom shook his head. "I was trying to pretend it's still night."

She nodded and continued on into the kitchen. Tom heard her rattling dishes as he checked another site. A minute later, she came back in and curled up on the couch beside him.

"What are you watching?" she asked, indicating the TV.

Tom glanced up. *"Deadliest Warrior,"* he answered. "It's like a hypothetical battle between the Mongols and the Comanches."

Erica made a sort of *hmm* sound as she yawned. "Is that like when Quint wants to know who would win if Superman and Batman fought each other?"

"Yes, exactly. I think this is the big-boy version," Tom answered. "And by the way, it would be Superman for sure."

She laughed lightly. Tom took one hand off his keyboard and snaked his arm around her shoulders. Pulling her close, he planted a kiss on her brow.

"I'm sorry I woke you," he said.

"It's okay," Erica answered. "You couldn't sleep?"

"No, I slept fine. I just woke up and I had stuff on my mind, so I got up."

Beside him, Erica nodded.

"Are you worried about something?" she asked. "Is there anything I can do?"

"Not worried, just thinking," he answered. "And you already 'do' everything. Without you, my life would just be a mess."

"Oh yeah, right. You didn't seem all that messed up when I met you."

"I was running on two spark plugs and a grimy air filter,"

he assured her. "You've tuned me up till I'm purring like an in-line six."

Erica laughed at that. "An in-line six, huh?"

Tom shrugged. "Okay, maybe more like a 350Z."

Erica grinned at him and shook her head. "Let me go see if the coffee is ready yet," she said, getting up from the couch.

Tom went back to his computer search. He found a very nice Buick, similar in age and model to Clara that had gone for a premium price at auction just two years earlier. It was salmon and white, which had been a much more typical color scheme for that year. And it didn't have the continental kit on the back. Both those things should have made Mrs. Gilfred's car more valuable. But a sales chart that Tom had studied indicated that the year the salmon-and-white sold had been the high point of Buick valuations. It would go back up there again, Tom was certain. However it was not going to be soon enough for Mrs. Gilfred.

Erica handed him a cup of steaming hot coffee, black, just the way he liked it. He took a sip and thanked her before setting it on the nearby table. Tom had just found a green-and-white Century hardtop that had sold the previous week. He was reading through the seller's details as his wife sat down beside him.

Erica began talking about something that had happened at work. Tom was sort of listening, but he was also reading through the engine specifications. She didn't sound really upset. It was a pretty matter-of-fact presentation. When she paused, Tom knew that he was expected to comment.

"So some guy hit on you and made this other crazy woman jealous," he said.

"He didn't hit on me," Erica corrected him firmly. "Everything we talked about was strictly work related, but apparently Callie didn't see it that way."

Tom discovered that the green-and-white's undercarriage had been replaced and there was some residual rust in the wheel wells that might indicate spots forming beneath the body paint. That was definitely not good and any experienced collector would have taken that into consideration while bidding.

"It's just craziness to assume that when I talk to some guy on the job, it's got to be some kind of flirty guy/girl thing."

Tom found the dead-ringer giveaway. The green and white's frame had been painted. A sure sign that somebody had been trying to cure corrosion.

"You'd think that everybody knowing the fact that I'm married and have a six-year-old at home would be enough to keep those gossips from going off the deep end."

"Nothing stops gossip," Tom told her. "And for a lot of people marriage and family doesn't even slow them down, let alone stop them."

He clicked off the green-and-white. It had way too many problems to be comparable to Mrs. Gilfred's Clara.

"Still, you'd think somebody there would know me better than that," Erica said.

"It takes time to know people and sometimes even when you think you do, they turn out to be a lot different."

"Yeah, I guess so," Erica agreed.

Tom took a slurp of his coffee as he thought about Cliff. "Besides, these days it's like everybody's cheating."

His wife made some sort of response, but Tom hardly heard it. He'd pulled up a gorgeous solid black Special with the continental kit. It wasn't for sale. It was a rental out in California, but it was a beauty and the owner had meticulously posted photos of it inside, outside and under the hood.

"Look at this," he said to Erica. "Isn't she a beauty?"

Erica leaned closer to view the screen. "She looks like the one you've got in the shop, except I think the blue one is prettier."

Tom nodded. "The blue one is prettier."

Erica rose to her feet.

"Where you going?" he asked.

"Hey, I've got a busy day ahead," she teased. "I can't sit here on the couch with you while you're looking at car porn."

"Car porn?" Tom chuckled. "Yeah, you've got that right. These are the kind of vehicles to get a man's pulse racing."

Erica rolled her eyes at him before she headed out the front door to get the newspaper. Tom was still clicking through Buick pages when she got back.

"Okay, okay," he told her, teasing, as he patted the place beside him. "I'm off the porn. You can sit with me, I'm just checking email."

"Your emails are all about cars, too," she stated correctly, and she flounced down next to him. She rifled though the paper. He knew she was looking for the crossword, she always did that first.

Tom read through the answers to a couple of parts inquiries. Some were good, some bad. He was surprised to see a message from Cliff. If he was late for work, Cliff might send a text, but usually if he had anything to say, he'd just call. Tom clicked on it. One sentence, short and to the point.

"If anybody asks, I was working late last night."

"Damn," Tom whispered under his breath.

"What?" Erica asked, glancing toward the laptop.

Tom slammed it shut. "Nothing," he answered, before

immediately realizing that he needed some explanation. "It was...uh...Cliff. He's going to be late this morning, overslept I guess."

Erica looked at Tom as if he'd lost his mind. "He can't have overslept. It's just now time to get up."

Tom could have cursed himself as an idiot. "He...uh...he got to bed late and he's...uh...he's planning to oversleep."

"Good grief, Tom," she said. "I know he's your friend, but you really shouldn't let him get away with that."

"No, no, of course not," Tom agreed, secretly wishing that if his friends were going to draw him into lies that he was actually a little better at it.

Chapter 10

ERICA'S IN-BOX PILED UP with charts faster than she could open them. There must be some kind of flu epidemic for the hospital to have ramped up its patient load. Surprisingly, the harried hustle and frayed tempers normally associated with maximum capacity seemed to be missing. Everyone seemed to be behaving normally. Still, she was working as fast as she could but getting further and further behind by the minute.

So when Letty called and wanted to go to lunch, Erica resisted.

"I'm so busy you would not believe it."

"You've still got to eat," her sister pointed out. "And I'm in the neighborhood."

Erica's computer made a tiny *ding* sound indicating new chart arrivals. She glanced up to see five more in her in-box. There was no way she could finish by the end of the day. She sighed in defeat.

"Okay, I'll meet you at Cha Cha's in ten minutes, but we'll have to be quick."

"Trust me, I can talk really fast," her sister assured her.

Erica was hungry and she didn't exactly look forward to the silence at her departmental lunch table. Dr. Glover hadn't ventured back into her territory, but the storm he'd stirred up was still churning. Erica was both ignoring it and waiting for it to blow over.

She logged off, grabbed her purse and headed out. Erica exited from the hospital's service entrance and cut across the green area of jogging trails between the University Hospital and the Audie Murphy VA. The air had turned cool, reminding everyone that it was autumn, even if there was very little color in the trees to indicate it. Students were out in jackets and running shorts as if they couldn't decide which season to dress for. Erica welcomed the crispness in the air. It reminded her of football games and pep rallies. Memories of Halloween also came to mind and she started thinking about a costume for Quint. She'd have to remember to ask his preference. Last year he'd been a ninja and the year before that he was a superhero. She wanted him to choose, something she had never had a chance to do. Every Halloween of her childhood, Erica had been a witch and Letty had been a princess. Those were the costumes easiest for Ann Marie. She'd go to her closet and pull out her black "funeral dress" for Erica. And one of her out-of-date cocktail gowns for her sister. Not that those were bad memories. Her mother never seemed as overwhelmed by trick-or-treat traditions as she often did at Christmas and Thanksgiving. And there was plenty of laughter and good feelings as she painted their faces and found just the right headgear, a rhinestone tiara for Letty and floppy black hat for Erica. Then the girls would get their paper grocery bags and head out into the neighborhood.

Ann Marie gave only one admonition. And it was not, "be careful," "look both ways before crossing the street" or even "be home before ten o'clock." Anne Marie simply said, "Erica, take care of your sister." And she always had.

The traffic on Babcock Road was typical enough that Erica felt a bit as if she was taking her life in her hands as she sprinted across. She had not quite reached the restaurant's front door when Letty drove up. She beeped the horn announcing her arrival, but Erica would have noticed anyway. Her younger sister's car was one that attracted attention whenever it passed.

Her aging Fiat was kept running by Tom's goodwill as a brother-in-law and it could, by some definition, be called a Classic Car. But most people spotting it would have more likely described it as some version of rusted junk heap. The much-dented rattletrap body was missing the front bumper. Although the car had at one time been blue, it had one orange door. And the one next to it was festooned with silver duct tape that secured the plastic where a window had once been. Their mother said it was an eyesore. *Student chic* was how Letty described it.

Erica preferred her sister's description and she loved how Ann Marie's emphasis on appearances had apparently made no impression on Letty at all.

Letty parked the car in the lot and emerged from behind the wheel. She was dressed in tight jeans and a faded T-shirt, her hair pulled back in a ponytail. Sensible shoes just added to the air of I-look-this-good-without-even-trying.

"I can't decide which makes me more jealous," Erica announced to her. "Your skinny jeans or your skinny genes."

The two sisters embraced.

"I bet we weigh exactly the same," Letty said. "I think Tom would say you're like a compact and I'm station wagon.

I've got a lot longer wheelbase, but we're cruising around with the same engine."

Erica laughed. "If we go with that analogy, does that mean I'm now running around with junk in my trunk?"

"You are exactly and it seems to me that Tom likes you just that way."

Erica wrapped her arm around her sister's waist.

"I'm glad you dragged me out here," she said as she pulled open the door. "I needed a break."

Cha Cha's was one of San Antonio's signature Tex-Mex restaurants. The decor was all twinkle lights and Talavera pottery, and the food tasted as good as it smelled. Scores of doctors, nurses, med students and the neighborhood locals had been getting their carb ration there for decades.

The hostess seated them in the little fake arbor secluded by webs of silk tree branches, and gave them menus. Erica wanted to order her favorite, *camarones de ajo*—shrimp in garlic sauce—but thought perhaps she shouldn't since she was going back to work.

"It will keep your coworkers at bay, for sure," Letty told her.

Erica chuckled. "I don't need garlic for that," she said. "Unless maybe I'm wearing it around my neck."

"Oh, yeah? What's up?"

With a rueful sigh, Erica quickly got her sister up to speed on the current Medical Records soap opera.

"So this Callie person thinks you stole her man."

Erica nodded. "Ridiculous, huh?"

"I don't know how ridiculous it is."

"What? You know it's completely nuts."

"I mean, yeah, sure, you're not very likely to go after some guy at work when you've got such a great husband at home,"

Letty said. "Still, just because he's not what you like, doesn't mean you wouldn't be *his* cup of tea."

"Thanks, I think," Erica answered. "Honestly, I'm hoping the two of them get together and walk hand in hand into the sunset," Erica said. "Of course the craziest part of it is the 'warning' from Melody that Callie is out to get me. I mean besides not being my BFF at the lunchroom table, what else is she supposed to do? Ban me from cheerleading practice?"

Erica laughed at her own little high school hijinks analogy.

Letty tutted and shook her head. "Just because this Melody person is one taco short of a Fiesta Platter doesn't mean she isn't right about Callie being dangerous."

"Dangerous? How could she be dangerous?"

"Oh, come on, Erica. Even somebody who's been in mommy-mode as long as you have can still remember that there are always women who see girl-on-girl retaliation as almost an art form."

"Well, yes, but that's kid stuff. By our age that kind of thing ought to be all over."

"Operative word *ought*," Letty said. "I don't think you can count on that. She could be very vindictive. And whether you're guilty or not, guilty won't change a thing."

Erica considered that thoughtfully, remembering the story about the woman from Admitting.

"It's all nonsense," Erica concluded. "Just office gossip ginned up to soap opera status."

Letty nodded agreement. "Still, keep your eyes open and your guard up," her sister told her. "Either that, or call me over. You've fought off the bullies for me all through childhood. I'd love to return the favor."

Erica ate her lunch as quickly as it arrived and, after a goodbye hug from her sister, hurried back to the hospital and the charts that were continuing to pile up. She worked as quickly and efficiently as she could, not taking time for so much as a sip of water or a bathroom break.

Just before quitting time, Mrs. Converse stepped into her cubicle, the computer generated production tally in her hand.

"What's going on?" she asked without preamble.

Erica could feel the heat of embarrassment stain her cheeks. She knew every coworker within earshot was listening.

"I don't know. I'm plowing through this stuff as fast as I can," she defended herself. "I've topped my best count, but I'm not going to be able to get my chart queue totally clear today. How long do you think this crowding will go on? I sure hope the patient load gets back to normal the next few days."

"The hospital isn't crowded," Mrs. Converse said. "Somehow the random sorter program is screwed up and the rest of the department has practically had the day off."

"What?"

Mrs. Converse showed Erica the day's tally. Almost all of the EMR charts had been routed to her in-box.

"How can that happen?" she asked.

Mrs. Converse shook her head. "I hate glitches and there is never a good explanation for them."

She turned out toward the passageway. "Callie? Callie Torreno?"

"Yes, Mrs. Converse," Callie answered as she emerged from her cubicle, wearing her jacket and with her purse already on her shoulder, obviously on her way out the door.

"Do you still have that friend who works in IT?"

Listening and watching, Erica was startled by the devious explanation that suddenly occurred to her. Deliberately she searched Callie's expression for signs of guilt.

"Javier? Uh...I think he still works here."

"Well, get him on the phone before you leave," Mrs. Converse said. "I want this routing mess fixed by the time the department opens in the morning."

"Yes, ma'am," Callie said, without making eye contact. She hurried back to her desk.

Mrs. Converse turned to Erica. She shook her head and chuckled lightly. "Well, *you* have certainly had a busy day. Trial by fire, I suppose. And you did well." She leaned forward and added with a whisper, "If this many charts had shown up in Lena's in-box, she would have been crying in my office in five minutes."

Mrs. Converse straightened immediately. She was all business and there was not a hint of the wink she'd just shared. "You'll certainly be able to catch up tomorrow."

Callie came back into view.

"Did you get hold of IT?"

"Yes, ma'am. Javiar said he'd get right on it."

"Good," Mrs. Converse said. "Have a nice evening, Callie, Erica."

"You, too."

"Good night."

As the older woman walked away, Erica looked straight at Callie. Had she somehow arranged the routing glitch? There was no clue on her face.

"Good night," Callie said simply, politely. There was nothing but cool civility in her tone. No hint of payback or triumph.

Still Erica couldn't quite shake her suspicions.

At the shop, mid-October turned crazy and more than a little frustrating. Cliff was sneaking off every time Tom's back was turned. Tom had tried reasoning, pleading, threatening, finally even docking his pay, but his best buddy and longtime employee seemed determined to screw up his life and had no problem making everyone at Bentley's Classic Car Care suffer as he did it.

The extra work and upheaval Cliff caused affected each of his fellow workers differently. Gus seemed to think that if Cliff didn't have to work, he didn't, either. He showed up on time and never left a minute early, but somehow he wasn't getting much accomplished for the eight hours he was putting in.

Hector was even worse. With Cliff and Gus leaving so much to be done, the pressure began to build. And Hector handled that pressure the same way he always had. Hector decided it was time to go on a bender. His meek little wife called with the bad news.

"I am so sorry," she told Tom.

He could hear the disappointment and fear in her voice. He couldn't do anything else but reassure her.

"I hired Hector knowing he had a drinking problem," Tom said. "Get him dried out and back to work as soon as you can. I'll hold his job open as long as I'm able to."

Tom had been busy enough handling the customers, the billing and locating parts. Adding most of the mechanic labor for the business just put him over the top. He didn't know how or when anything could get done.

In the past, when things were busy, he'd simply take home most of the paperwork. He still did that, but he couldn't take home a muffler installation for a Camaro. He needed to do that in the shop. So Tom began working late.

Which was why Tom was doing a brake job on a Mark VII at eight o'clock at night.

"Do you want me to bring you a plate of supper?" Erica asked him the first night he called home with an excuse.

He thought of what that would entail. Erica would have

changed into her hanging-around clothes and would be padding around in slippers through the house. She was undoubtedly tired from her own day on the job. And she'd want to have some quality time with her son. Instead, she would have to pack up the food, drag Quint from his favorite game or TV show and drive up to West Avenue. Tom wouldn't have any time to talk to either of them, so they'd just have to turn around and drive home.

"I've still got most of what you packed for my lunch," he said. "When I get hungry I'll just finish that up."

"Okay," she said. "Don't work too late."

"I won't," he promised.

But he did.

The late nights became a very regular thing. In the mornings, before he left the house, he'd check the contents of his dinner bucket. He would add whatever extra food would fit and then plan to put in a ten- or twelve- or sixteen-hour day.

"We've just got a lot of work coming in," he told Erica.

Even to his own ears it sounded like a lame excuse. He wanted to tell his wife what was going on. But he had never been good at lying. He was especially not good at telling half-truths. If he started to explain what was going on, the facts about Cliff would come out. And the fact that this had been going on—and he'd kept it a secret—would also come out. He didn't understand a lot about how Erica's mind worked. But he knew enough to know that she would not find his loyalty much of a virtue in this situation.

Trish and Erica knew each other. At first that had been reason enough not to come clean. He wanted to give Cliff a chance to straighten up without Trish ever knowing how bent he'd gotten. Tom had become convinced, however, that Trish finding out was just a matter of time.

Now, it was all about how Cliff was behaving and how Tom was handling it. Tom knew he should fire his friend. And if Erica found out what was going on, she would agree with him. The last thing Tom wanted was to appear, in his wife's eyes, as less than competent, as less than a responsible businessman. Erica believed in him when no one else really did. He didn't want to disappoint her. She set her standards very high. And he set his own to what he imagined she expected of him.

Tom examined the rotor for corrosion and warp. It looked surprisingly good for a twenty-year-old brake, undoubtedly the reason Lincolns had a reputation for a smooth ride. A warped or scarred rotor transferred its vibration all the way to the steering column. That kind of rattle not only put age on a car, but it compromised safety. This time, thankfully, Tom decided that replacing the disc pads would do the job.

I've got to let Cliff go, he thought to himself. That was what a businessman had to do when an employee was flagrantly taking advantage of a friendship with the boss.

It wasn't about moral judgments versus boys-will-be-boys. In fact, Cliff cheating on his wife didn't even add into the equation. Cliff was not at work when he was assigned to be there. Not showing up or sneaking off were both termination offenses. He'd been warned. He should be fired.

Tom's head was clear on that. But his heart, not so much. Cliff wasn't just an employee, he was a friend, his oldest friend. The two had met at Job Corps a dozen years ago. Cliff had been sent there by his working-class mom and dad to straighten him out. And Cliff had been determined not to let that happen.

For Tom, Job Corps was a dream come true. From the moment he'd volunteered himself as a ward of the state, he'd been looking for a place to fit in. That just hadn't happened in foster care. Tom was too big and too blunt not to stand out. He'd worked hard at being polite, at being agreeable, respectful. But it didn't come naturally to him. And he knew he looked scary. At sixteen he was already six-three and 190 pounds of pure muscle. The scarred, broken nose had been acquired when attempting to stop a fight, not start one. Still, people saw what they saw. And most thought he looked like trouble.

After drifting in and out of temporary placements he decided to request emancipation. Child Protective Services got him legal help and the lawyer came up with the idea of Job Corps. Tom needed to prove to the judge that he had a place to live and could support himself. The Job Corps program offered room and board while he took technical training and studied for a GED.

Cliff had been his roommate. The staff had placed Tom into computer-tech classes, but Cliff urged him to switch to auto mechanics. Up until that time Tom has mostly been interested in the outside of cars. But from the first moment he put his hands on an engine, he loved everything about it.

Today's brake job did not have the allure of working on a beautiful engine, but good brakes were absolutely essential.

So was a functioning washing machine, Tom reminded himself.

Erica hadn't breathed a word about any problem with the washer. But Quint had mentioned, almost in passing, his most recent trip to the coin laundry. Tom had immediately felt guilty. There were so many things around the house that he was just letting go. He'd gotten used to allowing Erica to manage on her own. He worked and somehow clothes got clean, groceries got bought, food got cooked, the bills got paid and the lawn got mowed. It wasn't such a bad division of labor when she was a stay-at-home mom, but she was working now. And Tom worried that she was still doing more than her share. But until he could get things squared up around the shop, he wasn't going to be much use to her at home.

Tom reattached the caliper, securing the new disc pads, and reconnected the bleeder valve.

He wanted to be a good husband, a good father, but it wasn't as easy as fixing cars. You couldn't just tighten things up or swap out the worn parts. You couldn't just list the tasks on the service log and mark them off one by one. It was constantly looking at two or ten places that you needed to be, two or ten things that you ought to be doing and then figuring out what had to be done now and what would have to wait.

Married life was not like auto mechanics. There were no gearboxes or flow valves. It was more like target practice with a grease gun. There was almost no chance to ever get a bull's-eye. And absolute certainty that you were going to make a mess in the attempt.

Chapter 11

AT WORK ERICA CONTINUED to keep her eyes open and her guard up. The incident with the EMR routing glitch really could not have been on purpose, she assured herself over and over again. Still, she began to suspect every chart miscode, every unlocatable file, every transferred phone call. Every snarl or stumble in her workday might be the underhanded efforts of Callie Torreno.

It occurred to her that she could take these suspicions to Mrs. Converse, but she thought better of it. The last thing she imagined a supervisor would want to do was intervene in a silly feud between two members of her staff. And the whole thing was so juvenile, Erica didn't even want her name associated with it.

She decided to simply work through it, let it die its own death for lack of attention. It took two to fight, and if Erica refused, then Callie would be left throwing punches at the air. Still, the thrill of being back on the job was being diminished day by day.

Erica deliberately pushed against these feelings. She knuckled down on her workday, determined to spend her time polishing her skills, improving her accuracy and picking up speed.

She maintained her silent presence at lunch. In truth, things around the table did not seem that much different than before. Erica began believing that it was all in Melody's imagination and that she'd been silly to give credence to the suggestion.

This certainty, however, was put to the test on Wednesday, the week after the routing glitch. Erica purchased her food and was headed to her regular spot at the table. The rest of the Medical Records team sat in their place. Callie at the head, with Darla and Rayliss on either side. Lena and Melody were seated across from each other. There was already laughter going on. Maybe they were sharing their typical stupid men jokes. The unsmiling visage of Melody caught her eye for a moment. Erica almost looked away, but she saw the woman's eyes widen in surprise. The women around her suddenly quieted. Erica followed their gaze and turned to bump lunch trays with Dr. Glover.

"Hi!" he said as exuberantly as if her presence in the cafeteria were unexpected.

"Oh, hi," she said.

"I've been wanting to talk with you," he said. "Why don't we share lunch?"

Erica was acutely aware of the silence at the nearby table and the dozen ears straining to hear what was being said.

"Well, I...uh..."

The doctor's boyish grin slid into a feigned plea. "Sit with me," he said. "Don't make me eat all by myself."

Erica couldn't help but smile back at him.

"Okay," she agreed after only a slight hesitation.

He directed her to a table for two and allowed her to seat herself before he lowered himself into the chair.

Erica could feel the collective gaze from the Medical Records table, but she chose to ignore it. With a smile on her face and a cheerfulness to her demeanor, she decided to tease him.

"Dr. Glover, I never would have imagined you as such a rebel."

"A rebel?"

"Rebel, rule breaker, enemy of the caste system."

"The caste system?"

"The rules on lunchroom status and affiliation segregation," Erica said. "No mixing among professions, job descriptions or pay scales. The white lab coats are strictly forbidden to eat with the polyester business suits."

Glover laughed. "Should I wait until the weather changes and you're wearing wool?"

Erica shook her head. "I doubt that would work, either, unless the cut was expensive enough to be exec staff. Then everybody would think you're either being called on the carpet or up for promotion."

"Alas, today it's neither one," the doctor answered. "I just get tired of eating alone and I thought the company of a smart, attractive woman might be better."

Erica ignored the compliment. She took a bite of her salad and chewed it for a moment. She sneaked a look up at him as he cut the chicken breast on his plate, one lock of brown hair straying down his forehead.

"Why do you eat alone?" she asked.

He was thoughtful for about a half minute.

"Lunchroom status and affiliation segregation," he answered, aping her description.

They grinned at each other. His was accompanied by a teasing wink.

Erica ignored that and forked another bite.

"It's not really considered the thing for me to eat with the techs that I supervise," he explained further. "And since we have to keep a pharmacist on duty at all times, we stagger lunch breaks. Each of us comes down here alone."

"Ah," Erica said. "I guess that makes sense."

"Don't look now," Glover said, glancing casually beyond her shoulder to the table of coders and transcriptionists behind her. "Your coworkers are looking daggers at us and whispering like crazy. What's that about?"

Erica could guess, but she wasn't willing to tell all. It was embarrassing. And if the young doctor knew he was a part of it, he might feel obliged to do something or say something. Erica couldn't allow that to happen.

"I'm the new girl," she said. "I think this is the Medical Records' version of hazing."

Dr. Glover nodded sympathetically. "Well, hang in there," he said. "We all go through it. And eventually even the newest new girl gets to be an old hand."

"Right," Erica agreed. "This is actually my second life at UTHSC," she said. "I worked here for three years back in the days before my son was born."

"Oh, yes, you said that you're a mom."

"Quint is six," she told him. "He's in first grade this year."

"So how's that going?"

"Pretty great," she said honestly. "I miss hanging out with him. But I really love being back at work."

Dr. Glover nodded as if that made perfect sense.

"Married?"

"Oh, yeah. You?"

"Not so much."

"That doesn't sound like a good answer."

"It's not," Dr. Glover answered, "but it's pretty accurate. My live-in girlfriend decided to live out about six months ago."

"Sorry."

He shrugged. "We were engaged for four years. You'd think I would have figured out that it really doesn't take that long to pick out a cake and a dress."

Erica nodded. "She could have borrowed mine. Tom and I got married on the courthouse steps while I was on my lunch break. After we said 'I do' we both went back to the job."

"That's efficient."

"We were saving money to start up a business," Erica said. "And it worked fine. We're just as married and just as committed, as if I'd worn a white dress and spent all our savings on flower arrangements and a dance band."

"True," Glover agreed. "So did you get that business started?"

"Yes, we did." Erica pulled her purse from the chair back and reached into the front flap. Pulling out one of the cards for Bentley's Classic Car Care, she handed it to Dr. Glover.

He surveyed it with interest.

"I drew the logo," she told him proudly, then felt a little embarrassed at having shared such a modest accomplishment.

"I like it," he told her, before slipping the card into his breast pocket. "Classic cars, huh. I always thought I might like to own one of those."

"There's a beauty at my husband's place for sale right now," she told him. "It's a vintage Buick convertible, great condition, really long, very stylish."

"A Buick, huh? I think I'm more the Mustang or T-Bird type," he said. "Or maybe that's just who I'd like to be."

His wry grin added an air of vulnerability to his very boyish attractiveness.

Nearby the scrape of chairs against the linoleum floor signaled the women from the Medical Records table were leaving. One by one each walked right by Erica's table without looking in her direction or speaking a word. It was meant as a deliberate snub. Erica was determined to ignored it. And she hoped that Dr. Glover didn't notice. But it was hard to miss.

"That seems like a bit more than just hazing," he said.

"No big deal," she assured him. "I got on somebody's wrong side. It'll blow over."

He nodded. The two of them ate in silence for a moment. "You know what they call you ladies, right?"

"What they call us? Who?"

"The other employees or at least the ones in Pharmacy," he answered. "Nearly every discipline in the hospital has a nickname."

"Really?"

He bobbed his head, verifying as he chewed. Once he'd swallowed, he spoke.

"We call the lab techs the Vampires, because they're always after people's blood. The guys in X-Ray are the Peeping Toms 'cause they want to see what people look like underneath their clothes."

Erica, smiling, shook her head.

"We say the Respiratory Therapists are the Perverts, 'cause everything they do is about heavy breathing," Dr. Glover continued. "And the physical therapists are known as the Sadists, 'cause what they do is sheer torture."

"And pharmacy?" Erica said. "You must be the Drug Dealers."

"A lucky guess," he declared. "But right on the money."

"So who are we?" she asked. "What's the nickname for Medical Records?"

"The Gossips," he answered. "You know everything about everybody and your whole job is making sure everybody else knows, too."

Erica laughed. "That's a better name for our department than you could even imagine."

He shrugged. "I could imagine a place a little more welcoming for the newest new girl, even if she has been here once before."

"Thank you, Dr. Glover. I appreciate the commiseration."

"Zac," he said. "Zac."

Erica shook her head. "That kind of informality is definitely a breach of hospital etiquette."

"I thought we were rebels," he said.

She grinned at him. "Okay, Zac, I'm Erica."

"Erica," he repeated, as if trying it on for size. "I like it. It suits you."

"Thanks," she answered. She imagined the pharmacist coming into the Medical Records department and addressing her by her first name. Such an event was sure to make heads spin.

Then she remembered something Mrs. Converse had said about professional distance. Was that what had happened to Callie? She hadn't kept professional distance with Dr. Glover? Erica had never heard her call him Zac, but Callie liked him enough that she probably did.

Chapter 12

FRIDAY MORNING DIDN'T start out that well. Tom had a big late-'80s Taurus up on the lift and was trying to locate a drip of power steering fluid. As he examined the small ribbed hose for damage, the seal gave way on the steering rack connection, spilling fluid on Tom's head.

He cursed vividly. Safety goggles protected his eyes, but he still got the foul liquid up his nose, across his face and in his hair. He finally managed to get a pan under it and drained it completely before heading to the bathroom to wash up the worst of the mess.

"If this is how my day is going to be," he said to his reflection in the mirror, "then God help me."

Heaven apparently heard. After weeks of feeling as if his business was becoming a one-man show, at five minutes before nine o'clock, a serious and subdued Cliff Aleman showed up and went right to work.

A sober Hector Ruiz turned up as well.

Even Gus seemed enthusiastic about ironing out the door panel on an '94 BMW.

Tom held his breath, thanking his good luck. This was how his shop was supposed to function. It was a four-man shop. He'd built the business to that level. In truth, he probably could have used some kind of helper to fetch, carry and clean up. He could certainly justify it with the quantity of work he'd been bringing in. He'd been carrying so much of it himself, lately, that he was more than aware of just how strong a customer base he had.

With his three employees all on task, Tom was free to pursue some of the jobs that he particularly wanted to do. And what he most particularly wanted to do was hang out with Clara, Mrs. Gilfred's Buick.

Since the morning sun filled the front driveway, Tom took that opportunity to pull her out into the sunshine for some digital photographs. He took dozens of shots, inside and out. He wanted any interested buyers to have no doubts about her exceptional condition. He got a close-up of the front grille. And a long shot of the driver's-side chrome from head to tail. He opened all the doors and stood on the back fender to get a perspective on the condition of the upholstery. Then he put the top up and took every angle again. The only pictures he didn't take were of the engine. He wasn't ready to show that off yet. He still had some cleaning up and spiffing up to do. Besides, he reasoned to himself, the prospective buyer that Mrs. Gilfred wanted could fall in love with Clara in a candid shot. Showing off the engine was like viewing the old girl in her underwear. That was for serious suitors only.

When he'd taken many more photos than he could use, Tom carefully backed the Buick into his fourth bay once more. He downloaded the pictures to his laptop and was eager for Mrs. Gilfred to see them.

But as he glanced around the shop that was finally functioning efficiently, he decided he couldn't risk leaving at the moment. Cliff was very much in the habit of disappearing when Tom left to get Quint from school. If he were to take off this morning, he might well lose Cliff for most of the day.

Tom decided to stay close and keep an eye on his team. There was still plenty of work to be done for all of them.

During lunch break, Tom called Christus Santa Rosa and was told that Mrs. Gilfred had been released from the hospital. He decided he would definitely go see her and show her what he was putting up on the website. He'd just wait until his employees had put in a full day on the job before he left.

Tom spent the afternoon working on a GMC. He thought he was just replacing a blown head gasket, but when he got into it he found damage to the rocker arm. It was more work, more time, more money and his customer was less than happy, as if the vehicle's problems were Tom's fault instead of just bad luck.

He was grateful to get away for the few moments it took to pick up Quint. And even more so when he returned to the shop to find Cliff still working.

He got Quint settled into the office. The little guy was full of excitement and chatter about Halloween, just a few days away.

"Cody Raza has got this cool *Scream* mask. It is so, so scary. I want to be scary this year," he said. "I want to be really scary, like a serial killer with an ax or something. You don't think Mom will make me be a minion or a fuzzy animal? That is so *baby!*"

He said the word "baby" with such inflection that it might have been a curse. It certainly sounded to be the worst thing on the planet.

"You'll need to ask Mom," Tom told him. "I'm not sure serial killer is totally okay for first grade, but Mom will know. And she won't make you do anything 'baby,' I'm sure of that."

"Okay," Quint agreed, though there was still some concern in his voice. "Are you going to have to work late on Halloween? I hope you don't. Please don't."

Tom glanced up from the refrigerator where he was retrieving Quint's after-school snack.

"I'll make a point not to."

"Good. Because if Mom can't get off to come to my party at school and you have to work when I'm trick-or-treating, then it won't be a very good time at all."

"It will definitely be a terrific Halloween," Tom assured him as he set an apple, some cheese crackers and a carton of milk on the service desk. He made a mental note to tell Erica what Quint had said. It wouldn't be long, Tom suspected, before the presence of his parents would be irrelevant to his son's estimation of a good time.

"Hey, we're going to be there. We wouldn't miss it," he assured his son. "Now eat your snack, get your homework done. Your mom will be here to get you in—" Tom glanced up at the clock "—an hour and ten minutes. Okay?"

The little boy nodded. "I'm good," he told his dad. Tom silently agreed wholeheartedly.

Back in the shop, Tom continued working on the GMC's valve assembly, though he was interrupted several times. The afternoon was always a little chaotic with customers calling about their cars or coming by to pick them up. And there was Quint as well. You couldn't just ignore a six-year-old, even if you did let him play with the intercom system.

Bugg Auflander showed up to talk about the prospect of getting some work done. Bugg always talked a lot more about getting work done than he ever talked about spending actual cash having something done. But today he seemed more serious about it than usual. And Tom really wanted to get Bugg's '66 Pontiac in the shop. It was a great car. But that wasn't all. There were a lot of guys among Bugg's friends who had classic cars that they'd kept up themselves over the years. But as eyesight and dexterity become more of a problem, they were going to need help. Tom thought that if he could do right by Bugg, bring him into the process and satisfy his expectations for a reasonable price, then all those old guys might look at Bentley's as the way to keep their classics a little bit longer.

Talking to Bugg, however, required some patience. The discussion of the problem with the fuel pump couldn't be contained with simple stories of engine misfire; instead he expanded into long wistful tales of driving the car out to the Grand Canyon in 1974.

Tom was listening, nodding, when he caught sight of Erica out of the corner of his eye. She approached hesitantly as Bugg droned on about the gas mileage he got using only first and second gear through the mountains.

Erica waited patiently a few paces behind Bugg for a couple of moments. When it became clear that the old man was not nearing a stopping place anytime soon, she mouthed to Tom, *Are you working late?* He made a slight nod to the affirmative. *Okay,* she mouthed further. *Extra food in your lunch box.* He gave her a thumbs-up. Bugg didn't even notice as he'd reached the part of the story that related the details of a right rear blowout on an icy Montana mountain pass.

Erica took Quint and headed for home. Tom continued to nod and listen for a very long ten minutes more, until Bugg got around to agreeing upon the repairs he wanted Tom to do and signing his name on the work order.

He still didn't have the valve train repair completely done when closing time arrived. Gus was completely cleaned up and ready to go at least fifteen minutes early. Hector carefully set up the pieces of a disassembled transmission so that he could get right on it the next morning. Cliff, who had basically said nothing to Tom all day, wrote his time out on the clipboard as 6:01.

Tom closed the gate and locked the door. In the quiet, solitary shop he was able to concentrate better and finish the work on the GMC. He cleaned and shined the pieces so that it looked almost as good as new. And, from the sound of the engine when he tested it, it was going to run better than it had in years.

He glanced at the task sheet and considered trying to get in a small, quick job. Then he decided against it. He should get to Mrs. Gilfred's house before dark. The woman might not answer her door if she saw a man on her porch.

He went into the shop's bathroom to wash off a little bit. In the mirror he spotted the dried, caked-on power steering fluid on his hair and face, a leftover from the Taurus that morning.

"Talk about scaring the woman on her own porch," he muttered to himself. "You look like a dirty homeless guy."

He tried to go after the sticky mess while leaning over the sink, but with little success. Then he glanced at Cliff's shower. A bar of soap and a bottle of shampoo were visible on the window shelf. With a shrug, he peeled off his coveralls. The water wasn't particularly hot, but it was good enough and after scrubbing his body and washing out his hair, he looked and felt more socially acceptable for visiting an elderly person.

With no bath towel available, he dried off with a handful of shop rags. He left his coveralls hanging in the bathroom and grabbed a new Bentley's Classic Car Care T-shirt from the office. Jeans and a T-shirt were always appropriate for a working man, he told himself. Especially so if they were clean.

He locked up and drove out to Leon Valley, his laptop on the seat beside him.

When he arrived at Mrs. Gilfred's house, he didn't need to knock on her door, or have her recognize him on the porch. The lady was out in her yard watering flowers with a garden hose.

Dressed in a pale lavender jogging suit that hung on her frame, she looked frail.

"Aren't you supposed to be resting?" he asked her after he stepped out of his truck.

The old woman smiled at him. "You sound like my doctor. And I'll tell you like I told him. I've got the longest rest of all coming up sooner than I like, so I'll wait till then."

"Hello! Hello!" From the neighbor's porch, Miss Warner called out and waved a handkerchief at him.

Tom smiled politely and waved. He tried to turn his attention back to Mrs. Gilfred, but it wasn't that easy.

"Oh, Mr. Bentley! Mr. Bentley. So good to see you again. Might I presume upon you for a little help, please. Please."

"Uh…" Tom began.

"Oh, good Lord," Guffy muttered under her breath. "You'd better go see what the silly fussbudget wants. We won't have any peace until you do."

"I'll be right back," Tom told her.

Mrs. Gilfred rolled her eyes. "Good luck with that."

Tom grinned at her before making his way over to Miss Warner's porch. And it wasn't that easy to get away. First she wanted a lightbulb changed. And then a picture moved.

When she requested that he retrieve a box from the attic, he balked.

"I really don't have time for that this evening," he told her. "I've got to see Mrs. Gilfred on business and then I have to get home to my family."

"Couldn't I tempt you with some tea and a brownie? I got a pan of those wonderful brownies from the grocery store."

"No, thank you," he repeated over and over, as he finally backed off the porch.

Guffy had gone into her house, so Tom grabbed his laptop from the porch and rang the doorbell. She let him inside with a wry grin. "I didn't expect you back until midnight. You must not be as polite as I think you are."

"I'm polite," Tom said. "But I'm not that crazy about roaming around a stranger's attic."

"Can't fault you there," she said. "I'm not even interested in roaming around my own."

He smiled at her humor. "I took some photos today of your car," he told her. "I came by to show them to you before I put them up on the internet."

"Come on into the kitchen," she said. "The folks at the church down the street came by with this pan of lasagna. I don't even go there. If I did, I'd tell them that I'm not that fond of Italian food. You'll have to share it with me, there's salad and bread, too."

It smelled so good, Tom didn't even think of uttering a polite refusal. He put the salad together while she dished the lasagna onto the plates. It tasted as fabulous and spicy as homemade lasagna can. Tom was scarfing it up when Mrs. Gilfred spoke.

"You've got a pretty healthy appetite."

"This is really, really good," he told her.

"Are you a man starved for home cooking?" she asked.

"I am these days."

"I thought you were married. Did she kick you out?"

Tom chuckled. "Not yet. But I've been working such long hours the past few weeks that I haven't been making it home for dinner."

"That's bad," Mrs. Gilfred said. "I hope it hasn't been my car keeping you from home."

"Oh, no, not at all," he assured her. "Besides your car doesn't seem as much work as it is pleasure."

"So, how is my Clara?" she asked. "Any buyers lined up yet?"

"Nothing yet," Tom told her. "But tomorrow she's making an international splash."

Tom opened his laptop and showed Guffy how to scroll through the photos.

"So, what do you think?"

"Oh, Clara looks lovely," Mrs. Gilfred told him. "She looks all shined up and ready for an adventure. I just wish I was still young enough to go with her."

The wistful sound in her voice caught Tom's attention.

"You know, you don't *have* to sell her," he reminded the woman. "Now that I've got her running, there's no reason why you shouldn't drive her around for another year or so. Then you could think about selling her again."

"No, no," Mrs. Gilfred said adamantly. "I want you to sell her. I'm too old to drive her and I want Clara to be driven around."

Tom nodded. Somehow he understood how she was feeling, while not knowing what he might feel in the same situation.

"So tell me about this wife of yours," Mrs. Gilfred said. "Why did the girl marry a big, rough-looking galoot like you?"

Mrs. Gilfred's criticism was made with such honesty and kindness, Tom couldn't help but laugh.

"I haven't got the faintest idea why Erica fell for me," he said. "But nobody would question why I fell for her."

Mrs. Gilfred smiled.

"She's smart, funny and kind and…quite a hottie," he explained. "I mean, even looking at it as a mechanic, how often can a guy come across a high-torque, smooth-running, low-maintenance vehicle with exceptional electronics and standard bodywork that looks like custom? When a fellow meets that girl, you know he's going to do whatever he can to try to park her in his own garage."

The old woman laughed aloud at that.

They began to talk. Tom told her about Erica and Quint, the struggles of opening his own shop. His luck in finding work that he liked to do and that he happened to be really good at.

Guffy talked about Clara and the places they'd been together, the people they'd known, things they had seen.

It was almost ten o'clock when he finally took his leave. He pulled his phone out of his pocket. He should have called Erica to let her know that he was going to be this late. But he hadn't. He hoped she hadn't worried. But he didn't want to take the time sitting at the curb calling. So he just drove home.

Tom let himself in through the garage door. He found his gorgeous wife sound asleep in front of reruns of *Dancing with The Stars*.

He went to the bedroom, stripped off his clothes and pulled back the sheets. In the bathroom he washed his hands and face and then returned to the living room where he leaned down and picked up Erica as if she were Quint. He carried her to bed and covered her up before slipping in beside her.

He spooned up against her back and wrapped his arms around her as she slept. Her body was warm, her skin soft. The scent of her enveloped him, clean and feminine. Tom nuzzled against her hair. He didn't want to wake her, but he couldn't resist just touching her.

"Future view—Tom Bentley," he whispered to himself. "Erica beside me for the rest of my life."

This was the best thing about being married, he thought. When he came in after a long day, without even the pleasure of talking to her, he felt loved and respected and safe. Safe. That was a word that caught him up a bit short. He was the protector. He was keeping his family from harm. Why did wrapping his arms around Erica make him feel safe as well? It was too big a question for as tired as he felt.

He sighed and drifted into sleep. But just in that middle place between conscious memory and slumber, he saw himself again in the backseat of that Buick with those people whose names he couldn't remember.

Erica mouthed the question, *Are you working late?*, hoping that the answer would be no. Tom's slight nod to the affirmative was a disappointment, but she understood. Or at least she thought she did. Tom had worked a lot of long hours during the start-up of the shop. But in the past year or so, that had become more and more infrequent. So much so that Erica had almost forgotten what it was like to *not* have her husband home for dinner, to give Quint a bath, to sit with her in front of the TV, to share the news of her day and to listen to the news of his.

The last few weeks, however, night after night after night, she and Quint were eating alone. Tom didn't get home before eight or eight-thirty. He always looked tired and he never had much to say.

It was curious, really, that such a change had occurred inexplicably. And even more so that Tom never offered any kind of explanation of what might be going on.

Her husband wasn't typically secretive, but Erica knew there were things in his past, hurts he had endured that crept into his day-to-day life. Sometimes those things would cast a shadow on him.

"Okay, Quint, have you got your backpack together? Are you ready to head home?" she asked her son as she returned to the shop's front office.

Quint was ready. He was tired, and on the short ride home he managed to nod off. He was too big for her to carry into the house, so she woke him up. The micro-nap seemed to have rejuvenated him and he talked a mile a minute for the next two hours, mostly following her around from room to room as she cleaned, giving her every possible piece of information on the upcoming Halloween celebration.

"There's going to be a costume contest and games and we can trick-or-treat right there in the gym," he said enthusiastically.

Erica made no attempt to dampen his excitement about the gym with the reality that the party had been put in place because parents no longer felt safe allowing their children to wander the neighborhood alone at night, even on a celebration night. Quint would get to knock on the doors of the houses of a few friends and then they'd spend time at the school.

His choice of costume, however, she did not encourage.

"I don't think serial killer is a good idea for a six-year-old," she told him.

"But Mom," he whined. "Cody Raza's going to be *Scream*."

The response that came to Erica's lips was, *If Cody Raza wanted to jump off a bridge...* But she managed to choke it back. It sounded too much like something Ann Marie would say. Erica was sure she never wanted to parent like her mother.

"*The Scream* is a famous painting," she said instead. "There is really nothing of educational value in being a serial killer."

Quint's brow furrowed in distress. "So I have to be something of educational value? I wanted to be scary."

He looked so disappointed Erica had to hide a smile. "Well, there are many scary characters in literature," she said. "I'm sure you can pick something that has educational value. Frankenstein or Dracula. Even vampires or mummies would have some merit, I think."

Her son's eyes widened. "You wouldn't let me watch the vampire movie," he pointed out.

"That was when you were five," she said. "You're six now. But I think you have to be able to read the scary stories before you can watch the movies."

"I'm getting better and better at reading," he assured her.

"Okay, and I can help you. So why don't we plan a trip to the library. You can pick out the book we want to read. But not at bedtime. This will have to be an afternoon or Saturday story."

Quint agreed and was placated enough to head off to his room and the toys there, leaving Erica free to sort the recycling for the next day's pickup as the pork chops cooked atop the stove.

When dinner was ready, she and Quint took their seats. The empty chair at the head of the table cast a pall on the meal. Erica looked down at her perfectly cooked meat and vegetables and felt little interest in eating.

Her son appeared equally unenthusiastic.

"It sure is quiet without Daddy here," he said.

Erica nodded agreement for a long moment and then went into action. She rose from her seat, retrieved another plate and a roll of aluminum foil from the kitchen.

"Let's drive up to the shop to eat."

"Yeah," Quint agreed enthusiastically.

Erica filled Tom's plate and covered it with foil. She did the same for her own and Quint's and then stacked all three into a box that would sit on the front floorboard. She got fresh silverware and napkins and then included a bag of cookies from the top of the cabinet for a special treat.

She and Quint were both laughing and happy as they ventured out. The sun setting on Woodlawn Lake was worth the trip outside, just for itself. They were both excited about their unexpected dining-out evening with Tom at his job.

Erica turned on some music and Quint was singing and rocking in his booster seat. She was moving her head to the rhythm herself.

When they arrived at the stop's gate, Erica punched in the code and the gate opened so she could pull the car into the drive. She was surprised that Tom didn't come out and greet them, but maybe he was way in the back. She used her key to open the office and then pressed the button to draw the gate closed.

"Go find your dad and tell him we've brought dinner," she told Quint. She went back out to the car and carried in the box of food, setting it on the desk. There were two chairs in the room, but she decided that she would need one of the work stools from the shop area. At the doorway, she ran into Quint.

"I can't find him," her son said. "I'm going to call him on the intercom."

Erica gave her son a wan smile. The building was not so big that her husband could get lost in it.

"I'll find him," she said. "You're strong enough to carry one of these stools into the office, right?"

Quint nodded his agreement. As he began half carrying, half dragging a third seat, Erica went looking for her husband. The shop seemed quiet and deserted.

"Tom?" she called out. "Tom?"

She reached bay four, where the Buick was parked, and still she hadn't found him. Erica walked the length of the Buick to the back wall. She no longer called out to him. She knew he wasn't there.

The door to the restroom was ajar. She flipped on the light and stepped inside. The heaviness of humidity and the scent of shampoo caught her attention. The place was steamy and the shower was wet. Erica's brow furrowed. The shower stall had always been there, but to her knowledge it had always just been used as a storage closet. It was obviously a functioning shower and someone had just used it.

"Weird," she muttered aloud.

What was even more peculiar was that Tom's coveralls hung on a hook on the back of the door. He'd taken a shower and changed clothes.

Erica left the restroom and walked to the building's back door, where she unlocked the dead bolt and stepped out into the back parking area. The light, a motion sensor, came on immediately, giving her an unrestricted view of a lot that was completely empty. Tom's truck was gone.

She carefully relocked the back door and returned to the front office where Quint had arranged their plates on the desk.

"Daddy's not here," she told him. "I guess he had an errand or something."

Her son's little face looked as puzzled as she felt. "Will he be back soon? Should we wait for him?"

No, Erica thought adamantly. Suddenly she wanted to be away from this place. She didn't want him to come back and find her here.

"Maybe we should go back home," she told Quint. "You know, we might have passed him on the road."

"Yeah," Quint agreed. "He's probably at home."

They quickly loaded up their box of food and returned it to the car. Erica double-checked the locks and the lights before they went through the security gate to the street.

From the backseat, her son was voicing thoughts very near her own.

"We would have seen his truck if we'd passed him on Fredericksburg or West Avenue," Quint said. "But he could have driven through the neighborhood or stopped at the gas station or the grocery store."

Erica nodded. "Absolutely," she agreed.

It was full darkness when they arrived back home and they were both disappointed when they pulled into the driveway to find that he was not there.

Enough of this, Erica scolded herself. It was getting late. Quint still hadn't eaten dinner and it was nearly time for his bath. Back in her own kitchen she reheated their dinner in the microwave and put the one she'd made for Tom into the refrigerator. She tried to be upbeat and eager, but she had lost her appetite. Dutifully she cut the meat, put pieces in her mouth and chewed.

"Where do you think he went?" Quint asked.

She didn't have an answer.

After the two of them had managed to finish their food, Erica cleaned up the kitchen, then supervised Quint in his bath. When he was finally in his pj's and settled into his bed, Quint read *The Very Hungry Caterpillar* aloud. He did a perfect job, but he knew the story so well that he hardly needed to read the words. Then Erica read to him from *The Wind in the Willows*. Normally the goings-on of Mole and Rat entertained them, but tonight they were both distracted and Erica replaced the bookmark after only a half-dozen pages.

"Good night," she told her son, planting a kiss on his forehead.

"Night, Mom," he replied. Then after a moment he added, "I bet I know where Daddy went."

"Oh?"

"I bet he went to see the woman at the hospital, the one he bought the flowers for."

Erica nodded vaguely. *What woman?* she was asking herself. And the phrase "woman at the hospital" brought to mind the image of Callie Torreno.

Quint yawned and settled into the covers as Erica tucked him in. She forced herself not to question her son, not to ask him what he was talking about. Those questions should be for Tom. She'd ask him herself as soon as he got home.

She turned off the light and closed the door. Erica wandered through the house, picking up trash, putting away toys, hanging up the towels in the aftermath of Quint's bath. Every few minutes she glanced out the front window expecting to see Tom's truck pull up into the driveway.

Finally, with nothing much left to do, she settled on the couch to watch television. He still hadn't called. She began to worry. Perhaps he'd been in an accident. What if he were lying in an emergency room somewhere and he wasn't able to speak? Of course, he'd still have his wallet on him. If he was hurt, someone would call. Maybe the shop had been broken into and some deranged criminal had taken him hostage.

There was nothing in the shop for a deranged criminal to want, she reminded herself. And it had been locked up tight when she'd arrived with Quint.

Undoubtedly, he'd simply gone out to see a client or to look at a car. That was part of his job, part of his business. He couldn't just wait for customers to come in the door— sometimes he had to go out and find them, wherever they were.

But why take a shower first?

She looked at her phone. She picked it up to check for messages. Nothing. She should just call him. If she wanted to know where he was, she should just call and ask.

What if he didn't take her call?

That was ridiculous, of course he would take it.

But she didn't want to be one of those wives. One of those crazy, paranoid wives who had to know where her husband was at every minute of every day. She had never been that woman. But she knew all about her.

She thought of Ann Marie. Her mother, ever distrustful and always done wrong. Man after man proving himself untrustworthy. Her mother never letting anything get by her.

Erica did not want to be her mother. She never wanted that life. When she'd sought love, she hadn't looked for handsome looks, family connections or a good income. She chose a man whose heart was true. Tom's heart was true. She'd always known that. Could time change such a thing?

She shivered in the living room darkness and dragged the throw off the back of the couch to wrap herself in.

In memory she could hear Melody's voice of warning. "Somebody from Admitting got under her skin and she ruined the woman's marriage."

"Nobody can ruin somebody else's marriage."

"She can if she targets the husband."

Erica shivered again and drew the blanket more tightly around her. *Tom would not be susceptible to the charms of some vengeful harpy,* she told herself.

Then her logic reminded her that she didn't have any ideas about what her husband might be susceptible to. Tom had had a long, complicated life before he met her. And not just his familiarity with the darker, more unsavory aspects of human existence with his addicted mother. But he'd also had his share of teenage passions and relationships of convenience. And although they had never discussed previous lovers, he had told her, "I've never been with anyone like you."

So the women that typically attracted him were nothing like Erica herself. She didn't know what they were like, so they could be exactly the kind of woman she feared.

"Stop it!" she said aloud. "Tom loves you."

She heard herself sounding more like Melody than like herself. And Melody, she's thought, always protested too much.

Erica covered her ears as if she could drown out the voices that were inside her head rather than around her. Once more she grasped at reason. There was a logical explanation about where Tom had spent the evening. One that did not, in any way, involve another woman.

Chapter 13

SOMEHOW, BETWEEN THE two of them, they forgot to set the alarm. The first hint of morning came as Quint padded into the bedroom.

"Mom, I'm going to be late for school."

Tom and Erica sat up in bed simultaneously.

"Oh, crap!" he heard his wife say.

A stronger word came to Tom's lips, but with Quint standing in the doorway, he managed not to say it.

"Go ahead, you can have the shower," he told his wife. "And don't worry about getting Quint to school. I'll take him."

As Erica rushed to the bathroom, Tom went to the kitchen and fixed Quint a hurry-up breakfast of cereal and milk. Once his son was dutifully eating, Tom went back to the bedroom and pulled on the clothes he'd taken off last night. He rubbed his chin, thinking of going without a shave, but the rough beard, along with the misshapen nose and the scar on his face, might be more than a new customer could get past. He traversed the steamy jungle of the bathroom, listening to his wife sloshing herself clean in the water as he scraped off the worst of his whiskers in a foggy mirror.

Quint was putting his bowl in the sink by the time Tom got back.

"I need to have a lunch," he told his father. With a sigh he added, "When we're late I always have to take peanut butter."

Tom nodded and opened the refrigerator. His own lunch from yesterday was sitting on the shelf.

"Why don't you take my leftovers from yesterday?" he suggested.

Quint looked skeptical.

"Why didn't you eat it?"

"Because a nice old woman fixed me dinner," he said. "Mom fixed this, so you know it's great. Roast beef, yum."

"Okay," Quint agreed.

Tom transferred the contents of his insulated carrier into Quint's lunchbox with the big yellow SpongeBob on the front. He added in a juice box and declared it complete.

"Go give your mom a kiss and let's get going," he said.

Erica was just coming out of the bedroom. She was dressed with her makeup done, but her hair was pulled up in a big clip on top of her head.

"Bye, Mom," Quint said, running toward her for a quick smooch.

"You need your lunch?"

"It's in my backpack," he told her. "Dad gave me his leftovers from yesterday."

"I'll catch lunch out somewhere," he told her. "And I've got my fingers crossed about making it home for dinner."

"Okay."

Tom stepped forward to say his goodbye as well. "Don't panic too much about getting there on time," he warned her. "I know you don't like being late, but better late than smashed up on the road."

"I'll be careful," she assured him.

Tom leaned down to place his lips on her own, but at the last minute she moved slightly and his little peck ended up on her cheek. It was unsatisfactory, but he thought they could make it up later when they had more time.

The drop-off line at the school in the mornings went far faster than the one in the afternoon and Tom arrived at his shop with time to spare. He unlocked everything, turned on the lights, checked the task sheets and penciled in who could do what. Then he went back to the restroom and pulled on his coveralls. He was tempted to open his laptop and check the site where he'd put up the photos of the Buick. But it was too soon to expect anything, he reminded himself. And since he couldn't be sure his employees would show up until they did, he didn't want to be distracted.

He raised the doors on bays one and two to let the morning sunshine in and allow the smells from cars, grease guns and motor oils to escape.

Bugg was supposed to bring in his vehicle and Tom was eager to get his hands on the 1966 Tempest. It was the lowest-priced model Pontiac had made that year, but it was still a DeLorean design and Tom was a fan.

As he expected, Bugg arrived before Hector, Gus or Cliff. Tom spotted him coming down West Avenue driving about fifteen miles per hour, annoying the commuters in the long line of cars behind him. He pulled into the driveway and Tom directed him into an empty bay.

"She's a beauty, a real beauty," Tom told the older man as he stepped out of the car. "And she sounds pretty good."

"Oh, she's missing," Bugg said. "She doesn't sound like herself at all. I don't know if it's a pump problem or something in the line or what."

Tom nodded. "Well, we'll figure it out and get her fixed up."

Bugg began to talk and talk. Tom knew he'd never get any work done if he didn't get the old guy home. Finally Gus showed up and Tom immediately dispatched him to return Bugg to his house.

"I'll call you as soon as I know anything," Tom assured him.

Bugg obviously wanted to hang around, but reluctantly followed Gus to his truck. Hector arrived and, with barely an acknowledgment, went right to work on an electronics problem left over from the day before. Tom had spoken only briefly to the man about his binge drinking and lost workdays. Hector was so embarrassed by his own behavior that he could hardly look Tom in the eye.

Not everybody was affected by the boss's displeasure. Cliff showed up just as Tom raised the Tempest on the lift. His friend had not uttered one word of apology or regret for his erratic behavior. And the thoughtful, reflective mood that Tom had seen yesterday was absent this morning. Cliff was cheerful, happy, joking as if nothing whatsoever was amiss.

"Nice car," he said, looking up into the undercarriage.

"It's Bugg's."

Cliff nodded. "I saw you talking to him yesterday. I'm glad you finally convinced him to bring it down here."

"It's missing a little. He thinks it's a fuel pump problem or maybe a dead cylinder, but it sounds more to me like a leaky valve," Tom said. "At least they're not that hard to fix and the parts are not that hard to find."

"Is it the same one that's in the GTO?"

"Uh-huh," Tom answered.

"Well, that should be pretty straightforward then," Cliff said. "Too bad this car isn't a GTO. Then it would really be worth something."

Tom hung the shop light on the frame before looking hard at Cliff. "This car is worth something to Bugg. It's worth a whole lot to him. He has a relationship with this car. You could bring the sweetest GTO on earth in here for an even trade and it could never mean as much to that old man as this car does. It's not just about the car's value, it's about its value to the owner."

"Still," Cliff pointed out, "some cars are more in demand. There are just some vehicles that everybody seems to want."

"I think it's more often that some cars have just survived better than others. Either because they were built tougher to begin with or they were treated better on the road. The fancier the car, the less likely the owner will use it for long-distance commutes or hauling heavy loads. And sporty muscle cars are more often bought by people who love tinkering with them, so they keep them up, serviced and never abuse them. Once you get forty or fifty years down the road, you begin to see that the only cars still out there are the lux vehicles and the sport models."

"Yeah, I guess there's some truth to that."

"But when you see a family car or a moderately priced car that makes it to vintage…" Tom said. "Then you know that somebody really had a connection with that vehicle."

Cliff shrugged and shook his head. "I guess that's why you're so taken with that old lady's Buick over that fast cool Shelby we had in here last week."

Tom nodded. "You're right," he said. "I'd rather have the Buick. It says something to me that the Shelby doesn't."

"Now the cars are talking to you?" Cliff chuckled.

"Yeah, maybe I should change the name of this place to 'The Car Whisperer.'"

"Oh, I like that, I truly like that," Cliff said. "Maybe I'll use it when I get my own shop."

Tom thought the possibility of Cliff getting his own shop was unlikely to happen anytime soon. Still, he played along with the dream, as he always had.

"Great idea," he said. "Feel free to use it. Just don't open up next door."

Cliff chuckled.

A small lull occurred in the conversation. Tom could tell that Cliff had something to say, so he just waited.

"Listen," Cliff said. "I know I've left you in the lurch a lot lately. I'm really sorry about that, and you've got a right to be sore at me."

Tom wasn't about to deny it or downplay it. Cliff was speaking the truth and he was walking on thin ice. Only their long friendship prevented him from being fired already.

"Things with Stacy have turned out...well, they've turned out differently than I expected. But the sneaking off and all that, I'm not going to be doing that anymore."

"Good," Tom said.

"I'm going to try to be here on time and stay until closing," Cliff said. "That's what I signed on for and that's what I need to do."

"Right," Tom agreed.

Cliff hesitated again. "But I need one more thing from you," he said. "Just one more and then I won't ask again."

"What?"

"If Trish calls you or comes by or has someone else talk to you," he said, "I need you to confirm that I was right here in the shop working last night."

Tom raised an eyebrow.

Cliff raised his hand like a Boy Scout. "Last time I'll ask, promise."

Tom didn't want to promise, but it sounded as if Cliff had finally come to his senses. That was maybe the best news that he'd had in a while.

"Okay, but this *is* the last time," Tom told Cliff firmly.

According to the clock, Erica arrived at work right on time. However, the fact that she typically showed up fifteen minutes early each day made her feel as if she was late.

After logging on to her computer she grabbed her coffee cup and hurried to the break room. She was starving as well as groggy, but she knew there would be nothing in their break room but microwave popcorn and maybe somebody's three-day-old leftovers. At ten she could go downstairs and grab a bite. Until then, she'd simply have to let her stomach growl.

Back at her desk, a cup of hot coffee beside her, Erica got to work, was eager to throw herself into it. During her morning shower, as well as on her commute, she berated herself for last night's indulgence. Sitting around stewing about her husband's faithfulness was beneath her. It was beneath their marriage. She could only blame this lapse in judgment on her mother whose bad luck with men was partially caused by her poor expectations. Erica had known only love and fidelity from her husband. She had never expected anything less and was not about to change.

She clicked on her in-box which was already filled with files on patients who'd come in during the night. Erica's job was to read what the doctors and nurses had reported, noting the patient's diagnosis and what treatments or procedures were undertaken. The usual and the unusual all needed to be recorded. It was Erica's challenge to find and enter the numerical codes for all of that. It was like translating information into a foreign language. The typical things, the diseases she saw every day, pneumonia, arrhythmia, diabetes, those numbers were as familiar to her as the back of her hand. But there were always unusual things, diseases or treatments that were rare or new. Those had to be looked up and verified. Getting that right could be a challenge. But whether it was experience or a natural gift, Erica thought she had a knack for understanding what people had written. Still, she never guessed and didn't hesitate to ask for help. And Mrs. Converse was a genius at interpretation.

When break time finally arrived, Erica was grateful for the walk to the vending machines. One of the most difficult back-to-the-job things to get accustomed to was the long hours seated in front of the computer screen. It made her neck and shoulders ache in a way that carrying a baby in a sling or lifting a toddler into a grocery cart never did.

She stood in front of the giant vending machine full of prepackaged snacks, a fistful of change in her hand. Cookies, chips or cheese crackers? Three bad choices. Did she want to stoke up her blood sugar? Or retain fluid? This was a downside of her job as well. A little bit of medical knowledge could be a dangerous thing.

"I always go for the peanuts," said a voice behind her. "At least there's protein in those oily, empty calories."

She turned to see Dr. Glover, standing behind her. He was only a couple of inches taller than she was. It was nice not having to really look up to meet a man's eyes.

"I overslept this morning," she admitted. "So I'm trying to make the least bad breakfast choice."

"Step away from the vending machine," he said, mimicking a cop on a megaphone. Then he added in a more traditional voice, "Seriously, go back to your desk, I'll bring you something better than this."

Erica hesitated, but his nod sent her back to the Medical Records office, where he showed up less than a minute later with a giant, warmed muffin.

"It's sweet potato," he told her. "Potassium, magnesium and beta carotene in a relatively low glycemic load."

To Erica's amazement, Dr. Glover actually sat down on the edge of her desk.

"Thank you," she said before eyeing the gift suspiciously. "Did you steal this out of the Doctor's Lounge?"

The cushy, private rest area down the hall was famous for the platters of fresh fruits and pastries still warm from the oven. However, pilfering the doctor's stash was expressly forbidden. Erica said as much to Glover.

"It's not stealing. They actually count me as one of the doctors."

"You are," she pointed out. "I'm not."

"Eat," he ordered. "We can't have you fainting on the job. You'd ruin the department's reputation as the one place that never has a crash cart."

Erica tutted at his joke and shook her head, but the muffin smelled wonderful, so she took a bite.

"Mmm, this is good," she admitted.

Dr. Glover nodded. "I know. It's my favorite. And I've tried all of them."

Erica decided she should just thank her good luck and enjoy her breakfast.

"So how late were you this morning? Did you get called on the carpet?"

She shook her head. "I made it here on time, but I'm usually early."

"Early, huh? I thought women were always late."

"That's a stereotype."

"They're always late when they're meeting me," he said. "Maybe they're reluctant."

"Or maybe you're dating the wrong women," Erica said.

He chuckled. "There's no maybe about that. All I ever seem to attract are the psycho-chicks. I must have a beacon shining above my head that says, 'Crazy ladies, apply for romance here!'"

Erica laughed.

"It must be true," he insisted.

"You just need to meet some different women," Erica said.

He shrugged. "I do. I meet nice women and they are always married. You are a case in point. Nice, funny, smart, easy to talk to and married. That's my luck."

Erica was flattered. Then a thought flickered through her mind. She almost let it go and then she reconsidered. Why not do something nice for someone else and perhaps she could even help herself in the bargain.

"Callie, the woman you worked with on this project before me," Erica said. "I kind of got the impression she was sort of interested in you."

He stared at her strangely for a moment and then laughed uproariously, loud enough to be heard in every corner of the department. But when he spoke it was only a little above a whisper.

"You kind of got that impression? I kind of got that impression, too. What did I tell you—psycho-chicks, they adore me." He rose to his feet. "I've got to get back to work. Thanks for the conversation."

"Thanks for the breakfast," she replied, indicating the half-eaten muffin she still held in her hand.

"Enjoy," he said as he walked away.

Erica finished her muffin and got back to work. At noon,

she logged off and had just unlocked the drawer to get her handbag when Melody stepped into her cubicle.

"Ready for lunch?"

Erica glanced up at her, puzzled. "You're in a good mood today," she pointed out.

Melody shrugged. "Callie's out sick. That's good news for you and me. We're the women she's targeting."

Erica mentally reminded herself that "targeting" was Melody's word choice. Erica had no evidence that Callie was upset with her at all.

"Okay," she said simply.

Melody looked positively exuberant. Erica felt less so, but she accompanied the woman downstairs and followed her through the cafeteria line.

When they carried their trays to the Medical Records table, Lena, Rayliss and Darla were already there. Callie's seat at the head of the table was empty. None of them had chosen to take it. Erica didn't, either.

They seated themselves. The atmosphere was a bit more quiet than usual, and everyone was relaxed.

"Callie's out sick today? I hope it's not serious."

"No, I don't think so," Darla replied.

Rayliss chuckled. "I'd bet on a bad case of anal astigmatism."

"Anal astigmatism?" Erica was certain she must have heard incorrectly.

"Yeah," Rayliss answered. "Callie probably couldn't see her butt coming in to work today."

Lena, Darla and Rayliss cackled as if that was the funniest joke they'd ever heard. Melody wasn't laughing, but she looked inexplicably pleased.

Erica smiled, but with uncertainty. She knew the group found it difficult to resist gossip. But this was more serious than silly rumors. It was very well known that Mrs. Converse was a stickler for appropriate use of sick leave. She took great pride knowing her department had the lowest absentee rate in the entire UTHSC institutional system.

If Callie, with her seniority and traits as a natural leader, was flouting the strict attendance policies, it would be noticed. And Erica was sure Mrs. Converse would not be happy and would be compelled to come down on it harshly.

Erica thought it might be in the best interest of the department to defend her.

"I'm sure if she called in sick, she truly is."

Darla looked up at her and then glanced over at Rayliss. The meaningful glance that passed between the two of them was completely uninterpretable to Erica.

"My guess is that Callie was pretty whipped this morning," Darla snorted. "Not to mean she was actually 'whipped'—I don't think the guy she's been doing is into that specifically."

Rayliss giggled at that and shot Erica a glance as if it was supposed to mean something to her.

"Oh…" Melody said, as if just getting the direction of the conversation.

Lena perked up as well. "I'd heard her bragging yesterday about her new boyfriend."

"I'm not sure you can call him a 'boyfriend,'" Rayliss said.

"Yeah," Darla agreed. "He was more like a reverse booty call. The toughest thing was getting him to meet her. When he showed up she jumped his bones."

"He told her he wasn't interested," Rayliss said. "But he couldn't turn it down."

"His lips said no, but his dick said yeah!"

Darla shot Erica another look and there was so much challenge in it, it took her breath away. Why was everyone looking at her? Darla was suggesting... What was she suggesting?

The memory of the steamy shower at the shop flashed in her mind. And Melody's words "targeted the woman's husband" reverberated through her head.

A sick pit of emptiness formed in her stomach. *No, no, no,* she assured herself. This had nothing to do with her. Callie may have hooked up with somebody, but that meant nothing to her. It had nothing to do with Tom. But still, Erica looked down at her salad and felt sick.

"Once was not enough, of course," Darla said. "He was reluctant to get going, but when she got him started, he really had an appetite. Callie said it was like he was starved for it. She gave him an A+ for technique and bonus points for stamina."

Erica looked up to see every face turned in her direction. Their expressions were curious, questioning, as if they were watching for her reaction. They seemed strangely amused, except for Melody, who was wide-eyed and shocked.

It's not true, she mentally chided her lack of faith. Tom would not, could not, be unfaithful. Their marriage mattered too much to them both.

But then why, *why* were these women looking at her? Why were they expecting some response from her? It was crazy. It was impossible. It was sickening.

How she got through the next few moments, she didn't know. She forced herself not to rise from her seat, not to run to the safety and solitude of the ladies' room or the familiar territory of her cubicle. She sat at the table, forking pieces of tasteless lettuce into her mouth.

It's a lie. It's a mean, cruel lie. Don't give anyone the satisfaction of seeing how their comments affect you.

These were lies, Erica assured herself over and over again.

They had to be lies. Although running alongside those mental expressions of certainty were tiny flashes of unhappy memory—the empty shop, the weeks of unexplained secretiveness and Quint's words, "the woman at the hospital that he bought flowers for."

Purposely she forced herself to recall another scene, now a decade old, standing on the courthouse steps. The wind blew through Tom's hair as he vowed, "to love, honor and cherish, as long as we both shall live."

Finally the seemingly unending lunch break was winding down and Erica was able to leave the table, still holding her head high. On her way back to the department, she stopped by the restroom, as she always did, but didn't even bother to repair her lipstick.

She looked at herself in the mirror. Her cheeks were pale. Her eyes looked hollow. Was this the look of a wronged woman?

"It's not true," she said aloud. Then she punctuated that comment by the sudden need to race to the commode, where she vomited the hateful lunch she'd just eaten.

Chapter 14

WITH SHEER FORCE OF WILL, Erica managed to avoid tearing up through the rest of workday. By the time she got on the bus, where theoretically she could have gone on a self-indulgent crying jag in front of strangers, she was no longer really in the mood.

She was sure it wasn't true. So instead of allowing the lie to eat at her and urge her to doubt, she would bring it right out in the open. She would share with Tom what her coworkers had suggested and ask him to tell her the truth.

The plan was a good one, she thought. And a very different approach than what her mother would have come up with. Ann Marie would already be playing private detective, borrowing a friend's car to shadow him. Searching through his laundry for phone numbers, lipstick stains or worse. She'd be tracking the mileage on his truck and checking his cell phone while he was in the shower for every number dialed or received.

Then, by the time Ann Marie notified her divorce lawyer, she'd have a complete list of her husband's assets and would know which ones she wanted for herself.

But that was Erica's mother. And those men were her mother's husbands. Erica knew she had chosen better. And she wasn't about to believe the worst of Tom.

She got off at her stop and walked to the shop, thinking about the discussion she and Tom would have. Maybe he would be home for dinner tonight and they would laugh together and listen to Quint. And then after their son was put to bed, it would be just the two of them. She'd tell him everything. He would be incredulous. He would hold her and explain everything to her and reassure her that it was all the worst kind of office gossip.

Yes, that was exactly how it was going to go. And she could hardly wait.

When she arrived at the shop, she went into the office to greet Quint. She kissed him on the top of the head and then listened as he related, in minute detail, how Maddycinn Guerra had "totally messed up" the spelling test.

"She forgot to write down the study words from the board," Quint said. "So she couldn't study and she missed three. Three! She never misses any. She started crying and she couldn't stop."

"Oh, that's too bad," Erica said.

"You're telling me," Quint agreed dramatically. "I never heard such boo-hooing in my whole life. It was awful. Cody stuffed tissues in his ears to shut out the sound."

Quint was grinning. "He had the big white tissues sticking out of his ears. It made him look like a rabbit or something. And everybody laughed. But Maddycinn thought they were laughing at her and she cried even more. That upset

Mrs. Salinas and she made Cody write 'I will be kind to sad friends' on the board *ten* times."

Erica managed to hide a smile.

"Being kind to sad friends is a good thing to practice," she told her son.

Quint nodded. "Yeah, I know. But you ought to be sad over serious stuff like your cat dying or something. Nobody cries over spelling words."

"Well, apparently Maddycinn does," Erica said. "Why don't you get your stuff together while I talk to your dad."

Just before she turned toward the side door, she noticed the pile of fliers and envelopes on the edge of the desk.

"Is this what the postman brought?" she asked Quint.

The boy nodded.

Erica absently flipped through the mail. She quickly sorted through it but one envelope caught her attention. It had the bank's return address but was too small to be the monthly statement. Erica opened it curiously. Inside she found a brand-new credit card, with a brand-new number. She hadn't gotten rid of the card they already had, so this must be an additional card. That surprised her. She and Tom were very careful with credit and tried to pay in full every month. And the account they had already had more available balance than they ever hoped to need. Why on earth would Tom have applied for an additional card? She turned the sheet over and then glanced inside the envelope. There was only one card, one card with Tom's name. That was curious as well. Every account they had ever had, had always been joint. Erica was an equal partner in Bentley's Classic Car Care. In truth, without *her* good credit and *her* life savings Tom would never have been able to approach the bank for the start-up money. But she had been happy to be a part of it. It was his dream. And when she'd fallen in love with him, it became her dream, too.

Erica put the card back in the envelope and set it on top of the other mail. She made no attempt to disguise the fact that she'd opened it. She and Tom had no secrets.

Yes, that was right, she reminded herself. She and Tom had no secrets.

Noise on the driveway drew her attention as a big silver SUV pulled into the parking spot in front of the door. Erica recognized the vehicle, of course.

Trish Aleman emerged from the driver's door. A minute later, her kids were climbing out of the back.

"It's Emily and Jordan," Quint said excitedly, leaping down from his own seat to join them.

He nearly barreled over Trish at the doorway as she called over her shoulder. "You kids stay outside, but keep away from the street."

She greeted Erica with a smile, though she seemed a bit more subdued than usual. Trish was one of those women who just seemed to have been born beautiful. She was a natural, with perfectly proportioned features, flawless skin and a lovely smile. Like a gifted artist she was able to improve that canvas by expert application of makeup, and perfectly coiffed long, thick dark hair that hung down to her waist in shiny ripples. Today she had those brunette tresses pulled up in a neat ponytail.

Why was it, Erica wondered, that when Trish put her hair in a ponytail, she looked young and vivacious? When Erica tried the same thing, she merely looked as if she hadn't had time to do her hair.

"Hey, Trish, what a nice surprise to run into you."

"We've got to make a point to see each other more often," Trish said. "The kids love to play together."

That was true. Her children and Quint always had a great time. For the adults, however, it wasn't always so perfect. The men worked together all week and had little or nothing left to say to each other at night or on a weekend. Trish and Erica should have lots in common, but Erica always felt as if she were in a competition and losing badly.

"How are you doing?" Trish asked.

"Great, great," Erica replied. "How's it going for you? Are the kids loving school this year?"

The conversational question seemed almost to catch her off guard, as if she hadn't really thought about it. "Yeah, I guess so," she said. "How is Quint?" she asked, almost as an afterthought.

"Doing great. He's very excited about Halloween this year."

"Halloween? Oh yeah, when is that?" Trish asked.

"Tomorrow," Erica answered, surprised that Trish didn't know. She seemed sort of out of it, distracted almost.

Tom walked through the door from the shop. "Hi," he said, including both women in the greeting. He snaked his arm around Erica's waist and gave her a little squeeze, but his eyes were on Trish.

"Do you need to talk to Cliff?" he asked. "I've got him… uh…in the middle of disassembling a transmission, but if it can't wait, of course I can interrupt him."

Erica immediately saw that there was something wrong with Tom's body language.

"No, no," Trish said. "It can wait. The kids and I were just out running around and I thought I'd stop in."

Erica raised an eyebrow at that. Trish and Cliff lived in Westover Hills, and there was no quick, easy or direct way to get from there to here. And there was no shopping over this way. If Trish stopped by, it had to be because she had made it her destination.

"I feel like I never see him anymore," she said. "The kids never see him anymore."

Erica nodded sympathetically. "Sometimes our lives just get so busy," she said, commiserating.

"Last night was Jordan's final PeeWee Football game and he really wanted his dad to be there," Trish said, and then looked directly at Tom. "Did he tell you that when you asked him to work late?"

Tom hesitated. "Uh…no, he didn't say anything," Tom replied. "I…uh…I'm sorry. I guess Cliff knew how desperate we were to get that…that work done. We were both here late."

Erica's world suffered a jolting and dramatic tilt and she was falling, dropping into unknown territory. Her husband was not looking at her, and his arm had left her waist. There was a falseness in his tone, but she didn't have to hear it to know that Tom was lying. She'd been here. The place had been empty. Her husband had been gone. And before he'd left, he'd cleaned up and taken a shower in the newly renovated facilities.

A memory of words spoken in passing, not even directed to her, suddenly appeared front and center in Erica's brain. She could hear her coworker, Rayliss, as clearly as if the woman was standing beside her.

"If a husband takes a shower before he comes home, then you know there's someone else."

Trish and Tom were still talking, but Erica could no longer hear what they were saying. It was as if there were some inexplicable ringing in her ears. But it wasn't physical, it was emotional.

She felt sick. The bottom had dropped out of her world, leaving only emptiness and nausea behind.

"I need to get home," she blurted, interrupting their conversation.

Both of them turned toward her, but Erica avoided their gaze. She didn't want either of them to see what was going on inside her.

"I'm so sorry you have to rush off," Trish said. "But I guess I should head out as well. If Halloween really is tomorrow, then I need to take the kids somewhere to get costumes."

"I'm sure you'll come up with something great," Erica said, without meeting her eyes. "Gotta go."

She grabbed up Quint's book bag and attempted to flee. Tom grabbed her hand.

"What? No goodbye kiss."

"Sorry," Erica said. She pecked him on the cheek with only a glance in his direction. He looked puzzled. That annoyed her. He should look guilty.

Out in front, Quint was not interested in a quick getaway.

"Aww, Mom" was his response to her request to get in the car. "I never get to see Jordon. Can't I stay and play a little longer."

"Jordon's got to leave, too," Erica said as a way to placate him. But it didn't work, and after a minute of back and forth, Erica sternly ordered him into the car.

Quint obeyed her, but was clearly put out. His brow was furrowed in an expression like a thundercloud. She'd seen that look on her own face enough times to recognize it. Still, she drove home, the two of them not speaking. Erica focused intently on the road in front of her. Concentrating on every move she needed to make. Her child was in the car. She couldn't allow emotion to take over. Keep a safe distance from the car in front. Check the mirrors. Check your speed. Slow for the stoplight. Signal with the blinker.

When she finally parked in her driveway, she felt so relieved that her eyes welled with tears.

Quint, still angry, went to his room and shut the door. He didn't slam the door—that was not allowed—but he shut it as forcefully as he thought he could get away with. Erica let him get away with it. She felt like slamming a few doors herself.

Instead she went into the privacy of the kitchen and tried to call her sister. The answering machine picked up.

"Hi, it's me, Letty. I'm either in class or way too busy to pick up the phone, but you can text me."

Erica did that.

Need U now

And then she stood in the kitchen, waiting, breathing, trying not to start screaming or crying. Tom was lying to her. He had a secret life with secret appointments and secret friends. He had a secret credit card. And he was taking showers at work—he was taking showers for some other woman.

Erica bit her lip, trying to hold back the wave of emotion that was about to swamp her. Her knees felt as if they were about to buckle and she leaned against the wall.

"It can't be true," she whispered to herself. "Tom is not that kind of guy. It can't be true."

She slid down the wall until she was sitting on the kitchen floor. The emptiness that had formed in her stomach had expanded to include her entire body.

The telephone rang. She crawled over to the counter and reached for it as if it were a lifeline.

"What's up?" her sister asked immediately.

"I think Tom is having an affair."

Tom's jaw was set hard and tight as he stepped up to Cliff. "I need to see you in the office, now," he said.

He turned without even waiting to make sure his friend followed. He was so mad that he needed the distance between them to keep from throwing a punch. Tom stood for a moment looking out the window, trying to get a grip on his anger.

He didn't turn until he heard Cliff enter the office and close the door behind him. Cliff's typical, cocky self-assurance was not in evidence. He was wide-eyed and worried. And that, at least, was as it should be.

"Don't you ever put me in that position again," Tom said. "I had to lie to your wife's face. That's the only time that's ever going to happen. If she calls me on the phone five minutes from now and asks 'What's up with Cliff?' I'm telling her that you're a cheating son of a bitch and that she needs to get herself a good lawyer."

"I'm sorry," Cliff said.

"Yeah, I'd have to agree with that. I can't believe you wouldn't come out and face her."

"You're right," Cliff said. "I'm going to have to do that sooner or later."

"And you missed the kid's game? That stuff is important. I thought it was over between you and Stacy."

"Over?" Cliff looked shocked at the suggestion. "No. I'd say it's over with me and Trish. I don't want to be married to her and living in some stupid suburb. What we had burned out a long time ago. I love Stacy now. I only want to be with her."

Tom's anger turned to shocked disbelief.

"You said she was just a fling."

"I was wrong. Stacy's my soul mate. I do not, will not, live my life without her."

Tom was almost speechless.

"What about your kids?" he demanded finally.

Cliff shrugged. "I think we're going to have to dump the kids. Stacy said her husband would never give her custody. So if she can't have hers, I won't have mine."

"That's crazy."

"It's not crazy to finally get something you want," Cliff said petulantly. "All my life I never got anything I wanted. Now I want Stacy and nobody is going to talk me out of having her."

Tom stared at his friend, thinking that all Cliff needed was to stamp his foot and it would be a full-blown tantrum. Deliberately Tom lowered his voice to a more reasonable pitch, with the hope that Cliff would listen.

"You're discounting some big things," he said. "You've got a wife who loves you, great kids, a nice house, a job you like. Your parents are proud of you. Your friends respect you. Are you sure this woman is worth all of that?"

Cliff raised his chin slightly, his expression almost con-descending. "You can't understand what I feel, what I want," he said. "You've always been so desperate to turn your son-of-a-junkie existence into some greeting card that you don't even see how boring it all is. I'm still young. I still want to have fun. Stacy's fun and we're going to have fun together."

Tom stood staring at his oldest friend, wondering when they had parted ways. Once they had only wanted the same things. Today they couldn't be more different.

"Fine," Tom told him. "Throw away your marriage with both hands if you want to. But don't ask me to lie to your wife, don't ask me to run interference. If you're going to leave her, then man up and tell her so. I think she deserves to hear it from you."

"That's none of your business."

"No, it's not. But *this place* is my business. So get back to work. Consider yourself on probation. If you miss one more day or duck out one more afternoon, you're gone."

Cliff was insulted. "You think I can't get a better job than this," he said with a sneer.

"I don't know, maybe you can," Tom answered. "If you don't want to work for me, all you have to do is say so."

Cliff turned on his heel and walked back into the shop. Tom half expected him to gather up his things and leave, but he didn't. He went back to work and stayed until quitting time. Hector and Gus, who'd been as quiet as church mice since the argument, left on time as well.

Tom walked through the quiet solitude of the place, picking up tools and rags and parts that somehow hadn't made it back to the places where they should have been.

Wanting to take his mind off Cliff for a moment, Tom walked over to the Buick, and he couldn't resist raising the hood. Little by little she was looking better and better. He'd completely redone her carburetor, replaced her hoses, greased every joint and connection on her frame. Her transmission was as smooth as a sewing machine. The 322 Nailhead was hitting perfectly on all eight cylinders. And her electrical system was probably better now than it ever had been. All she needed was a good scrub underneath the hood and a little bit of shiny bling. Some lucky man was going to fall in love with Clara, just as he had.

He'd just received a request for further information from his online posting. He suspected the inquiry was from a dealer rather than an individual. Tom had answered the questions, but made it clear that the car was special to the owner and to himself and that they were not desperate to let her go, and that they'd be waiting for the right buyer at the right price.

Tom considered starting her up, just to hear the engine purr and to…to escape into whatever it was about the car that almost made him feel good. There was something about that memory that triggered something within him. He didn't know what it was, but he liked it.

For just a moment he recalled Cliff's angry words and he considered them. He had always believed it was the truth in accusations that hurt more than the lies. And there was certainly some truth to what Cliff had said. Tom's life with his mother had been bad. He'd once described it as "abandonment in plain sight." Tom had been right under his mother's nose and she still didn't notice him. He, however, learned to keep his eye on her. If she decided to pick up stakes, she wouldn't think to bring him with her. And he couldn't trust her to find her way back to him.

Tom didn't feel sorry for himself. He'd known plenty of kids in that life who'd had it worse. His mother hadn't taken care of him, but she hadn't abused him, either.

And if he'd had dreams of another kind of life, he'd got them from her.

"I'm going to find a nice family for you," she'd tell him on nights when she was mellow and they were safe.

"You'll have a mama who bakes pies and a daddy who goes to work. You'll go to school and learn things. Did I tell you that I was the fourth grade spelling champion at Crockett Elementary?"

"Yeah, Mama, you did."

"You're going to have clean clothes every day. Hot meals that you have to eat at the table. And you'll go to church every Sunday."

His mother had never been able to follow through on her plans. By the next day, she would already be back on the cycle of cash, buy, use, crash. But at least he'd known she'd wanted a different life for him, even if she couldn't manage to provide it.

Tom had found that life for himself. He found Erica and together they had made it happen. And if Cliff thought that it was dull or boring or an imitation of a greeting card, well that was Cliff's problem.

Tom shut the hood. Tomorrow's Halloween craziness would make for a far-from-typical evening. But tonight it would be just his little family around the dinner table.

It was then that he heard a noise out front. It was still twilight outside, but the motion sensors flooded the front driveway with illumination. Tom didn't consider this neighborhood to be dangerous, but he knew that thieves and addicts and crazy people did not limit themselves to any particular part of town.

He grabbed a tire iron from the wall and carried it like a weapon. It wouldn't fend off a bullet, of course, but slammed down on a man's arm, it could certainly spoil his aim.

The would-be intruder seemed to be banging on one of the bay doors. If it was a burglar, he certainly wasn't a very stealthy one.

"Hello, hello, Tom Bentley, are you in there?"

"Who wants to know?"

"It's Briscoe," the voice answered. "Briscoe Garrity. You helped me fix my truck."

Tom's brow furrowed thoughtfully and then he remembered the young guy with the busted radiator hose and the pregnant girlfriend.

"I'll meet you at the office door," Tom said, and walked in that direction, still carrying the tire iron.

Through the windows he could see the kid was alone. And in the parking area behind him, the old SUV was recognizable. Tom unlocked the door.

"Have you got car trouble?"

The kid shook his head. "I'm a dad," he answered.

From his shirt pocket he retrieved a cigar. In the dim light of the office Tom could read the writing on the blue band. *It's a Boy!*

"Congratulations," Tom said.

"Thanks."

The young guy looked happy, eager and very, very young. In the garish overhead light, he looked thin and his clothes looked slept-in. His hair was shaggy and he hadn't shaved in a couple of days.

"I guess I didn't realize it was happening so soon," Tom said.

"She was due about Thanksgiving, so this is, like, way early. But he's okay. He looks really tiny, and he only weighs five pounds. But that's a decent size, the doctor told us."

Tom managed not to shake his head. Two kids who couldn't keep a car running were now going to be in charge of a five-pound preemie. He sure hoped they were tough enough to step up to the challenge.

"They grow fast," Tom told him, hoping to encourage optimism. "They don't stay that small for very long."

The kid nodded. "We named him Briscoe Andrew Garrity, Jr. Isn't that wild!"

Tom wasn't sure. Fortunately the kid explained.

"That makes me Briscoe Andrew Garrity, Sr. Me, a senior somebody." He chuckled as if it were very amusing.

"Well, good. Great," Tom said. It was the kid's cue to wrap it up and make his exit, but Briscoe wasn't doing that. Instead, his expression became more serious. He was hesitating as if he had something he wanted to say.

Tom waited.

"I...I wanted to tell you that we *did* get married," he managed finally. "And I think you were right about that. Kera never acted like she cared, but when we finally did it, she cried. Her mom cried, too, and her mom never liked me, not for a minute."

"Mothers-in-law can be like that," Tom agreed.

The kid nodded. "The husband thing is all good. When we went to the hospital and everything I got right in there. They made her mom wait outside, but I was there. I felt like...like a dad, I guess. More than I felt before. I can't really explain that."

Tom shrugged. "Some things don't need to be explained," he said. "It can be okay just to know them."

Briscoe appeared in agreement with that.

"Anyway, so now I got this wife and kid," he said, allowing his words to sort of drift off thoughtfully.

Tom recalled that moment in his own life. He'd been excited about it in anticipation. He'd thought he was so ready. But the sudden reality of it, the wave of weighty responsibility had been scary and unexpected.

"You'll get used to it," he told Briscoe. "It's like building a car from the frame up. If you think about all you'll have to do, it's overwhelming. But if you take it one bolt at a time and keep working, you can get it done."

The kid nodded as if taking in the sage advice.

"I've got a job," he said. "I deliver pizza. I can do that and the boss likes me okay, I guess. I make less than minimum wage, but I get to keep all my tips. So that's been fine."

Tom nodded in tacit approval.

"Kera's mom says we can live with her, as long as I pay

our share of the rent. But I worry, what if my car goes bad and I can't work? And, you got to know that sooner or later my car is going to go bad."

Tom figured that was probably right. Especially true as he knew the kid didn't have a clue about taking care of a vehicle.

"So, you want me to have a look at your car?"

"Uh…well, that would be great," Briscoe said. "But what I'd really like is a job."

"A job?"

"Yeah, I thought, 'wouldn't it be cool if I could learn how to work on my car and get paid for it at the same time.'"

Tom's jaw fell open. His instant reaction was incredulity. *Yeah, wouldn't that be cool, and wouldn't it be cool if every time he was hungry, hamburgers just started to fall from heaven.*

After that first sarcastic moment however, Tom considered it more seriously.

"Are you interested in cars?"

The kid was honest enough to shrug.

If a person doesn't grow up around guys who work on cars, then they never really learn anything about them. That was as true of Tom as it was of Briscoe. When he first went to Job Corps the only thing he'd known about cars was how to drive one. He wouldn't have pursued the career if Cliff hadn't been interested and urged him in that direction. But he'd learned. And he'd gotten good at it. Better than Cliff, better than lots of guys who grew up with a wrench in their hands. Briscoe couldn't be much older than Tom was when he worked on his first engine.

"Do you have any skills you can bring to my shop?" he asked the kid.

Briscoe looked momentarily disheartened, immediately followed by a reaction that was part defiance, part defensiveness.

"I'm not stupid," Briscoe stated with matter-of-fact directness. "And I'm not afraid of work. I dropped out of high school, but I thought about studying for my GED."

Tom barely managed to stifle a grin. *Thinking* about *studying* wasn't much of a recommendation. Still, the kid had gone ahead and married his girlfriend, just on the advice of a stranger. Maybe there was something there, something teachable, that a guy could work with.

"I've been kicking around the idea of taking on some help," Tom admitted. "But I'll have to talk it over with my wife. She and I are partners in this business and I count on her to be the levelheaded one and keep me straight."

Briscoe nodded.

"Come back tomorrow and I'll let you know what she thinks."

The relief and elation in the kid's eyes was evident.

"I'm not promising anything," Tom clarified.

"I get it," the kid said. "I'm not big on promises anyway. I'll be back tomorrow."

Chapter 15

THE TEARS HAD DRIED ON Erica's cheeks, but her heart still ached. The catharsis of confessing all her fears aloud was freeing, but her sister wouldn't allow her to wallow in her tears.

"You're talking crazy," Letty told her. "Tom is not cheating on you. He loves you. This is all about those stupid women at your job."

"I know it's about them," Erica admitted. "But that doesn't explain why he lied. Remember that comic's line, 'just because you're paranoid doesn't mean people aren't out to get you.'"

"I'm not saying they're not out to get you," Letty said. "But I am saying that Tom would never be a part of anything he knew would hurt you."

"That's what I keep telling myself," Erica admitted. "But what if I'm one of those wives who never saw it coming? One who gets completely blindsided by infidelity?"

"Oh," Letty said, feigning agreement. "You might be one of *those* wives as opposed to being a wife like our mom who always sees it coming even when it's not even on the horizon. I think she subconsciously encourages the men in her life to be unfaithful."

"She doesn't do that."

"I think maybe she does," Letty said. "If you enter a relationship already planning for the breakup, I think the outcome is inevitable."

Erica thought maybe her sister had a point, but they weren't talking about Ann Marie and her two-timing husbands. Her mother's love life was like an ongoing soap opera. Erica's marriage was a happily-ever-after. She didn't live from crisis to crisis.

"What am I going to do, Letty?" she asked. "I love him. I don't want to lose him. But I don't know if I can forgive him."

"Forgive him? Erica! Get ahold of yourself. You don't know that there is anything to forgive. I highly doubt it. And you should, too."

"But what about the lie and the flowers and the credit card and the shower? How do you explain all of that?"

"I can't explain it," Letty said. "I don't know anything about it. But Tom does and you've got to talk to him."

They had already covered this ground a couple of times. Letty was absolutely convinced that a heart-to-heart talk between husband and wife would solve everything. And the sooner that happened, the better for all concerned.

But Letty hadn't heard the sound of Tom's voice as he lied to Trish. Erica had heard it. She'd heard it perfectly. And the last thing in the world she wanted was to hear it directed at her.

Letty was sure it was all a simple misunderstanding that could be cleared up.

Erica hoped, desperately hoped, that her sister was right.

But knowing for sure, required taking the risk. Risk was fine for Letty or Ann Marie. Erica didn't take risks. She didn't like them.

What would happen if she confronted Tom and he confessed all? What would she do then? She would have to forgive him or leave him. Those were the only choices a wife had. And even if she chose to forgive, could a woman ever really do that? She wasn't sure.

Even more frightening was the realization that it wasn't all up to her. What if she confronted Tom and he was relieved to confess? What if the only thing keeping him at home was his fear of hurting her?

"Letty, it's just not as simple as you make it out to be," Erica hedged. "Marriage is a lot more complicated than you think."

"What I think is that you're letting silly gossip and mean-spirited nastiness poison what should be a happy, fulfilling time for you."

"My husband is lying. There is no excuse for that in a marriage," Erica stated without equivocation.

"Oh, really?" Letty said, sarcasm evident in her voice. "Then what about the money that you're secreting away? Mom is so proud of you for that. But in my book it sounds the same as a lie."

Erica didn't get to comment on that. When she glanced up she saw Quint standing in the doorway. The side of his face had pillow marks, as if he'd taken his anger to his room, only to fall into an accidental nap.

"Oh, hi, Quint."

She was still seated on the kitchen floor. Hurriedly she

wiped her cheeks to make sure that no telltale signs lingered there. Her son silently looked around the kitchen.

"What's for dinner?" he asked finally.

Dinner? Somehow she'd forgotten about dinner.

"Got to go," she said into the phone, one second before hanging it up. She stood and hurried to the refrigerator, casting one quick glance toward the clock. Tom would be home in ten minutes. This morning she'd planned to bake chicken, but it was too late for that now. She pulled open the pantry and rooted around for a moment, considering one thing and then another. Finally she pulled out a dusty jar of bargain red sauce.

"How about spaghetti?"

"All right!" Quint responded enthusiastically and pumped his fist in the air.

Erica managed a wan smile as she retrieved her pasta pot from the bottom cabinet and began filling it with water. Quint came up behind her and wrapped his arms around her legs.

"I'm not mad at you anymore, Mom," he said.

"Good."

"Are you mad at me?"

"No, of course not. Why would I be mad at you?"

Quint didn't quite answer that question, but his response suggested his reasoning.

"I'm...I'm sorry I made you cry."

Erica shut off the water and knelt down to take her son in her arms.

"You did not make me cry," she assured him. "I made myself cry."

"How come?"

"I...I..." Erica searched for the right answer. One that was true, but didn't draw her son into an adult world he didn't need to understand. "Someone said something at work and it hurt my feelings."

Quint's eyes widened. "Was it a bully? We learned all about bullies in kindergarten. Bullies like *intimidation*," her son said with great emphasis on the large word.

"No, not exactly a bully," Erica assured him. "Just a gossip."

"Is that worse?"

"No," she admitted. "But maybe it is just as bad. A gossip spreads stories that may or may not be true."

Quint's brow furrowed. "You shouldn't spread around stories that aren't true," he said. "You'd get in trouble for that in first grade."

"Yes, I suppose you would," Erica said.

"Maybe you should get in trouble when you do it at work, too."

Her son's wise advice put an actual smile on her face.

"I think you may be right about that," she told him. "Do you want to set the table for me?"

"Sure."

Tom was a bit late, making her last-minute dinner right on time. He arrived home, loving and happy and normal. He came into the kitchen to give her a big hug and a kiss. She turned her head slightly, pretending distraction, to insure that his lips made contact with her cheek and not her mouth. If he noticed, he didn't indicate it.

"Dinner smells good," he said. Then he nuzzled her neck. "You smell even better."

"Quint set the table," she said. "And he had a short nap, so he's probably going to have some energy."

"Quint, have you got energy?" he called out. "Can you loan me some?"

He was talking and laughing with Quint, feigning a sword

fight with an invisible light saber as he headed in to take a quick shower.

At least he's washing up at home, Erica thought to herself.

Over dinner Erica could hardly eat. She still felt shell-shocked. She closely observed her husband, looking for signs of duplicity, indications of guilt. She didn't see any. This should have comforted her; instead it made her wonder if he was better at hiding his feelings than she'd thought. Or perhaps his conscience didn't prick him. After all, he'd been raised among addicts and criminals. With no moral foundation, he could be completely unconcerned with vows of fidelity or the basis of trust.

You're talking about Tom, here, your Tom, remember.

Letty's word sounded loud in her memory. The rabbit hole where her thoughts were headed bore no resemblance to the man she'd been in love with for ten years. He was the most honest, conscientious, trustworthy man she'd ever met. And none of that was out of habit, it was out of deliberate choice. If he had become involved with another woman, there would be nothing casual or careless about it.

She watched him eat his unmemorable, mediocre meal with the gusto of a man who labored for a living. He was so carefree and full of life. He didn't seem at all like a man who was risking his marriage.

"So this kid came in this evening and asked me for a job," he said.

"A kid?" Quint asked eagerly.

"Not a kid like you," Tom clarified. "A kid like a teenager."

"Oh, you mean *figuratively* a kid," Quint said.

"Yes," Tom agreed, smiling at his son. "Figuratively he's a kid. But I *actually* want to hire him. I wanted to get your thoughts on it."

Erica's thoughts were a quick, knee-jerk no, but she managed to keep from voicing that aloud. She tried to refocus her attention from marital catastrophe to the subject of conversation, their business. Tom was thinking of hiring a new employee. Employees were necessary to the business, and without them the business couldn't grow and thrive. But they were also a liability. Hiring meant employees got paid even if receipts were off, or payments went uncollected. In a bad month it would be Tom and Erica who would have to scrimp by. The guys who worked for them would receive their usual wages.

"Do you think the business can support another guy?"

Tom sighed and shook his head. "Barely," he said. "We're doing about what we did last summer."

Erica nodded slowly. If the shop was putting through the same amount of work as a few months ago, then there was no explanation for all the overtime Tom was putting in.

"Do you think he could be a help to you?"

Tom shook his head. "Not anytime soon. The kid doesn't know anything about cars."

Erica's brow furrowed. "Then he's not the kid to hire. There are tons of teenagers with experience."

"I know," he agreed. "But I think I like this one."

Why hire someone who wouldn't cut down on the workload? That didn't make sense, unless Tom wanted the workload to continue to be an excuse.

"I met this kid right here, on our street," he said. "His car broke down."

Erica listened to the story, but her thoughts were swirling again. Why did everything he said feel suspect? Why did she search every word for hidden meaning? Because there was a lie between them and she was too much of a coward to confront it.

"He reminds me of myself," Tom said. "Not that he's anything like me. I guess I identify with his ignorance. I've been as dumb as he is now and I know how far he's got to go."

Tom chuckled at that. Erica could barely manage a smile.

"He's got a wife and newborn baby to support, so it's not like he'll be out partying at night and hungover at work. Of course, a guy can be just as tired after walking the floor with a colicky baby."

Erica nodded.

"I think it wouldn't be such a bad idea to have more staff as backup in case things change in the future," he said. "If one of the guys left us tomorrow, it would take time to replace him. It would be best to have another pair of skilled hands to count on. We can't afford more skilled hands, but we can get willing hands a lot cheaper. If the kid can listen to me and follow directions, at least I could count on that."

"Do you think one of the men might be leaving?" she asked.

That's when she saw it. A blush rushed to his cheeks and there was a hesitation in his speech as if to deliberately avoid stammering.

"No, no, of course not."

There was a lie somewhere in there. Erica saw it as clearly as she saw the uneaten spaghetti on her plate.

"Hector was off the wagon for a few days," he said. "He's sobered up and back to work now. So that's good."

Erica nodded. Tom still couldn't quite meet her eyes. There was something there and it wasn't about Hector.

"And you know how hard it is to keep Gus on task, even at best of times."

It wasn't about Gus, either. There was a lie that was eating at Tom and Erica was scared, really scared, that she might already know what it was.

Ask him. Ask him. Ask him! her rational brain demanded. *The worst thing is not knowing. Not knowing for sure.* But she was too afraid to take the chance. What if he confessed? He was a terrible liar, what if he just blurted out his infidelity, his betrayal. Could she forgive him? Could their marriage ever be the same? Or would she have to do what her mother had always done? Would she have to destroy it all to keep her self-respect?

Ask him! the voice in her head screamed at her. *It's better to know. Don't be that woman who looks like a fool. The one who lies to herself.*

"He's not going to work at my desk, is he?" Quint piped up. "Even if I like him, I gotta have my desk to do my homework after school."

Tom chuckled and the tension across the table shattered.

Of course he's not going to confess in front of Quint. She wouldn't even want him to. She would talk to him later. She would talk to him when they were alone.

"I couldn't let him have that desk," Tom assured his son. "That desk is for you and me. Briscoe would be working out in the shop."

"Okay then," Quint said, and then looked toward his mother. Erica realized that both of them were waiting for her to comment.

"Hire him if you think that's the thing to do," Erica said.

"I do. I do think it might help." The overlay of deception was back in her husband's voice, but it evaporated as he talked about his new hire. "It would certainly help him," Tom said. "I wonder all the time what my life might have been if I hadn't learned how to do something to earn a living."

Erica nodded absently.

"All I have—our home, our business, even you and Quint—would never have happened if I hadn't learned a trade," Tom said. "It's scary really, when you think about it. How the direction of your life can just turn on a dime and everything that happens thereafter is totally dependent on what you chose to do in that one situation, in that one moment. If I hadn't learned how to work on cars, I never would have stopped to help you. And without you, nothing else could have happened."

Erica watched his face and listened to his voice. There was nothing false or insincere in either one of them. He did love her, she was certain of it. And he valued her. But he still could have made a mistake. Did one mistake mean a change in life trajectory was unavoidable?

With her mother it had been. Yet despite all the family challenges Erica had had growing up, having Letty as her sister had made her childhood worth living. She would never have traded her for a "normal" family unit.

After dinner Tom and Quint cleaned the kitchen together. It sounded as if they were having a lot of fun that included a water fight. She could hear Tom's deep laughter and her son was screeching with joy. She would never do anything to put a wall between those two. It was as much a vow as a call to action. She wanted this family and she wasn't willing to let anything destroy it.

Erica was supposed to be working on her presentation for the EMR workshop, but her thoughts were so scattered that she quickly gave up. She took Tom's laptop from the coffee table and tried to distract herself with what had become her secret pleasure during the past few weeks—looking at washing machine reviews on the internet. She tried to get into the excitement of shopping. She was actually going to buy something she wanted and needed, but the concerns that continued to nag at her stole all of the pleasure out of her potential purchase.

Having had a nap before dinner, Quint was not easy to get to bed. They let him stay up an extra half hour. He showered forever and then talked Tom into reading him chapter after chapter.

Erica looked at websites on Tom's laptop until she thought she could write a thesis entitled: *Washers: A Comparison of Prices and Features on Standard Models.*

When she couldn't read another word about high capacity or spin effectiveness, she found herself reading news headlines and checking activity on the social networks.

Pulling up Tom's email was something she did with deliberate casualness. She knew exactly what she was doing and why.

She glanced through the subject headings, careful not to open anything. It was mostly notification of shipped orders with tracking numbers or responses to searches for hard-to-find car parts.

But one heading, right in the middle of what were obviously work-related messages, stabbed like a knife in Erica's heart.

Sounds like you are in love with Clara.

Erica eyed the sender. It was an email address she didn't recognize. She looked at the heading again. *Sounds like you are in love with Clara.* She hadn't read it wrong. That's what it said. Her heart was in her throat. She heard Tom's step in the hallway and she snapped the computer shut.

Tom walked into the living room. "Finally, Quint's sleeping. I thought I might have to read the whole book before he nodded off."

"Uh-huh." Erica nodded vaguely.

Tom came over and sat down beside her. She still had his laptop in her hands. He took it from her and set it on the coffee table. "Surfing the net?"

"Uh, yeah."

"Did you find what you were looking for?" he asked.

She had. She had found exactly what she'd been looking for. It was the kind of evidence that her mother would use in divorce court. But Erica looked into the eyes of her husband and knew that she wasn't her mother. She didn't want to confront her husband, she didn't want to accuse him or punish him. She wanted to keep him.

"Future view—The Bentleys," she said. "Five years from today."

Tom grinned at her. "Five years."

"Yes."

"Our small business loan will be paid off," he mused thoughtfully. "So that should be a big burden lifted."

"Uh-huh."

"Quint will be in middle school," he said. "So we'll probably be doing soccer or band concerts or science fairs. You know he's bound to be into something."

"Of course."

Tom stared off into space for a moment and then shrugged. "I guess I'm tired tonight. I can't think of anything else."

"Will you still be here with me?" Erica asked. The minute she heard the question leave her lips, she wanted to pull it back. But she couldn't.

Tom's expression was momentarily puzzled. Then a smile spread across his face and a bubble of laughter escaped his throat. "I will be unless this house burns down. And if we have to move into a tent in the backyard, I'll be there, too."

Erica felt an unreasonable sense of relief. She reached for him and began tugging at his clothes.

Tom began his workday whistling. *Nine years of marriage and his lovely, devoted wife still had some new tricks up her sleeve or, more accurately, in her jeans.* Erica had put a smile on his face last night, and it was still there this morning.

Today was Halloween and Quint was giddy with excitement. There would be a costume contest in his classroom and he was ready for it, dressed as Dracula with a knee-length black cape that Erica had fashioned from an old skirt and ninety-nine cents' worth of vampire teeth purchased at the supermarket. She was using her own makeup to paint his face. She dusted on some very, very pale base that seemed to drain all the color out of his face. Then she used eyebrow pencil to create wrinkles on his forehead. The dark, almost black lipstick applied to his mouth drew attention to his fang teeth, which he joyfully bared for his father while voicing the threat "I'm going to suck your blood!"

Tom thought his son looked more cute than scary, but he kept that opinion to himself.

Erica was in costume as well. With a black suit, black stockings and black shoes, all she needed to add was a pointy witch's hat and a broom to complete the outfit.

She was, Tom decided, the best-looking witch he'd ever encountered. And he told her so.

She thanked him with feigned casualness, but she was a little shy with him this morning. Tom thought that might be a good observation to have in the bridegroom's handbook. *You've outdone yourself in the sack when your wife can't meet your eyes without blushing.*

"I'm coming right home after work," he promised Quint. "I won't allow you out in the neighborhood sucking blood without me."

Quint giggled.

Tom kissed Erica on the top of the head. "I guess it's too late to warn you to behave," he said. "You cast a spell on me last night."

Erica's cheeks immediately flushed a vivid scarlet and she widened her eyes and gave a scandalized nod toward Quint. As if their six-year-old would some how figure out what mommy and daddy had been doing while he'd been fast asleep.

Tom winked at her. "See you this evening, witch," he said.

He was whistling on the road, all the way to the shop.

It looked like it was going to be a great day. All his employees showed up on time ready to work. Hector was quiet once again. He looked pale, Tom thought. His recent bender hadn't done him any good, that was for certain. Gus, on the other hand, appeared to be in a very lighthearted mood and was anxious to complete the job from the day before. Cliff was back to being strange and secretive.

And the newest member of Tom's team showed up looking clean shaven and, if not neatly pressed, at least mostly unwrinkled.

"You told me to come back today," he said, as if Tom might have forgotten their conversation of the previous evening.

He nodded to Briscoe, acknowledging their discussion. "I talked it over with my wife," Tom said. "We're going to give you a shot at this."

He saw the reaction in the young guy's shoulders that could only be relief.

"I'm starting you out at minimum wage, so I don't know that you'll do much better than you did at the pizza place," Tom said. "But if you work hard and show yourself to be able to learn, we may be able to do better."

"Okay," Briscoe said. "That sounds all right to me."

"You're on probation for the first couple of months," Tom said. "If it doesn't work out, then it doesn't work out. You may not like this kind of job or you might not be able to pick it up."

The young guy nodded, adopting a casual unconcern that was at odds with his eagerness.

"Let me get you a T-shirt with our logo," Tom said. "That'll make you look more official. And you need to get yourself a better pair of shoes, something that you can accidentally drop a transmission on without breaking your foot."

Briscoe looked down at his dirty sneakers and nodded.

Tom took him out and introduced him around. All the guys were initially friendly.

"Where'd you work before?" Gus asked him.

"Pizza Village."

The silence in response to that revelation was to be expected. Cliff gave Tom a look of disapproval.

"Briscoe is going to be a helper to all of us until he finds his feet. He's going to free you up to do the jobs you do best."

It was an overly optimistic interpretation, but he wanted all of them to understand that he wasn't taking on a new mechanic, he was just hiring a hand.

"I guess if we get hungry, we can always send him out for a fourteen-inch Supreme," Cliff said.

Gus snickered in appreciation.

"I don't expect he'll be rebuilding an engine by this afternoon," Tom said. "But he's young and willing to learn. I think we've all been there."

Tom's tone was deliberately stern. He wanted this to work and it wouldn't if the other guys treated Briscoe as if he wasn't part of the team.

"You can follow me around today," Tom said. "You'll get a chance to find out what these other fellows know soon enough."

For Tom, of course, the downside of having a new and untrained employee was that he would have to let the guy shadow him for the next few days, maybe for a few weeks. Even after that he'd have to watch him closely for a good long while. It was a risk and an inconvenience. But everything about business, especially a business with employees, involved risk and inconvenience.

He took Briscoe to the fourth bay.

The young guy whistled. "Nice car," he said.

At least the kid had some taste.

"You'll see a lot of nice cars here," Tom told him. "Not all of them will be in pristine condition. Some of them are going to be so modified that they're unrecognizable as the vehicle they started out to be. Some will look so rough, you'll wonder how they made it out of the junkyard. But no matter what they're like or what they've been, you can't disrespect them. They mean a lot to their owners, so they need to mean a lot to us."

Lovingly, Tom threaded his fingers through the Buick grill and opened Clara's hood.

Damn, I love this car, Tom thought to himself. Deliberately he pushed the thought away. It wasn't his car and it never would be. He was fixing it up for Guffy and she was going to sell it to somebody probably very far away. In fact, he'd received another email from the guy in Seattle who was interested in the Buick. Tom still thought the guy was a dealer, but he portrayed himself as simply the middleman for an interested buyer.

Tom leaned over the engine for a long moment before resuming his talk with Briscoe.

"My wife tells me that doctors have a motto, something like, 'First do no harm,'" Tom told him. "Here in my shop, I like to think the same way. If you're working over the side of the car, or on the front of the car, we don't want to be scratching the paint with a belt buckle or a dropped wrench or whatever. We always hang some padding for protection."

Tom indicated the pile of grease-and-oil-smeared fender protectors. The quarter inch of padding, covered by vinyl, had magnets sewn into the hem to help them cling to the car.

Briscoe followed the direction of Tom's gaze as if taking note.

"When we're washing things, we need to be careful, too. Harsh soaps and chemicals can be just as damaging to the finish as a metal tool. But when we're working with water, it's not like we can use a big old bath mat."

Briscoe nodded.

"So what I do is spray wax all around the edges of the engine, the tops of the fenders, and the front grille. This creates a barrier in case we have something splashing out."

Tom liberally sprayed the right side of the Buick with the wax and then handed the can to Briscoe. The younger guy applied it to the left side and the front grille. He worked much more slowly than he really needed to and Tom had to bite his tongue from rushing the kid. It was just wax and any excess would just be buffed off. But it was better that the guy was cautious than quick, Tom reminded himself.

Although it was hard to be patient, watching someone take ten minutes to do a job that Tom could do in two.

"That looks good," Tom said, once the waxing was done. "That's exactly how it needs to be."

With plenty of explanation and hands-on help, the two of them went through the proper steps for washing an engine. Tom mostly watched and supervised. However, he was also repeatedly interrupted by customers as people stopped by to leave their cars, inquire about the business or schedule service.

Tom kept a close eye on his new employee, not allowing any of the other distractions of his job to get in the way of what he was teaching the young guy to do.

As he watched Briscoe work, Tom's mind wandered. He recalled the previous evening with his wife and smiled. Erica was always good in bed. And if he was honest with himself, he'd have to admit he wasn't that difficult to please. Last night, however, there had been something new, something different.

When the two of them had first hooked up, she'd been hesitant and skittish. Erica hadn't trusted men very easily. Tom had played it safe to win her over. Still, she'd been pretty wide-eyed when it came to sexuality. That was okay with Tom. Vanilla was actually his favorite flavor. And if, like last night, it sometimes showed up with surprisingly hot and spicy toppings, so much the better.

It took the best part of an hour to wash and shine up the Buick's engine. But the convertible now looked as good under the hood as she did on the street. In fact, she looked good enough to show to the would-be suitor in Seattle. The guy would be a fool if he couldn't appreciate such a beauty.

Chapter 16

HALLOWEEN WAS, FOR MOST of the University Hospital employees, the best holiday at the hospital because it was the one holiday when everybody was on the job. And all these very serious adult people got the opportunity to behave like children. Doctors were writing notes wearing werewolf gloves, nurses were flitting from room to room with angel wings upon their backs. Funny shoes, pumpkin hats and candy corn were the order of the day.

In the Medical Records department, Mrs. Converse was a Dutch girl complete with wooden shoes, an apron and a bonnet. Rayliss was in a bee costume that showed off her legs while disguising her lack of waistline. Lena was a Southern belle in a hoop skirt that made it very difficult to sit in her cubicle. Darla wore her cheerleading uniform from her high school days. And Callie was some sort of vampire vamp with purple hair extensions and a frothy black-and-gray dress that seemed like some sort of ball gown/lingerie hybrid.

There was lots of laughter and camaraderie in the building, but there was also plenty of work to do. No one had the luxury of losing sight of that.

Erica was especially busy. Her in-box continued to provide an endless collection of charts. As well, her first workshop on electronic medical records was rapidly approaching, which was why Melody had decided to arrange a meeting.

Her coworker had been decidedly cool since the horrible lunch when some kind of indiscretion involving Tom had been suggested.

Erica assumed Melody was embarrassed to be associated with the group. Those same gossipy women had suggested things about her own husband, Gabe, in the past. Undoubtedly she understood exactly how that felt.

As a result Erica had expected a newfound bond between the two of them, but, so far, she hadn't seen any evidence of empathy.

Her Tom, her wonderful, loving, caring Tom, could not be having any sordid affair. And she chose to believe in Tom, to believe that he was true. Any shakiness in her faith in him had been overcome last night. Her husband may be having temptations, but Erica was sure that he'd not been with anybody else.

Still, there was something going on. And this "Clara" person could be a plant or even a fake identity, but Erica wasn't going to give up without a fight.

She and Melody laid out the syllabus on the conference table. They had a lot of material to cover and not that much time. Melody was dressed as some sort of sprite-like creature with gossamer wings. Erica didn't know if she was supposed to be Tinkerbell or a dragonfly, and she didn't ask.

"I don't know if we'll have time for this overview," Melody said. "Maybe we should just stick to the what and let them figure out the why on their own."

Erica shook her head. "Everything we know about training tells us that staff members comply better when they understand the reasons for doing it. Maybe we can borrow time from one of the other speakers."

"We can't cut Radiology or the Labs," Melody said. "Mrs. Maizika in Nursing is just terrible."

"Well, maybe we could cut her short," Erica suggested. "Just ten or fifteen minutes would be all we'd need."

Melody shook her head. "Think of the politics of that. Mrs. Maizika would have the Vice President for Nursing on the line before you even got off the phone."

Erica thought about that. Melody was probably right.

"Let me talk to Dr. Glover," she suggested. "I'll see if he can give us some of his scheduled time."

Melody looked up at her with surprise. "You're still talking to him?"

"Talking to him? Of course, I'm talking to him. That's part of my job."

The look on Melody's face was one of distaste. "Well, I'd never speak to him again," she said sharply. "But obviously I'm not you and I would never have gotten myself in that kind of situation."

Erica was confused. It seemed odd to put blame on Dr. Glover. The man might have been the catalyst for Callie's anger, but he certainly wasn't responsible for anything going on among employees of the Medical Records department.

"I like Dr. Glover," she told Melody. "It's not like I'm going to give up a relationship with him just because of something Callie did."

Callie had apparently lost her position on the EMR team

because she didn't keep her professional relationship with Dr. Glover professional enough. Erica knew from her own experience that Dr. Glover did want to be called Zac and talk like friends.

"Of course, he's partly to blame as well," Erica admitted. "But from my point of view, it was really Callie's responsibility to hold the line."

Melody raised an eyebrow, her expression disapproving.

"Anyway, I *am* talking to Dr. Glover," Erica stated flatly. "I can keep my remarks to less than ten minutes. I'll ask him if he'll let me have that."

Which was exactly what Erica did less than an hour later. It was her break time, but due to tons of trick-or-treat snacks everywhere, she had absolutely no need for anything to eat. She made a quick stop off at the ladies' room and then went downstairs to the Pharmacy.

As soon as she came around the corner, she saw Dr. Glover. He was standing at the counter tapping into a tablet-style computer. He was wearing his white pharmacist coat and through his head there appeared to be an oversize femur that went in one side of his skull and out the other.

He glanced up and smiled.

"Hello," he said. "To what do I owe the pleasure of this visit from…the Wicked Witch of the West?"

Erica grinned at him. "Not the Wicked Witch of the West, just the Less Than Nice Witch of Medical Records," she answered. "And what are you supposed to be?"

He reached up to touch his unusual head ornament and chuckled. "Pretty much what I am every day," he said. "I'm a bonehead."

Erica laughed as she was intended to.

"Have you got a minute? I need to ask a favor."

Dr. Glover was immediately serious. "One second," he

told her. She watched as he approached one of the other employees and then he disappeared into the back of the work area, only to reemerge through a nearby door marked Employees Only.

He'd removed the bone headband and was looking like his usual self. He was smiling, but his manner was cautious. She had asked him for a favor, she remembered. Maybe he thought it was a much more serious one than she wanted to put to him. They walked to an empty waiting area off the far side of the hallway that contained a half-dozen uncomfortable chairs.

"How is your workshop presentation coming along?" Erica asked.

"Mine?" He seemed surprised by the question. "I'm basically done."

"Do you think you could give me some of that time? I'm in the first slot with the welcome and the get-acquainted, and then I'm sharing a short overview of health data collection and inventory. I'm running long on content and short on minutes."

"Sure, I can do that. How much do you need?"

"Ten minutes," she answered. "Fifteen on the outside. When we're asking people to make such big changes in things that they've done every day for years, it's important to give them a clear understanding of why the change furthers the goals."

Dr. Glover nodded. "And you can do that in fifteen minutes?" His statement was both genuine and laced with humor.

Erica grinned at him. "I guess I've got to try," she said. "I'm just going to remind them that it's the 'why' that's important in the job and not the 'how.' In Medical Records, we chronicle the events of a person's lifetime. We do it because we know that to have any chance of moving forward in the right direction, caregivers have to understand where a patient, *a person,* has been."

Tom had promised to be on time and for once, it was going to happen. At the end of the day he hurried his guys off, but they didn't need a lot of persuasion. Gus hadn't really done a lick of work since about three o'clock. Hector was exhausted after spending most of the afternoon wrestling a damaged axle boot. Cliff had spent the day in a better mood. Tom hoped that was tied to anticipating Halloween with his kids.

Which was what Briscoe had been thinking and talking about all day.

One of Kera's cousins had shown up with a hand-me-down baby pumpkin costume. Briscoe was excited about taking it to the hospital, dressing his son in it and getting out of the NICU to trick-or-treat at the nursing station.

"You know he won't remember anything about this," Tom pointed out.

"But we'll have pictures," Briscoe said.

Tom hurried them all out and double-checked the lock on the gate before driving home. The evening's adventure was already in full swing. Little kids in disguises were going house to house, flitting in and out of the street at their own peril, their mamas and grandmas chasing after them with admonishments. Tom managed to slowly make it to his house without incident.

His wife and son were eagerly waiting in the kitchen. They both looked relieved when he walked through the door.

Quint's vampire cape had been given some quick repairs

after a hard day at school. Erica had changed out of her witch outfit into more comfortable jeans.

"Quint's already eaten everything I'm going to be able to get him to eat," she said. "I've got a plate of leftovers for you to stick in the microwave. Could you man the doorbell while our vampire tries to get candy from our neighbors?"

"Sure," Tom answered. "Do I have time to take a shower?"

Erica answered, "Yeah, of course."

But the crestfallen expression on his son's face said otherwise.

"I'll wash up in the sink. Why don't you two go ahead," he suggested. "Somebody might run out of candy."

Quint was horrified at the thought. "They don't run out, do they, Mom?"

"Not this early," she reassured him.

They headed off into the night while Tom attempted to clean up the worst of his workday grime. He was interrupted about every five minutes by another trio or quartet of princesses, dinosaurs or superheroes. When he finally felt degreased enough to eat, he heated his dinner. Seated at the table alone, he opened up his laptop and checked his email. He had a new inquiry on the Buick, but it was from an auto auction. They were impressed by the photos, and suggested that they could bring the owner a top price.

Guffy had already made clear that she wanted more control of Clara's fate than an auction could offer.

There was also another email from the dealer supposedly negotiating for a private customer. The guy was big on cutesy subject headings. This one read: Sleepless in Seattle Seeks Long-Term Relationship with Clara.

As he took a bite of his dinner, he examined the direction of his thinking. Did he not want her to sell the car? Being honest with himself, he really didn't. If he had his druthers, that car would never leave this town. And he'd do service on it for the rest of his life. But, of course, he didn't have his druthers. It was Mrs. Gilfred's car and she was ready to sell. He was pushing as hard as he could locally, but more than likely it would be a buyer from far away who would finally claim the old girl.

Tom found that inordinately sad, as if something really valuable, really special, was being ripped away. That was silly. It was just a car.

Once more he recalled being in the backseat of that unknown Buick with unknown people driving to an unknown location. He could see his sneakers perfectly. They weren't dirty and worn as they always had been during his childhood. These were new and clean and they were on his feet. These people had bought him the shoes. He suddenly knew that with complete certainty. Why? Who were they? Why had they done that?

Concentrating on the memory didn't bring it into focus. He just couldn't remember, and trying to do so only increased his frustration.

The doorbell rang again and he went to distribute more candy.

Quint and Erica arrived home a few minutes later. His son was excited about the impressive assortment of chocolate, lollipops and bubble gum in his bag. But he was also anxious to get to the party at the school gym where he was sure everything fun was happening.

Tom locked up, turned off the lights and they headed that way.

"There are like big kids who trick-or-treat, too," Quint was explaining to him. "Like from junior high or something. And they don't carry a sack with a pumpkin on it, they have pillowcases. Imagine that, Dad. A whole pillowcase just full of candy."

"Wow, that's a lot of candy," Tom agreed.

"Did you do that, Dad? When you were bigger than me did you ever get that much?"

Tom shook his head. "I never went on trick-or-treat."

"Never?"

"Never. I was in Mexico a lot. They don't do trick-or-treat there."

"That sucks."

"Quint!" Erica's voice was scolding. "I don't want to hear you say that. That's not a word we're going to use."

"Cody says it all the time," Quint complained. "He even says it to Mrs. Salinas. He told her that 'social studies sucks' and she didn't send him to the principal's office or nothing."

"I'm not Cody's teacher or his mother," Erica answered. "But I am yours and you're not going to use that word."

"Dad?" Quint pleaded for him to overrule.

Tom shook his head. "Your mom knows what words are best. So I won't say it if you won't, pardner."

Quint sighed heavily. "Well that...stinks. That stinks!"

"Yes, I guess it does," Erica admitted.

"But anyway, Quint likes big words," Tom said. "That one only has five letters. Five letters is nothing."

"Stinks has six," Quint announced, as if it were a personal victory.

Tom shot his wife a secret grin. He knew his son could not appreciate the ordinariness of his middle-class life, but Tom truly did. Quint might never understand how lucky he was. And that was the sweetest thing about having a childhood. Only those who missed it could really imagine its value.

The school gym was decorated with orange and black

crepe paper. There was music and games and snacks. Quint tossed some beanbags, spun a prize wheel and bobbed for apples. He took a turn in the "haunted house" set up within a maze of room dividers near the bleachers.

"It's kind of *baby* scary," he told Tom. "It's not really scary, but it was fun."

As Erica's attempts at makeup were long gone, Quint decided to get his face painted. The artist was surprisingly good putting a putrid green pallor on his child's face, white around the eyes to make them seem hollow and drips of blood trailing down from the sides of his red lips.

Looking at himself in the mirror, Quint was very impressed. "This is so cool. I'm like total vampire or something."

"Yes, you are," Tom agreed.

It took less than an hour for Quint to experience all the Halloween party had to offer. Erica suggested it was time to visit his grandmother.

"I'm sure Ann Marie has a special Halloween gift for you," Erica said. "And you know how much she'll love your Dracula costume."

Quint was easily persuaded.

Tom kept a smile on his face, as if he were delighted about the visit as well.

The thing about Ann Marie was that she was definitely not Erica. Tom saw her as a different version of his own mother. Always distracted by her ever dramatic relationships with men, nevertheless, she had a great sense of what families *should* be doing. And when it came to holidays, a visit to see her was nonnegotiable. Tom didn't mind that. In truth, he liked having obligations to fulfill. Ann Marie didn't like him very much. But that didn't bother him. She thought her daughter could have done better. Tom kind of agreed with her. Erica could have had any man she wanted. He felt extremely lucky that she'd wanted him. And if other men might have been better able to provide for her, no one else would ever love her or value her more than he did. He was certain of that.

Back in the car the three of them carefully picked their way through the neighborhood, deliberately avoiding Donaldson Avenue where the annual street party would be getting into full swing.

Without incident they made it into Monte Vista, where the boulevards were wider and better lit.

The front walk of the house was lined with long rows of jack-o'-lanterns and the seating area on the porch was swathed in fake webs and giant spiders. Melvin was doling out the candy along with tongue depressors advertising his son's medical supply store.

"Oh, you look so scary!" Ann Marie raved about Quint's costume. "Doesn't he look scary, Melvin?"

"Very frightening," the old man agreed.

"And the makeup is perfect, absolutely perfect," Ann Marie said. "I know your mother didn't do that."

"I had my face painted at the Halloween carnival at my school."

"Well, you look so impressive, I don't want to mess you up," Ann Marie told him, offering her usual air kiss as a greeting.

"I look impressive," Quint repeated.

"Let's take this vampire out to knock on some doors," Ann Marie suggested.

"Quint's already done trick-or-treating in our neighborhood," Erica told her.

"In *your* neighborhood?" her mother said disparagingly. "In your neighborhood they only give out jawbreakers and caramelos. In these houses he'll pick up actual chocolate bars or better. The Warricks across the street are giving out tickets to Sea World."

Quint's eyes got as big as saucers. "Oh, Mom, can I go there? I wanna go to Sea World. Can I please?"

Erica rolled her eyes at her mother, but agreed to let Quint go.

Ann Marie wanted to take Quint herself, but Erica decided to go with them rather than worry the whole time they were gone.

Tom took a seat on the chair next to Melvin. He liked the old guy. Much superior, he thought, to Ann Marie's last husband who Tom had only met once toward the end of their short marriage. Erica tended to give all her mother's husbands the benefit of the doubt. And she undoubtedly knew better than Tom but, still, he sensed Melvin was a cut above Ann Marie's typical catch.

"I've got some sodas here in the cooler," the older man offered. "Or there's probably a beer in the fridge if you want one."

"Soda's fine," Tom told him. "I only drink beer on hot days or after I mow the lawn."

Melvin chuckled. "It's not my favorite either, but it is certainly the social drink of South Texas."

He handed Tom a wet can of soda.

"How's everything?" Melvin asked.

"Good," Tom answered. "We're making the adjustment with Erica going back to work. So far, that's been working out fine. She likes her job and Quint's doing okay hanging out at the shop in the afternoons. It seems to be working."

"How are things with the business?"

"Going okay," Tom answered. "I just hired somebody new. He's a helper, not a mechanic. I can't really afford another mechanic, but I've been having some serious absentee problems the last couple of months, so I needed some help. Either that or work sixteen-hour days."

"That can be rough," Melvin said.

Tom nodded. "I don't mind doing them," he said. "Long hours means more business, more business more money, and that's a good thing. But I can't do it every day. I don't want to do it every day. I want to be with Erica and Quint. Erica's the center of my life. And Quint, he's growing up fast. And you can't get that back."

"True."

"Still, I like what I do," Tom admitted. "And if you've got that, if you do work that you're proud of, it makes a difference."

Melvin nodded. "And all those beautiful cars you get to be with, that's just a nice plus."

Tom laughed and took a swig of his soda. "You are right about that. I've got a beauty in the shop right now. I'm selling her on consignment and I can barely stand to part with her."

"Oh, yeah?"

"Fifty-six Buick Roadmaster, a convertible with a continental kit. It sounds like a cliché, but she's a one-owner by a little old lady in Leon Valley."

"And she only drove her to church on Sundays?"

Tom shook his head at Melvin's question. "I think she had a bit more fun with her than that. But she was in really good condition when I got her. Now I've put her even closer to perfect and I've shined her up like a new penny."

"It sounds like it was a labor of love," Melvin said.

"It felt like it, too," Tom agreed. "She reminds me of something. Back when I was a kid I rode in a car just like her, but I can't recall where exactly or when, but it was a really happy time, a celebration or something."

Tom paused, once more trying to recall this vision from his past. He shook his head in failure.

"Anyway, I think that's why the car appeals to me. Because of something I wish I could remember."

"Oh, I hate that," Melvin said. "When you almost have the memory, but you just don't quite. It's in your head somewhere, but you can't roll it out on demand. That gets worse with age, you know."

"Well, if I'm already suffering from it, my future doesn't look too bright," Tom joked. "Still, I love that Buick."

"I guess you're not that eager to sell her."

Tom shrugged. "The owner's giving me a nice commission. And when it happens I'm going to buy my wife a new fancy washer and dryer. The rusty old buckets she's trying to work with now are beyond fixing."

Melvin was quiet, thoughtful for a moment. "Does she know you're planning to buy that for her?"

"No, it's a surprise. Selling cars is not part of the business, it's really an extra. And I figure the extra money probably ought to be spent on stuff for the family, not just plowed back into the business."

Melvin nodded.

A group of children, with parents in tow, came racing up the walk. Melvin doled out the candy and tongue depressors. Every child said thank-you before hurrying off to the next destination.

"So, are you interested in buying a really beautiful Buick convertible?" Tom asked when they were alone again.

The older man laughed. "I'm not really an auto collector kind of guy. I've got more vehicles in my garage than I can drive. And I haven't even opened up a hood in twenty years or more."

"I'll throw in free maintenance for the life of the car," Tom said.

"Really?"

"I'd love to," he confessed. "I'd like nothing better than to get to work on this beauty for the next fifty years."

"Why don't you buy her yourself?" Melvin asked.

Tom shook his head. "You know better than that, Melvin," he said. "This is a rich man's hobby. I'm a regular family guy with a small business and a lot of obligations."

"It could be an investment."

"Collectibles are not like other investments, they are not money in the bank. You can only get out of them what someone is willing to pay," Tom said.

Melvin chuckled. "Have you looked at money in the bank lately?" he said. "It's not that much of an investment, either."

Tom laughed along with him, which was all a guy could do these days with the uncertainty of the current recession.

"The most sage advice from brokers and speculation experts is to put your money into commodities that you understand," Melvin told him. "Classic cars are your business. You're involved in that market much more closely than the average guy."

"Maybe so," Tom agreed. "But a guy would have to be able to view the car as little different than cold, hard cash on the hoof. He couldn't be emotionally involved with it. I am so…so nuts about this car. It reminds me of something I just want to hold on to. That makes it not an investment, but an expensive souvenir."

Melvin tutted disapprovingly. "You are too hard on yourself, Tom," he said. "I own the apartment building where my parents lived, where I grew up. That old brick place has a million memories of family and holidays and I think of it every time I remember my father, my mother or my brother, all long dead. It's a piece of investment real estate that I just happen to care about, and it is something I want to keep."

Tom nodded thoughtfully, then answered. "I have a great kid and a woman I love. I'd never jinx that by being greedy for more."

"It's not greedy to try and look ahead," Melvin said. "It's smart. Anybody who buys that car is going to be looking at it more or less the same way you are. They're wanting to enjoy it while driving it around, with hopes that it will rise in value as time goes on."

"Right," Tom agreed. "But that buyer will likely have a lot more disposable income than I do."

"Maybe so," Melvin agreed. "But he won't have as much control of his asset as you would. Every hiccup in the engine, every minute of road wear, every scratch that gets on the door panel adds to the cost of his investment. Most likely he'll have to pay somebody to keep it running, pay somebody to keep it looking good, maybe even pay somebody to safely store it."

Tom nodded. "Yeah, I guess so," he said. "Even those collectors who have big warehouse garages mostly hire help to keep the cars maintained and driven on a regular basis."

"All of that you'd be able to do yourself," Melvin pointed out. "You're not just able to do it, you're eager to do it. There is value to that. And I'm not just talking intangible value, which is a lot, but actual dollars and cents."

"Still, it's buying and owning a classic car," Tom said. "That's not something a working man should do."

Melvin shrugged. "Unless maybe a working man can figure a way to make it pay."

Chapter 17

CALLIE RETURNED FROM sick leave and either Mrs. Converse didn't know or didn't care about the rumored cause of her absence. The mood in the department returned to normal. Or perhaps even better than normal. Callie seemed a little full of herself and a bit condescending to Erica. Deliberately Erica decided not to notice.

At the noon lunch table almost nothing had changed.

"Did you hear the one about the guy who got a call from the lawyer?" Rayliss asked.

Erica glanced up, as did everyone at the table.

"The lawyer told him, 'I've got some good news and some bad news.'"

Rayliss was grinning broadly. She had the attention of the whole table. "The good news is that your wife found a picture that's worth at least a million dollars. 'Wow, that's great,' the guy says. 'What's the bad news?' 'The bad news is, it's a photo of you screwing her best friend.'"

Everybody laughed as they were expected to. Everybody except Melody, of course. The woman haughtily looked down her nose at her coworker. "Why on earth would you people think that is funny?" she asked. "It is mean-spirited and slightly sick."

"It's a joke," Callie explained with deliberate coldness. "Humor is good for people. It's good for us."

"Taking delight in other people's misery is not humor," Melody said. "My husband, Gabe, says that it's evidence of low intellect and I should avoid it."

"By all means, avoid it," Rayliss said.

"Yeah," Callie agreed. "Avoid it, avoid us. In fact, I think I'd prefer that. You've really been pretty high on yourself since you got me bounced from the EMR workshop. But the truth is, I don't care. Teaming up with you has become a pain. Erica is welcome to it."

Callie's annoyance proved that Melody had been partially right about her. She was not happy about Erica taking her place. And if Melody was right about that, maybe her other suppositions about Callie weren't quite as wild as they seemed. Erica felt herself being drawn back into the fear and doubt. She couldn't just sit there and let that happen. She couldn't listen to another word.

"Excuse me," Erica said, rising to her feet. "I think I'll take this food back to my desk."

She didn't wait for reactions. She left the table and walked back to the Medical Records department.

Mrs. Converse was in her office, thumbing through a professional journal and munching on a sandwich. She glanced up but didn't invite Erica in. Perfect. Erica decided Mrs. Converse had the right idea. Better to eat lunch alone than to get drawn into the gossip and petty office politics that could so easily turn on anyone.

At her cubicle, Erica spread her napkin across her lap and surveyed her salad. She couldn't quite shake the fears she fought against. She needed reassurance and decided to get it from the one person who really had it to offer. She dug her cell phone out of her purse and called Tom.

"Hey, babe," he answered on the third ring. "I love hearing the sound of your voice."

"That's why I called," she told him. "So you could hear the sound of my voice when I wasn't scolding my son or arguing with my mother."

"Ann Marie only wants the best for you," he answered.

"Which I think can be summed up as marrying a wealthy doctor and taking him for all he's worth," Erica replied.

Tom feigned a long-suffering sigh. "I'm not a doctor, but I can play one when we get home."

"Are you requesting a V72.3?"

"I'm like an art illiterate," he said. "I don't know the codes, I just know what I like."

Erica laughed. "I wish we could just go home and play all afternoon."

Tom tutted. "Now, now, we're got to keep up our working class work ethic so we can pass it on to our son."

"Yeah, I know," she answered. "What do you want for supper? Do you think you'll be home on time."

"No, I'll probably be pretty late. Go ahead and fix Quint something he likes."

Erica hesitated. Her pulse began pounding in her throat.

"Is Hector out again today?" she asked.

"Oh, no," Tom answered. "You know how he is. Once he'd dried out it's months, maybe years, before he messes up again."

"You just have a lot of extra work?"

"Not too much," he said. "Mostly I'm slow because I'm training Briscoe."

"I thought he was supposed to make it better, not worse," Erica said.

"He is. And he will. But not quite yet."

"Okay. I understand," she said. "Maybe I should fix a plate and bring something up there for you."

"No, don't bother. I'll get something. Besides, I have to go out and see a customer."

A hard knot formed in Erica's stomach. It made her a bit queasy.

"What kind of customer do you have to see after hours?" she asked.

"Oh, I don't *have* to see her after hours. I could go to see her during the day," Tom replied. "But it's hard to get away. And I hate to leave these guys unsupervised."

"Let Cliff take charge, he's the one to do that when you go to pick up Quint."

Erica heard it then. Her husband didn't say one word, but the lie that came through the phone receiver was loud and clear. There was definitely something he was not telling. Something he was keeping from her. And whatever it was, it was not good.

"Cliff's not really that good at taking charge," he managed finally. There was not one syllable of conviction in his statement. Erica wanted to call him on it, but she was too afraid.

"Okay, then," she said. "I'll see you when I pick up Quint and then...well, I'll see you when I see you."

"Right."

"Guess I've got to go," she said.

"Okay, love you," he said.

"I love you, too," she told him before clicking the end button.

Erica sat there for a long moment, staring at the plate of food on her desk. A million thoughts were scrambling in her brain all at once and she didn't want to focus on any of them.

Her husband was meeting a customer after work. The customer was a she. Her husband was lying to her about something. And apparently he would rather spend the evening with somebody else than with her.

She took the plate of food and dumped it into her trash can. Then she stared at her empty desk. Was this how her mother had felt? This sense of disconnection with the world around you. Was that what had kept her mother so distant?

Erica picked up her phone. For a long moment she actually considered calling her mother. But she managed to resist the impulse. She called Letty instead.

When her sister picked up, she was obviously eating lunch as well and in a place that was busy and noisy.

"Could you babysit for me tonight?"

"Tonight's not the best," her sister said. "I was going to work on my nanowire transistors project."

"The nanowires will have to wait," Erica insisted. "I've... I've got something critical I have to do."

"Oh, okay." Letty's voice was hesitant, curious.

"Come over to my house this afternoon as soon as you can," Erica said. "Wait, go by and borrow a car from Mr. Schoenleber."

"Borrow a car from Melvin?"

"Tell him...tell him that your car is messing up and that Tom can't work on it until tomorrow, but that you need to go somewhere tonight. He'll be okay with that."

"What is going on?"

"Don't ask a lot of questions, Letty. Just do what I ask you. I need a car that won't be recognized. You know I'd do it for you."

"Oh my God, you are having a Mom incarnation."

"No, of course not."

"You are. I know you are. What are you planning? Are you going to stake out Tom's workplace or follow him?"

"A little of both."

"Don't do it, Erica. He loves you. You've got to trust him. Don't do it."

"I have to. I can't not know. I just have to."

Erica could hear other women returning to the department. "I can't talk now," she said. "Just get the car and be there."

Her sister reluctantly agreed and, in fact, when Erica and Quint arrived home, Letty was standing in the driveway next to a gray minivan that Melvin's business used for cargo.

"You didn't tell me Aunt Letty was coming to play with me," Quint said excitedly.

"It's a surprise. Just promise me you won't drive her crazy and that you'll go to bed on time."

Her son promised sincerely, but she was pretty sure he'd completely forgotten about it by the time they got into the house.

He and Letty were playing in his room, while Erica picked out a dinner menu of frozen fish sticks, spinach and mac and cheese. While the water was boiling, she went into the bedroom and changed into what she hoped could be described as nondescript clothing. She wore dark jeans, a black knit shirt and a jacket. Erica put her hair into a knot on the top of her head and then covered it with a San Antonio Spurs ballcap. She put on sunglasses and looked at herself in the mirror. She could have been anybody, she decided. She also might as well have been blind. The dark glasses were too dark for indoors. They'd be even worse at night. She took them off then looked through the drawer until she found a pair she didn't like as well. With the help of a rattail comb and some nail clippers she managed to break out the lenses. Then she put the empty frames on her face and looked in the mirror again.

"Harry Potter," she said aloud. "Now what I really need is my invisibility cloak."

It was then that her sister came into the bedroom. "Oh, wow, this is totally serious, isn't it? You've turned into Mom."

"No, I'm still me. I'm just me being careful and not being stupid," Erica said.

Letty shook her head. "You are not this person," she insisted. "You do not stalk the people you love, trying to get dirt on them."

"I'm not looking for dirt," Erica assured her. "I'm looking for truth. That's it. I know that he's lying to me and I can't stand it. I have to find out the truth."

Her sister shook her head. "What's that Lincoln quote?" Letty said. "If you look for the bad in people expecting to find it you surely will."

"I'm going to do this," Erica said. "Making me feel guilty about it is not helpful."

"I *really* wish you wouldn't," her sister said.

"I don't know what time I'll be back. Thanks for doing this and for getting the car."

"I picked it out deliberately," Letty said. "Melvin wanted me to take the BMW, but I thought this thing looked a lot more like something a stalker would drive."

It did. And despite her sister's sarcasm, it was exactly the vehicle Erica needed. Letty was not happy. But Erica didn't have time for her disapproval. She hurried out to the driveway.

Her plan, as much as there was of it at least, was to watch the shop until Tom left and then follow him to see where he went. Beyond that, she didn't let her mind wander. She just needed to see where he went after work.

She drove the gray minivan to the shop and just as she got close she lost her nerve and drove right by. Two blocks later she turned around in a parking lot and went back. She passed by once more, but this time more slowly. Tom always parked his truck in the back, so she couldn't know for certain that he was still inside. But there was obvious activity going on, with two of the bay doors open.

She needed a place to park which would be close enough to see, but far enough away that no one would notice her. She found it across the street and fifty feet south of the Bentley entrance, directly in front of an *aguas frescas* stand. The site was perfect for easy access and line of sight. It wasn't so perfect if one were trying to be discreet. A half-dozen Hispanic guys sipped *tamarindos* or *sandías* in the chairs or on the benches in front of the tiny building. A lone *gringa* sitting in a minivan wouldn't go unnoticed.

At first Erica thought she would simply ignore them. After more than few curious looks, she decided to become just another customer. She got out of the car and went up to the screened serving window to order. As she waited, she worried that Tom might suddenly drive away from the shop and she'd be unable to catch up with him. Nervously she stood on one foot and then another as the slowest Mexican woman on earth moved around in a space no larger than a good-size closet.

Erica was about to just say *Forget it* and leave, when the old lady lifted the screen and slid a cold, wet bottle of *horchata* and a slurpy straw in her direction. Erica paid for the drink, carefully counting out the correct change so she wouldn't have to wait and then hurried back to the minivan.

She caught the sight of movement at the shop's entrance and her heart was in her throat. Gus was leaving. When he turned his car toward her, she kept her head down, not wanting to be recognized.

Cliff took off next. Erica expected him to pass by as well, since that was the direction that took him home. But he turned up the street instead and she was glad there was no chance for him to catch sight of her.

Erica sipped her drink. She was jittery. The SUV belonging to the new guy, Briscoe, came out next. And then Hector.

Erica's heart was racing.

She watched the Bentley entrance, expecting at any moment to see her husband's truck emerge.

The afternoon sun was pouring down on the metal roof of the minivan, making it hot. Erica started up the engine just long enough to lower windows, hoping to catch a breeze floating by. Her drink, a kind of cinnamon-flavored rice milk, was rich and tasty, but she was wishing she'd made a lighter, cooler choice.

She was beginning to think Tom had left early. Maybe he'd been gone before she even got there. Then she reminded herself that he would not leave the gate open like that. If he were gone, the business would be locked up and secure. It was not, so he must be there. She sipped her drink.

Erica hadn't taken her eyes off the place, yet when her husband pulled out of the driveway onto West Avenue, she was caught up short. She jerked into action, spilling the last of her *horchata* on her jeans. Her immediate reaction was to try to clean it up, which got the sticky substance on her hands, which then got it on the steering wheel.

She glanced up the street. He was going to get away. Quickly she put the minivan in Reverse and stepped on the gas. A horn blared and she braked, as a fast-moving low-to-the-ground vehicle swerved around her. She heard someone yell out a rude female epithet.

"Sorry," she answered to the universe in general.

A minute later she was racing in traffic, trying not to be left behind. Erica was praying she would not get delayed by a red light. At the first two intersections her luck held, then she ran through on a yellow.

Then she got trapped behind a poky old grandma in an aging Crown Vic, and decided she had to pass on the right. But just as she successfully got in that lane to pass, she saw Tom's truck a half block ahead of her turning left onto the freeway.

Erica cursed loudly and put the pedal to the metal and, at the last minute, was able to zip over in front of another car to make the turn. This earned her a one-finger salute from an irate driver.

Once on I-10 she was able to easily accelerate beyond anything she would have ever done with her son in the car and catch up to her husband, who was cruising at the speed limit. She made the 410 interchange one-and-a-half car lengths behind him and followed him west for another couple of miles until they exited at Bandera Road. The traffic here was nearly bumper to bumper as Leon Valley residents made their way home from jobs and school and shopping. Erica used the stop-and-go driving conditions as an opportunity to find the wipes in her purse and tried to clean up the spilt *horchata* that was now a major part of her fashion statement.

Tom turned off into a subdivision of aging '60s dream

houses. Erica held back a little as he made several turns un-erringly, obviously knowing his way around.

When Erica turned a corner, she found that he'd pulled to a stop in front of a house further down the block. She parked, too. She didn't really need the shade of the syca-more she'd pulled under, but she hoped it made the minivan looked less conspicuous than if she was next to the sign pole on the corner that read Helm Street.

Apparently she needn't have worried. Tom got out of his truck, and without even one guilty glance around strode up the walk.

He was flagged down midway by an older heavy-set woman who'd apparently been sitting on the porch next door. Tom stood and talked to her for several minutes. An-other woman walked by with her dog. She waved at the two of them, but it was only Tom who waved back.

Did everybody on Helm Street know him? He must come up here all the time. Erica tried to put the brakes on that thought. He might have lived around here during one of his foster home placements, she suggested to herself. Or maybe…or maybe…

Erica couldn't think of another excuse. But she was wish-ing she'd brought binoculars. Tom began to head toward the front door of the house but the older woman was still talking to him. He slowly but surely kept putting distance between them. Finally he gave her a little wave and climbed the front steps to ring the doorbell. It was loud enough for Erica to hear it all the way down the street. He waited a couple of minutes, cooling his heels on the front porch.

That's an old female trick, Erica thought to herself. Making them wait was supposed to hone a man's ardor. Cause him to desire you that much more.

Finally somebody opened the door, but Tom's body was

in the way and Erica couldn't see who it was. She unhooked her seat belt and quickly climbed over into the passenger seat attempting to get a better look, but to no avail. Then, Tom walked inside and the door closed. Erica sat there.

The old woman who had spoken to Tom in the yard was leisurely making her way back to her own house. Then abruptly she turned down the driveway that divided the two properties.

Erica sat in the minivan.

She began to wish she hadn't drunk the *horchata*. And not just because the spill had caused her jeans to adhere uncomfortably to her thighs. She needed to go to the bathroom. But if she left, she might miss Tom's departure. She might miss the chance to see the woman he was with.

In the wild fear of her own imagination she could picture the scene now: Tom would emerge from the front door, disheveled. Behind him a busty beauty wearing only a see-through negligee and fur mules would hurry after him, loath for him to leave. She'd throw her arms around him for one last passionate kiss. Then Tom would press the woman, this stranger, up against the wall, the way he had done with Erica just three nights ago, and have sex with her right there.

"Stop it!" she demanded of herself aloud.

Under no circumstances would Tom have sex with some strange woman on her front porch.

Erica continued to sit and watch and plan her next move, but she really needed to go to the bathroom. The street had to be one of the most boring in America. A few people came home, parked in their driveways and went into their houses. She saw one more dog walker. And witnessed a package delivery down the block. Nothing was happening and she had to go to the bathroom.

Erica wondered about her mother and how she had done

this very thing. How had she sat in unfamiliar neighborhoods waiting in silence as she imagined her husband with another woman?

Unpleasantly Erica recalled the incident when she'd first realized that her mother had tapped their phone. Erica had joked about an indiscretion at a party and her mother had cautioned her about it.

"You listened to my private calls!" Erica had accused.

"Believe me it's much more of a chore than a pleasure," her mother answered. "I record it all and browse though it while I'm exercising at the gym."

"That's illegal," Erica challenged.

"I pay for the phone, I can record conversations on it if I want," Ann Marie said. "I don't know why you're so upset. I didn't deliberately spy on you."

"Why are you spying on anybody?"

"I'm a wife," she'd answered. "If I'm not proactive, then I'll get played."

Erica crossed her legs and was shaking her foot to distract herself from the need to pee. She wanted to call Letty. She wanted to talk to her sister, share this crappy miserable moment with her, the way they'd shared so many crappy miserable moments in the past. But she didn't. Letty was against this. If Erica called, her sister would tell her to get out of there.

Perhaps she should leave, Erica thought. She'd found out what she wanted to know. She'd found out where Tom was spending his evenings. What more did she need to know?

She needed to see the woman. She needed to see Tom with her.

The sun was now cutting through the trees in colors of brilliant orange. It would be dark soon, very soon. And unless the lovers had the good sense to turn on the porch light, Tom's retreat would be completely shadowed.

"Okay, time to make a move," Erica announced aloud to herself.

She put on her jacket and raised her collar to disguise her profile. She pulled the bill of the baseball cap lower on her face and opened the door of the minivan. She stepped outside and glanced around furtively. No one was observing her. She locked the vehicle and put the keys in her pocket before stealthily crossing the street. Not a soul in sight. In the distance she could hear the sound of traffic, but it was far away and her footfalls on the pavement made almost no noise at all.

As she approached the house, she saw that it was longer than it was wide. From the driveway beside it she could see only one light shining out from a pair of windows. Beneath those windows was a hedge of overgrown nandina. Erica realized immediately that she could hide in the cover of that hedge and peek into those windows.

She hesitated. Was she into window peeping now? She didn't want to be this person. But she had to know. And she couldn't wait much longer, she had to go somewhere to pee.

Glancing around once more, she headed down the driveway, carefully keeping to the shadows of the house. She slipped in between the hedge and the house and took her first glance through the window. She saw Tom.

He was sitting at a table with a plate of food in front of him. He was talking, laughing. His fork paused in the air, his conversation directed at someone else in the room. Someone that Erica couldn't see. She had to move farther down the hedge to be able to get a full view of the room. She took a couple of slow, silent steps in that direction and was surprised to find the old woman she'd seen from the house next door crouched down peeping in the same windows.

The two women, shocked, stared at each other's faces for only a half an instant. Just long enough for Erica to recognize her. The woman, of course, did not recognize Erica. She began screaming at the top of her lungs.

Erica heard movement inside the house. She turned and ran. No stealth and shadows now. She sprinted up the street as if all the demons of hell were after her. She heard the front door of the woman's house slam against the siding as it was thrown open. That wasn't the only door. Porch lights all over the neighborhood were going on and husbands, fathers, sons and brothers were rushing outside. Erica reached the minivan and fumbled for the keys in her pocket. Frantically she looked back the way she'd come to see that most of the would-be rescuers had rushed toward the sound of the screaming. She did hear somebody holler and saw somebody pointing in her direction.

She got the key into the door lock and got it open. Inside she fumbled for the ignition. Once the engine had turned over she jerked the transmission into Drive and made a quick, wide U-turn that involved bouncing over the curb. As soon as she was on the road, she accelerated sharply, leaving a strip of rubber on the road and the screech of tires in her wake. Erica's heart was pounding. She was cursing her stupidity. She was desperately trying to drive slowly and unsuspiciously. After a couple of turns, she realized that she was lost in the subdivision. And somewhere in the last two minutes, she'd peed herself.

Tom was still yawning as he walked into the kitchen the next morning.

"Shower's empty," he announced.

"I took a bath last night before I went to bed," Erica answered without turning to face him.

On the way to the coffeepot, he planted a kiss on the back of her head. "You're fixing eggs this morning? It really smells good."

Tom poured the first cup of the day and savored it. The first sip was far and away the best. It just made the mornings start out right.

"Do you want me to put toast in?"

"Sure."

The bread was already on the counter and he loaded it into the toaster and pushed down the lever. "Sorry I was so late getting in last night," he said. "You'll never believe what happened."

When Erica didn't respond or comment, he figured it must be a critical moment for the sunny-sides.

"I was at my customer's house and apparently she's got a next-door neighbor who is a busybody and she wanted to know who was visiting, so she decided to peek into the windows." Tom shook his head as he thought of it. "So while this old gal is looking in, a *real* Peeping Tom shows up. Unbelievable!" Tom laughed at the memory. "So the woman lets out this bloodcurdling scream. If I was an older guy I would have had a heart attack."

The toast popped up and Tom got the butter out of the refrigerator.

"It's funny now, but it sure wasn't funny last night," he said. "For a single woman living alone, the idea of some guy looking in her windows is scary. So we called the police."

Erica carried a plate of eggs to the table. Tom followed with the toast and seated himself.

"They weren't able to catch the guy," Tom continued. "The cops didn't actually show up for twenty minutes. But they got a description from the crazy lady next door and the other neighbors who saw him driving off. He looked like a teenager with glasses and a ball cap. He was driving a minivan, probably his parents'."

"Did anybody get the license number?" Erica asked.

"No," Tom answered. "It all happened pretty fast and he was parked up the street."

Tom took a bite of his eggs. They were cooked exactly as he liked them. "Mmm, these are great," he said.

Quint came bouncing in and sat down in front of his own breakfast. "Can I wear the new shirt that Aunt Letty and I made?" he asked. "It's not a new shirt, really. It's a shirt I had. But Aunt Letty wrote my name on it in glue and we put glitter on it and it looks so cool. Aunt Letty knows how to do everything and I love it when she comes to babysit me."

"Eat your eggs," Erica said, too sharply.

Tom and Quint both glanced up.

"I'll let you wear the shirt if you stop talking and eat your eggs."

"Okay," Quint said quietly. He focused on his plate. After a couple of moments he tentatively asked, "Did I do something, Mom? Are you mad at me?"

Tom was wondering the same thing himself.

"Of course not," Erica answered more evenly. "I'm not mad at all. I...I have a headache and I need a quiet breakfast."

"Okay," Quint whispered.

Erica was not a woman who was particularly prone to headaches.

"Do you think you're coming down with something?" Tom asked. "Should you call in sick today? Stay home?"

"I took an aspirin," she answered hastily. "I'll be fine."

They ate the rest of the meal in silence. Quint finished first and hurried to wash up and dress. Tom cleared the table.

"Drink your coffee," he told Erica. "I can put this stuff in the dishwasher." It only took him a couple of minutes, but she was not at the table when he got back. He found her in the bathroom, already dressed in her underwear and putting on makeup.

"Are you feeling better?"

"I'm fine," she assured him. "I just couldn't take Quint's chatter this morning."

Tom stepped behind her and wrapped his arms around her waist. He could see both their faces in the mirror, but she wouldn't meet his eyes. Something was wrong, but he didn't know what. That was the way it was with wives, he'd discovered. There were lots of times that a husband just couldn't get a handle on what was going on. She might be having her period. Or not having her period. Maybe she didn't sleep well. Or she was simply annoyed about not having a decent washing machine. It was hard for a husband to know.

He nuzzled her temple with his freshly shaved cheek. "Would it help if I said I love you?"

She did look at him them. There was something strange in her eyes, beautiful but with an intensity that wasn't typical. Inexplicably the memory of the interior of the Buick flashed in his mind. But the answer was more confusing than the question.

"Are you going to say it?" Erica asked.

"Yeah, yeah, of course," Tom stumbled slightly on his own thoughts. "I love you, Erica. I love you. Don't ever doubt it."

"I love you, too," she answered.

The moment was so serious that it felt uncomfortable. In defense Tom stepped back, wrapped a towel around his neck like a silk scarf and burst into song mimicking the low-timbred smoothness of *The King*.

"Hah-va I told...you—lately that I love you..."

Tom had just managed to put a smile on her face when a small voice called out from the vicinity of the living room.

"I'm ready!"

"Your son awaits," Tom said.

"Thank goodness. It's way too early in the morning for Elvis impersonations," Erica teased.

He swatted his wife playfully on the backside.

They finished dressing. The family headed off to work, to school, to the shop. As he opened up for business and got ready for his day, Tom thought again about how the look in her eyes reminded him of that time in his childhood when he rode in the Buick.

"It was a wedding," he murmured aloud to himself. He got the new sneakers because he was going to a wedding.

That was probably what it meant, he thought. He'd been on his way to a wedding and looking at his wife made him think of marriage.

Not all that strange and complicated, he assured himself. He put it out of his mind as he concentrated on the work at hand.

Briscoe and Hector showed up at few minutes early. Gus wandered in about twenty minutes late. When nine o'clock rolled around and Cliff hadn't showed up, he phoned his cell. No answer.

Maybe he's late and doesn't want to have to apologize twice.

A half hour later he was ready to call the home number, when Trish called him.

"Is Cliff there?"

Tom hesitated. He really hated to lie for this guy, even if he was his best friend.

"I guess he's running late this morning, Trish. Must have got into some traffic going through downtown."

On the other end of the line she burst into tears. "He didn't come home last night. I don't know where he is or what happened. I thought he must be working late again and got too busy to call. But this morning…he didn't come home at all."

Tom was momentarily speechless as he warred between which was worse to say to a sobbing wife, *Have you checked the hospitals?* or *Don't worry, he's probably shacked up with his girlfriend.*

"I woke up this morning and he wasn't here," Trish said. "I phoned his cell and no one answered. I phoned and phoned and phoned. I had to keep it together for the kids. I couldn't afford to fall apart until they were safely at school."

Tom hated the whole idea of her trying valiantly to remain stoic while her cheating husband probably overslept in a cheap motel.

"Let me make some calls, Trish," he said. "I don't know where he is, but let me call around. I'll get back to you as soon as I can."

Tom hung up the phone and privately cursed Cliff. He flipped through the office Rolodex until he found the parts store. He dialed the number. A woman answered the phone, but it was not the woman he was searching for.

"Hi, this is Tom Bentley at Bentley's Classic Car Care. Is Stacy in this morning?"

"No, she's not here today."

"Is she coming in later?"

"No, she's taking a few days off for vacation. She should be back at the store on Monday. Can somebody else help you?"

"No, no, that's fine. Thank you."

Tom hung up and cursed again. He paced a couple of times back and forth in the office and then went out into the shop to talk to Gus and Hector.

"Did Cliff say anything about not being here today?" he asked.

The two men glanced at each other first, shaking their heads.

"He's been pretty quiet the last week or so," Gus said. "Not very interested in shooting the bull around here."

"What about this girlfriend of his, Stacy?" Tom asked, not even bothering to pretend that they didn't know. "What's her last name?"

Again they were short on information.

"Call the place where she works," Gus said.

Tom sighed. "I did, but I didn't think to ask that question. I guess I'll call again."

He went back into the office and re-called the parts store. "This is Tom Bentley again. What is Stacy's last name?"

The woman replied without hesitation.

"Do you have her home phone number?" Tom asked.

"She's not there. I told you, she's on vacation."

"I could leave a message on her voice mail," Tom fudged.

"Oh yeah, sure."

He heard the woman clicking through a couple of screens before she gave him the number. Tom wrote it down and then made a mental note to remind his own employees not to give out personal information on each other.

After ending the call to the parts store, he phoned the number he'd been given, not knowing what he might encounter or what he even had to say. When a man's voice picked up on the third ring, he decided that honesty had to be the best policy.

"Hi," he said. "This is Tom Bentley from Bentley's Classic Car Care. I'm trying to find Stacy."

There was a hesitation on the end of the line.

"So you've lost her, too."

"Huh?"

"Aren't you the son of a bitch who's been screwing my wife for months?"

Tom was momentarily speechless. Had Cliff somehow thrown suspicion on Tom? Was that how he'd been doing it? Was that how he'd been keeping his wife from suspecting anything? Why Trish had been so angry at him?

"No, I'm not," Tom replied firmly. "I am the boss of the son of a bitch who's been screwing your wife for months. He didn't show up for work this morning and *his* wife is terrified."

Stacy's husband was silent for a moment and then gave a disgusted snort. "Now that figures," he said. "The creep isn't even man enough to face his own wife. What Stacy sees in these low-life cowards I'll never understand."

Tom noticed the plural. "Cowards?" he repeated. "More than one."

The man didn't answer directly. "She always comes back to me," he said. "Once things get out in the open, she'll run off with the guy for a week or two. But she always comes back. Stacy won't leave the kids for long. And I'm not about to give them up. I shouldn't have to give them up, not even part-time. I've done nothing to be punished for."

Tom didn't understand the man's logic, or whether he was right or wrong or both. And he didn't care.

"Do you have any idea where they are?" he asked.

"Not for sure. She loves South Padre. I've found her before down there at a place called Coronodo Condos."

"Thank you," Tom said before hanging up.

Briscoe was standing in the doorway. Tom went out and found the kid another task he could do without help. He talked with a customer and then finally got back to the office to open up his laptop and check the internet for the beach property.

When he had the number he opened the bay four door and got into the Buick. The engine turned over like butter and hummed as sweetly as a sewing machine. He put the top down and drove the vehicle to the back lot where he parked in the crisp cool sunshine of a November morning, and the memory of his childhood came flooding back.

He'd ridden in a car like this to Delila Vera's wedding. He remembered it now and was astonished that he'd forgotten it. They had lived with Delila for a while in Colombia and she'd shown up later in Mexico, like so many did. But Delila had changed. She had fallen in love with a man who owned a shoe store. It was a small, insignificant shoe store. And he was an older, ordinary man, a widower with two young children. But she had fallen in love with him and it had changed her. She had given up the drugs and the street life. She had worked for him in his store. And on that beautiful autumn day, they had driven in his beautiful old car to the tiny church in his village to get married.

Tom and his mother had been Delila's only guests. They'd washed and dressed in the rooms above the store. Delila had loaned her mother a dress. And there was a clean shirt and trousers that belonged to the man's son. Tom's feet were bigger than the son's, so the man had given him a pair of sneakers to keep.

The wedding had been simple and sweet. Afterward, Tom had never seen any of them again. But that day, that wedding day, had been one of hope. It had been one Tom had put his faith in. If finding love and family could give Delila a new life, then it was possible for anyone. Even his mother. Even himself.

Tom leaned back into the Buick's aging upholstery and allowed the sun to shine on his face. The world could be a terrible place. There was sadness everywhere and lives that were destroyed, people who were wounded. Traps that snared. Dreams that died.

He found himself smiling. Because there was hope. Delila's wedding had proved that to him. And every day his own marriage to Erica reinforced it.

I love you, he'd said that morning to his wife. Those were very small words that couldn't begin to encompass the fullness of his feelings for her, about her. It was too big a meaning to be held in his brain. Too grand a concept for a regular guy to be able to express. He loved her. And that was a driving force, an engine, that could never be contained with internal combustion.

Tom sat there in the sun for a few more minutes before he heaved a sigh, pulled out his cell phone and got to the business at hand. He dialed the number of Coronodo Condos on his cell phone.

He went through a couple of layers of trouble. The property manager was loath to verify who was staying where. The condos did not have private phones in the rooms. Finally he convinced the lobby superintendent that it was an emergency and he agreed to check the apartment while Tom waited on the phone.

Tom grabbed a chammy and began one-handedly wiping down the Buick as he waited. Finally Cliff was on the phone.

"Hello."

"Cliff, this is Tom," he said. "Don't talk. Listen. You're fired. Now, I'll give you fifteen minutes to call your wife. And I'll even give you a hint of what you might say. You might say that you lost your job and you were afraid to face her. You just started driving and kept on going. Tell her that you're coming home now and you'll be there in a couple of hours. That you love her and that you're sorry and that you want to work things out." Tom barely paused. "If you go that route, then I'll keep your secret until I go to my grave. I'll give you a good recommendation and you can blame everything on me." Tom thought it was a very fair offer. "As I said, you've got fifteen minutes. If you don't call your wife, then I will and I'll tell her what a lying, cheating bastard you really are. And I'll also tell her where her divorce lawyer can find you. Fifteen minutes."

Tom didn't wait for a response. He clicked the phone off and looked at his watch.

Chapter 18

ERICA AND MELODY WERE having one final meeting on the EMR workshop, but it was not going well at all. Erica could barely focus on the material in front of her. She was still reeling from her spying fiasco of the night before. She replayed her whole crazy behavior over and over in her head. She was as bad as her mother. No, she was worse. Her mother would never have gotten that close without actually getting some information.

And Tom, this morning, talking about it as if there was nothing out of the ordinary about him visiting a customer at home. He'd even let it slip that it was a "single female, living alone." Did he not think she noticed! Did he think she was stupid!

The wave of irrational anger was followed by a pit of fear in her stomach. "I love you," he'd said. And his expression was as open and honest and sincere as it had been on their wedding day. Could he be lying? Had he always been lying?

Erica managed to get a grip on her imagination. Tom was a car mechanic and a loving husband and father. If he had strayed, it was not some diabolical plot. It was…it was… Erica couldn't quite complete the thought. Was it a deal breaker? If her husband had been unfaithful would she leave him?

She didn't know. She was her mother's daughter. Ann Marie had no respect for women who stayed with philandering husbands. Still, Erica could not contemplate a life without Tom. Could not imagine Quint bouncing back and forth between her place and Tom's. Lots of women did it. But lots of them didn't have a choice. Erica didn't know if she had a choice. If she did, she couldn't be sure what it would be.

She'd read the same sentence in her notes three times. Finally she underlined it and looked over at Melody.

Her workshop leader didn't seem much better off than she did. Melody seemed nervous, edgy, uncomfortable She had an open bag of M&M's on the table and she was scarfing them down by the handful.

"Did you get the extra time?" she asked Erica.

Erica glanced up.

"From Dr. Glover," Melody clarified her question.

"Oh yeah, of course," she answered.

"Of course," Melody repeated in a tone that was snide. Then she got up and left the room.

Erica didn't know what that was about, but she decided to ignore it. With everything going on at home and the workshop happening tomorrow, she simply couldn't take on Melody's drama right now. The woman would have to learn to deal on her own.

Erica decided that an hour or so of letting tempers cool would be the best thing for both of them. Deliberately she tried to focus on the presentation. She assumed that Melody would eventually be back to the conference room. But when she didn't return and Erica had done all she could do, she put the papers back in order and carried everything to her desk.

In her cubicle, she pulled up her in-box and began coding charts. She figured she'd need to play catch-up. Melody would undoubtedly want to finish up the meeting this afternoon. Erica didn't want to lose any more time than she already had.

She didn't see Melody at the lunch table, but decided to take her sandwich back to her desk. Erica toyed with the idea of calling her sister, or even her mother, but ultimately decided to leave the phone in her purse. She did click open her screen and was reading and making notations between bites.

"Are you working or breaking?"

The question came from Mrs. Converse, who was standing at the entrance to the cubicle.

"Actually, I'm breaking," Erica said. She held up her sandwich as proof.

"You'll recall that I have strict rules about taking scheduled breaks," she said. "Downtime is vital to maintain quality work. My employees are not machines. Your brains require rest."

"Sorry," Erica said. "We have the workshop tomorrow and I thought Melody might want to do some last-minute polishing this afternoon, so I was trying to cover a few more charts."

"Melody told me the workshop was ready to go," Mrs. Converse said.

Erica thought that was probably debatable, but she wasn't about to dispute the project leader's judgment.

"She's gone for the day," Mrs. Converse continued. "She

wasn't feeling very well and she wants to be her best tomorrow."

"Melody went home?"

Mrs. Converse nodded. "So you'll have all afternoon to
work on your charts."

At that moment Erica wasn't worried about the charts.
There were a million small details that needed to be taken
care of before the participants showed up the next day. The
list of follow-up calls alone would take a couple of hours.
Maybe Melody was making the follow-up calls from home.
Or maybe she wasn't. Erica thought about asking Mrs. Converse and decided against it. If Melody forgot about the fol-
low-ups, that was really dropping the ball. Erica wouldn't
even suggest to the supervisor that her coworker had done
such a thing.

"Okay then," Erica said, forcing a big smile on her face
that she hoped wasn't too fake. "Maybe I'll just turn the
screen off and call my sister for a lunchtime chat."

Mrs. Converse smiled.

Erica, of course, didn't call Letty. She pulled out the follow-up list and started with the Dietary Department, verifying the catered lunch. Then she placed a call to the Physical
Plant double-checking that the room they were using was
still available for their use and that the appropriate tables
and chairs would be set up in the positions they'd requested.
She checked with all the speakers, making sure they knew
when they were to speak and where. It didn't take her long
to realize that she wasn't duplicating Melody's work. Melody
hadn't contacted anyone. She must have simply neglected it
completely.

Erica managed to get some charts done late in the afternoon. She decided to take the presentation home and
polish it up as best she could. By the end of the day, she was

exhausted. Also slightly grateful. She'd been so frantic trying to get everything done, that her worries about her marriage and her husband had been put on the back burner.

However they came front and center when she went to pick up Quint.

"I'm working late again tonight," Tom told her. "I'll be home as soon as I can."

She wanted to argue with him. But she could see how busy he was. He had two cars up on lifts. He was working on one and supervising Briscoe as he did work on the other.

"I've got something important I need to talk to you about," he said.

The seriousness of his tone made her heart catch in her throat.

"What is it?" she asked him.

Tom shook his head. "We'll talk tonight, at home."

Erica agreed. She took Quint home. He was even more talkative than usual, perhaps he sensed that his mother was hardly listening.

She tried to get back into the workshop presentation, but was actually grateful when the phone rang, even if it was her mother.

"So, have you thought about your entry for the Christmas parade?" she asked.

"Uh…no."

"Well, it doesn't have to be a float, you know. It can be something else. Quint's not in a tumbling group, I suppose. What about his Little League team?"

"What about his Little League team?"

"They could march in the parade as your entry," her mother said, in a tone that suggested the answer was obvious.

"You told me that we wouldn't have to have an entry,"

Erica reminded her. "You said if we just signed our name and you paid our fee that would be the end of it."

"Well, of course it's not the end of it," Ann Marie said. "You can't just not show up. You'll have to come up with some kind of entry. But you have a month and you're so creative about these things. What's happening with the car?"

"The car?"

"Yes, Letty's car. She left that horrible excuse for a car in our driveway and borrowed the van from Melvin."

"Oh, yes, Letty's car." Erica dragged herself quickly into the lie. "Yeah, I expect her to bring the van back this afternoon."

"That's good," her mother said. "She told Melvin she would bring it back this morning."

"I'm sure she just got busy and couldn't get over there," Erica said.

"I don't want you girls taking advantage of Melvin," Ann Marie said. "He is very easy to manipulate and I don't want you doing that."

"We wouldn't manipulate the poor man. We know that's your job."

Her mother's sharp intake of breath was indication of a direct hit. If she'd had any doubt, the sudden dial tone she heard a second later confirmed her aim.

Erica grinned at the phone. But it was short-lived. Her mother's life was such a long-term, unending mess. It was easy to take potshots. Erica reminded herself that her own little nest might not be quite as perfect as she'd always thought.

A few minutes later Letty called.

"Have you lost your mind?" she asked. "Why would you start a fight with Mom? Do you not have enough trouble already?"

"I was defending you," Erica answered. "At least I sort of was. She suggested that borrowing Melvin's minivan was somehow manipulating him."

"It wasn't my idea to borrow a car so you could spend the night stalking your husband."

"I was not stalking. And I couldn't take my own car. Why didn't you return it this morning like you said you would?"

"Because I might get a question or two if I returned a car that smells like spilt milk and urine. What the heck did you do in there anyway?"

"It's a long story," Erica said.

"I thought you were always willing to share with your sister."

"Some things my sister doesn't need to know."

"Like why you would pee in the car," Letty said.

"I didn't pee in the car, I peed on myself and then I had to sit in the car."

Letty laughed.

"I can't believe you find this funny," Erica said. "My husband was in the house with a strange woman. I nearly got caught. There were people screaming and chasing me. Seriously, it was not funny."

"If you don't want me to laugh, then you have to tell me everything," she said.

Reluctantly, Erica gave her a condensed version of her personal nightmare on Helm Street. When she finished, Letty actually laughed harder than she had before.

"I am having a crisis in my marriage and you find it funny," Erica accused.

"You're not having a crisis," Letty assured her. "You're seeing a mirage."

"He said he has something serious he needs to discuss with me," Erica told her. "What if he confesses? He may be coming home to tell me everything, get it off his chest, beg for forgiveness."

"I don't think so."

"But what if he does?"

"Then you'll deal with it," Letty said.

"I don't know how," Erica said. "I don't know what I'd do. I love him. I don't want to lose him. But if he cheated on me, I don't know if I could forgive him."

"I doubt anybody knows that until they've been in that situation," Letty said.

"Mom does," Erica pointed out. "I think this is the only time in my life that I'd want to be Mom. That I want to be so sure of myself and certain about what is the right thing to do."

"I am certain of you," Letty said. "I would trust your decision making over anyone I know. But I don't buy into your speculation. Tom is not a cheater. He's just not a run-around-on-your-wife kind of guy."

"He is visiting some woman on that street," Erica said. "That's not my imagination or speculation. He's admitted it. He's visiting a woman. He's been visiting her long enough that people on the street stop and talk to him. He's eating dinner with her. He's eating with her instead of with me and Quint."

"I don't have an explanation," Letty told her. "But I do have the facts. Fact is, the guy is the truest man I've ever met. He is the only reason I still believe that it's possible in this crazy world to find happiness out there. He has made my sister happy. And nobody I know deserves it more."

Erica felt the tears pooling in the corners of her eyes.

"I want to believe in him," she said to Letty.

"Then do. Mom always thinks men are cheating on her. And somehow that always turns out to be right. Please don't fall into the trap of having those expectations. You are better than that. Tom is better than that."

It was almost nine when Tom arrived home. He'd been so tired he'd started making mistakes and that was when it was past time to quit. For once, he wasn't eager to face his wife. Well, he might have been eager if he could just curl up with Erica in his arms. But it had been a sad, disappointing day. And Erica was going to have to share in that.

He came in through the garage door, secretly hoping that she'd be sound asleep and he'd have a great excuse not to talk to her. But she was sitting at the kitchen table, papers spread out in front of her. He walked over and kissed her on the top of the head.

"Still hard at work, huh?"

"I've got that workshop presentation tomorrow," she said.

"Oh, right, that's tomorrow," he said. "I'm sure it will be great."

"Melody left early today and left a lot of stuff hanging."

He nodded sympathetically. "Well, your part will be great."

"I probably need to go in early in the morning," she said. "Can you take Quint to school?"

"Sure."

He watched her gather all her papers together. She was careful and methodical. She kept everything in order. Tom only wished that his own thoughts were the same. He waited until she was completely finished. He would have waited indefinitely if there had been any chance of that.

Tom took her hand and led her into the living room to get comfortable on the couch. Erica had her back against the cushions. He sat on the edge turned in her direction so that he could look directly at her.

When he did, he saw that her jaw was set tight and her expression was guarded. She knew it was bad news. And Tom hated being the one to bring it.

"Cliff and Trish are splitting up," he said, getting the punch line out of the way first.

Erica looked puzzled for a moment as if she didn't know who he was talking about. That announcement came as a complete surprise.

"Oh my God, what happened?"

Tom didn't want to get into a lot of details. "He didn't come home last night. Trish was frantic. She called me this morning. When I tracked him down, he was at the beach in South Padre."

Erica's eyebrows went up at that.

"He was with a woman from the Auto Parts Store down the street."

"Oh, no," she said.

"I talked to him myself," Tom said. "I told him to call Trish and tell her that he was fired, because I did fire him, and that he'd driven all night and now he was on his way home. I gave him fifteen minutes to fix it. I actually waited twenty. When I called Trish back, she hadn't heard from him, so I told her where he was and who he was with."

Tom heaved a heavy sigh and shook his head. "I still can't believe he didn't take the chance I offered him. I threw the guy a lifeline and he let it drag in the water."

"Wait a minute," Erica said, and edged forward in her seat. "You were trying to get the guy to lie to his wife?"

"He was already lying to his wife," Tom said. "And he's been lying to her for, I don't know how long. But he's my friend and I wanted to let him know he still had an option to save his marriage."

"So, he's been having this affair, lying to his wife, and you knew about it," she said.

Tom nodded.

From her expression he could see that Erica didn't like that. He thought he'd better try to explain. He rose to his feet and began to pace the living room as he talked.

"I caught them together in the parking lot behind the shop," he said. "This was a couple of months ago. Cliff said it was just a sex thing. He begged me not to say anything. And then the woman told me she had kids, too. She asked me not to say anything. I was just hoping the whole mess would blow over."

"Why didn't you tell *me?*" Erica asked.

"Because I knew it would put you in the same position I was in," Tom said. "Trish is your friend. I knew you'd feel you should tell her."

"Of course, I would have told her. She deserved to know."

Tom shrugged. "I was hoping she would never find out."

"So Cliff lied to his wife," Erica said slowly, critically.

Tom was surprised by his wife's tone. Erica had risen to her feet and was standing right in front of him, her arms tightly crossed against her chest.

"Cliff lied to his wife and not only didn't you stop him, you lied to her, too."

"What was I supposed to do?" Tom asked. "Should I jump in and break up someone else's marriage? Cliff was my friend, my oldest friend. I thought it was a slipup, a stupid mistake. I wanted him to get his act together. And I've always liked Trish. I think she's been good for him, steadied him. They're our friends. I wasn't exactly anxious to rip her heart out and stomp on it."

Tom ran his fingers through his hair and then rubbed his eyes tiredly. "What a day!" he said. "Trish's whole world got turned upside down. The lives of her kids, changed forever. She was hurt and scared and angry. And I'm the lucky bastard who got to make all that happen."

Tom shuddered at the memory of it. "Oh my God, Erica, you can't even imagine how terrible I felt. I literally got queasy talking to her. And, trust me, Trish sure didn't see my spilling the beans as any great favor. I think she may be as mad at me as she is at him. I doubt she will ever speak to me. Cliff won't either for that matter. Of course, I knew that was going to happen as soon as I knew I'd have to fire him."

"As soon as you knew you'd have to fire him?" Erica repeated his words in the form of a question.

"Yeah," Tom said. "Things had just gotten worse and worse. In fact, I think my knowing about Stacy may have thrown gasoline on the fire. What he'd originally described as a 'Saturday thing' quickly became almost an everyday. He was constantly sneaking off the job to meet her. It made running the shop sheer hell. I couldn't count on him. He just wasn't being responsible. Now I'm thinking if he'd had to keep the secret from me, too, he would never have been able to get so deeply involved with her so quickly."

"So, you actually *helped* him cheat on his wife," Erica said.

"It wasn't intentional," Tom said.

"Wasn't it? It sounds pretty intentional to me. You find out Cliff is screwing some slut in the parking lot and instead of making him stop, you cover for him."

"'Making him stop'—how could I have made him stop?" Tom asked. "Men don't tell other men what to do. Especially about that kind of stuff."

"You mean sex kind of stuff?"

"Yeah, sex, marriage, relationships," Tom said. "I know

you women talk to each other and advise each other and are in each other's business all the time. Men don't do that."

"Men are afraid to do that," Erica said. "They all want to act so *macho*."

"It's not fear and it has nothing to do with macho," Tom stated. "Men just don't care. We don't care. What Cliff thinks about my marriage, about me and you, is not even on my radar. I don't need his opinion. And he doesn't need, or want, mine."

"You could have tried."

"I did try. I told him that he was playing with fire. That he was risking everything. He agreed with me. He already knew it. But it didn't stop him. He didn't want to stop. If you don't want to stop, nothing can stop you."

"You could have told Trish," Erica said.

"Do you think she would have been any happier finding out about it two months ago than she was today?"

"But if she'd found out earlier, before he was so involved, and she'd confronted him, maybe they could have worked it out, gone to counseling, saved the marriage."

"Yeah, maybe," Tom admitted. "But I thought that, maybe, giving him some time, he might come to his senses, get back on fidelity highway and become the husband he used to be, without her ever having to know, or having to be hurt."

"So you're saying that it's okay to cheat, as long as the stupid, trusting wife doesn't find out."

"I never said that."

"You'd want them to live a marriage that's a lie."

"Well, yeah, if that would work," Tom said. "Trust me, the truth isn't always what it's cracked up to be."

"Oh, so you think it's okay to lie," she said.

"I don't think it's okay. But there are lies in every marriage, every relationship."

"In our marriage? In our relationship?"

"Yeah. Sure. Little things, big things, you know that as well as I do."

"What are you lying to me about?"

Tom searched his brain for an example. It was probably a testament to the strength of their bond that nothing immediately came to mind.

"Okay," he said finally. "I lied about kids."

"About kids?"

"Actually I lied over and over about kids," Tom said. "At first when you wanted to try and have a kid, I wasn't sure I would be any good at it. So while we were trying, I was secretly hoping that we wouldn't get pregnant. And then when we did, I lied for the next nine months about how happy I was. I wasn't happy, I was scared. The whole financial thing and the parenting thing and the whole thing. I didn't want any of it, but I knew that you did so I lied about it."

"You didn't want kids?"

"I didn't then. After Quint was born and he was so terrific and we are such a great family together, then I wanted kids. I wanted more kids. But then you wanted to go back to work. I know you like your job. You feel good about what you do. It gives you lots of personal success and a feeling of achievement. So you said, you thought one child was enough and I said okay, so I lied again."

"You want more children?"

"No, I mean I did, I would, but I don't. Our family is great like it is. What I'm just saying is that for two people to get along together for the long haul, being a stickler for the absolute truth can make more trouble than it does good."

"So you're going to tell me what you think I want to hear." Erica's tone was strident and snide.

"No, sometimes I'm going to tell you things that you *don't* want to hear. Like how unreasonable you sound. I've already had one woman yell at me today. I was hoping to come home to one who would at least try to understand."

"What's going on?" a small, sleepy voice asked from the door to the hallway. "Why are you shouting at each other?"

Tom hadn't realized they'd gotten so loud. Quint was a sound sleeper. If they'd awakened him, they were really screaming.

"Nothing, sweetie," Erica assured him quickly. "Just grown-up stuff."

"Come on, buddy," Tom told him. "I'll put you back into bed."

Tom could feel the blood pumping through his veins and deliberately calmed himself as he followed his son back to his room.

In the dim glow of the night-light, Quint climbed back into his bed. Tom covered him up and tucked him in on the sides, the way Erica had shown him.

"Are you mad at Mom?" Quint asked him.

"No," Tom answered. "I'm just tired and grouchy."

The little boy nodded and closed his eyes.

Tom wondered if, in Erica's view, he should have been honest with his son. Yes, he was mad at Erica. She refused to see his side of it and she'd dragged their marriage into Cliff and Trish's mess. Or maybe he had dragged them into it. At that moment, he was too exhausted to know. But he was certain he didn't want to argue about it anymore.

He took off his shoes. He needed to make up with Erica. He needed to take a shower. And he needed to go to bed. The morning would be coming around too soon.

Quint had his eyes closed, but Tom was listening for the change in the sound of his breathing that would tell him that his son was sleeping. While he waited, he stretched out across the top of the bedspread. And he promptly fell asleep.

Chapter 19

HER PERSONAL LIFE FELT shaky and scary, but Erica dragged herself out of bed the next morning. That's what responsible people do. She had obligations at her job. It didn't matter that she'd had a big fight with her husband, and that it had ended with him choosing not to sleep in their bed. None of that could matter this morning, because there were thirty-seven medical-records professionals taking time out of their own busy careers to attend a workshop at University Hospital.

This was Melody's project and it would be Melody who took the bows or the criticism for how it went. Still, Erica had signed on to help make it work. Mrs. Converse was counting on her. She wouldn't let anybody down.

She was dressed and ready to head out the door when Tom got up. He was groggy and smelly, still dressed in his work clothes. Erica let him get a cup of coffee before she spoke.

"You said you'd take Quint to school this morning."

"Right. Got it, no problem."

They looked at each other across the width of the kitchen. Should she say something to him? She could apologize. Of course, she wasn't actually wrong. Any apology would be for the argument, and not for the content. She would have to explain that. If she did, they'd be right back where they were last night and she didn't have time for that right now.

"I've got to go."

Tom nodded.

"Wish me luck."

He shook his head. "My Erica doesn't need *luck*. She makes planning and hard work pay off."

Tom took the two paces across the room to kiss her goodbye. His target suggested her brow or temple. Erica raised her face offering her lips and he pressed his own to hers for one brief sweet moment.

"Knock 'em dead," he told her.

Erica nodded. "I'll do my best."

She grabbed up her stuff from the table and headed out.

As she opened the garage, he called out to her from the doorway. "Erica, I love you."

She turned and nodded. "I know you do," she answered.

Since she was leaving so early, missing all the commuter traffic, she took the sedan instead of the bus. Erica drove to the hospital and actually found a good parking space. She deliberately tried to focus her thoughts on the day ahead and not on the husband and child she left behind. In a leadership seminar she'd taken years ago, the speaker had stressed the importance of compartmentalizing. While you were on the job, you put your family life in a box that you only opened for emergencies. Erica really tried to do that. This morning, however, the lid kept snapping open and her husband would pop into her thoughts like a jack-in-a-box. A Tom-in-a-box.

Erica went to the department. The place was dark and completely deserted. She locked her purse in her drawer, grabbed up the box with the registration materials and headed down to the classroom.

The lights were on, which was a positive sign. She opened the door, expecting Melody to be there. She was not. Instead, she found the setup crew getting the tables put up. Either they hadn't seen the schematic or they couldn't read it, because they started facing everything longwise in the room, when the more discussion-friendly plan had them going the other direction. Erica was so glad she was there before they got it all done incorrectly and left for their next task.

Once that crisis was averted, the AV guy showed up with the wrong projector. He argued, Erica stood her ground. They weren't showing vacation slides. These were computer screens and technical forms, and everybody in the room had to be able to see them perfectly.

As soon as the tablecloths were laid, Erica began setting up the sign-in area. *Where in the heck is Melody?* she wondered. She didn't really know how Melody wanted it done. It was such a minor thing, they hadn't ever discussed it. Erica didn't want to take over her coworker's project, but a quick check of her watch suggested that for better or worse it needed to be done.

She laid the ID pins out alphabetically and decided that the info packets were so bulky she'd just place them at every seat at the tables.

Dietary was setting up the coffee, juice and cookies when Melody finally made it through the door. She looked terrible. Her skirt was wrinkled. She'd pulled her hair up into an untidy clip. And except for a smear of lipstick, she wasn't wearing any makeup at all.

"I overslept," she said by way of explanation.

Erica stifled the urged to scream at her. Instead, recalling how easily Melody had gone over the deep end the day before, she spoke as professionally and evenly as she could.

"None of the attendees are here yet. There's still plenty of time for you to fix your hair and makeup."

Melody reached up to touch her hair, as if she just remembered she had it.

"Go on," Erica prodded gently. "I've got things covered here."

Melody went off to the bathroom and Erica continued to get everything ready. The guy from AV finally showed up with the right projector, but was teed off at having to make a second trip. He just set it down on the floor inside the door and left.

Erica was annoyed, but knew that it would be quicker to just set it up herself than to try to find the man and force him to do his job. She was pretty good at figuring out how things worked and had it set up to her satisfaction just half a minute before the early arrivals walked in the door.

For the next twenty minutes Erica was greeting people, checking them off the list, handing out name tags and offering refreshments.

As ten o'clock got closer and closer and Melody hadn't returned, Erica began to worry. At three minutes before the scheduled start time, the last person checked in. Melody still hadn't returned.

Erica kept her smile firmly plastered on her face as she edged out the doorway. She hurried down the hallway as quickly and unobtrusively as possible.

She could hear Melody sobbing as soon as she opened the door to the ladies' room.

"Melody. Melody," she said firmly as she walked to the

origin of the sound in the furthermost stall. "It's time to start the workshop. You've got to come out of there."

"I can't do it," she said, whining through her tears. "I can't face all those people."

"Yes, you can. Of course you can. Open the door."

Melody hesitated.

"Please, open the door," Erica said.

She heard the metal click of the latch and then pulled it open. Melody sat atop the toilet seat. She hadn't combed her hair and any makeup had disappeared amid her tear-stained face, swollen eyes and red nose.

"I'll go on first," Erica suggested. "You've got time to pull yourself together. We're going to be fine."

"I can't do this," Melody said. "I had a terrible fight with Gabe last night. I just can't do this today."

"Of course you can," Erica assured her. "You'll have to put your personal concerns aside for a few hours. Nobody knows more about EMR than you do. They want to learn. They're here to learn. All you've got to do is tell them what you know."

"I can't. You don't understand."

"What don't I understand?"

"I had a fight with my husband," Melody repeated. "I love him and he's angry at me. I can't think about anything else. I can't do anything else."

"Is that what you're going to tell Mrs. Converse? That you can't do your job because you've got troubles at home?" Erica asked. "It just so happens that I had a fight with my husband last night, too. This is not the best day of my life, either. But I took on this responsibility and I've got to follow through with it."

Melody waved away her comparison. "It's not the same,"

she said. "Gabe is my whole life. You…you're hardly even married. Just a divorce waiting to happen."

Erica was incredulous. "Why would you say something like that? You know nothing about me and nothing about my marriage."

Even with a red, runny nose, Melody managed a haughty expression.

"I know that you lie and cheat and pretend to be happily married while you screw around behind your husband's back."

"What?" Completely clueless, Erica looked at the woman. "You are completely off base with that."

Melody rolled her eyes. "Denial is more than a river in Egypt," she said snottily.

"I have no idea what you're talking about," Erica said.

"Oh, you don't? You forget. I was there." Melody rose to her feet and pointed her finger in Erica's face. "When Rayliss and Darla said what they said, *I saw your face.*"

Erica searched her brain trying to recall whatever Melody was talking about, what she was so furious about. The thing about "seeing her face" and Rayliss and Darla. That could only have been when Callie called in sick and those two harpies suggested that she'd been with Tom. Melody was there, but surely she couldn't know about that.

Erica had completely discounted anything happening between her husband and Callie. Was Melody suggesting she was wrong about that?

"What do you know about Tom?" she demanded.

Erica's harsh tone temporarily sobered Melody. "I…I don't know anything about him. Except that he's married to a faithless woman like you."

"What? Faithless?" Erica repeated. "I love my husband."

"Yeah, sure," Melody said. "But not so much that you wouldn't get involved with Dr. Glover."

"Dr. Glover?" Erica was incredulous. "You think I'm involved with Dr. Glover? That is simply ridiculous."

"There's no use in denying it," Melody said. "Callie slept with him to get back at you. I saw your face. I know you were having an affair."

"I was not, am not, having an affair with anybody," Erica stated firmly, loudly, harshly. "I am sick to death of the gossip in this place. And I'm not going to listen to another word of it." She stiffened her backbone. "I have a roomful of women waiting on a workshop. So I'm going back in there to do what I get paid for. You need to straighten up, get your head together and get in there or go tell Mrs. Converse why not."

Erica stormed out. As she walked down the hall she deliberately tried not to think about what Melody had said. It was just too confusing. And she also tried not to speculate on whether or not her coworker might show up to help her. She would do what she had to do and figure everything out later.

By the time she got to the workshop classroom, she had her game face on. With a smile, she walked through the door and calmly made her way directly to the podium.

"Good morning, Medical Records Professionals."

Erica finished her presentation and thought it had gone well, even if she did say so herself. She introduced Dr. Glover, the first speaker, and made her way to the back of the room near the doorway.

Dr. Glover was, of course, young and charming and the women in the room immediately adored him. He also seemed to be a natural at teaching, with a knack for anticipating the right questions and boiling down explanations as he presented the ins and outs of e-script prescription practices.

Erica took the opportunity to quietly step out to go to the ladies' room. She pretended to herself that she simply needed to use the facilities. But she was also curious to see if Melody was still in the bathroom stall.

She was not. The place was quiet and deserted. Erica was relieved at first, but then posed a question to herself. If Melody wasn't in the workshop and she wasn't in the restroom, where in the devil was she?

Maybe she was hanging back until Glover finished. She obviously had a problem with the guy.

Erica glanced at herself in the mirror and shook her head. Could that thing in the cafeteria really have been about Glover? Did those women really think she would have an affair with him? She found the whole idea incredulous. She was simply not the kind of person who would cheat. How could anyone think that she was? And a rumor like that could be dangerous. What if Glover had been married? People could be hurt by things like that. Or the story could have gotten back to Tom, though she was sure he would never believe it for an instant.

The idea that Callie might have had sex with Glover to get back at her was a wild idea. Callie had a crush on the guy. If she got involved with him, it was for herself, not as some kind of payback to Erica.

By the time Erica made it back to the workshop, the pharmacy presentation was winding down and Mrs. Maizika from the Department of Nursing was waiting in the wings.

Dr. Glover finished to enthusiastic applause and as he gathered up his materials, Erica went up and introduced Mrs. Maizika. The rugged old nurse took her place behind the podium and began reading in a monotone voice, instructions for interpreting electronic nursing notes.

Erica mentally rolled her eyes. *Next time they have to come up with someone better than this,* she told herself.

She saw Dr. Glover waiting just outside the doorway and she joined him as he walked down the hall.

"How'd I do?" he asked.

"You were great and you know it," she answered. "The ladies love you."

"Yep, it's the story of my life," he quipped. "I'll bet every one of them in there is married."

Erica nodded vaguely and gave him a half smile.

"Callie Torreno isn't married," she said.

He was caught up short, but only for an instant. "Ah," he said. "So you finally heard. You may be the last person in the hospital to know."

"It's true then?"

He nodded. "I'm afraid so."

"Wow. I didn't even think that you liked her," Erica said.

"I don't," he answered. "It just…it just happened."

"Having sex with people doesn't 'just happen,'" she pointed out.

"This time it did," Glover said. "The woman shows up at my door one night, completely uninvited and unannounced. She just throws herself at me. She obviously wanted sex, pure and simple. She was not asking for a relationship or even a date. It was just sex. I admit, she's got a nice body. And it had been a while for me. We were both free. I had a condom. I couldn't think of a reason not to."

"So you did."

Glover nodded. "I'm not proud of it," he said. "But I'm not ashamed, either. We're both adults. Adults do that kind of thing. I generally don't do it with people from the workplace. It can make things awkward, as it has this time. She apparently offered the details all over the hospital, with lots of embarrassing anecdotes."

"Not too embarrassing," Erica said. "If I remember correctly, she gave you pretty high marks in the loverboy department."

Erica looked at the man's face. He was blushing.

She thought about telling him what Melody suspected, what maybe everybody suspected. But she decided against it. Erica liked him. She enjoyed his company. It wasn't really his fault that some gossipy people had misinterpreted her relationship with him. Still it was probably a good idea to keep a bit more professional distance between them.

"I've got to get back," she said. "Thank you for an excellent presentation."

Her grinned that boyish grin at her. She gave a little wave and headed back up the hall.

Erica returned to the workshop, where Mrs. Maizika's monotone continued. Glancing around the room, Erica decided it was safe to say that a lot of the attendees were nodding off or tuning her out. Erica grabbed up one of the notepads and wrote some suggestions for things that were absolutely essential to know about electronic nursing notes. When the question and answer period came and nobody raised a hand, Erica posed the queries herself, one by one. Mrs. Maizika was better off-the-cuff than she was reading from her text. That even spurred some inquiries from the audience. Ultimately, Erica thought it hadn't turned out as badly as it could have.

The Dietary Department showed up with lunch trays and everyone got up to stretch, visit the bathroom and chat among themselves.

Melody still hadn't shown up. Erica went down to the

department to look for her. The staff had already gone to the cafeteria. Mrs. Converse was in her office eating a sandwich and she waved Erica inside.

"I was going to come down to the workshop as soon as I finished eating," she said. "It's just going to be you and me."

"What?"

"Melody has gone home for the day," Mrs. Converse said. "In fact, she's on a three-day suspension for insubordination."

"Oh my God," Erica said.

"I think it will be all right, ultimately. She's got some kind of family crisis. That happens to her periodically. I'm sure she'll be back here next week doing what she does best."

"What about the workshop?"

"You've got the syllabus," Mrs. Converse said. "You simply teach the material to the best of your ability. I'll be there to answer any questions that you can't handle."

Erica felt a momentary knot of fear. "I haven't rehearsed Melody's presentation," she confessed. "I've only read over it a couple of times."

"Well, a couple of times will have to be enough."

"I can't believe that Melody would walk out on me like this," Erica said.

Mrs. Converse shook her head. "I blame myself," she said. "I know what she's like. It's one thing to admire and respect your husband—it's quite another to let him make every plan, every choice, every decision. That can undermine a woman's belief in herself. Melody is, by far and away, the most knowledgeable employee I have on EMR. I really thought it might be an excellent opportunity for her to broaden herself as a person and heighten her value in this department as an employee." The woman shook her head. "But I was wrong about her. At least I am for now. She's doesn't have enough faith in herself to grow into the kind of leader we need."

Erica had no comment. She was still reeling from the reality of having to do the entire afternoon presentation by herself and with her boss watching.

Chapter 20

TOM CHECKED HIS EMAIL at lunch to find two more messages about the Buick. One was from the guy he'd already been communicating with, and he was willing to come closer to the asking price, pay cash and was ready to take possession sight unseen. Those three things together convinced Tom that he was a dealer, and that he was trying to pick up a bargain to hold on to through the recession. Tom didn't like it. He didn't think Mrs. Gilfred was going to like it. But it was her call, not his.

The second email was a new nibble. This guy was a regular handyman car buff in Maryland. He liked the pictures, was very interested in the car, but he also sounded a little scared of the price. Tom was sure he was more the kind of person Mrs. Gilfred had in mind. And he wanted to check him out before Guffy felt obligated to take the dealer's offer.

The shop was busy and he'd let the guys know that Cliff would not be coming back. The two experienced guys weren't surprised. He imagined they'd seen it coming for a while.

Briscoe was shocked, but pleasantly so.

"Does this mean I can get his job, maybe?" he asked Tom.

"By the time you know enough to do his job, you won't have to ask me, I'll be asking you."

Still, he liked the kid's enthusiasm. Briscoe was trying and he was learning. He wasn't afraid to ask questions. He was deferential to the other guys and to the customers who came in. It was a positive start. He also had pictures of the baby to show. Coe, as they were calling him, looked to Tom pretty much like every other baby in the world. But Briscoe thought he was amazing. Tom found that to be an admirable quality.

At three he went over to the elementary school. Quint was all a-chatter about Cody Raza being sent to the principal's office for punching a second-grader during playground time. Quint was very disappointed that he'd been on the jungle gym and had missed the whole thing.

"That guy got what he deserved," Quint assured his father. "He said that first-graders were babies. Babies! Like we are in kindergarten or something. Cody really showed him."

"You know, Quint," Tom told him, "it would have been better if Cody had made his point with words rather than with his fists."

"I know, Dad," Quint said. "But Cody's not really a words guy. He's a slug 'em kind of guy."

"Well, I'm not Cody's dad," Tom said. "But I'm your dad and I'd rather you were a 'words kind of guy.' Fighting is always the last resort."

Quint agreed. Or at least agreed to try to agree.

It was a half block later before Tom realized that at no time in that father-son discussion had he suggested that

Quint should get Erica's opinion. That they should hear her thoughts on the matter. That they should rely on her judgment. Erica was his parenting expert. But he hadn't needed her on this one. He was finding his feet. He was beginning to know the answers without having to pose the questions.

He thought about what he'd said to Briscoe that morning about knowing how to do the job. Tom was finally able to listen to his son, like he would to a misfiring engine, and know without looking which spark plug was connected to the wrong wire.

Once Quint was eating his snack and doing his homework, Tom was back on the job. He had to pull the engine out of a Firebird. Heaving out an 800-pound chunk of machinery was always fraught with potential problems. But it was one of those afternoons when everything worked the way it was supposed to. He had it locked down and secured on the hoist in no time.

When he turned to see Erica standing at the doorway, he left it where it was and walked over, wiping his hands.

"How did your EMR thing go?" he asked her.

"Great," she answered. "Better than great. Spectacular."

She was grinning ear to ear, looking happier than he'd seen her in a week or more.

"Well, I'm proud of you," he said.

"You should be even more proud than you know," she told him. "Melody chickened out on me and I had to do her part and my part all on my own. And Mrs. Converse was seated in the room, watching me the whole time."

"Wow. You go, girl," he said, and raised his hand for a fist bump.

Erica laughed and tapped his knuckles with her own.

"So I'm going home, fixing us a celebratory dinner and planning a fantastic weekend."

Tom winced. "I'm going to be late," he said. "I've got to go by and see the owner of the Buick. Working shorthanded like this, I'm not going to have any other time. But I'd love to celebrate with you when I get there."

He watched the sparkle drain out of her smile and he hated having to do it. The whole argument from the night before might have blown over, but he was sure their emotions were both still bruised.

Momentarily he thought about just letting go of the whole problem of the Buick while so much was going on. Then he reminded himself that tomorrow was Saturday again. And it was another Saturday when his wife was going to have to drag their dirty clothes and their six-year-old to some coin-operated laundry. The commission on the Buick would buy her a new washer and dryer. In the long run, his wife would appreciate that a lot more than having her husband show up for dinner.

"I'll try not to be too late," he told her.

Erica nodded and left.

With a sigh, Tom went back to work. The Firebird's engine was still in fair shape. Fair enough that he thought it could be salvaged for parts. The owner wanted to replace the 250 straight six with the much more prized 5.7-liter small block V-8. He had it buckled in by closing time. He locked up and headed to Leon Valley.

Tom pulled into his usual spot in front of Mrs. Gilfred's home. For once he was able to get to the front door without being waylaid by Miss Warner. Tom chuckled to himself as he thought of the woman's run-in with the peeper. The lady was certainly dancing around the fact that she was so nosy she was looking in her neighbor's window. The policemen didn't find it at all amusing. Neither did Guffy, who publicly scolded the woman as a busybody.

"If you want to know what's going on in my house," she told Miss Warner sharply, "then knock on the door. I'd be happy to let you inside to eavesdrop in safety and comfort."

Half the folks on the street had a hard time keeping a straight face.

Which was good. Having some creep stalking the neighborhood, even assuming he was a harmless creep, is unsettling for everybody. A bit of comic relief was very welcome.

Guffy answered the door and, as always, she seemed delighted to see him.

"Can you stay to supper?" she asked him immediately. "I'm thawing out a bit of stew that was pretty good the first time around. And it would only take me a minute to stir up a pan of corn bread."

"No, no dinner for me tonight," he told her. "My wife is fixing something special and I promised that I'd be home as soon as I could."

"All right then," she said. "So what have you got to show me? More cheesecake photos of my Clara?"

Tom laughed. "No more hot pics," he said. "But the photos are working. We've got a firm offer from the Seattle guy. And we've caught the eye of a genuine romantic in Maryland."

The two walked into the kitchen and sat down together at the table. Tom pulled up the email he'd received and turned the computer toward her so that she could read the words for herself.

He took a slip of paper and a pencil out of his pocket to make note of Mrs. Gilfred's comments or counteroffer.

The old woman sighed heavily. "I like this new fellow better than the first one," she said. "That first one is too smooth. That always makes me nervous."

"I think the smoothness is part of being in sales," Tom

said. "He's trying to make a living. It's hard to fault a man for that."

"True," Guffy agreed. "Still, selling to him is not a lot different than putting Clara up for auction."

"Except you'd know the price you're going to get."

Mrs. Gilfred waved that away. "The money never mattered that much. When you get to be my age, there's really not a lot of things that you really want or need to buy. My house is paid off and I've got my pension. I wanted to sell her because I want somebody to have her."

Tom nodded. "I know that's what you want," he confirmed. "And that's what makes the handyman in Maryland look so much more attractive."

"Yes, I suppose so," she said. "But Maryland is very far away."

"You knew we'd have to look nationally," he reminded her. "Classic cars rarely bring a good price if you sell them locally. It would have just been really great luck to find somebody in San Antonio."

"You explained that," Mrs. Gilfred said. "I wish you would buy her. The photographs alone tell me how much you love her."

Tom sighed and shook his head. "Guffy, it's like I told you," he said. "I'm a family man. I'm too honest with myself to consider a purchase like this as anything but a man-toy. And I've got too many responsibilities to treat myself to such a gift."

"You're too stubborn to see a good deal when one stumbles into the room," Mrs. Gilfred told him. "I'll let you have Clara at a bargain price. You can even pay her off over time."

"You don't want to do that," Tom said.

"Don't tell me what I do and don't want to do," Guffy said. "I wouldn't be making such a deal for nothing. I'd

expect you to take me out on a Sunday afternoon drive with
the top down now and again."

Tom grinned at her. The old lady had become a friend to
him. And he hadn't expected that. He'd met plenty of old
guys coming into the shop, but Mrs. Gilfred could talk about
things other than automobiles. And sometimes he needed
that. She had a lifetime of experience to share. And she had
an ear for listening as well.

"I did finally recall the entire Buick memory that's been
nagging me," he said.

"See, didn't I tell you it would come back to you when
you least expected."

"It certainly did that," he admitted. "I was in the middle
of firing one of my mechanics and it all came pouring in."

"And was it as nice a memory as you'd thought?"

"Yes, it kind of was," he said. Briefly he related the events
that he'd remembered. Deliberately leaving out the unnecessary details. He made it what it really was. A story of a
sunny day, a lovely wedding and a little boy with a new pair
of shoes.

She heard him out, somehow managing to hear between
the lines of the facts he stated.

"The car wasn't new even then," Tom said. "It had to be
thirty years old at the time. But I remember that the engine
was quiet and it didn't smoke, the upholstery was still nice
and the body was clean and waxed. The shoe-store man had
obviously valued it even back when it was just another old
car. He treated it with respect and attention and care."

"Which was why," Guffy said, "even as a little boy, you
knew instinctively that he was going to be a wonderful husband for your mother's friend."

Tom thought about that for a moment and then shrugged.
"I guess you're right about that. I guess the shoes meant he

could provide for her. And the car proved that he could love her."

Mrs. Gilfred smiled at him as if he were her star pupil and had just gotten the most important questions absolutely right.

"It's a wonderful memory, Tom," she said. "It's one you should hold close and cherish. Sometimes you remind me of myself. I don't have a lot of nice images from childhood. I had a mean, abusive bastard of a father. He nearly put me off men for a lifetime. The only way I could get free of him was to marry someone more powerful than he was."

She tutted to herself, shaking her head.

"I bought Clara just weeks after our divorce was final. For me that car meant I traveled the road alone. No one was ever going to put me in the passenger seat again. She was a symbol for me of all I'd achieved."

Tom nodded thoughtfully.

"For you this Buick represents the family life that you'd always wished you had," she said.

"Yes," he agreed. "It probably does. But I don't have to wish anymore. I have that family life. I have it with my own family."

"I can see that you do," Guffy said. "Although I never think it's a bad idea to have a reminder parked in the garage."

Erica rolled over in the bed and winced. She and Tom had perhaps overdone it last night with the celebratory sex, but they were making up for their argument the previous night. And Erica had her own agenda. She used the occasion as a roundabout way to suggest to her husband that whatever spicy dish he might be hungry for, was as good or better, home cooked.

"It was certainly roundabout," she muttered to herself as she grinned and blushed in the privacy of her own bed.

She could hear the water running in the shower and, from the living room, the distinctive high-pitched sounds of Saturday morning cartoons. It was the weekend and she could lie in bed if she wanted. And although she was still yawning and groggy, she was excited as well.

The water stopped running in the bathroom. A minute later a naked Tom came into the bedroom headed for his underwear drawer. Silently she admired her husband's form. His waistline was not as slim as when she married him. But his arms, his thighs, his sculpted abs and tight butt, those still looked very, very good to her. *He was her husband,* she thought. *Hers!* If that was too possessive, then so be it.

Tom must have felt her gaze upon him. He glanced in her direction.

"Did I wake you? I wanted to let you sleep."

"Just admiring the view," she said.

He turned toward her, giving her a full frontal and held his arms out on either side of him to give a "wild and crazy guy" wiggle. She groaned with humor.

Laughing, Tom pulled on his boxers and left the room. He was back a couple of minutes later, carrying two cups of coffee. He sat down on the side of the bed and handed one to her. Erica scooted up into a sitting position and brought the dark brew to her lips for the first, the best, sip of the day.

"Mmm, this is so good," she said.

"Better than what you got last night?"

"Now you're fishing for compliments," she said.

"I can dish 'em out as well as take 'em," he told her. "I walk in the door and my wife jumps my bones. Now that's a 'welcome home' that a guy could get used to."

Erica blushed a bit. "Yeah, well I was so busy with the welcome that you didn't hear all the news, what was really the best part of yesterday."

"I'm all ears," her husband said.

"Don't lie to me, Tom Bentley," Erica teased, running her hand lovingly along the clean-shaven jawline. "I just saw you without your clothes on."

He laughed. "So, tell me the best news."

"Mrs. Converse was really, really impressed with how I handled myself."

"Of course, she was," he said. "Smart woman."

"She came to the workshop to back me up and answer questions, and to take over if I stumbled. And she was just able to sit there and watch me."

"You sound surprised at that," Tom said. "But it's exactly what I would have expected. You know your stuff and you're very good at expressing yourself in a way that people can understand."

Erica liked his praise. "Thanks," she said. "Anyway, afterward Mrs. Converse told me that she's put in a proposal for a new midlevel position next year as an EMR Outreach Coordinator."

"Oh, yeah?"

"This person would actually take the training out to the small hospitals, doctors' offices, nursing homes, wherever."

Tom was nodding. "That sounds like a good idea."

"It hasn't been okayed yet," Erica said. "But she thinks, because it's self-funding, that it probably will be approved. And she said she thought I would be an excellent candidate for the job."

He raised a quizzical eyebrow. "Do you think you would like that?"

Erica nodded. "It would move me into a management bracket, so there would be slightly higher pay. I'd have a more flexible time schedule, though there would certainly be a lot of local travel involved. But I think what I like most about it is that we would have an opportunity to really put our stamp on the changes coming."

"That is pretty cool," Tom said.

"It is. Very," Erica agreed. "I like coding. I like what I'm doing now. But this would be really challenging."

"And you're just the woman to take on a challenge," Tom said. "I mean, you married me, didn't you?"

She laughed.

"Future view—The Bentleys," Tom said. "Three years from today."

"Okay," Erica said. "I've gotten the outreach position and I've trained people all over our part of the state. I've been able to take my own philosophy of medical records—and how it improves the standards of care—to the entire region."

"Sounds good," Tom said.

"And I also get to spend all my future Saturday mornings being served coffee in bed," she added.

"Hey, now," he feigned complaint. "You're lucky you're sitting on your backside, 'cause talk like that could definitely earn you a husbandly swat."

"Ooh, promise?" she teased.

They continued to talk and laugh and speculate as Tom got ready for work. By the time he left, Erica was humming and feeling optimistic about the adventure of applying for a new kind of job.

Her thoughts drifted to Melody. Her coworker had more seniority on the job and a better grasp of EMR. Erica was pretty sure that when Mrs. Converse had written the proposal for the new position, she'd had Melody in mind. But Melody's self-image had been too small to combine both devoted wife and responsible employee.

Melody's loss was Erica's gain. She had no problem expanding the view of herself as wife, mother and successful professional. And she couldn't even feel bad about it.

She shook her head thinking about what she'd discovered yesterday. Melody believed that Erica was having an affair with Dr. Glover. That was totally ridiculous. Why on earth would a woman buy into such a silly notion on such flimsy evidence? Believing in gossip could become an addiction as bad as smoking or drinking.

Erica took her last sip of coffee, luxuriating in her leisure.

Wife, mother, medical records professional, sex goddess.

She laughed aloud at her own musings. Then she got up and dutifully began her day. She fixed breakfast for Quint, picked up the house and took care of her regular Saturday chores. Quint had to give up cartoons for room cleaning. And, of course, Quint cleaning his room meant Erica could get nothing else done between the encouragement, questions about where things go and unsuccessful inspections.

"Mom?" his voice rang through the house time and time again.

At noon Erica put together what she thought of as a compromise lunch: tuna patties with spinach, for brain power and iron. Macaroni and cheese, to satisfy her son's palate. She began gathering up the laundry. Still dreading the nearby coin-op, she called her mother to see if she could bring it over to Mr. Schoenleber's house.

"When are you buying yourself that new washer?" her mother demanded.

"Soon," Erica promised. "Very soon. But today I'd love to borrow the laundry room."

Her mother humphed unhappily. "Well, all right, I suppose."

"I'm bringing Quint," Erica warned.

"Well, Melvin's here, maybe he can entertain him."

Erica gathered up everything and loaded it into the car. She and Quint drove over to the house in Monte Vista. Melvin came out to help them carry everything into the laundry room.

Ann Marie was on her phone, but interrupted the call long enough to suggest to Melvin that he entertain Quint.

Melvin looked intently at him for a moment. "What would you like to do?" he asked.

Quint shrugged his small shoulders. "Anything," he answered honestly.

"There's a dinosaur exhibit at the Witte Museum, would you like to go?"

Erica watched her son's eyes widen with excitement. "Could we?" He turned toward her. "Could we, Mom?"

"You sure you're up for that, Mr. Schoenleber?"

"Call me Melvin," he answered. "And I've been wanting an excuse to go see it myself."

Erica gave Quint a stern lecture about being on his best behavior, but she knew he would be. She waved goodbye as they headed off. Her mother was still chatting in the solarium. Erica went to the laundry room to get started on the dirty clothes.

She filled the washer with light-colored things, a couple of her blouses, a few of Quint's shirts, various kinds of underwear and pajamas. She started that up and then began sorting through some of the more heavily soiled items. Tom's work clothes were, of course, the worst. With all the grease and oil and various motor fluids, they were always a challenge. As were the superfluous items he always left in his pockets. Early in their marriage she often complained about his jeans in the laundry basket with loose change or a pencil or, worst of the worst, a tissue hiding in the pocket. Over time she'd discovered that it was easier to train herself to check the pockets than to train him to leave them empty. Today her surprises included a tire valve stem, a lug nut, a half-dozen receipts and a business card for a new auto glass shop. Erica piled the saved items atop the dryer. She always took them home and put them on his dresser, which is where he would look for something if he lost it.

A word on one of the loose pieces of paper caught her eye. She stared at it for a long moment and then slowly, hesitantly, she picked it up and read what Tom had written in his own handwriting.

Clara
doesn't like smooth
keep close
somebody to love her like I do

Erica stared at the paper, reading and rereading it. What did it mean? The last line needed no explanation. Tom, her Tom, actually *loved* somebody else.

Tears stung her eyes, but she blinked them back. She'd already cried too much over this. She'd already moaned and grieved and sobbed. The image of Melody caught in her mind—sitting on the toilet, red nosed and mascara streaked. It was not as if there weren't choices in the world. A woman could live in fear and curse the fates or she could take action on her own behalf. Erica recalled that morning in the bedroom when she'd looked at her husband, casually naked, and had felt that sense of ownership. He was *her* husband. Couples did not own each other, but they did pledge to each other. Until he renounced that bond, it was still there. And Erica was not giving up or giving in without a fight.

She grabbed her purse. Her mother was still in the solarium, still on the phone.

"When my clothes finish, put them in the dryer," Erica ordered.

Her mother's startled face said everything about the uniqueness of such a request. "All right, dear," Ann Marie answered in a voice that was both shocked and conciliatory.

Erica walked out the back door to her car. She got in and drove toward Leon Valley and a confrontation with the other woman.

Chapter 21

THE SUBDIVISION LOOKED different during the day-time. Erica made several wrong turns before she finally turned onto Helm Street. She pulled up and parked in the place where Tom's truck had been a few nights ago. Then she began to second-guess herself. Everything looked different in the clear light of midday. What if this wasn't the right house and she went to the door and confronted the wrong woman?

As she was considering such a scenario, the neighbor came out of her house carrying a broom to sweep her driveway. Erica remembered the neighbor perfectly. She just hoped the woman wouldn't remember her. Steeling her nerves, she got out of the car and went directly up the sidewalk to the front porch that Tom had stood upon himself.

She rang the doorbell. It was the overwhelmingly loud sound that Erica recalled from her night as a neighborhood peeper. The wait seemed just as long as well. The neigh-bor, still sweeping, made a sound as if she wanted to say something. Erica was not going to waste one word on the nosy busybody. She froze the woman out with a look as sharp as an ice pick.

On the drive Erica had imagined what she would say to her rival.

Perhaps she should pour on the guilt. *Tom not only has a wife, but he's got a little boy who adores him. You mustn't destroy that.*

Or maybe a threat like her mother might make. *I'll take him for everything he's got and the two of you will be left with nothing.*

But what she really wanted to say was pure Loretta Lynn, *You ain't woman enough to take my man!*

Erica heard the dead bolt click. She stiffened her spine and set her jaw tightly, ready for battle.

The door yawned open and standing on the threshold was a tiny old woman in men's trousers and a cardigan sweater.

"Whatever you're selling, I'm not buying," she said directly.

"I'm a…"

"And if you're wanting me to go to some church, well, religion and I parted ways some time back."

"No, I'm…"

"Speak up! I can't make out a blame thing if you mumble."

Erica did speak up, loud and clear. "I'm here to see Clara."

"Clara?" The woman appeared momentarily caught off guard before she answered. "Clara's not here."

"Where is she?"

Erica's sharp, unfriendly tone was contagious.

"What's it to you?" the old woman asked.

"I…I am *Mrs. Tom Bentley,*" she declared. Erica rarely used the old-fashioned, formal description of herself. But at this moment she felt certain it was called for.

The woman's brow furrowed for a moment and then the expression on her face changed completely into a warm, welcoming smile.

"You're Tom's wife?" she said. "Well, come in, come in. No sense standing on the porch. There is such a chill in the air today."

Erica hadn't noticed any chill. And the woman's unexpected friendliness was more disconcerting than her hostility. However she was determined to confront Clara and this woman knew where to find her, so Erica followed her inside.

"Come on back into the kitchen," the woman said. "It's a bit early, I guess, but I'm having my afternoon toddy."

The kitchen was retro, not by design but by default. The dark wood cabinets and green appliances were relics of a bygone era. But the place was clean and the sun streaming through the double windows, where Erica had gained her experience as a peeper, made the room cheerful.

"Sit, sit," the woman insisted.

Erica took the same chair she'd seen her husband occupying.

On the table a tall green bottle with the name Laphroaig took center stage.

The woman tapped the whiskey adoringly on its cap. "This is my absolute favorite. In my opinion it's the best scotch malt money can buy." She laughed lightly. "Of course my money doesn't buy a lot of whiskey, but I drink one bottle a year of this and we're nearly to Thanksgiving. Let me get you a glass."

"No, thank you," Erica told her quickly. "I don't care for any."

"Oh, you've got to try it," she insisted. "Good whiskey is

the best thing in the world. It doesn't give you a headache like wine, or make you sick to your stomach like mixed drinks. And don't even talk to me about beer. A woman just can't drink that and keep her girlish figure."

From the cupboard, the woman produced a square and stubby glass into which she splashed about a quarter of an inch of the liquor.

"Just have a taste," the woman said.

"Look, Mrs...." Erica hesitated.

"Oh, call me Guffy," the woman said. "My friends call me Guffy and I am absolutely certain you and I are going to be great friends."

Erica could not imagine such a circumstance. The mere suggestion of it caused her to bring the glass of whiskey to her lips.

The taste was not at all what Erica expected. She'd always found alcohol to be kind of medicinal, best when disguised by orange juice or tabasco or blended into the official drink of San Antonio, a margarita, essentially a limeade Sno-Kone. But this ten-year-old scotch was smooth and smoky. It smelled like the ocean, but the warmth and sweetness on her tongue was strangely invigorating. Erica felt more alert, more in control. She'd always thought that the term "liquid courage" meant too drunk to think straight. But this was different and immediate. It was like the alertness of coffee with the addition of self-assurance. Erica needed both.

"The whiskey is very nice, Mrs....uh...Guffy. But I am not here to socialize."

She nodded. "Of course not, you're here about Clara," she said. She clucked her tongue. "I have to admit, I'm surprised he even mentioned her to you. Or maybe he didn't," she suggested, looking at Erica questioningly. "Maybe he just told you about her generally and not how much I think the two of them belong together."

Erica nearly choked on her whiskey. "I'm his *wife*," she said. "You can hardly expect him to say something like that to me."

Guffy shrugged. "I suppose you're right," she said. "But now that you know I hope you would consider it."

"Consider what?"

"Letting Tom take Clara off my hands," the woman answered. "I love her, she's important to me and we've had a lot of great times together. But the future is not so bright for me as it once was. My doctors tell me that these seasons of feeling okay will get to be fewer and fewer as this endgame proceeds. I want to make sure that Clara goes on. That someone who loves her is taking care of her. And I'm convinced that the person who can best do that is your Tom."

Erica didn't know what to say. She drank her scotch instead of speaking.

"I truly like and admire your husband," Guffy told her. "And I'm not particularly partial to men. If you want the truth, I've been quietly batting for the other team for the last sixty years."

Erica wondered if the whiskey was numbing her brain. "Batting for the other team?" she repeated.

Guffy nodded. "I'm a lesbian," she answered. "Isn't it interesting that I can just say that out loud. When I first knew I was one, I couldn't even whisper the word to my girlfriend. Now they say it on TV."

The woman chuckled as if delighted by the idea.

Erica was trying to take this information in and sort it with what little she already knew. Somehow it was not adding up easily.

"Is…uh…is Clara a lesbian as well?"

The older woman seemed momentarily stunned and then literally guffawed.

"You are funny," she said. "You are really funny. You seem very proper, but what a dry wit. No wonder Tom is so in love with you."

"He *is* in love with me," Erica stated firmly.

"I know," Guffy agreed. "He talks about you and your boy all the time. Everything he says and does is about you. Even his decision to reject Clara is all about that. But I don't want you to let him do it. He and Clara have a special bond. I understand that. She has great meaning to me, too. That meaning is important to preserve. It may be as important as preserving Clara herself."

Erica repeated the words that rang loudest to her. "Tom rejected Clara."

Guffy nodded. "Oh, yes. And more than once. He keeps saying how he's a family man and he has responsibilities. I believe in that. I applaud it, but these two just belong together and I'm going to do everything I can to make that happen."

"You can say that, right to my face!"

"Well, I wouldn't say it behind your back," Guffy told her. "I'd think you'd welcome it. An honest hardworking man, who cares so much about his family deserves a reward."

"Not a reward like that!"

"I'll make it as easy on you as I can," the old woman said. "But your Tom is a proud man with a strong sense of what's right. He didn't take advantage of me, even when he could have. I don't expect he'd do that now."

"No, he would not," Erica said. "Tom doesn't 'take advantage' of women. He looks tough and he's a man's kind of man, but he's a protector when it comes to women and children."

Guffy nodded. "Probably because he grew up taking care of his mother and fending for himself."

Erica tried to keep her jaw from dropping. Tom *never* talked about his early life or his mother. He deliberately kept his past in the past. And even direct questions from curious neighbors and acquaintances earned answers that were vague enough to be meaningless.

"He told you about his mother?"

"Not too much," Guffy answered. "Tom's childhood is not a place he wants to revisit. But we've spent a good deal of time together, talking about Clara. Things come out."

Guffy shrugged as if that meant nothing. But it was something to Erica.

"I think perhaps he sees me as the grandmother he never had," Guffy said. "I'm sure I would have loved to have a son or grandson like him."

And what would that make Clara? Erica thought to herself. His sister? Or his wife?

"I need to go," Erica told the older woman. "Do you know where I can find Clara?"

"She's at your husband's shop."

"She's with Tom." Erica stood up so quickly she spilled the rest of the liquor in her glass. She quickly began sopping it up with the tiny cocktail napkin she'd been given.

"Grab that dish towel hanging on the drawer handle," Guffy said. "This whiskey hits you kind of quick if you're not used to it."

"I didn't drink enough for it to hit me," Erica assured her. "Now thank you for your hospitality, but I really must go."

"You're going to see Clara, aren't you?"

"Yes, if you must know, I am going to see her and my husband," she said. "I believe I have the right."

Guffy nodded. "Sit back down," she said. "I'm going to

call him and tell him to bring her over here. You shouldn't be out on the road in your condition."

"I'm not in any condition," Erica insisted. "I hardly drank any of this at all."

"Well, I'm going to pretend that you did," Guffy said. "It's time that this discussion was out in the open and I'm not going to be left out."

Tom couldn't have been any more startled by the call from Mrs. Gilfred. Stranger yet was the conversation. It wasn't really much of a conversation, more of a dialogue with responses from Tom that were either ignored or met with a "what did you say?"

"Your wife is here at my house," Guffy told him. "I've plied her with liquor to get on her good side. Now bring my Clara home and let's see if the three of us can work something out."

"I think I've been very clear," Tom said. "I'd love to buy this car, but I just don't think I should."

"What was that?"

Tom raised his voice. With her hearing problem and the noise of the shop he was practically yelling into the phone. "I said I'd...I'll come over there."

"Good, good. And bring Clara. Pretty day like this would be perfect for getting her out into the sunshine."

Tom was shaking his head and muttering under his breath as he went back into the work area. What on earth was going on? And why was Erica up in Leon Valley talking with Mrs. Gilfred? The old woman must have gone around him. She'd really become too fond of the idea of Tom buying the Buick. Now she'd probably roped Erica into agreeing with her.

He found Briscoe where he'd left him, beneath the chassis of an '86 Fiero.

"I'm going to have to leave for an hour or so," he said. "Do you think you can finish this on your own?"

The young guy glanced into the undercarriage of the vehicle and then over at Tom. "Uh…yeah…yeah, I think I can."

Tom nodded. "Don't trust yourself completely yet," he cautioned him. "Get Gus or Hector to take a look before you call it done."

Briscoe nodded.

"I've got to take the Buick up to her owner," Tom announced. "I guess it's time for her to get a road trial anyway. Gus, you're in charge. Keep everybody working, we've got too much to do to have anybody slacking off today."

The man nodded with a solemnity that was unexpected. "You do what you have to do, Tom. I can keep this crew on task. And nobody's a better teacher than Hector. He'll probably be better for the youngster than you are."

Tom nodded. "Okay, then," he said.

In bay four, Tom raised the door. He grabbed a chamois and wiped the dust off the car as he put down the convertible top. She was looking good. Her heavy amounts of polished chrome were like a beautiful woman covered in expensive jewels. She didn't need the bling, but it was certainly eye-catching. Her new wide-stripe whitewalls, recently arrived from the antique tire distributor in Tennessee, added the kind of elegant glamour that one associated with famous actresses of a bygone era walking carefree in impossibly high heels.

Tom opened the driver's-side door and sat down inside. He slid the key into the ignition and turned it over. She started up immediately and purred with the smooth efficiency that defined the Nailhead V-8. He slipped her out of the bay and into the front lot, allowing her a minute and a half to warm-up, a necessity for vintage engines.

It was a gorgeous afternoon, the air was dry and crisp, but the sun shining directly down on him was warm. In San Antonio, convertibles were not a summer vehicle. And summer was often the longest season. But there were plenty of wonderful days in spring and fall and even the depths of winter when an open car was exactly the right thing.

Tom slid the variable pitch Dynaflow transmission into Drive and pulled out onto West Avenue. He felt as if he were playing hooky. He should be back in the shop with his head up a busted muffler. Instead he was cruising down the road on the finest set of wheels he would never own. He was loving it. And it was part of his job, he reminded himself. An old car was like an old person, life was pretty much use it or lose it. Clara had already spent too much time being carefully garaged. She needed to be driven. And he wanted to be the person to do that. At least while he could.

Tom tried not to speculate on Erica and Mrs. Gilfred. What if the old lady had convinced Erica? What if she was going to push Tom to buy Clara?

That scenario was too pleasant to be seriously considered. Tom had learned early to take a healthy dose of reality with all his dreams. Santa Claus didn't really leave stuff for kids on December 24. And his smart, sensible Erica wasn't going to throw judgment out the window just because an old lady asked her to. Even if Erica was convinced, Tom had known all along that owning classic cars was too rich for his blood. That's why he'd wanted to open his kind of shop. He got to care for them, repair them, restore them without having to pay for the upkeep.

He pulled to a stop at a red light. The brakes were almost

completely silent. All the sound was in the pedal not the rotors or the pads. And they responded efficiently, just as they should without the slightest veer to the left or right.

The driver of the compact Honda next to him rolled down the passenger window.

"Great car!"

"Thanks," Tom answered.

"Did you restore it yourself?"

"It's mostly original," Tom told the guy. "I did some work on it. It belongs to one of my customers."

"You a mechanic?"

Tom pulled one of his cards out of his shirt pocket and leaned left as far as he could to hand it through the guy's window. He took it and glanced at it quickly.

"My father-in-law has an old Shelby he's been working on for years," the guy said. "He's always complaining about not being able to find the right mechanic."

"Tell him to drop by," Tom said. "And bring his Shelby if it's drivable. If nothing else I'd be happy to admire it."

Behind them a car honked. The light had changed.

"Thanks," the guy called out before he continued on.

Word of mouth was the best advertising. If the guy's father-in-law liked working on cars, he would probably have friends who did, too. And often they were in that age group where they had more money to have things fixed than time to fix it themselves.

Tom entered the freeway, eager to blow the cobwebs out of Clara's tailpipe and see how she liked it. She accelerated with all the power he'd expect of the 322 and she was up to sixty by the time he left the ramp. It was hard to hear engine noise over the noise of the wind, but she was driving smoothly, with no rattles or vibrations. Tom couldn't keep from smiling.

He exited the interstate at Bandera, wove his way through the traffic to Mrs. Gilfred's subdivision. Once there he leisurely took the twists and turns, not detecting any jerkiness or whine in the power steering.

When he got to Mrs. Gilfred's house, sure enough, he saw Erica's car parked in front. He turned into the driveway that had been Clara's for many decades.

He turned the car off and walked to the front door. Tom glanced in the direction of Miss Warner's house and caught her peeking out from between the plants on her porch. He smiled and waved before pressing the button on the doorbell for the hard-of-hearing.

The old woman opened the door, looking, as she always did these days, happy to see him. Behind her, standing near the kitchen, Erica did not look so pleased. Even from this distance he could see the lines in her forehead and the set of her jaw. She had her hands clasped together tightly. Guffy must have upset her somehow. He hoped she hadn't been pressuring her to buy the Buick. Surely she knew he wouldn't push for that. Of course Erica would know that his responsibility to his wife and son came *way* ahead of his love of any car.

He gave her a big smile, hoping that it offered reassurance. She returned one that was more tentative.

"Come on in the kitchen, Tom," Mrs. Gilfred said to him. "You've been here enough that you surely know the way."

"Yes, ma'am, I do," he said, but he let her go first. Her gait was still hesitant, as if she was measuring every step.

Tom followed slowly as she went into the kitchen. Erica still stood by the doorway.

"Is Quint here?" he asked her.

"He's gone to the museum with Melvin," she answered. "Who's running the shop?"

"I left Gus in charge," he answered.

Directly in front of her, the concern he'd seen from across the room was clearly visible. Hoping to dispel it, he wrapped an arm around her waist and gave her a peck on the lips. He tasted liquor on her breath, an unexpected surprise.

"So you've been sampling the Scotch whiskey. That's pretty wild for my Erica on a Saturday afternoon," he teased.

She didn't seem to see the humor in it.

"Where's Clara?" Her tone was defensive, almost harsh. It was out of character and puzzling.

"Out in the driveway," he answered. "Look, I don't know what Mrs. Gilfred has said or how hard she's tried to push this on you, but I'm not crazy. I'm not about to mess things up for us."

Tom saw Erica's brow furrow. "Mrs. Gilfred?" she asked. "Where have I heard that name before?"

"That's Guffy's name," he answered.

"I didn't hear it here," she said.

Tom shrugged. "Let's sit down and talk," he said. "There are some things I've been thinking about."

"No," Erica answered. "I'm not talking about anything before I meet Clara."

He eyed his wife for a moment, and then chuckled at her choice of words. "Honey, you actually have met her," he said. "But I'm happy to introduce you again. Besides, we probably do need to talk first in private. Guffy, we'll be back."

"Take all the time you need, talk it out. I want you kids to be happy with Clara. It would please me a lot."

"We'll talk," Tom told the older woman. "We're not making any promises, so don't get your heart set on it."

He grabbed Erica's hand and led her out. He felt strangely young and exuberant. He was excited to be with Erica, just the two of them. The two of them and a gorgeous car. He rushed her across the porch and down the steps and didn't stop until they were standing in the driveway next to the Buick. Parked out in bright sunshine, Clara was even more beautiful than she had been sitting in the shop. He'd waxed the paint job to a near clear-coat finish and the chrome gleamed like mirrors. He glanced over at Erica to see if she was as taken by the sight.

His wife was looking all around, everywhere but at the car. That wasn't a good sign. But Tom was determined to show the vehicle at its best. And its best, of course, was out on the road.

"Erica, meet Clara," he said as he opened the passenger door. "Hop in, baby, and we'll take her for a spin."

She hesitated for a long moment and then slid into the seat. Tom shut the door and then ran around to get behind the wheel. He put the key in the ignition and turned it over. He had to stop himself from pointing out how good the engine sounded. Erica needed to appreciate it herself, not simply to know how much he appreciated it.

He backed the car out of the narrow driveway and headed down the street. Tom glanced in her direction to see the wind blowing through her hair. He loved that feeling, but he knew some women weren't crazy about it, so he modulated the speed, keeping a leisurely pace down the city streets.

Beside him, Erica suddenly started laughing.

"What is it?" he asked, but she just shook her head.

Tom pulled to a stop at a red light on Bandera Road. In the crosswalk at the curb an old man with a walker ignored his turn to make his way to the other side of the street for the pleasure of simply staring at Clara.

"I had a car just like that once," he called out to them. "It was green and a hardtop, but it was just like yours."

Tom smiled at him and looked over at Erica. She was grinning, too.

"I wish I still had that car," the old man said.

"I wish you did, too," Tom told him. He pulled a business card out of his pocket and gave it to Erica. "He might have friends."

Erica bounded out of the Buick, handed it to the old man and was back in her seat before the light changed. They waved at the guy as they drove off.

Tom made his way though the streets, turning this way and that. At first he thought he was just wandering, then he realized that he had a destination in mind. As he had in his life, as soon as he figured out where he wanted to go he drove there directly. When he arrived at Woodlawn Lake he parked in the smallest, most distant lot from the clubhouse and docks. It was bereft of trees, making it the a perfect spot for private, nighttime stargazing. It wasn't so bad on a Saturday afternoon, either.

Tom remembered the exact location of their long-ago tryst and put the Buick in that very place. He turned off the ignition, replacing the sound of the motor with the flutter of the breeze through the leaves and the distant squeals of children at play down at the lake.

He turned to his beautiful wife, attractive and desirable in jeans and a T-shirt with her ponytail slightly windblown. She was running her hands along the chrome trim on the dashboard. His eyes were drawn not to the shiny metal but to the hands, long and slim and loving hands that were so familiar to him and so dear.

"What are you thinking?" he asked her.

Erica looked up at him, her gaze so direct, so open, so contented with her life.

"Guffy says that you're in love with Clara," she stated.

"I am in love with Erica," he answered. "I do love Clara, she's a beautiful Buick. But that's what she is, a Buick. I figured out some time ago that I want more in my life than a gorgeous car. I want my wife. I want my son. I want our family to be together. And then I want our business, our friends, our relatives. Any and all of that means more to me than this very pretty vehicle."

"But you would like to own the car."

Tom nodded. "I would, I admit that. And I feel like half the town has been trying to talk me into buying it."

"I'm listening," Erica said.

"Okay," Tom began, sighing heavily. "There is the investment aspect of owning her. You know how I feel about investing in classic cars. But it is true that in the collection market right now, Buicks are still among the best bargains. Their prices haven't started to rise like the costs of those muscle cars. I think that's temporary, I think the value is going to go up. No one knows how soon or how far, but it's going to happen. For almost no cost, except my own time, I can keep her in top shape almost indefinitely. We could sell her at any time and most likely get at least as much as we paid for her."

Erica was nodding.

"As just an investment, however, I couldn't justify buying her," he said. "She might actually work better for us as an advertisement. You've seen for yourself how much attention she generates just rolling down the street. I can have magnetic signs made for her doors with our logo and phone number. It's better than a billboard, because you might see it anywhere in town."

Erica appeared to consider that thoughtfully.

"And there are also ways for a beautiful vehicle like this to pay its own way," Tom said. "I wouldn't want to rent it out—I think the insurance for something like that would just be prohibitive. But I could do some chauffeuring. If you had business associates in town and you needed to give them a tour of the city, what better way to do it than in a fabulous, comfortable vintage convertible?"

Erica was smiling at him now.

"And for weddings," he said. "You know the first time I ever rode in a car like this was at a wedding. Can't you just picture it with some tasteful strings of tin cans attached to the bumper."

Erica laughed aloud. "I can see half the young women in this town opting for blue-on-blue as her bridal colors."

"You think so?"

She slid across the seat to wrap her arms around his neck. "I do think so," she said. "It's such a romantic automobile. Somehow it just says love and commitment and…and sex."

Erica brought her mouth to his and the kiss was hot, passionate, luscious, tugging at his mouth. She was the aggressor again and Tom was immediately, delightedly, turned-on. He liked this change in his wife. He liked having her stroke him, seduce him. She straddled him, pressing their bodies as closely together as fabric would allow. She rocked atop him until he moaned aloud. Then she pulled her lips from his. She kissed him on his cheek, his jaw. Her teeth tugged lightly on his ear before she whispered in warm breath that raised hackles all over his body.

"Tell me that you love me."

"I love you," he said as she kissed his throat. "I love you," he said as she lingered at his collarbone. "I love you," he said as she pressed her lips to the top of his sternum. She began undoing the buttons on his shirt and moving down his chest as his "I love you" mantra continued. The soft touch of her mouth was enticing. When she moved on, the moisture of her kiss tingled in the hint of breeze. His nipples were as hard as bearings but with the sensitivity of spark plug wires. The hair on his chest stood as taut as suspension springs, but instead of being relegated to supporting the frame they were roaring to combustion like a carburetor. When Erica unbuckled his belt and reached for the button on his jeans, he had just enough sense left to grab her hands.

"We're in an open vehicle in a public place," he pointed out.

"I know," she told him. "And normally I wouldn't say this, but can you make it quick?"

She didn't wait for his answer as she unzipped his pants and put her head in his lap.

He was easily able to comply.

Erica repaired her makeup in the rearview mirror as best she could. Tom had gone up to the clubhouse and came back with a soda from the vending machine. She took a grateful sip.

He was looking at her in the intense, knowing way that was the hallmark of their intimacy. She felt herself blushing. Deliberately she mustered her almost-ten-years-a-married-woman sophistication and drew it around her like a cloak.

"Well, I suppose we have to buy this car," she said. "I only have sex with men in cars we actually own."

Tom chuckled. "Are you sure, Erica?" he asked more seriously. "Because there are still a lot of arguments against it."

"What arguments?"

"Well, there's Quint's college fund, for one. Our mortgage. Putting more money into the business. Getting a more practical car for the family, a minivan or something."

"Quint's college fund is a monthly automatic draw," she

said. "As is the mortgage. I like taking public transportation. And buying this car will be putting money in the business."

"There's one other thing I haven't told you that may change your mind," he said.

"What?"

"Guffy was going to give me ten percent commission on the sale," he said. "I was hoping to use that money to buy you a new washer and dryer. The ones we have are completely shot and ready for the junkyard. If we don't get that ten percent, it'll be that much longer before we can afford to replace them."

Erica looked at her husband for a long minute. "You were going to buy me a washer and dryer?"

"Well, not you so much as us," he answered. "You may *do* most of the laundry, but Quint and I *create* most of it."

That was certainly true.

"I've priced some models, but of course, I'd want you to pick the one you like best."

"I have," she answered. "I've been looking, too, and I've found exactly the ones I want."

Tom nodded slowly. "But if we buy this car..." He let the obvious hang out incomplete.

"We're buying this car, mister," she said. "Don't try to wiggle out of it by saying you didn't mean to have sex here and that I led you astray."

He was grinning again.

"And we'll buy the washer and dryer, too," she said. "The hospital made an error when they first calculated my pay. I'm making more than we'd budgeted for, and I've been putting that excess in a new savings account just for household stuff. By my next paycheck, I'll be able to buy exactly what I want."

"Wow, I can't believe that," Tom said. "That's great."

"Thanks."

"I can't believe you didn't tell me," he said. "You've been keeping this to yourself all this time."

"Are you mad?" she asked him.

"No, just a little confused. You've always had such a thing about honesty. Remember how mad you got at me about not sharing what I knew about Cliff and Trish's marriage."

"I was wrong about that," Erica said. "People, even married people, have to be allowed to hold confidences. That's part of having friends. If a husband or wife can't let each other do that, it's almost like they insist on being the only friend. It's not right and it's not fair."

"I was not quite fair, either," Tom said. "It was not a confidence I wanted to have. I should have insisted to Cliff immediately that I would not keep it for him."

"Unlucky them," Erica said.

Tom nodded. "And lucky us."

"Careful, committed us," Erica corrected. "I love you very much, Tom. It would hurt me very much if you were ever unfaithful to me. But I'm not going to look for lies. I'm going to trust you to tell me the truth."

"I promise I will," he said. "At least as much as I can. The big things are so obvious, it makes it easy. But it's the little things that sometimes trip me up. I know that you've always been such a stickler for having everything out in the open."

"I've changed my mind about that," Erica said.

"Really?"

"Big important things really should be shared, but small secrets can sometimes add up to wonderful surprises."

He grinned at her.

"Future view—The Bentleys," she said. "Fifty years from now."

"Fifty!" Tom's jaw dropped for a moment. "Will we still be alive?"

"We can try," Erica told him.

He was thoughtful for a long moment. "Fifty years from now, the business and the hospital and all that career stuff will be behind us. Quint will be taking care of two old, retired people."

"True," Erica agreed.

"He'll be successful doing...whatever he wants to do. He'll be married to some great woman a lot like his mama and he'll take us for Sunday outings, since you and I won't be able to drive anymore."

"You're right," Erica agreed. "Neither of us will be able to drive. So...I guess we'll have to push this Buick down here to the parking lot from time to time to stir up the passion we'll still have together."

Epilogue

THE ENTIRE STREET OF west Fair Oaks was blocked off, as were all the nearby parking lots of the school. It was a balmy seventy-seven degrees, but the floats, the marchers, the decorations all featured brilliantly white snow, frost-glistened trees and characters costumed in red fur. With a shrill whistle, the policeman waved the lead, a very businesslike patrol car, onto the parade route. The lights were flashing to warn off any errant vehicle who might not have noticed the crowds, the barricades and the dozens of officers securing the route. Behind the leader was the color guard from Fort Sam Houston, moving in the elegant solemnity expected of those representing the men and women in uniform. They carried the national flag and one for each branch of service.

The high school marching band elected to forgo the flashy capes and striped trousers they typically wore, for matching shorts and T-shirts, each head topped with a jaunty Santa cap. They played "Sleigh Ride" with enough enthusiasm that onlookers found themselves singing along.

The pug owners' club pulled a series of minifloats in wagons, each featuring his or her pet besplendored in kingly or queenly garb. The Shriners wheeled in crazy commotion in their go-carts. There were clowns on stilts, politicians in motor cars and an army of *Star Wars* characters wielding light sabers.

Almost half of the parade had already headed south on Broadway when the cop waved entrant number 27, a shiny blue-on-blue 1956 Buick Roadmaster convertible with a continental kit onto the street. The vehicle was lightly festooned with silver garland and shiny stars twinkling over the dark blue fenders. Magnetic signs on the doors advertised Bentley's Classic Car Care with the familiar logo, the address, phone number and website. Inside the vehicle four occupants waved at the crowd. In the front seat a married couple, in their early thirties, looked happy, eager and slightly harried, as would be expected of ambitious young people operating a business and raising a family.

In the backseat a wide-eyed laughing little boy sat next to a thin, frail, older woman with a crew cut as silver as the holiday decor. She was grinning as broadly as the child. Her wave was perhaps a bit shaky and she needed to rest her arm in her lap every few minutes, but she was obviously enjoying her day in the sun, riding in a beautiful car that was as familiar to her as anything in her life.

A few blocks ahead of them, seated on the rooftop of the single-floor building that housed one of the Schoenleber Medical Supply stores, Ann Marie Maddock was dressed in an elegant summer linen suit of brilliant red. If one looked closely at the silk scarf around her throat, it featured the tiniest of red, green and gold poinsettias, her only concession to the season. She watched the passing celebration with moderate interest, sipping on a glass of white wine. Every few moments she glanced up the street anxious for the sight of her daughter and grandson who were to be in the parade for the first time.

With disdain she noted the number of plump thirtyish and fortyish women in holiday T-shirts featuring reindeer, snowmen and assorted elves of several varieties. She hoped against hope that Erica had not chosen to wear something so inarguably tacky. But both her daughters had minds of their own, and fashion seemed never to enter them.

Letty was at the far end of the balcony, socializing with other younger people invited to view the occasion. She was dressed, very typically for her, in skinny jeans and a layered top. Fortunately, Letty had the body type to get away with wearing almost anything. One of the young men in attendance seemed particularly taken with her. He was nice looking, perhaps a bit boyish in appearance but life certainly had a cure for that. She'd heard him say that he worked at University Hospital and if he was a friend of Melvin's son, then he could at least afford to take her daughter out for a nice dinner.

"Doctor?" she'd asked Melvin pointedly. He knew her well enough not to require any further explanation of her interest.

He glanced over in the direction of the two.

"Uh…pharmacist, I think," Melvin answered. "I'm pretty sure he said pharmacist."

She turned her attention back to the street in time to see a float that was merely a couple of pieces of blow-up lawn decoration pulled on a trailer. Apparently the standards for what qualified as an entry were very low.

"I have a little holiday gift for you," Melvin said.

That got her full attention. She loved getting presents. Especially the kind given by wealthy men that came in small blue jewelry boxes.

She smiled at him when he handed it to her. It was tiny and square. About the perfect size for earrings. She had seen some gorgeous sapphires at Penaloza. Maybe the owner had called Melvin and mentioned them. No, that would be too lucky. She girded herself for disappointment as she untied the bow and opened the little box.

To Ann Marie's surprise it wasn't earrings at all but a huge square-cut diamond in a breathtaking antique setting.

"What's this?" she asked him.

"Exactly what it looks like," Melvin answered. "But before you say anything, one way or another, you have to know that I want a very strict pre-nup. If you divorce me, you don't take anything that I've bought, including this ring. If you stay with me, everything I have is yours for the rest of your life. A lot of women would think that's a very good deal."

Ann Marie just stared at him, shocked, her thoughts shooting out in a hundred different directions.

"Ann Marie! Ann Marie! Mr. Melvin!" The sound of a little voice permeated the noise all around her. She turned her eyes toward the street just in time to see Quint waving up at her from the backseat of the very beautiful, very romantic Buick.

★ ★ ★ ★ ★

We hope you enjoyed this novel from Pamela Morsi.
Overleaf are some discussion questions that we hope will
further enhance your enjoyment of this novel.

QUESTIONS FOR DISCUSSION

1. We're a culture that loves gossip. Where does it cross the line between entertaining pastime and harmful influence?

2. Erica is back to work after a stint as a stay-at-home mom. Have you been there and done that? What kind of challenges did you face that she did not?

3. Is a successful marriage a matter of luck, hard work or compatibility of personalities over time?

4. Erica loves her son, but also loves having a job. Is she everywoman or simply a type?

5. Conventional wisdom suggests that family dysfunction gets repeated in successive generations. Yet Tom's childhood created a longing for sanity and stability. Is that true to life?

6. Is infidelity a challenge or a deal breaker in marriage?

REQUEST YOUR
FREE BOOKS!

2 FREE NOVELS
FROM THE ROMANCE COLLECTION
PLUS 2 FREE GIFTS!

YES! Please send me 2 FREE novels from the Romance Collection and my 2 FREE gifts (gifts are worth about $10). After receiving them, if I don't wish to receive any more books, I can return the shipping statement marked "cancel." If I don't cancel, I will receive 4 brand-new novels every month and be billed just $5.99 per book in the U.S. or $6.49 per book in Canada. That's a saving of at least 25% off the cover price. It's quite a bargain! Shipping and handling is just 50¢ per book in the U.S. and 75¢ per book in Canada.* I understand that accepting the 2 free books and gifts places me under no obligation to buy anything. I can always return a shipment and cancel at any time. Even if I never buy another book, the two free books and gifts are mine to keep forever.

194/394 MDN FELQ

Name _____ (PLEASE PRINT)

Address _____ Apt. #

City _____ State/Prov. _____ Zip/Postal Code

Signature (if under 18, a parent or guardian must sign)

Mail to the **Reader Service:**
IN U.S.A.: P.O. Box 1867, Buffalo, NY 14240-1867
IN CANADA: P.O. Box 609, Fort Erie, Ontario L2A 5X3

Not valid for current subscribers to the Romance Collection
or the Romance/Suspense Collection.

Want to try two free books from another line?
Call 1-800-873-8635 or visit www.ReaderService.com.

* Terms and prices subject to change without notice. Prices do not include applicable taxes. Sales tax applicable in N.Y. Canadian residents will be charged applicable taxes. Offer not valid in Quebec. This offer is limited to one order per household. All orders subject to credit approval. Credit or debit balances in a customer's account(s) may be offset by any other outstanding balance owed by or to the customer. Please allow 4 to 6 weeks for delivery. Offer available while quantities last.

Your Privacy—The Reader Service is committed to protecting your privacy. Our Privacy Policy is available online at www.ReaderService.com or upon request from the Reader Service.

We make a portion of our mailing list available to reputable third parties that offer products we believe may interest you. If you prefer that we not exchange your name with third parties, or if you wish to clarify or modify your communication preferences, please visit us at www.ReaderService.com/consumerschoice or write to us at Reader Service Preference Service, P.O. Box 9062, Buffalo, NY 14269. Include your complete name and address.

ROM11

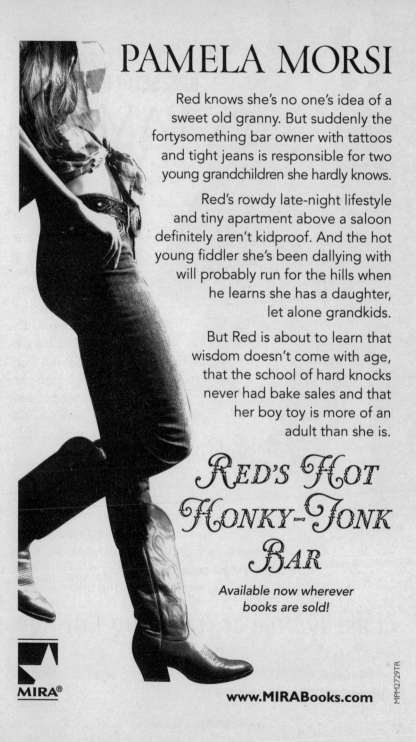